WH

&

ODDS AGAINST

Dick Francis has written over forty-one international best-sellers and is widely acclaimed as one of the world's finest thriller writers. His awards include the Crime Writers' Association's Cartier Diamond Dagger for his outstanding contribution to the crime genre, and an honorary Doctorate of Humane Letters from Tufts University of Boston. In 1996 Dick Francis was made a Mystery Writers of America Grand Master for a lifetime's achievement and in 2000 he received a CBE in the Queen's Birthday Honours list.

Dick Francis

WHIP HAND

&

ODDS AGAINST

PAN BOOKS

Whip Hand first published 1979 by Michael Joseph.
First published in paperback 1981 by Pan Books in association with Michael Joseph.
Odds Against first published 1965 by Michael Joseph.
First published in paperback 1967 by Pan Books in association with Michael Joseph.

This omnibus first published 2006 by Pan Books
an imprint of Pan Macmillan Ltd
Pan Macmillan, 20 New Wharf Road, London N1 9RR
Basingstoke and Oxford
Associated companies throughout the world
www.panmacmillan.com

ISBN-13: 978-0-330-44670-9
ISBN-10: 0-330-44670-3

1 3 5 7 9 8 6 4 2

A CIP catalogue record for this book is available from
the British Library.

Printed and bound in Great Britain by
Mackays of Chatham plc, Chatham, Kent

WHIP HAND

this book is for
Mike Gwilym *Actor*
and
Jacky Stoller *Producer*
with gratitude and affection

Prologue

I dreamed I was riding in a race.

Nothing odd in that. I'd ridden in thousands.

There were fences to jump. There were horses, and jockeys in a rainbow of colours, and miles of green grass. There were massed banks of people, with pink oval faces, indistinguishable pink blobs from where I crouched in the stirrups, galloping past, straining with speed.

Their mouths were open, and although I could hear no sound I knew they were shouting.

Shouting my name, to make me win.

Winning was all. Winning was my function. What I was there for. What I wanted. What I was born for.

In the dream, I won the race. The shouting turned to cheering, and the cheering lifted me up on its wings, like a wave. But the winning was all; not the cheering.

I woke in the dark, as I often did, at four in the morning.

There was silence. No cheering. Just silence.

I could still feel the way I'd moved with the horse, the

1

ripple of muscle through both of the striving bodies, uniting in one. I could still feel the irons round my feet, the calves of my legs gripping, the balance, the nearness to my head of the stretching brown neck, the mane blowing in my mouth, my hands on the reins.

There came, at that point, the second awakening. The real one. The moment in which I first moved, and opened my eyes, and remembered that I wouldn't ride any more races, ever. The wrench of loss came again as a fresh grief. The dream was a dream for whole men.

I dreamed it quite often.

Damned senseless thing to do.

Living, of course, was quite different. One discarded dreams, and got dressed, and made what one could of the day.

CHAPTER ONE

I took the battery out of my arm and fed it into the recharger, and only realized I'd done it when ten seconds later the fingers wouldn't work.

How odd, I thought. Recharging the battery, and the manoeuvre needed to accomplish it, had become such second nature that I had done them instinctively, without conscious decision, like brushing my teeth. And I realized for the first time that I had finally squared my subconscious, at least when I was awake, to the fact that what I now had as a left hand was a matter of metal and plastic, not muscle and bone and blood.

I pulled my tie off and flung it haphazardly on to my jacket, which lay over the leather arm of the sofa: stretched and sighed with the ease of homecoming: listened to the familiar silences of the flat; and as usual felt the welcoming peace unlock the gritty tensions of the outside world.

I suppose that that flat was more of a haven than a home. Comfortable certainly, but not slowly and lovingly put together. Furnished, rather, on one brisk unemotional afternoon in one store: 'I'll have that, that, that and that . . . and send them as soon as possible.' The collection had gelled, more or less, but I now owned nothing whose loss I would ache over; and if that was a defence mechanism, at least I knew it.

Contentedly padding around in shirt sleeves and socks, I switched on the warm pools of tablelights, encouraged the television with a practised slap, poured a soothing Scotch, and decided not to do yesterday's washing up. There was steak in the fridge and money in the bank, and who needed an aim in life anyway?

I tended nowadays to do most things one-handed, because it was quicker. My ingenious false hand, which worked via solenoids from electrical impulses in what was left of my forearm, would open and close in a fairly vice-like grip, but at its own pace. It did *look* like a real hand, though, to the extent that people sometimes didn't notice. There were shapes like fingernails, and ridges for tendons, and blue lines for veins. When I was alone I seemed to use it less and less, but it pleased me better to see it on than off.

I shaped up to that evening as to many another. On the sofa, feet up, knees bent, in contact with a chunky tumbler and happy to live vicariously via the small screen: and I was mildly irritated when halfway through a decent comedy the door bell rang.

With more reluctance than curiosity I stood up, parked the glass, fumbled through my jacket pockets for the spare battery I'd been carrying there, and snapped it into the socket in my arm. Then, buttoning the shirt cuff down over the plastic wrist, I went out into the small hall and took a look through the spyhole in the door.

There was no trouble on the mat, unless trouble had taken the shape of a middle-aged lady in a blue headscarf. I opened the door and said politely, 'Good evening, can I help you?'

'Sid,' she said. 'Can I come in?'

I looked at her, thinking that I didn't know her. But then a good many people whom I didn't know called me Sid, and I'd always taken it as a compliment.

Coarse dark curls showed under the headscarf, a pair of tinted glasses hid her eyes, and heavy crimson lipstick focused attention on her mouth. There was embarrassment in her manner and she seemed to be trembling inside her loose fawn raincoat. She still appeared to expect me to recognize her, but it was not until she looked nervously over her shoulder, and I saw her profile against the light, that I actually did.

Even then I said incredulously, tentatively, 'Rosemary?'

'Look,' she said, brushing past me as I opened the door more widely. 'I simply must talk to you.'

'Well . . . come in.'

While I closed the door behind us she stopped in front of the looking glass in the hall and started to untie the headscarf.

'My God, whatever do I look like?'

I saw that her fingers were shaking too much to undo

the knot, and finally with a frustrated little moan she stretched over her head, grasped the points of the scarf, and forcefully pulled the whole thing forward. Off with the scarf came all the black curls, and out shook the more familiar chestnut mane of Rosemary Caspar, who had called me Sid for fifteen years.

'My God,' she said again, putting the tinted glasses away in her handbag and fetching out a tissue to wipe off the worst of the gleaming lipstick. 'I had to come. I had to come.'

I watched the tremors in her hands and listened to the jerkiness in her voice, and reflected that I'd seen a whole procession of people in this state since I'd drifted into the trade of sorting out trouble and disaster.

'Come on in and have a drink,' I said, knowing it was what she both needed and expected, and sighing internally over the ruins of my quiet evening. 'Whisky or gin?'

'Gin . . . tonic . . . anything.'

Still wearing the raincoat she followed me into the sitting room and sat abruptly on the sofa as if her knees had given way beneath her. I looked briefly at the vague eyes, switched off the laughter on the television and poured her a tranquillizing dose of mother's ruin.

'Here,' I said, handing her the tumbler. 'So what's the problem?'

'Problem!' She was transitorily indignant. 'It's more than that.'

I picked up my own drink and carried it round to sit in an armchair opposite her.

'I saw you in the distance at the races today,' I said. 'Did the problem exist at that point?'

She took a large gulp from her glass. 'Yes, it damn well did. And why do you think I came creeping around at night searching for your damn flat in this ropey wig if I could have walked straight up to you at the races?'

'Well . . . why?'

'Because the last person I can be seen talking to on a racecourse or off it is Sid Halley.'

I had ridden a few times for her husband a way back in the past. In the days when I was a jockey. When I was still light enough for flat racing and hadn't taken to steeplechasing. In the days before success and glory and falls and smashed hands . . . and all that. To Sid Halley, ex-jockey, she could have talked publicly for ever. To Sid Halley, recently changed into a sort of all-purpose investigator, she had come in darkness and fright.

Forty-fivish, I suppose, thinking about it for the first time, and realizing that although I had known her casually for years I had never before looked long enough or closely enough at her face to see it feature by feature. The general impression of thin elegance had always been strong. The drooping lines of eyebrow and eyelid, the small scar on the chin, the fine noticeable down on the sides of the jaw, these were new territory.

She raised her eyes suddenly and gave me the same sort of inspection, as if she'd never really seen me before: and I guessed that for her it was a much more radical reassessment. I was no longer the boy she'd once rather brusquely issued with riding instructions, but a man she had come to in trouble. I was accustomed, by now, to seeing this new view of me supplant older and easier relationships, and although I might often regret it, there seemed no way of going back.

'Everyone says . . .' she began doubtfully. 'I mean . . . over this past year, I keep hearing . . .' She cleared her throat. 'They say you're good . . . very good . . . at this sort of thing. But I don't know . . . now I'm here . . . it doesn't seem . . . I mean . . . you're a jockey.'

'Was,' I said succinctly.

She glanced vaguely at my left hand, but made no other comment. She knew all about that. As racing gossip goes, it was last year's news.

'Why don't you tell me what you want done?' I said. 'If I can't help, I'll say so.'

The idea that I couldn't help after all reawoke her alarm and set her shivering again inside the raincoat.

'There's no one else,' she said. 'I can't go to anyone else. I have to believe . . . I have to . . . that you can do . . . all they say.'

'I'm no superman,' I protested. 'I just snoop around a bit.'

'Well . . . Oh God . . .' The glass rattled against her teeth as she emptied it to the dregs. 'I hope to God . . .'

'Take your coat off,' I said persuasively. 'Have

8

another gin. Sit back on the sofa, and start at the beginning.'

As if dazed she stood up, undid the buttons, shed the coat, and sat down again.

'There isn't a beginning.'

She took the refilled glass and hugged it to her chest. The newly revealed clothes were a cream silk shirt under a rust-coloured cashmere-looking sweater, a heavy gold chain, and a well-cut black skirt: the everyday expression of no financial anxieties.

'George is at a dinner,' she said. 'We're staying here in London overnight . . . He thinks I've gone to a film.'

George, her husband, ranked in the top three of British racecourse trainers and probably in the top ten internationally. On racecourses from Hong Kong to Kentucky he was revered as one of the greats. At Newmarket, where he lived, he was king. If his horses won the Derby, the Arc de Triomphe, the Washington International, no one was surprised. Some of the cream of the world's bloodstock floated year by year to his stable, and even having a horse in his yard gave the owner a certain standing. George Caspar could afford to turn down any horse or any man. Rumour said he rarely turned down any woman: and if that was Rosemary's problem it was one I couldn't solve.

'He mustn't know,' she said nervously. 'You'll have to promise not to tell him I came here.'

'I'll promise provisionally,' I said.

'That's not enough.'

'It'll have to be.'

'You'll see,' she said. 'You'll see why . . .' She took a drink. 'He may not like it, but he's worried to death.'

'Who . . . George?'

'Of course George. Who else? Don't be so damned stupid. For who else would I risk coming here on this damn charade?' The brittleness shrilled in her voice and seemed to surprise her. She visibly took some deep breaths, and started again. 'What did you think of Gleaner?'

'Er . . .' I said. 'Disappointing.'

'A damned disaster,' she said. 'You know it was.'

'One of those things,' I said.

'No, it was *not* one of those things. One of the best two-year-olds George ever had. Won three brilliant two-year-old races. Then all that winter, favourite for the Guineas and the Derby. Going to be the tops, everyone said. Going to be marvellous.'

'Yes,' I said. 'I remember.'

'And then what? Last spring he rán in the Guineas. Fizzled out. Total flop. And he never even got within sight of the Derby.'

'It happens,' I said.

She looked at me impatiently, compressing her lips. 'And Zingaloo?' she said. 'Was that, too, just one of those things? The two best colts in the country, both brilliant at two, both in our yard. And neither of them won a damn penny last year as three-year-olds. They

10

just stood there in their boxes, looking well, eating their heads off, and totally damn bloody useless.'

'It was a puzzler,' I agreed, but without much conviction. Horses which didn't come up to expectations were as normal as rain on Sundays.

'And what about Bethesda, the year before?' She glared at me vehemently. 'Top two-year-old filly. Favourite for months for the One Thousand and the Oaks. Terrific. She went down to the start of the One Thousand looking a million dollars, and she finished tenth. *Tenth*, I ask you!'

'George must have had them all *checked*,' I said mildly.

'Of course he did. Damn vets crawling all round the place for weeks on end. Dope tests. Everything. All negative. Three brilliant horses all gone useless. And no damned explanation. Nothing!'

I sighed slightly. It sounded to me more like the story of most trainers' lives, not a matter for melodramatic visits in false wigs.

'And now,' she said, casually dropping the bomb, 'there is Tri-Nitro.'

I let out an involuntarily audible breath, halfway to a grunt. Tri-Nitro filled columns just then on every racing page, hailed as the best colt for a decade. His two-year-old career the previous autumn had eclipsed all competitors, and his supremacy in the approaching summer was mostly taken for granted. I had seen him win the Middle Park at Newmarket in September at a

record-breaking pace, and had a vivid memory of the
slashing stride that covered the turf at almost incredible
speed.

'The Guineas is only a fortnight away,' Rosemary
said. 'Two weeks today, in fact. Suppose something
happens . . . suppose it's just as bad . . . what if he fails,
like the others . . .?'

She was trembling again, but when I opened my
mouth to speak she rushed on at a higher pitch. 'Tonight
was the only chance . . . the only night I could come
here . . . and George would be livid. He says nothing can
happen to the horse, no one can get at him, the security's too good. But he's scared, I know he is. Strung up.
Screwed up tight. I suggested he called you in to guard
the horse and he nearly went berserk. I don't know why.
I've never seen him in such a fury.'

'Rosemary,' I began, shaking my head.

'Listen,' she interrupted. 'I want you to make sure
nothing happens to Tri-Nitro before the Guineas. That's
all.'

'All . . .'

'It's no good wishing afterwards . . . if somebody tries
something . . . that I'd asked you. I couldn't stand that.
So I had to come. I had to. So say you'll do it. Say how
much you want, and I'll pay it.'

'It's not money,' I said. 'Look . . . there's no way I can
guard Tri-Nitro without George knowing and
approving. It's impossible.'

'You can do it. I'm sure you can. You've done things

before that people said couldn't be done. I had to come. I can't face it . . . George can't face it . . . not three years in a row. Tri-Nitro has got to win. You've got to make sure nothing happens. You've got to.'

She was suddenly shaking worse than ever and looked well down the road to hysteria. More to calm her than from any thought of being able in fact to do what she wanted, I said, 'Rosemary . . . all right. I'll try to do something.'

'He's got to win,' she said.

I said soothingly, 'I don't see why he shouldn't.'

She picked up unerringly the undertone I hadn't known would creep into my voice: the scepticism, the easy complacent tendency to discount her urgency as the fantasies of an excitable woman. I heard the nuances myself, and saw them uncomfortably through her eyes.

'My God, I've wasted my time coming here, haven't I?' she said bitterly, standing up. 'You're like all bloody men. You've got menopause on the brain.'

'That's not true. And I said I'd try.'

'Yes.' The word was a sneer. She was stoking up her own anger, indulging an inner need to explode. She practically threw her empty glass at me instead of handing it. I missed catching it, and it fell against the side of the coffee table, and broke.

She looked down at the glittering pieces and stuffed the jagged rage halfway back into its box.

'Sorry,' she said shortly.

'It doesn't matter.'

'Put it down to strain.'

'Yes.'

'I'll have to go and see that film. George will ask . . .'
She slid into her raincoat and moved jerkily towards the
door, her whole body still trembling with tension. 'I
shouldn't have come here. But I thought . . .'

'Rosemary,' I said flatly. 'I've said I'll try, and I will.'

'Nobody knows what it's like.'

I followed her into the hall, feeling her jangling des-
peration almost as if it were making actual disturbances
in the air. She picked the black wig off the small table
there and put it back on her head, tucking her own
brown hair underneath with fierce unfriendly jabs,
hating herself, her disguise and me: hating the visit, the
lies to George, the seedy furtiveness of her actions. She
painted on a fresh layer of the dark lipstick with
unnecessary force, as if assaulting herself; tied the knot
on the scarf with a savage jerk, and fumbled in her
handbag for the tinted glasses.

'I changed in the lavatories at the tube station,' she
said. 'It's all revolting. But I'm not having anyone see
me leaving here. There are things going on. I know
there are. And George is scared . . .'

She stood by my front door, waiting for me to open it;
a thin elegant woman looking determinedly ugly. It
came to me that no woman did that to herself without a
need that made esteem an irrelevance. I'd done nothing
to relieve her distress, and it was no good realizing that

it was because of knowing her too long in a different capacity. It was she who was subtly used to being in control, and I, from sixteen, who had respectfully followed her wishes. I thought that if tonight I had made her cry and given her warmth and contact and even a kiss, I could have done her more service; but the block was there, and couldn't be lightly dismantled.

'I shouldn't have come here,' she said. 'I see that now.'

'Do you want me . . . to take any action?'

A spasm twisted her face. 'Oh God . . . Yes, I do. But I was stupid. Fooling myself. You're only a jockey . . . after all.'

I opened the door.

'I wish,' I said lightly, 'that I were.'

She looked at me unseeingly, her mind already on her return journey, on her film, on her report of it to George.

'I'm not crazy,' she said.

She turned abruptly and walked away without a backward glance. I watched her turn towards the stairs and go without hesitating out of sight. With a continuing feeling of having been inadequate I shut the door and went back into the sitting room; and it seemed that the very air there too was restless from her intensity.

I bent down and picked up the larger pieces of broken glass, but there were too many sharp little splinters for total laziness, so I fetched dustpan and brush from the kitchen.

Holding the dustpan could usefully be done left-handed. If I simply tried to bend backwards the real hand that wasn't there, the false fingers opened away from the thumb. If I sent the old message to bend my hand inwards, they closed. There was always about two seconds' delay between mental instruction and electrical reaction, and taking that interval into account had been the most difficult thing to learn.

The fingers could not of course feel when their grip was tight enough. The people who fitted the arm had told me that success was picking up eggs: and I'd broken a dozen or two in practising, at the beginning. Absent-mindedness had since resulted in an exploding light bulb and crushed-flat cigarette packets and explained why I used the marvels of science less than I might.

I emptied the bits of glass into the dustbin and switched on the television again; but the comedy was over, and Rosemary came between me and a cops-and-robbers. With a sigh I switched off, and cooked my steak, and after I'd eaten it picked up the telephone to talk to Bobby Unwin, who worked for the *Daily Planet*.

'Information will cost you,' he said immediately, when he found who was on his line.

'Cost me what?'

'A spot of quid pro quo.'

'All right,' I said.

'What are you after, then?'

'Um,' I said. 'You wrote a long piece about George

16

Caspar in your Saturday colour supplement a couple of months ago. Pages and pages of it.'

'That's right. Special feature. In-depth analysis of success. The *Planet*'s doing a once-a-month series on high-flyers, tycoons, pop-stars, you name it. Putting them under the cliché microscope and coming up with a big yawn yawn exposé of bugger all.'

'Are you horizontal?' I said.

There was a short silence followed by a stifled girlish giggle.

'You just take your intuitions to Siberia,' Bobby said. 'What made you think so?'

'Envy, I dare say.' But I'd really only been asking if he was alone, without making it sound important. 'Will you be at Kempton tomorrow?'

'I reckon.'

'Could you bring a copy of that magazine, and I'll buy you a bottle of your choice.'

'Oh boy, oh boy. You're on.'

His receiver went down without more ado, and I spent the rest of the evening reading the flat-racing form books of recent years, tracing the careers of Bethesda, Gleaner, Zingaloo and Tri-Nitro, and coming up with nothing at all.

CHAPTER TWO

I had fallen into a recent habit of lunching on Thursdays with my father-in-law. To be accurate, with my *ex*-father-in-law: Admiral (retired) Charles Roland, parent of my worst failure. To his daughter Jenny I had given whatever devotion I was capable of, and had withheld the only thing she eventually said she wanted, which was that I should stop riding in races. We had been married for five years; two in happiness, two in discord, and one in bitterness; and now only the itching half-mended wounds remained. Those, and the friendship of her father, which I had come by with difficulty and now prized as the only treasure saved from the wreck.

We met most weeks at noon in the upstairs bar of the Cavendish Hotel, where a pink gin for him and a whisky and water for me now stood on prim little mats beside a bowl of peanuts.

'Jenny will be at Aynsford this weekend,' he said.

Aynsford was his house in Oxfordshire. London on Thursdays was his business. He made the journey between the two in a Rolls.

'I'd be glad if you would come down,' he said.

I looked at the fine distinguished face and listened to the drawling noncommittal voice. A man of subtlety and charm who could blast through you like a laser if he felt the need. A man whose integrity I would trust to the gates of hell, and whose mercy, not an inch.

I said carefully, without rancour, 'I am not coming to be sniped at.'

'She agreed that I should invite you.'

'I don't believe it.'

He looked with suspicious concentration at his glass. I knew from long experience that when he wanted me to do something he knew I wouldn't like, he didn't look at me. And there would be a pause, like this, while he found it in him to light the fuse. From the length of the pause, I drew no comfort of any sort. He said finally, 'I'm afraid she's in some sort of trouble.'

I stared at him, but he wouldn't raise his eyes.

'Charles,' I said despairingly. 'You *can't* . . . you can't ask me . . . You know how she speaks to me these days.'

'You give as good as you get, as I recall.'

'No one in their senses walks into a tiger's cage.'

He gave me a brief flashing upward glance, and there was a small twitch to his mouth. And perhaps it was not the best way of referring to a man's beautiful daughter.

'I have known you, Sid,' he said, 'to walk into tigers' cages more than once.'

'A tigress, then,' I amended, with a touch of humour.

He pounced on it. 'So you'll come?'

'No . . . Some things, honestly, are too much.'

He sighed and sat back in his chair, looking at me over the gin. I didn't care for the blank look in his eyes, because it meant he was still plotting.

'Dover sole?' he suggested smoothly. 'Shall I call the waiter? We might eat soon, don't you think?'

He ordered sole for both of us, and off the bone, out of habit. I could eat perfectly well in public now, but there had been a long and embarrassing period when my natural hand had been a wasted, useless deformity, which I'd self-consciously hidden in pockets. At about the time I finally got used to it, it had been smashed up again, and I'd lost it altogether. I guessed life was like that. You gained and you lost, and if you saved anything from the ruins, even if only a shred of self-respect, it was enough to take you through the next bit.

The waiter told us our table would be ready in ten minutes and went quietly away, hugging menus and order pad to his dinner jacket and grey silk tie. Charles glanced at his watch and then gazed expansively round the big, light, quiet room, where other couples, like us, sat in beige armchairs and sorted out the world.

'Are you going to Kempton this afternoon?' he said.

I nodded. 'The first race is at two-thirty.'

'Are you working on a job?' As an enquiry, it was a shade too bland.

'I'm not coming to Aynsford,' I said. 'Not while Jenny's there.'

After a pause, he said, 'I wish you would, Sid.'

I merely looked at him. His eyes were following the track of a bar waiter delivering drinks to distant customers; and he was taking a great deal too much time thinking out his next sentence.

He cleared his throat and addressed himself to nowhere in particular. 'Jenny has lent some money . . . and her name, I'm afraid . . . to a business enterprise which would appear to be fraudulent.'

'She's done *what*?' I said.

His gaze switched back to me with suspicious speed, but I interrupted him as he opened his mouth.

'No,' I said. 'If she's done that, it's well within your province to sort it out.'

'It's your name she's used, of course,' Charles said. 'Jennifer Halley.'

I could feel the trap closing round me. Charles studied my silent face and with a tiny sigh of relief let go of some distinct inner anxiety. He was a great deal too adept, I thought bitterly, at hooking me.

'She was attracted to a man,' he said dispassionately. 'I didn't especially like him, but then I didn't like you, either, to begin with . . . and I have found that error of judgement inhibiting, as a matter of fact, because I no longer always trust my first instincts.'

I ate a peanut. He had disliked me because I was a jockey, which he saw as no sort of husband for his well-bred daughter; and I had disliked him right back as an intellectual and social snob. It was odd to reflect that he was now probably the individual I valued most in the world.

He went on, 'This man persuaded her to go in for some sort of mail order business . . . all frightfully up-market and respectable, at least on the surface. A worthy way of raising money for charity . . . you know the sort of thing. Like Christmas cards, only in this case I think it was a sort of wax polish for antique furniture. One was invited to buy expensive wax, knowing that most of the profits would go to a good cause.'

He looked at me sombrely. I simply waited, without much hope.

'The orders rolled in,' he said. 'And the money with them, of course. Jenny and a girl friend were kept busy sending off the wax.'

'Which Jenny,' I guessed, 'had bought ready, in advance?'

Charles sighed. 'You don't need to be told, do you?'

'And Jenny paid for the postage and packing and advertisements and general literature?'

He nodded. 'She banked all the receipts into a specially opened account in the name of the charity. Those receipts have all been drawn out, the man has disappeared, and the charity, as such, has been found not to exist.'

I regarded him in dismay.

'And Jenny's position?' I said.

'Very bad, I'm afraid. There may be a prosecution. And her name is on everything, and the man's nowhere.'

My reaction was beyond blasphemy. Charles observed my blank silence and nodded slowly in sympathy.

'She has been exceedingly foolish,' he said.

'Couldn't you have stopped her? Warned her?'

He shook his head regretfully. 'I didn't know about it until she came to Aynsford yesterday in a panic. She has done it all from that flat she's taken in Oxford.'

We went in to lunch, and I couldn't remember, afterwards, the taste of the sole.

'The man's name is Nicholas Ashe,' Charles said, over the coffee. 'At least that's what he said.' He paused briefly. 'My solicitor chap thinks it would be a good idea if you could find him.'

I drove to Kempton with visual and muscular responses on auto-pilot and my thoughts uncomfortably on Jenny.

Divorce itself, it seemed, had changed nothing. The recent antiseptic drawing of the line, the impersonal court to which neither of us had gone (no children, no maintenance disputes, no flicker of reconciliation, petition granted, next case please) seemed to have punctuated our lives not with a full stop but with hardly a comma. The legal position had not proved a great liberating open door. The recovery from emotional cataclysm seemed a long slow process, and the certificate was barely an aspirin.

Where once we had clung together with delight and

passion, we now, if we chanced to meet, ripped with claws. I had spent eight years in loving, losing and mourning Jenny, and although I could wish my feelings were dead, they weren't. The days of indifference still seemed a weary way off.

If I helped her in the mess she was in, she would give me a rotten time. If I didn't help her, I would give it to myself. *Why*, I thought violently, in impotent irritation, had the silly bitch been so *stupid*.

There was a fair attendance at Kempton for a weekday in April, though as often before I regretted that in Britain the nearer a racecourse was to London, the more vulnerable it became to stay-away crowds. City-dwellers might be addicted to gambling, but not to fresh air and horses. Birmingham and Manchester, in days gone by, had lost their racecourses to indifference, and Liverpool had survived only through the Grand National. Most times it took a course in the country to burst at the seams and run out of racecards; the thriving plants still growing from the oldest roots.

Outside the weighing room there was the same old bunch of familiar faces carrying on chats which had been basically unchanged for centuries. Who was going to ride what, and who was going to win, and there should be a change in the rules, and what so-and-so had said about his horse losing, and wasn't the general outlook grim, and did you know young fella-me-lad has left his wife? There were the scurrilous stories and the slight exaggerations and the downright lies. The same mingling of honour and corruption, of principle and expediency. People ready to bribe, people with the ready palm. Anguished little hopefuls and arrogant big guns. The failures making brave excuses, and the successful hiding the anxieties behind their eyes. All as it had been, and was, and would be, as long as racing lasted.

I had no real right any longer to wander in the space outside the weighing room, although no one ever turned me out. I belonged in the grey area of ex-jockeys: barred from the weighing room itself but tolerantly given the run of much else. The cosy inner sanctum had gone down the drain the day half a ton of horse landed feet first on my metacarpals. Since then I had come to be glad simply to be still part of the brotherhood, and the ache to be riding was just part of the general regret. Another ex-champion had told me it took him twenty years before he no longer yearned to be out there on the horses, and I'd said thanks very much.

George Caspar was there, talking to his jockey, with three runners scheduled that afternoon; and also Rose-mary, who reacted with a violent jerk when she saw me at ten paces, and promptly turned her back. I could imagine the waves of alarm quivering through her, although that day she looked her usual well-groomed elegant self: mink coat for the chilly wind, glossy boots, velvet hat. If she feared I would talk about her visit, she was wrong.

There was a light grasp on my elbow and a pleasant voice saying, 'A word in your ear, Sid.'

I was smiling before I turned to him, because Lord Friarly, earl, landowner, and frightfully decent fellow, had been one of the people for whom I'd ridden a lot of races. He was of the old school of aristocrats: sixty-ish, beautifully mannered, genuinely compassionate, slightly eccentric, and more intelligent than people expected. A slight stammer was nothing to do with speech impediment but all to do with not wanting to seem to throw his rank about in an egalitarian world.

Over the years I had stayed several times in his house in Shropshire, mostly on the way to northern race-meetings, and had travelled countless miles with him in a succession of elderly cars. The age of the cars was not an extension of the low profile, but rather a disinclination to waste money on inessentials. Essentials, in terms of the earl's income, were keeping up Friarly Hall and owning as many racehorses as possible.

'Great to see you, sir,' I said.

'I've told you to call me Philip.'

'Yes . . . sorry.'

'Look,' he said. 'I want you to do something for me. I hear you're damned good at looking into things. Doesn't surprise me, of course, I've always valued your opinion, you know that.'

'Of course I'll help if I can,' I said.

'I've an uncomfortable feeling I'm being *used*,' he said. 'You know that I'm a sucker for seeing my horses run, the more the merrier, and all that. Well, during the past year I have agreed to be one of the registered owners in a syndicate ... you know, sharing the costs with eight or ten other people, though the horses run in my name, and my colours.'

'Yeah,' I said nodding. 'I've noticed.'

'Well ... I don't know all the other people, personally. The syndicates were formed by a chap who does just that – gets people together and sells them a horse. You know?'

I nodded. There had been cases of syndicate-formers buying horses for a smallish sum and selling them to the members of the syndicate for up to four times as much. A healthy little racket, so far legal.

'Those horses don't run true to form, Sid,' he said bluntly. 'I've a nasty feeling that somewhere in the syndicates we've got someone fixing the way the horses run. So will you find out for me? Nice and quietly?'

'I'll certainly try,' I said.

'Good,' he said, with satisfaction. 'Thought you would. So I brought the names for you, of the people in the syndicates.' He pulled a folded paper out of his inner pocket. 'There you are,' he said, opening it and pointing. 'Four horses. The syndicates are all registered with the Jockey Club, everything above board, audited accounts, and so on. It all looks all right on paper, but, frankly, Sid, I'm not *happy*.'

'I'll look into it,' I promised, and he thanked me profusely, and also genuinely, and moved away, after a minute or two, to talk to Rosemary and George.

Further away, Bobby Unwin, notebook and pencil in evidence, was giving a middle-rank trainer a hard-looking time. His voice floated over, sharp with northern aggression and tinged with an inquisitorial tone caught from tele-interviewers. 'Can you say, then, that you are perfectly satisfied with the way your horses are running?' The trainer looked around for escape and shifted from foot to foot. It was amazing, I thought, that he put up with it, even though Bobby Unwin's printed barbs tended to be worse if he hadn't the personal pleasure of intimidating his victim face to face. He wrote well, was avidly read, and among most of the racing fraternity was heartily disliked. Between him and me there had been for many years a sort of sparring truce, which in practice had meant a diminution of words like 'blind' and 'cretinous' to two per paragraph when he was describing any race I'd lost. Since I'd stopped riding I was no longer a target, and in consequence we had developed a perverse satisfaction in talking to each other, like scratching a spot.

Seeing me out of the corner of his eye he presently released the miserable trainer and steered his beaky nose in my direction. Tall, forty, and forever making copy out of having been born in a back-to-back terrace in Bradford: a fighter, come up the hard way, and letting no one ever forget it. We ought to have had much in common, since I too was the product of a dingy back street, but temperament had nothing to do with environment. He tended to meet fate with fury and I with silence, which meant that he talked a lot and I listened.

'The colour mag's in my briefcase in the Press room,' he said. 'What do you want it for?'

'Just general interest.'

'Oh, come off it,' he said. 'What are you working on?'

'And would you,' I said, 'give me advance notice of your next scoop?'

'All right,' he said. 'Point taken. And I'll have a bottle of the best vintage bubbly in the members' bar. After the first race. OK?'

'And for smoked salmon sandwiches extra, would I acquire some background info that never saw the light of print?'

He grinned nastily and said he didn't see why not; and in due course, after the first race, he kept his bargain.

'You can afford it, Sid, lad,' he said, munching a pink-filled sandwich and laying a protective hand on the gold-foiled bottle standing beside us on the bar counter. 'So what do you want to know?'

'You went to Newmarket . . . to George Caspar's yard . . . to do this article?' I indicated the colour magazine, which lay, folded lengthwise, beside the bottle.

'Yeah. Sure.'

'So tell me what you didn't write.'

He stopped in mid-munch. 'In what area?'

'What do you privately think of George as a person?'

He spoke round bits of brown bread. 'I said most of it in that.' He looked at the magazine. 'He knows more about when a horse is ready to race and what race to run him in than any other trainer on the Turf. And he's got as much feeling for people as a block of stone. He knows the name and the breeding back to the flood of every one of the hundred and twenty plus horses in his yard, and he can recognize them walking away from him in a downpour, which is practically impossible, but as for the forty lads he's got there working for him, he calls them all Tommy, because he doesn't know tother from which.'

'Lads come and go,' I said neutrally.

'So do horses. It's in his mind. He doesn't give a bugger's damn for people.'

'Women?' I suggested.

'Uses them, poor sods. I bet when he's at it he's got his mind on his next day's runners.'

'And Rosemary . . . what does she think about things?'

I poured a refill into his glass, and sipped my own. Bobby finished his sandwich with a gulp and licked the crumbs off his fingers.

'Rosemary? She's halfway off her rocker.'

'She looked all right yesterday at the races,' I said. 'And she's here today, as well.'

'Yeah, well, she can hold on to the grande dame act

30

in public still, I grant you, but I was in and out of the house for three days, and I'm telling you, mate, the goings-on there had to be heard to be believed.'

'Such as?'

'Such as Rosemary screaming all over the place that they hadn't enough security and George telling her to belt up. Rosemary's got some screwy idea that some of their horses have been got at in the past, and I dare say she's right at that, because you don't have a yard that size and that successful that hasn't had its share of villains trying to alter the odds. But anyway . . .' he drank deep and tipped the bottle generously to replenish his supplies ' . . . she seized me by the coat in their hall one day . . . and that hall's as big as a fair-sized barn . . . literally seized me by the coat and said what I should be writing was some stuff about Gleaner and Zingaloo being got at . . . you remember, those two spanking two-year-olds who never developed . . . and George came out of his office and said she was neurotic and suffering from the change of life, and right then and there in front of me they had a proper slanging match.' He took a breath and a mouthful. 'Funny thing is, in a way I'd say they were fond of each other. As much as he could be fond of anybody.'

I ran my tongue round my teeth and looked only marginally interested, as if my mind was on something else. 'What did George say about her ideas on Gleaner and Zingaloo?' I said.

'He took it for granted I wouldn't take her seriously,

but anyway, he said it was just that she had the heebie-jeebies that someone would nobble Tri-Nitro, and she was getting everything out of proportion. Her age, he said. Women always went very odd, he said, at that age. He said the security round Tri-Nitro was already double what he considered really necessary, because of her nagging, and when the new season began he'd have night patrols with dogs, and such like. Which is now, of course. He told me that Rosemary was quite wrong, anyway, about Gleaner and Zingaloo being got at, but that she'd got this obsession on the subject, and he was ready to humour her to some degree to stop her going completely bonkers. It seems that both of them . . . the horses, that is . . . proved to have a heart murmur, which of course accounted for their rotten performances as they matured and grew heavier. So that was that. No story.' He emptied his glass and refilled it. 'Well, Sid, mate, what is it you *really* want to know about George Caspar?'

'Um,' I said. 'Do you think there's anything he is afraid of?'

'George?' he said disbelievingly. 'What sort of thing?'

'Anything.'

'When I was there, I'd say he was about as frightened as a ton of bricks.'

'He didn't seem worried?'

'Not a bit.'

'Or edgy?'

He shrugged. 'Only with his wife.'

'How long ago was it, that you went there?'

'Oh . . .' He considered, thinking. 'After Christmas. Yes . . . second week in January. We have to do those colour mags such a long time in advance.'

'You don't think, then,' I said slowly, sounding disappointed, 'that he'd be wanting any extra protection for Tri-Nitro?'

'Is that what you're after?' He gave the leering grin. 'No dice, then, Sid, mate. Try someone smaller. George has got his whole ruddy yard sewn up tight. For a start, see, it's one of those old ones enclosed inside a high wall, like a fortress. Then there's ten-foot-high double gates across the entrance, with spikes on top.'

I nodded. 'Yes . . . I've seen them.'

'Well, then.' He shrugged, as if that settled things.

There were closed-circuit televisions in all the bars at Kempton to keep serious drinkers abreast of the races going on outside, and on the nearest of these sets Bobby Unwin and I watched the second race. The horse which won by six lengths was the one trained by George Caspar, and while Bobby was thoughtfully eying the two inches of fizz still left in the bottle, George himself came into the bar. Behind him, in a camel-coloured overcoat, came a substantial man bearing all the stigmata of a satisfied winning owner. Cat-with-the-cream smile, big gestures, have this one on me.

'Finish the bottle, Bobby,' I said.

'Don't you want any?'

'It's yours.'

He made no objections. Poured, drank, and comfortably belched. 'Better go,' he said. 'Got to write up these effing colts in the third. Don't you go telling my editor I watched the second in the bar, I'd get the sack.' He didn't mean it. He saw many a race in the bar. 'See you, Sid. Thanks for the drink.'

He turned with a nod and made a sure passage to the door, showing not a sign of having dispatched seven eighths of a bottle of champagne within half an hour. Merely laying the foundation, no doubt. His capacity was phenomenal.

I tucked his magazine inside my jacket and made my own way slowly in his wake, thinking about what he'd said. Passing George Caspar I said, 'Well done,' in the customary politeness of such occasions, and he nodded briefly and said 'Sid,' and, transaction completed, I continued towards the door.

'Sid . . .' he called after me, his voice rising.

I turned. He beckoned. I went back.

'Want you to meet Trevor Deansgate,' he said.

I shook the hand offered: snow-white cuff, gold links, smooth pale skin, faintly moist; well-tended nails, onyx and gold signet ring on little finger.

'Your winner?' I said. 'Congratulations.'

'Do you know who I am?'

'Trevor Deansgate?'

'Apart from that.'

It was the first time I'd seen him at close quarters. There was often, in powerful men, a give-away droop of the eyelids which proclaimed an inner sense of

34

superiority, and he had it. Also dark grey eyes, black controlled hair, and the tight mouth which goes with well-exercised decision-making muscles.

'Go on, Sid,' George said into my tiny hesitation. 'If you know, say. I told Trevor you knew everything.'

I glanced at him, but all that was to be read on his tough weathered countenance was a sort of teasing expectancy. For many people, I knew, my new profession was a kind of game. There seemed to be no harm, on this occasion, in jumping obligingly through his offered hoop.

'Bookmaker?' I said tentatively; and to Trevor Deansgate directly, added, 'Billy Bones?'

'There you are,' said George, pleased. 'I told you so.'

Trevor Deansgate took it philosophically. I didn't try for a further reaction, which might not have been so friendly. His name at birth was reputed to be Shummuck. Trevor Shummuck from Manchester, who'd been born in a slum with a razor mind and changed his name, accent and chosen company on the way up. As Bobby Unwin might have said, hadn't we all, and why not?

Trevor Deansgate's climb to the big league had been all but completed by buying out the old but ailing firm of 'Billy Bones', in itself a blanket pseudonym for some brothers called Rubenstein and their uncle Solly. In the past few years 'Billy Bones' had become big business. One could scarcely open a sports paper or go to the races without seeing the blinding fluorescent pink advertising, and slogans like 'Make no Bones about it,

Billy's best' tended to assault one's peace on Sundays. If the business was as vigorous as its sales campaign, Trevor Deansgate was doing all right.

We civilly discussed his winner until it was time to adjourn outside to watch the colts.

'How's Tri-Nitro?' I said to George, as we moved towards the door.

'Great,' he said. 'In great heart.'

'No problems?'

'None at all.'

We parted outside, and I spent the rest of the afternoon in the usual desultory way, watching the races, talking to people, and thinking unimportant thoughts. I didn't see Rosemary again, and calculated she was avoiding me, and after the fifth race I decided to go.

A racecourse official at the exit gate stopped me with an air of relief, as if he'd been waiting for me for a shade too long.

'Note for you, Mr Halley.'

'Oh? Thanks.'

He gave me an unobtrusive brown envelope. I put it in my pocket and walked on, out to my car. Climbed in. Took out, opened, and read the letter.

Sid,
I've been busy all afternoon but I want to see you. Please can you meet me in the tea room? After the last?
Lucas Wainwright

Cursing slightly, I walked back across the car park, through the gate, and along to the restaurant, where lunch had given place to sandwiches and cake. The last race being just finished, the tea customers were trickling in in small thirsty bunches, but there was no sign of Commander Lucas Wainwright, Director of Security to the Jockey Club.

I hung around, and he came in the end, hurrying, anxious, apologizing and harassed.

'Do you want some tea?' He was out of breath.

'Not much.'

'Never mind. Have some. We can sit here without being interrupted, and there are always too many people in the bar.' He led the way to a table and gestured to me to sit down.

'Look, Sid. How do you feel about doing a job for us?' No waster of time, Commander Wainwright.

'Does "us" mean the Security Service?'

'Yes.'

'Official?' I said, surprised. The Racecourse Security people knew in moderate detail what I'd recently been doing and had raised no objections, but I hadn't imagined they actually approved. In some respects, I'd been working in their territory, and stepping on their toes.

Lucas drummed his fingers on the tablecloth.

'Unofficial,' he said. 'My own private show.'

As Lucas Wainwright was himself the top brass of the Security Service, the investigative, policing arm of the

Jockey Club, even unofficial requests from him could be considered to be respectably well-founded. Or at least, until proved otherwise.

'What sort of job?' I said.

The thought of what sort of job slowed him up for the first time. He hummed and hah'ed and drummed his fingers some more, but finally shaped up to what proved to be a brute of a problem.

'Look, Sid, this is in strictest confidence.'

'Yes.'

'I've no higher authority for approaching you like this.'

'Well,' I said. 'Never mind. Go on.'

'As I've no authority, I can't promise you any pay.'

I sighed.

'All I could offer is . . . well . . . help, if you should ever need it. And if it was within my power to give it, of course.'

'That could be worth more than pay,' I said.

He looked relieved. 'Good. Now . . . this is very awkward. Very delicate.' He still hesitated, but at last, with a sigh like a groan, he said, 'I'm asking you to make . . . er . . . discreet enquiries into the . . . e . . . background . . . of one of our people.'

There was an instant's silence. Then I said, 'Do you mean one of *you*? One of the Security Service?'

'I'm afraid that's right.'

'Enquiries into exactly what?' I said.

He looked unhappy. 'Bribery. Backhanders. That sort of thing.'

'Um,' I said. 'Have I got this straight? You believe one of your chaps may be collecting pay-offs from villains, and you want me to find out?'

'That's it,' he said. 'Exactly.'

I thought it over. 'Why don't you do the investigating yourselves? Just detail another of your chaps.'

'Ah. Yes.' He cleared his throat. 'But there are difficulties. If I am wrong, I cannot afford to have it known that I was suspicious. It would cause a great, a very great deal of trouble. And if I am right, which I fear I am, we . . . that is, the Jockey Club . . . would want to be able to deal with things quietly. A public scandal involving the Security Service would be very damaging to racing.'

I thought he was perhaps putting it a bit high, but he wasn't.

'The man in question,' he said miserably, 'is Eddy Keith.'

There was another countable silence. In the hierarchy of the Security Service then existing, there was Lucas Wainwright at the top, with two equal deputies one step down. Both of the deputies were retired senior-rank policemen. One of them was ex-Superintendent Eddison Keith.

I had a clear mental picture of him, as I had talked with him often. A big bluff breezy man with a heavy hand for clapping one on the shoulder. More than a trace of Suffolk accent in a naturally loud voice. A large flourishing straw-coloured moustache, fluffy light brown hair through which one could see the pink scalp shining, and fleshy-lidded eyes which seemed always to be twinkling with good humour, and often weren't.

I had glimpsed there occasionally a glint as cold and unmerciful as a crevasse. Very much a matter of sun on ice: pretty but full of traps. One for applying the handcuffs with a cheery smile; that was Eddy Keith.

But crooked . . .? I would never have thought so.

'What are the indications?' I said at last.

Lucas Wainwright chewed his lower lip for a while and then said, 'Four of his inquiries over the past year have come up with incorrect results.'

I blinked. 'That's not very conclusive.'

'No. Precisely. If I were sure, I wouldn't be here talking to you.'

'I guess not.' I thought a bit. 'What sort of inquiries were they?'

'They were all syndicates. Inquiries into the suitability of people wanting to form syndicates to own horses. Making sure there weren't any undesirables sneaking into racing through the back door. Eddy gave all-clear reports on four proposed syndicates which do in fact all contain one or more people who would not be allowed through the gates.'

'How do you know?' I said. 'How did you find out?'

He made a face. 'I was interviewing someone last week in connection with a dope charge. He was loaded with spite against a group of people he said had let him down, and he crowed over me that those people all owned horses under false names. He told me the names, and I checked, and the four syndicates which contain them were all passed by Eddy.'

'I suppose,' I said slowly, 'they couldn't possibly be syndicates headed by Lord Friarly?'

He looked depressed. 'Yes, I'm afraid so. Lord Friarly mentioned to me earlier this afternoon that he'd asked you to take a look-see. Told me out of politeness. It just reinforced the idea I'd already had of asking you myself. But I want it kept quiet.'

'So does he,' I said reassuringly. 'Can you let me have Eddy's reports? Or copies of them? And the false and true names of the undesirables?'

He nodded. 'I'll see you get them.' He looked at his watch and stood up, the briskness returning to his manner like an accustomed coat. 'I don't need to tell you . . . But do be discreet.'

I joined him on his quick march to the door, where he left me at an even faster pace, sketching the merest wave of farewell. His backview vanished uprightly through the weighing room door, and I took myself out again to my car, reflecting that if I went on collecting jobs at the present rate I would need to call up the troops.

CHAPTER THREE

I telephoned the North London Comprehensive School and asked to speak to Chico Barnes.

'He's teaching judo,' a voice said repressively.

'His class usually ends about now.'

'Wait a minute.'

I waited, driving towards London with my right hand on the wheel and my left round the receiver and a spatter of rain on the windscreen. The car had been adapted for one-handed steering by the addition of a knob on the front face of the wheel's rim: very simple, very effective, and no objections from the police.

'Hello?'

Chico's voice, cheerful, full of his general irreverent view of the world even in one single word.

'Want a job?' I said.

'Yeah.' His grin travelled distinctly down the line. 'It's been too dead quiet this past week.'

'Can you go to the flat? I'll meet you there.'

'I've got an extra class. They lumbered me. Some

other guy's evening class of stout ladies. He's ill. I don't blame him. Where are you phoning from?'

'The car. From Kempton to London. I'm calling in at Roehampton, at the limb centre, as it's on the way, but I could be outside your school in . . . say . . . an hour and a half. I'll pick you up. OK?'

'Sure,' he said. 'What are you going to the limb centre for?'

'To see Alan Stephenson.'

'He'll have gone home.'

'He said he'd be there, working late.'

'Your arm hurting again?'

'No . . . Matter of screws and such.'

'Yeah,' he said. 'OK. See you.'

I put the phone down with the feeling of satisfaction that Chico nearly always engendered. There was no doubt that as a working companion I found him great: funny, inventive, persistent, and deceptively strong. Many a rogue had discovered too late that young slender Chico with his boyish grin could throw a twenty-stone man over his shoulder with the greatest ease.

When I first got to know him he was working, as I was, in the Radnor detective agency, where I had learned my new trade. At one point there had been a chance that I would become first a partner and eventually the owner of that agency, but although Radnor and I had come to an agreement, and had even changed the agency's name to Radnor-Halley, life had delivered an earthquake upheaval and decided things otherwise.

It must have been only a day before the partnership agreements were ready to be signed, with finances arranged and the champagne approaching the ice, that Radnor himself sat down for a quiet snooze in his armchair at home, and never woke up.

Back from Canada, as if on stretched elastic, had immediately snapped an unsuspected nephew, brandishing a will in his favour and demanding his rights. He did not, he said forthrightly, want to sell half his inheritance to a one-handed ex-jockey, especially at the price agreed. He himself would be taking over and breathing new life into the whole works. He himself would be setting it all up in new modern offices, not the old crummy bomb-damaged joint in the Cromwell Road, and anyone who didn't like the transfer could vote with his feet.

Most of the old bunch had stayed on into the new order, but Chico had had a blazing row with the nephew and opted for the dole. Without much trouble he had then found the part-time job teaching judo, and the first time I'd asked for his help he'd joined up with enthusiasm. Since then I myself seemed to have become the most regularly employed investigator working in racing, and if Radnor's nephew didn't like it (and he was reputed to be furious) it was just too bad.

Chico bounced out through the swinging glass doors of the school with the lights behind him making a halo round his curly hair. Any resemblance to sainthood stood precisely there, since the person under the curls was in no way long-suffering, God-fearing or chaste.

He slid into the car, gave me a wide grin, and said, 'There's a pub round the corner with a great set of bristols.'

Resignedly I pulled into the pub's car park, and followed him into the bar. The girl dispensing drinks was, as he'd said, nicely endowed, and moreover she greeted Chico with telling warmth. I listened to the flirting chit-chat and paid for the drinks.

We sat on a bench by the wall, and Chico approached his pint with the thirst brought on by too much healthy exercise.

'Ah,' he said, putting down the tankard temporarily. 'That's better.' He eyed my glass. 'Is that straight orange juice?'

I nodded. 'Been drinking on and off all day.'

'Don't know how you bear it, all that high life and luxury.'

'Easily.'

'Yeah.' He finished the pint, went back for a refill and another close encounter with the girl, and finally retracked to the bench. 'Where do I go then, Sid? And what do I do?'

'Newmarket. Spot of pub-crawling.'

'Can't be bad.'

'You're looking for a head lad called Paddy Young.

45

He's George Caspar's head lad. Find out where he drinks, and sort of drift into conversation.'

'Right.'

'We want to know the present whereabouts of three horses which used to be in his yard.'

'We do?'

'He shouldn't have any reason for not telling you, or at least, I don't think so.'

Chico eyed me. 'Why don't you ask George Caspar, right out? Be simpler, wouldn't it?'

'At the moment we don't want George Caspar to know we're asking questions about his horses.'

'Like that, is it?'

'I don't know, really.' I sighed. 'Anyway, the three horses are Bethesda, Gleaner, and Zingaloo.'

'OK. I'll go up there tomorrow. Shouldn't be too difficult. You want me to ring you?'

'Soon as you can.'

He glanced at me sideways. 'What did the limb man say?'

'Hello, Sid, nice to see you.'

He made a resigned noise with his mouth. 'Might as well ask questions of a brick wall.'

'He said the ship wasn't leaking and the voyage could go on.'

'Better than nothing.'

'As you say.'

*

I went to Aynsford, as Charles had known I would, driving down on Saturday afternoon and feeling the apprehensive gloom deepen with every mile. For distraction I concentrated on Chico's news from Newmarket, telephoned through at lunchtime.

'I found him,' he said. 'He's a much-married man who has to take his pay packet home like a good boy on Friday evenings, but he sneaked out for a quick jar just now. The pub's nearly next door to the yard; very handy. Anyway, if you can understand what he says, and he's so Irish it's like talking to a foreigner, what it boils down to is that all three of those horses have gone to stud.'

'Did he know where?'

'Sure. Bethesda went to some place called Garvey's in Gloucestershire, and the other two are at a place just outside Newmarket, which Paddy Young called Traces, or at least I think that's what he said, although as I told you, he chews his words up something horrible.'

'Thrace,' I said. 'Henry Thrace.'

'Yeah? Well, maybe you can make sense of some other things he said, which were that Gleaner had a tritus and Zingaloo had the virus and Bruttersmit gave them both the turns down as quick as Concorde.'

'Gleaner had a what?'

'Tritus.'

I tried turning 'Gleaner had a tritus' into an Irish accent in my head and came up with Gleaner had arthritis, which sounded a lot more likely. I said to

Chico, ' . . . and Brothersmith gave them the thumbs down . . .'

'Yeah,' he said. 'You got it.'

'Where are you phoning from?'

'Box in the street.'

'There's a bit of boozing time left,' I said. 'Would you see if you can find out if this Brothersmith is George Caspar's vet, and if so, look him up in the phone book and bring back his address and number.'

'OK. Anything else?'

'No.' I paused. 'Chico, did Paddy Young give you any impression that there was anything odd in these three horses going wrong?'

'Can't say he did. He didn't seem to care much, one way or the other. I just asked him casual like where they'd gone, and he told me, and threw in the rest for good measure. Philosophical, you could say he was.'

'Right, then,' I said. 'Thanks.'

We disconnected, but he rang again an hour later to tell me that Brothersmith was indeed George Caspar's vet, and to give me his address.

'If that's all, then, Sid, there's a train leaving in half an hour, and I've a nice little dolly waiting for me round Wembley way who'll have her Saturday night ruined if I don't get back.'

The more I thought about Chico's report and Bobby Unwin's comments the less I believed in Rosemary's suspicions; but I'd promised her I would try, and try I still would, for a little while longer. For as long as it took me, anyway, to check up on Bethesda, Zingaloo and Gleaner, and talk to Brothersmith the vet.

Aynsford still looked its mellow stone self, but the daffodil-studded tranquillity applied to the exterior only. I stopped the car gently in front of the house and sat there wishing I didn't have to go in.

Charles, as if sensing that even then I might back off and drive away, came purposefully out of his front door and strode across the gravel. Watching for me, I thought. Waiting. Wanting me to come.

'Sid,' he said, opening my door and stooping down to smile. 'I knew you would.'

'You hoped,' I said.

I climbed out on to my feet.

'All right.' The smile stayed in his eyes. 'Hoped. But I know you.'

I looked up at the front of the house, seeing only blank windows reflecting the greyish sky.

'Is she here?' I said.

He nodded. I turned away, went round to the back of the car, and lugged out my suitcase.

'Come on, then,' I said. 'Let's get it over.'

'She's upset,' he said, walking beside me. 'She needs your understanding.'

I glanced at him and said, 'Mm.' We finished the short journey in silence, and went through the door.

Jenny was standing there, in the hall.

49

I had never got used to the pang of seeing her on the rare occasions we had met since she left. I saw her as I had when I first loved her, a girl not of great classical beauty, but very pretty, with brown curling hair and a neat figure, and a way of holding her head high, like a bird on the alert. The old curving smile and the warmth in her eyes were gone, but I tended to expect them, with hopeless nostalgia.

'So you came,' she said. 'I said you wouldn't.'

I put down the suitcase and took the usual deep breath. 'Charles wanted me to,' I said. I walked the steps towards her, and, as always, we gave each other a brief kiss on the cheek. We had maintained the habit as the outward and public mark of a civilized divorce; but privately, I often thought, it was more like the ritual salute before a duel.

Charles shook his head impatiently at the lack of real affection, and walked ahead of us into the drawing room. He had tried in the past to keep us together, but the glue for any marriage had to come from the inside, and ours had dried to dust.

Jenny said, 'I don't want any lectures from you, Sid, about this beastly affair.'

'No.'

'You're not perfect yourself, even though you like to think so.'

'Give it a rest, Jenny,' I said.

She walked abruptly away into the drawing room, and I followed more slowly. She would use me, I thought, and discard me again, and because of Charles I would let her. I was surprised that I felt no tremendous desire to offer comfort. It seemed that irritation was still well in the ascendancy over compassion.

She and Charles were not alone. When I went in she had crossed the room to stand at the side of a tall blond man whom I'd met before; and beside Charles stood a stranger, a stocky young-old man whose austere eyes were disconcertingly surrounded by a rosy country face.

Charles said in his most ultra-civilized voice, 'You know Toby, don't you, Sid?', and Jenny's shield and supporter and I nodded to each other and gave the faint smiles of an acquaintanceship we would each have been happier without. 'And this, Sid, is my solicitor, Oliver Quayle. Gave up his golf to be here. Very good of him.'

'So you're Sid Halley,' the young-old man said, shaking hands. There was nothing in his voice either way, but his gaze slid down and sideways, seeking to see the half-hidden hand that he wouldn't have looked at if he hadn't known. It often happened that way. He brought his gaze back to my face and saw that I knew what he'd been doing. There was the smallest flicker in his lower eyelids, but no other remark. Judgement suspended, I thought, on either side.

Charles's mouth twitched, and he said smoothly, 'I warned you, Oliver. If you don't want him to read your thoughts, you mustn't move your eyes.'

'Yours don't move,' I said to him.

'I learned that lesson years ago.'

He made courteous sit-down motions with his hands, and the five of us sank into comfort and pale gold brocade.

'I've told Oliver,' Charles said, 'that if anyone can find this Nicholas Ashe person, you will.'

'Frightfully useful, don't you know,' drawled Toby, 'having a plumber in the family, when the pipes burst.'

It was a fraction short of offensiveness. I gave him the benefit of a doubt I didn't have, and asked nobody in particular whether the police wouldn't do the job more quickly.

'The trouble is,' Quayle said, 'that technically it is Jenny alone who is guilty of obtaining money by false pretences. The police have listened to her, of course, and the man in charge seems to be remarkably sympathetic, but...' he slowly shrugged the heavy shoulders in a way that skilfully combined sympathy and resignation, '... one feels they might choose to settle for the case they have.'

'But I say,' protested Toby, 'it was that Ashe's idea, all of it.'

'Can you prove it?' Quayle said.

'Jenny says so,' Toby said, as if that were proof enough.

Quayle shook his head. 'As I've told Charles, it would appear from all documents that she signed that she did know the scheme was fraudulent. And ignorance, even if genuine, is always a poor, if not impossible, defence.'

I said, 'If there's no evidence against him, what would you do, even if I did find him?'

Quayle looked my way attentively. 'I'm hoping that if you find him, you'll find evidence as well.'

Jenny sat up exceedingly straight and spoke in a voice sharp with perhaps anxiety but certainly anger.

'This is all rubbish, Sid. Why don't you say straight out that the job's beyond you?'

'I don't know if it is.'

'It's pathetic,' she said to Quayle, 'how he longs to prove he's clever, now he's disabled.'

The flicking sneer in her voice shocked Quayle and Charles into visible discomfort, and I thought deject-edly that this was what I'd caused in her, this compulsive need to hurt. I didn't just mind what she'd said, I minded bitterly that because of me she was not showing to Quayle the sunny-tempered person she would still be if I wasn't there.

'If I find Nicholas Ashe,' I said grimly, 'I'll give him to Jenny. Poor fellow.'

None of the men liked it. Quayle looked disil-lusioned, Toby showed he despised me, and Charles sorrowfully shook his head. Jenny alone, behind her anger, looked secretly pleased. She seldom managed nowadays to goad me into a reply to her insults, and counted it a victory that I'd done it and earned such general disapproval. My own silly fault. There was only one way not to let her see when her barbs went in, and that was to smile . . . and the matter in hand was not very funny.

I said, more moderately, 'There might be ways . . . if I can find him. At any rate, I'll do my best. If there's anything I can do . . . I'll do it.'

Jenny looked unplacated, and no one else said anything. I sighed internally. 'What did he look like?' I said.

After a pause Charles said, 'I saw him once only, for about thirty minutes, four months ago. I have a general impression, but that's all. Young, personable, dark-haired, clean-shaven. Something too ingratiating in his manner to me. I would not have welcomed him as a junior officer aboard my ship.'

Jenny compressed her lips and looked away from him, but could not protest against this judgement. I felt the first faint stirrings of sympathy for her and tried to stamp on them: they would only make me more vulnerable, which was something I could do without.

I said to Toby, 'Did you meet him?'

'No,' he said loftily. 'Actually, I didn't.'

'Toby has been in Australia,' Charles said, explaining.

They all waited. It couldn't be shirked. I said directly to her, neutrally, 'Jenny?'

'He was *fun*,' she said vehemently, unexpectedly. 'My God, he was fun. And after you . . .' She stopped. Her head swung round my way with bitter eyes. 'He was full of life and jokes. He made me laugh. He was terrific. He lit things up. It was like . . . it was like . . .' She suddenly faltered and stopped, and I knew she was thinking, like us when we first met. Jenny, I thought desperately, don't say it, please don't.

Perhaps it was too much, even for her. How could people, I wondered for the ten thousandth useless time, how could people who had loved so dearly come to such a wilderness; and yet the change in us was irreversible, and neither of us would even search for a way back. It was impossible. The fire was out. Only a few live coals lurked in the ashes, searing unexpectedly at the incautious touch.

I swallowed. 'How tall was he?' I asked.

'Taller than you.'

'Age?'

'Twenty-nine.'

The same age as Jenny. Two years younger than I. If he had told the truth, that was. A confidence trickster might lie about absolutely everything as a matter of prudence.

'Where did he stay, while he was ... er ... operating?'

Jenny looked unhelpful, and it was Charles who answered. 'He told Jenny he was staying with an aunt, but after he had gone, Oliver and I checked up. The aunt, unfortunately, proved to be a landlady who lets rooms to students in north Oxford. And in any case ...' he cleared his throat, ' ... it seems that fairly soon he left the lodgings and moved into the flat Jenny is sharing with another girl.'

'He lived in your flat?' I said to Jenny.

55

'So what of it?' She was defiant. And something else . . .

'So when he left, did he leave anything behind?'

'No.'

'Nothing at all?'

'No.'

'Do you want him found?' I said.

To Charles and Quayle and Toby the answer to that question was an automatic yes, but Jenny didn't answer, and the blush that started at her throat rose fast to two bright spots on her cheekbones.

'He's done you great harm,' I said.

With stubbornness stiffening her neck, she said, 'Oliver says I won't go to prison.'

'Jenny!' I was exasperated. 'A conviction for fraud will affect your whole life in all sorts of horrible ways. I see that you liked him. Maybe you even loved him. But he's not just a naughty boy who pinched the jampot for a lark. He has callously arranged for you to be punished in his stead. *That*'s the crime for which I'll catch him if I damned well can, even if you don't want me to.'

Charles protested vigorously, 'Sid, that's ridiculous. Of course she wants to see him punished. She agreed that you should try to find him. She wants you to, of course she does.'

I sighed and shrugged. 'She agreed, to please you. And because she doesn't think I'll succeed; and she's very likely right. But even *talk* of my succeeding is putting her in a turmoil and making her angry . . . and it's by no means unknown for women to go on loving scoundrels who've ruined them.'

Jenny rose to her feet, stared at me blindly, and walked out of the room. Toby took a step after her and Charles too got to his feet, but I said with some force, 'Mr Quayle, please will you go after her and tell her the consequences if she's convicted. Tell her brutally, make her understand, make it shock.'

He had taken the decision and was on his way after her before I'd finished.

'It's hardly kind,' Charles said. 'We've been trying to spare her.'

'You can't expect Halley to show her any sympathy,' Toby said waspishly.

I eyed him. Not the brightest of men, but Jenny's choice of undemanding escort, the calm sea after the hurricane. A few months earlier she had been thinking of marrying him, but whether she would do it post-Ashe was to my mind doubtful. He gave me his usual lofty look of non-comprehension and decided Jenny needed him at once.

Charles watched his departing back and said, with a tired note of despair, 'I simply don't understand her. And it took you about ten minutes to see ... what I wouldn't have seen at all.' He looked at me gloomily. 'It was pointless, then, to try to reassure her, as I've been doing?'

'Oh, Charles, what a bloody muddle ... It won't have done any harm. It's just given her a way of excusing him . . . Ashe . . . and putting off the time when she'll have to admit to herself that she's made a shattering . . . shaming . . . mistake.'

The lines in his face had deepened with distress. He said sombrely, 'It's worse. Worse than I thought.'

'Sadder,' I said. 'Not worse.'

'Do you think you can find him?' he said. 'How on earth do you start?'

CHAPTER FOUR

I started in the morning, having not seen Jenny again, as she'd driven off the previous evening with Toby at high speed to Oxford, leaving Charles and me to dine alone, a relief to us both; and they had returned late and not appeared for breakfast by the time I left.

I went to Jenny's flat in Oxford, following directions from Charles, and rang the doorbell. The lock, I thought, looking at it, would give me no trouble if there was no one in, but in fact, after my second ring, the door opened a few inches, on a chain.

'Louise McInnes?' I said, seeing an eye, some tangled fair hair, a bare foot and a slice of dark blue dressing gown.

'That's right.'

'Would you mind if I talked to you? I'm Jenny's . . . er . . . ex-husband. Her father asked me to see if I could help her.'

'You're Sid?' she said, sounding surprised. 'Sid Halley?'

'Yes.'

59

'Well . . . wait a minute.' The door closed and stayed closed for a good long time. Finally it opened again, this time wide, and the whole girl was revealed. This time she wore jeans, a checked shirt, baggy blue sweater, and slippers. The hair was brushed, and there was lipstick: a gentle pink, unaggressive.

'Come in.'

I went in and closed the door behind me. Jenny's flat, as I would have guessed, was not constructed of plasterboard and held together with drawing pins. The general address was a large Victorian house in a prosperous side street, with a semi-circular driveway and parking room at the back. Jenny's section, reached by its own enclosed, latterly added staircase, was the whole of the spacious first floor. Bought, Charles had told me, with some of her divorce settlement. It was nice to see that on the whole my money had been well spent.

Switching on lights, the girl led the way into a large bow-fronted sitting room which still had its curtains drawn and the day before's clutter slipping haphazardly off tables and chairs. Newspapers, a coat, some kicked-off boots, coffee cups, an empty yoghurt carton in a fruit bowl, with spoon, some dying daffodils, a typewriter with its cover off, some scrunched-up pages that had missed the waste-paper basket.

Louise McInnes drew back the curtains, letting in the grey morning to dilute the electricity.

'I wasn't up,' she said unnecessarily.

'I'm sorry.'

The mess was the girl's. Jenny was always tidy, clearing up before bed. But the room itself was Jenny's. One or two pieces from Aynsford, and an overall similarity to the sitting room of our own house, the one we'd shared. Love might change, but taste endured. I felt a stranger, and at home.

'Want some coffee?' she said.

'Only if . . .'

'Sure. I'd have some anyway.'

'Can I help you?'

'If you like.'

She led the way through the hall and into a bare-looking kitchen. There was nothing precisely prickly in her manner, but all the same it was cool. Not surprising, really. What Jenny thought of me, she would say, and there wouldn't be much that was good.

'Like some toast?' She was busy producing a packet of white sliced bread and a jar of powdered coffee.

'Yes, I would.'

'Then stick a couple of pieces in the toaster. Over there.'

I did as she said, while she ran some water into an electric kettle and dug into a cupboard for butter and marmalade. The butter was a half-used packet still in its torn greaseproof wrapping, the centre scooped out and the whole thing messy: exactly like my own butter packet in my own flat. Jenny had put butter into dishes automatically. I wondered if she did when she was alone.

'Milk and sugar?'

'No sugar.'

When the toast popped up she spread the slices with butter and marmalade and put them on two plates. Boiling water went on to the brown powder in mugs, and milk followed straight from the bottle.

'You bring the coffee,' she said, 'and I'll take the toast.' She picked up the plates and out of the corner of her eye saw my left hand closing round one of the mugs. 'Look out,' she said urgently, 'that's hot.'

I gripped the mug carefully with the fingers that couldn't feel.

She blinked.

'One of the advantages,' I said, and picked up the other mug more gingerly by its handle.

She looked at my face, but said nothing: merely turned away and went back to the sitting room.

'I'd forgotten,' she said, as I put down the mugs on the space she had cleared for them on the low table in front of the sofa.

'False teeth are more common,' I said politely.

She came very near to a laugh, and although it ended up as a doubtful frown, the passing warmth was a glimpse of the true person living behind the slightly brusque façade. She scrunched into the toast and looked thoughtful, and after a chew and a swallow, she said, 'What can you do to help Jenny?'

'Try to find Nicholas Ashe.'

'Oh . . .' There was another spontaneous flicker of smile, again quickly stifled by subsequent thought.

'You liked him?' I said.

She nodded ruefully. 'I'm afraid so. He is . . . was . . . such tremendous fun. Fantastic company. I find it terribly hard to believe he's just gone off and left Jenny in this mess. I mean . . . he lived here, here in this flat . . . and we had so many laughs . . . What he's done . . . it's incredible.'

'Look,' I said, 'would you mind starting at the beginning and telling me all about it?'

'But hasn't Jenny . . .?'

'No.'

'I suppose,' she said slowly, 'that she wouldn't like admitting to you that he made such a fool of us.'

'How much,' I said, 'did she love him?'

'Love? What's love? I can't tell you. She was *in* love with him.' She licked her fingers. 'All fizzy. Bright and bubbly. Up in the clouds.'

'Have you been there? Up in the clouds?'

She looked at me straightly. 'Do you mean, do I know what it's like? Yes, I do. If you mean, was I in love with Nicky, then no I wasn't. He was fun, but he didn't turn me on like he did Jenny. And in any case, it was she who attracted him. Or at least . . .' she finished doubtfully, ' . . . it seemed like it.' She wagged her licked fingers. 'Would you give me that box of tissues that's just behind you?'

I gave her the box and watched her as she wiped off

the rest of the stickiness. She had fair eye-lashes and English-rose skin, and a face that had left shyness behind. Too soon for life to have printed unmistakable signposts; but there did seem, in her natural expression, to be little in the way of cynicism or intolerance. A practical girl, with sense.

'I don't really know where they met,' she said, 'except that it was somewhere here in Oxford. I came back here one day, and he was *here*, if you see what I mean. They were already ... well ... interested in each other.'

'Er,' I said, 'have you always shared this flat with Jenny?'

'More or less. We were at school together ... didn't you know? Well, we met one day and I told her I was going to be living in Oxford for two years while I wrote a thesis, and she said, had I anywhere to stay, because she'd seen this flat, but she'd like some company ... So I came. Like a shot. We've got on fine, on the whole.'

I looked at the typewriter and the signs of effort. 'Do you work here all the time?'

'Here or in the Bodleian ... er, the library, that is ... or out doing other research. I pay rent to Jenny for my room ... and I don't know why I'm telling you all this.'

'It's very helpful.'

She got to her feet. 'It might be as well for you to see all the stuff. I've put it all in his room ... Nicky's room

. . . to get it out of sight. It's all too boringly painful, as a matter of fact.'

Again I followed her through the hall, and this time on further down the wide passage, which was recognizably the first-floor landing of the old house.

'That room,' she said, pointing at doors, 'is Jenny's. That's the bathroom. That's my room. And this one at the end was Nicky's.'

'When exactly did he go?' I said walking behind her.

'Exactly? Who knows? Some time on Wednesday. Two weeks last Wednesday.' She opened the white painted door and walked into the end room. 'He was here at breakfast, same as usual. I went off to the library, and Jenny caught the train to London to go shopping, and when we both got back, he was gone. Just gone. Everything. Jenny was terribly shocked. Wept all over the place. But of course, we didn't know then that he hadn't just left her, he'd cleared out with all the money as well.'

'How did you find out?'

'Jenny went to the bank on Friday to pay in the cheques and draw out some cash for postage, and they told her the account was closed.'

I looked round the room. It had thick carpet, Georgian dressing chest, big comfort-promising bed, upholstered armchair, pretty, Jenny-like curtains, fresh white paint. Six large brown boxes of thick cardboard stood in a double stack in the biggest available space; and none of it looked as if it had ever been lived in.

I went over to the chest and pulled out a drawer. It was totally empty. I put my fingers inside and drew them along, and they came out without a speck of dust or grit.

Louise nodded. 'He had dusted. And hoovered, too. You could see the marks on the carpet. He cleaned the bathroom, as well. It was all sparkling. Jenny thought it was nice of him ... until she found out just why he didn't want to leave any trace.'

'I should think it was symbolic,' I said absently.

'What do you mean?'

'Well ... not so much that he was afraid of being traced through hair and fingerprints ... but just that he wanted to feel that he'd wiped himself out of this place. So that he didn't feel he'd left anything of himself here. I mean ... if you want to go back to a place, you subconsciously leave things there, you "forget" them. Well-known phenomenon. So if you subconsciously, as well as consciously, don't want to go back to a place, you may feel impelled to remove even your dust.' I stopped. 'Sorry. Didn't mean to bore you.'

'I'm not bored.'

I said matter-of-factly, 'Where did they sleep?'

'Here.' She looked carefully at my face and judged it safe to proceed. 'She used to come along here. Well ... I couldn't help but know. Most nights. Not always.'

'He never went to her?'

'Funny thing, I never ever saw him go into her room,

even in the daytime. If he wanted her, he'd stand outside and call.'

'It figures.'

'More symbolism?' She went to the pile of boxes and opened the topmost. 'The stuff in here will tell you the whole story. I'll leave you to read it . . . I can't stand the sight of it. And anyway, I'd better clean the place up a bit, in case Jenny comes back.'

'You don't expect her, do you?'

She tilted her head slightly, hearing the faint alarm in my voice. 'Are you frightened of her?'

'Should I be?'

'She says you're a worm.' A hint of amusement softened the words.

'Yes, she would,' I said. 'And no, I'm not frightened of her. She just . . . distracts me.'

With sudden vehemence she said, 'Jenny's a super girl.' Genuine friendship, I thought. A statement of loyalties. The merest whiff of challenge. But Jenny, the super girl, was the one I'd married.

I said, 'Yes,' without inflection, and after a second or two she turned and went out of the room. With a sigh I started on the boxes, shifting them clumsily and being glad neither Jenny nor Louise was watching. They were large, and although one or two were not as heavy as the others, their proportions were all wrong for gripping electrically.

The top one contained two foot-deep stacks of office-size paper, white, good quality, and printed with what looked like a typewritten letter. At the top of each sheet there was an impressive array of headings, including, in the centre, an embossed and gilded coat of arms. I lifted out one of the letters, and began to understand how Jenny had fallen for the trick.

Research into Coronary Disability it said, in engraved lettering above the coat of arms, with, beneath it, the words *Registered Charity*. To the left of the gold embossing there was a list of patrons, mostly with titles, and to the right a list of the charity's employees, one of whom was listed as Jennifer Halley, Executive Assistant. Below her name, in small capital letters, was the address of the Oxford flat.

The letter bore no date and no salutation. It began about a third of the way down the paper, and said:

So many families nowadays have had sorrowful first-hand knowledge of the seriousness of coronary artery disease, which even where it does not kill can leave a man unable to continue with a full, strenuous working life.

Much work has already been done in the field of investigation into the causes and possible prevention of this scourge of modern man, but much more remains still to be done. Research funded by Government money being of necessity limited in today's financial climate, it is of the utmost import-ance that the public should be asked to support directly the essential programmes now in hand in privately run facilities.

We do know, however, that many people resent receiving straightforward fund-raising letters, however worthy the cause, so to aid 'Research into Coronary Disability' we ask you to buy something, along the same principle as Christmas cards, the sale of which does so much good work in so many fields. Accordingly the Patrons, after much discussion, have decided to offer for sale a supply of exceptionally fine wax polish, which has been especially formulated for the care of antique furniture.

The wax is packed in quarter-kilo tins, and is of the quality used by expert restorers and museum curators. If you should wish to buy, we are offering the wax at five pounds a tin; and you may be sure that at least three-quarters of the revenue goes straight to research.

The wax will be good for your furniture, your contribution will be good for the cause, and with your help there may soon be significant advances in the understanding and control of this killing disease.

If you should wish to, please send a donation to the address printed above. (Cheques should be made out to Research into Coronary Disability.) You will receive a supply of wax immediately, and the gratitude of future heart patients everywhere.

Yours sincerely

Executive Assistant

I said 'Phew' to myself, and folded the letter and tucked it into my jacket. Sob stuff; the offer of something tangible in return; and the veiled hint that if you didn't cough up it could one day happen to you. And, according to Charles, the mixture had worked.

The second big box contained several thousand white envelopes, unaddressed. The third was half full of mostly hand-written letters on every conceivable type of writing paper; orders for wax, all saying, among other things, 'cheque enclosed'.

The fourth contained printed Compliments slips, saying that *Research into Coronary Disability* acknowledged the contribution with gratitude and had pleasure herewith in sending a supply of wax.

The fifth brown box, half empty, and the sixth, unopened and full, contained a number of flat white boxes about six inches square by two inches deep. I lifted out a white box and looked inside. Contents, one flat round unprinted tin with a firmly screwed-on lid. The lid put up a fight, but I got it off in the end, and found underneath it a soft mid-brown mixture that certainly smelled of polish. I shut it up, returned the tin to its package, and left it out ready to take.

There seemed to be nothing else. I looked into every cranny in the room and down the sides of the armchair, but there wasn't as much as a pin.

I picked up the square white box and went back slowly and quietly towards the sitting room, opening the closed doors one by one, and looking at what they concealed. There had been two which Louise had not identified: one proved to be a linen cupboard, and the other a small unfurnished room containing suitcases and assorted junk.

Jenny's room was decisively feminine; pink and white, frothy with net and frills. Her scent lay lightly in the air, the violet scent of *Mille*. No use remembering the first bottle I'd given her, long ago in Paris. Too much time had passed. I shut the door on the fragrance and the memory and went into the bathroom.

A white bathroom. Huge fluffy towels. Green carpet, green plants. Looking glass on two walls, light and bright. No visible tooth brushes: everything in cupboards, very tidy. Very Jenny. Roger & Gallet soap.

The snooping habit had ousted too many scruples. With hardly a hesitation I opened Louise's door and put my eyes round, trusting to luck she wouldn't come out into the hall and find me.

Organized mess, I thought. Heaps of papers, and books everywhere. Clothes on chairs. Unmade bed; not surprising, since I'd sprung her out of it.

A washbasin in a corner, no cap on the toothpaste, pair of tights hung to dry. An open box of chocolates. A haphazard scatter on the dressing chest. A tall vase with horse-chestnut buds bursting. No smell at all. No long-term dirt, just surface clutter. The blue dressing gown on the floor. Basically the room was furnished much like Ashe's; and one could clearly see where Jenny ended and Louise began.

I pulled my head out and closed the door, undetected. Louise, in the sitting room, had been easily sidetracked in her tidying, and was sitting on the floor intently reading a book.

'Oh, hello,' she said, looking up vaguely as if she had forgotten I was there. 'Have you finished?'

'There must be other papers,' I said. 'Letters, bills, cash books, that sort of thing.'

'The police took them.'

I sat on the sofa, facing her. 'Who called the police in?' I said. 'Was it Jenny?'

She wrinkled her forehead. 'No. Someone complained to them that the charity wasn't registered.'

'Who?'

'I don't know. Someone who received one of the letters, and checked up. Half those patrons on the letterhead don't exist, and the others didn't know their names were being used.'

I thought, and said, 'What made Ashe bolt just when he did?'

'We don't know. Maybe someone telephoned here to complain, as well. So he went while he could. He'd been gone for a week when the police turned up.'

I put the square white box on the coffee table. 'Where did the wax come from?' I said.

'Some firm or other. Jenny wrote to order it, and it was delivered here. Nicky knew where to get it.'

'Invoices?'

'The police took them.'

'These begging letters . . . who got them printed?'

She sighed. 'Jenny, of course. Nicky had some others, just like them, except that they had his name in the space where they put Jenny's. He explained that it was no use sending any more letters with his name and address on, as he'd moved. He was keen, you see, to keep on working for the cause . . .'

'You bet he was,' I said.

She was half-irritated. 'It's all very well to jeer, but you didn't meet him. You'd have believed him, same as we did.'

I left it. Maybe I would have. 'These letters,' I said. 'Who were they sent to?'

'Nicky had lists of names and addresses. Thousands of them.'

'Have you got them? The lists?'

She looked resigned. 'He took them with him.'

'What sort of people were on them?'

'The sort of people who would own antique furniture and cough up a fiver without missing it.'

'Did he say where he'd got them from?'

'Yes,' she said. 'From the charity's headquarters.'

'And who addressed the letters and sent them out?'

'Nicky typed the envelopes. Yes, don't ask, on my typewriter. He was very fast. He could do hundreds in a day. Jenny signed her name at the bottom of the letters, and I usually folded them and put them in the envelopes. She used to get writers' cramp doing it and Nicky would often help her.'

'Signing her name?'

'That's right. He copied her signature. He did it hundreds of times. You couldn't really tell the difference.'

I looked at her in silence.

'I know,' she said. 'Asking for trouble. But, you see, he made all that hard work with the letters seem such fun. Like a game. He was full of jokes. You don't understand. And then, when the cheques started rolling in, it was so obviously worth the effort.'

'Who sent off the wax?' I said gloomily.

'Nicky typed the addresses on labels. I used to help Jenny stick them on the boxes and seal the boxes with sticky tape, and take them to the post office.'

'Ashe never went?'

'Too busy typing. We used to wheel them round to the post office in those shopping bags on wheels.'

'And the cheques . . . I suppose Jenny herself paid them in?'

'That's right.'

'How long did all this go on?' I said.

'A couple of months, once the letters were printed and the wax had arrived.'

'How much wax?'

'Oh, we had stacks of it, all over the place. It came in those big brown boxes . . . sixty tins in each, ready packed. They practically filled the flat. Actually in the end Jenny wanted to order some more, as we were running very low, but Nicky said no, we'd finish what we had and take a breather before starting again.'

'He meant to stop anyway,' I said.

Reluctantly, she said, 'Yes.'

'How much money,' I said, 'did Jenny bank?'

She looked at me sombrely. 'In the region of ten thousand pounds. Maybe a bit more. Some people sent much more than a fiver. One or two sent a hundred, and didn't want the wax.'

'It's incredible.'

'The money just came pouring in. It still does, every day. But it goes direct to the police from the post office. They'll have a hell of a job sending it all back.'

'What about that box of letters in Ashe's room, saying "cheques enclosed"?'

'Those,' she said, 'are people whose money was banked, and who've been sent the wax.'

'Didn't the police want those letters?'

She shrugged. 'They didn't take them, anyway.'

'Do you mind if I do?'

'Help yourself . . .'

After I'd fetched them and dumped them in their box by the front door, I went back into the sitting room to ask her another question. Deep in the book again, she looked up without enthusiasm.

'How did Ashe get the money out of the bank?'

'He took a typewritten letter signed by Jenny saying she wanted to withdraw the balance so as to be able to give it to the charity in cash at its annual gala dinner, and also a cheque signed by Jenny for every penny.'

'But she didn't . . .'

'No. He did. But I've seen the letter and the cheque. The bank gave them to the police. You can't tell it isn't Jenny's writing. Even Jenny can't tell the difference.'

She got gracefully to her feet, leaving the book on the floor. 'Are you going?' she said hopefully. 'I've got so much to do. I'm way behind, because of Nicky.' She went past me into the hall, but when I followed her she delivered another chunk of dismay.

'The bank clerks can't remember Nicky. They pay out cash in thousands for wages every day, because there's so much industry in Oxford. They were used to Jenny in connection with that account, and it was ten days or more before the police asked questions. No one can remember Nicky there at all.'

'He's professional,' I said flatly.

'Every pointer to it, I'm afraid.' She opened the door while I bent down and awkwardly picked up the brown cardboard box, balancing the small white one on top.

'Thank you,' I said, 'for your help.'

'Let me carry that box downstairs.'

'I can do it,' I said.

She looked briefly into my eyes. 'I'm sure you can. You're too damned proud.' She took the box straight out of my arms and walked purposefully away. I followed her, feeling a fool, down the stairs and out on to the tarmac.

'Car?' she said.

'Round the back, but . . .'

As well talk to the tide. I went with her, weakly

gestured to the Scimitar, and opened the boot. She dumped the boxes inside, and I shut them in.

'Thank you,' I said again. 'For everything.'

The faintest of smiles came back into her eyes.

'If you think of anything that could help Jenny,' I said, 'will you please let me know?'

'If you give me your address.'

I forked a card out of an inner pocket and gave it to her. 'It's on there.'

'All right.' She stood still for a moment with an expression I couldn't read. 'I'll tell you one thing,' she said. 'From what Jenny's said . . . you're not a bit what I expected.'

CHAPTER FIVE

From Oxford I drove west to Gloucestershire and arrived at Garvey's stud farm at the respectable visiting hour of eleven-thirty, Sunday morning.

Tom Garvey, standing in his stable yard talking to his stud groom, came striding across as I braked to a halt.

'Sid Halley!' he said. 'What a surprise. What do you want?'

I grimaced through the open car window. 'Does everyone think I want something, when they see me?'

'Of course, lad. Best snooper in the business now, so they say. We hear things, you know, even us dim country bumpkins, we hear things.'

Smiling, I climbed out of the car and shook hands with a sixty-year-old near-rogue who was about as far from a dim country bumpkin as Cape Horn from Alaska. A big strong bull of a man, with unshakable confidence, a loud domineering voice, and the wily mind of a gypsy. His hand in mine was as hard as his business methods and as dry as his manner. Tough with men, gentle with horses. Year after year he prospered, and if I would have had every foal on the place exhaustively blood-typed before I believed its alleged breeding, I was probably in the minority.

'What are you after, then, Sid?' he said.

'I came to see a mare, Tom. One that you've got here. Just general interest.'

'Oh yes? Which one?'

'Bethesda.'

There was an abrupt change in his expression from half-amusement to no amusement at all. He narrowed his eyes and said brusquely, 'What about her?'

'Well . . . has she foaled, for instance?'

'She's dead.'

'*Dead?*'

'You heard, lad. She's dead. You'd better come in the house.'

He turned and scrunched away, and I followed. His house was old and dark and full of stale air. All the life of the place was outside, in fields and foaling boxes and the breeding shed. Inside, a heavy clock ticked loudly into silence, and there was no aroma of Sunday roast.

'In here.'

It was a cross between a dining room and an office: heavy old table and chairs at one end, filing cabinets and sagging armchairs at the other. No attempts at cosmetic decor to please the customers. Sales went on outside, on the hoof.

Tom perched against his desk and I on the arm of one

of the chairs: not the sort of conversation for relaxing in comfort.

'Now then,' he said, 'why are you asking about Bethesda?'

'I just wondered what had become of her.'

'Don't fence with me, lad. You don't drive all the way here out of general interest. What do you want to know for?'

'A client wants to know,' I said.

'What client?'

'If I were working for you,' I said, 'and you'd told me to keep quiet about it, would you expect me to tell?'

He considered me with sour concentration.

'No, lad. Guess I wouldn't. And I don't suppose there's much secret about Bethesda. She died foaling. The foal died with her. A colt, it would have been. Small, though.'

'I'm sorry,' I said.

He shrugged. 'It happens sometimes. Not often, mind. Her heart packed up.'

'Heart?'

'Aye. The foal was lying wrong, see, and the mare, she'd been straining longer than was good for her. We got the foal turned inside her once we found she was in trouble, but she just packed it in, sudden like. Nothing we could do. Middle of the night, of course, like it nearly always is.'

'Did you have a vet to her?'

'Aye, he was there, right enough. I called him when

we found she'd started, because there was a chance it would be dicey. First foal, and the heart murmur, and all.'

I frowned slightly. 'Did she have a heart murmur when she came to you?'

'Of course she did, lad. That's why she stopped racing. You don't know much about her, do you?'

'No,' I said. 'Tell me.'

He shrugged. 'She came from George Caspar's yard, of course. Her owner wanted to breed from her on account of her two-year-old form, so we bred her to Timberley, which should have given us a sprinter, but there you are, best laid plans, and all that.'

'When did she die?'

'Month ago, maybe.'

'Well, thanks, Tom.' I stood up. 'Thanks for your time.'

He shoved himself off his desk. 'Bit of a tame turn-up for you, asking questions, isn't it? I can't square it with the old Sid Halley, all speed and guts over the fences.'

'Times change, Tom.'

'Aye, I suppose so. I'll bet you miss it, though, that roar from the stands when you'd come to the last and bloody well lift your horse over it.' His face echoed remembered excitements. 'By God, lad, that was a sight. Not a nerve in your body . . . don't know how you did it.'

I supposed it was generous of him, but I wished he would stop.

'Bit of bad luck, losing your hand. Still, with

steeplechasing it's always something. Broken backs and such.' We began to walk to the door. 'If you go jump-racing you've got to accept the risks.'

'That's right,' I said.

We went outside and across to my car.

'You don't do too badly with that contraption, though, do you, lad? Drive a car and such.'

'It's fine.'

'Aye, lad.' He knew it wasn't. He wanted me to know he was sorry, and he'd done his best. I smiled at him, got into the car, sketched a thank-you salute, and drove away.

At Aynsford they were in the drawing room, drinking sherry before lunch: Charles, Toby and Jenny.

Charles gave me a glass of fino, Toby looked me up nd down as if I'd come straight from a pigsty, and Jenny said she had been talking to Louise on the telephone.

'We thought you had run away. You left the flat two hours ago.'

'Sid doesn't run away,' Charles said, as if stating a fact.

'Limps, then,' Jenny said.

Toby sneered at me over his glass: the male in possession enjoying his small gloat over the dispossessed. I wondered if he really understood the extent of Jenny's attachment to Nicholas Ashe, or if knowing, he didn't care.

I sipped the sherry: a thin dry taste, suitable to the occasion. Vinegar might have been better.

'Where did you buy all that polish from?' I said.

'I don't remember.' She spoke distinctly, spacing out the syllables, wilfully obstructive.

'Jenny!' Charles protested.

I sighed. 'Charles, the police have the invoices, which will have the name and address of the polish firm on them. Can you ask your friend Oliver Quayle to ask the police for the information, and send it to me.'

'Certainly,' he said.

'I cannot see,' Jenny said in the same sort of voice, 'that knowing who supplied the wax will make the slightest difference one way or the other.'

It appeared that Charles privately agreed with her. I didn't explain. There was a good chance, anyway, that they were right.

'Louise said you were prying for ages.'

'I liked her,' I said mildly.

Jenny's nose, as always, gave away her displeasure. 'She's out of your class, Sid,' she said.

'In what way?'

'Brains, darling.'

Charles said smoothly, 'More sherry, anyone?' and, decanter in hand, began refilling glasses. To me, he said, 'I believe Louise took a first at Cambridge in mathematics. I have played her at chess . . . you would beat her with ease.'

'A Grand Master,' Jenny said, 'can be obsessional and stupid and have a persecution complex.'

Lunch came and went in the same sort of atmosphere, and afterwards I went upstairs to put my few things into my suitcase. While I was doing it Jenny came in to the room and stood watching me.

'You don't use that hand much,' she said.

I didn't answer.

'I don't know why you bother with it.'

'Stop it, Jenny.'

'If you'd done as I asked, and given up racing, you wouldn't have lost it.'

'Probably not.'

'You'd have a hand, not half an arm . . . not a stump.'

I threw my spongebag with too much force into the suitcase.

'Racing first. Always racing. Dedication and winning and glory. And me nowhere. It serves you right. We'd still have been married . . . you'd still have your hand . . . if you'd have given up your precious racing when I wanted you to. Being champion jockey meant more to you than I did.'

'We've said all this a dozen times,' I said.

'Now you've got nothing. Nothing at all. I hope you're satisfied.'

The battery charger stood on a chest of drawers, with two batteries in it. She pulled the plug out of the mains socket and threw the whole thing on the bed. The batteries fell out and lay on the bedspread haphazardly with the charger and its flex.

'It's disgusting,' she said, looking at it. 'It revolts me.'

'I've got used to it.' More or less, anyway.

'You don't seem to care.'

I said nothing. I cared, all right.

'Do you enjoy being crippled, Sid?'

Enjoy . . . Jesus Christ.

She walked to the door and left me looking down at the charger. I felt more than saw her pause there, and wondered numbly what else there was left that she could say.

Her voice reached me quite clearly across the room.

'Nicky has a knife in his sock.'

I turned my head fast. She looked both defiant and expectant. 'Is that true?' I asked.

'Sometimes.'

'Adolescent,' I said.

She was annoyed. 'And what's so mature about hurtling around on horses and knowing . . . *knowing* . . . that pain and broken bones are going to happen?'

'You never think they will.'

'And you're always wrong.'

'I don't do it any more.'

'But you would if you could.'

There was no answer to that, because we both knew it was true.

'And look at you,' Jenny said. 'When you have to stop racing, do you look around for a nice quiet job in stockbroking, which you know about, and start to lead a normal life? No, you damned well don't. You go straight into something which lands you up in fights and beatings and hectic scrambles. You can't live without danger, Sid. You're addicted. You may think you aren't, but it's like a drug. If you just imagine yourself working in an office, nine to five, and commuting like any sensible man, you'll see what I mean.'

I thought about it, silently.

'Exactly,' she said. 'In an office, you'd die.'

'And what's so safe about a knife in the sock?' I said. 'I was a jockey when we met. You knew what it entailed.'

'Not from the inside. Not all those terrible bruises, and no food and no drink, and no damned sex half the time.'

'Did he show you the knife, or did you just see it?'

'What does it matter?'

'Is he adolescent . . . or truly dangerous?'

'There you are,' she said. 'You'd prefer him dangerous.'

'Not for your sake.'

'Well . . . I saw it. In a little sheath, strapped to his leg. And he made a joke about it.'

'But you told me,' I said. 'So was it a warning?'

She seemed suddenly unsure and disconcerted, and after a moment or two simply frowned and walked away down the passage.

If it marked the first crack in her indulgence towards her precious Nicky, so much the better.

I picked Chico up on Tuesday morning and drove north to Newmarket. A windy day, bright, showery, rather cold.

'How did you get on with the wife, then?'

He had met her once and had described her as unforgettable, the overtones in his voice giving the word several meanings.

'She's in trouble,' I said.

'Pregnant?'

'There are other forms of trouble, you know.'

'Really?'

I told him about the fraud, and about Ashe, and his knife.

'Gone and landed herself in a whoopsy,' Chico said.

'Face down.'

'And for dusting her off, do we get a fee?'

I looked at him sideways.

'Yeah,' he said. 'I thought so. Working for nothing again, aren't we? Good job you're well-oiled, Sid, mate, when it comes to my wages. What is it this year? You made a fortune in anything since Christmas?'

'Silver, mostly. And cocoa. Bought and sold.'

'Cocoa?' He was incredulous.

'Beans,' I said. 'Chocolate.'

'Nutty bars?'

'No, not the nuts. They're risky.'

'I don't know how you find the time.'

'It takes as long as chatting up barmaids.'

'What do you want with all that money, anyway?'

'It's a habit,' I said. 'Like eating.'

Amicably we drew nearer to Newmarket, consulted the map, asked a couple of locals, and finally arrived at the incredibly well-kept stud farm of Henry Thrace.

'Sound out the lads,' I said, and Chico said, 'Sure', and we stepped out of the car on to weedless gravel. I left him to it and went in search of Henry Thrace, who was reported by a cleaning lady at the front door of the house to be 'down there on the right, in his office'. Down there he was, in an armchair, fast asleep.

My arrival woke him, and he came alive with the instant awareness of people used to broken nights. A youngish man, very smooth, a world away from rough, tough, wily Tom Garvey. With Thrace, according to pre-digested opinion, breeding was strictly big business: handling the mares could be left to lower mortals. His first words, however, didn't match the image.

'Sorry. Been up half the night . . . Er, who are you, exactly? Do we have an appointment?'

'No.' I shook my head. 'I just hoped to see you. My name's Sid Halley.'

'Is it? Any relation to . . . Good Lord. You're him.'

'I'm him.'

'What can I do for you? Want some coffee?' He rubbed his eyes. 'Mrs Evans will get us some.'

'Don't bother, unless . . .'

'No. Fire away.' He looked at his watch. 'Ten minutes do? I've got a meeting in Newmarket.'

'It's very vague, really,' I said. 'I just came to enquire into the general health and so on of two of the stallions you've got here.'

'Oh. Which two?'

'Gleaner,' I said. 'And Zingaloo.'

We went through the business of why did I want to know, and why should he tell me, but finally, like Tom Garvey, he shrugged and said I might as well know.

'I suppose I shouldn't say it, but you wouldn't want to advise a client to buy shares in either of them,' he said, taking for granted this was really the purpose of my visit. 'They might have difficulty in covering their full quota of mares, both of them, although they're only four.'

'Why's that?'

'They've both got bad hearts. They get exhausted with too much exercise.'

'Both?'

'That's right. That's what stopped them racing as three-year-olds. And I reckon they've got worse since then.'

'Somebody mentioned Gleaner was lame,' I said.

Henry Thrace looked resigned. 'He's developed arthritis recently. You can't keep a damn thing to yourself in this town.' An alarm clock made a clamour on his desk. He reached over and switched it off. 'Time to go,

I'm afraid.' He yawned. 'I hardly take my clothes off at this time of the year.' He took a battery razor out of his desk drawer, and attacked his beard. 'Is that everything then, Sid?'

'Yes,' I said. 'Thanks.'

Chico pulled the car door shut, and we drove away towards the town.

'Bad hearts,' he said.

'Bad hearts.'

'Proper epidemic, isn't it?'

'Let's ask Brothersmith the vet.'

Chico read out the address, in Middleton Road.

'Yes, I know it. It was old Follett's place. He was our old vet, still alive when I was here.'

Chico grinned. 'Funny somehow to think of you being a snotty little apprentice with the head lad chasing you.'

'And chilblains.'

'Makes you seem almost human.'

I had spent five years in Newmarket, from sixteen to twenty-one. Learning to ride, learning to race, learning to live. My old guv'nor had been a good one, and because I saw every day his wife, his lifestyle, and his administrative ability, I'd slowly changed from a boy from the backstreets into something more cosmo-politan. He had shown me how to manage the money I'd begun earning in large quantities, and how not to be corrupted by it; and when he turned me loose I found he'd given me the status that went with having been taught in his stable. I'd been lucky in my guv'nor, and lucky to be for a long time at the top of the career I loved; and if one day the luck had run out it was too damned bad.

'Takes you back, does it?' Chico said.

'Yeah.'

We drove across the wide Heath and past the race-course towards the town. There weren't many horses about: a late morning string, in the distance, going home. I swung the car round familiar corners and pulled up outside the vet's.

Mr Brothersmith was out.

If it was urgent, Mr Brothersmith could be found seeing to a horse in a stable along Bury Road. Otherwise he would be home to his lunch, probably, in half an hour. We said thank you, and sat in the car, and waited.

'We've got another job,' I said. 'Checking on syndicates.'

'I thought the Jockey Club always did it themselves.'

'Yes, they do. The job we've got is to check on the man from the Jockey Club who checks on the syndicates.'

Chico digested it. 'Tricky, that.'

'Without him knowing.'

'Oh yes?'

I nodded. 'Ex-Superintendent Eddy Keith.'

Chico's mouth fell open. 'You're joking.'

'No.'

'But he's the fuzz. The Jockey Club fuzz.'

I passed on Lucas Wainwright's doubts, and Chico said Lucas Wainwright must have got it wrong. The job, I pointed out mildly, was to find out whether he had or not.

'And how do we do that?'

'I don't know. What do you think?'

'It's you that's supposed to be the brains of this outfit.'

A muddy Range Rover came along Middleton Road and turned into Brothersmith's entrance. As one, Chico and I removed ourselves from the Scimitar, and went towards the tweed-jacketed man jumping down from his buggy.

'Mr Brothersmith?'

'Yes? What's the trouble?'

He was young and harassed, and kept looking over his shoulder, as if something was chasing him. Time, perhaps, I thought. Or lack of it.

'Could you spare us a few minutes?' I said. 'This is Chico Barnes, and I'm Sid Halley. It's just a few questions . . .'

His brain took in the name and his gaze switched immediately towards my hands, fastening finally on the left.

'Aren't you the man with the myoelectric prosthesis?'

'Er . . . yes,' I said.

'Come in, then. Can I look at it?'

He turned away and strode purposefully towards the side door of the house. I stood still and wished we were anywhere else.

'Come on, Sid,' Chico said, following him. He looked back and stopped. 'Give the man what he wants, Sid, and maybe he'll do the same for us.'

Payment in kind, I thought; and I didn't like the price. Unwillingly I followed Chico into what turned out to be Brothersmith's surgery.

He asked a lot of questions in a fairly clinical manner, and I answered him in impersonal tones learned from the limb centre.

'Can you rotate the wrist?' he said at length.

'Yes, a little.' I showed him. 'There's a sort of cup inside there which fits over the end of my arm, with another electrode to pick up the impulses for turning.'

I knew he wanted me to take the arm off and show him properly, but I wouldn't have done it, and perhaps he saw there was no point in asking.

'It fits very tightly over your elbow,' he said, delicately feeling round the gripping edges.

'So as not to fall off.'

He nodded intently. 'Is it easy to put on and remove?'

'Talcum powder,' I said economically.

Chico's mouth opened, and shut again as he caught my don't-say-it stare, and he didn't tell Brothersmith that removal was often a distinct bore.

'Thinking of fitting one to a horse?' Chico said.

Brothersmith raised his still-harassed face and answered him seriously. 'Technically it looks perfectly possible, but it's doubtful if one could train a horse to activate the electrodes, and it would be difficult to justify the expense.'

'It was only a joke,' Chico said faintly.

'Oh? Oh, I see. But it isn't unknown, you know, for a horse to have a false foot fitted. I was reading the other day about a successful prosthesis fitted to the fore-limb of a valuable broodmare. She was subsequently covered, and produced a live foal.'

'Ah,' Chico said. 'Now that's what we've come about. A broodmare. Only this one died.'

Brothersmith detached his attention reluctantly from false limbs and transferred it to horses with bad hearts.

'Bethesda,' I said, rolling down my sleeve and buttoning the cuff.

'Bethesda?' He wrinkled his forehead and turned the harassed look into one of anxiety. 'I'm sorry. I can't recall . . .'

'She was a filly with George Caspar,' I said. 'Beat everything as a two-year-old, and couldn't run at three because of a heart murmur. She was sent to stud, but her heart packed up when she was foaling.'

'Oh dear,' he said, adding sorrow to the anxiety. 'What a pity. But I say, I'm so sorry, but I treat so many horses, and I often don't know their names. Is there a question of insurance in this, or negligence, even? Because I assure you . . .'

'No,' I said reassuringly, 'nothing like that. Can you remember, then, treating Gleaner and Zingaloo?'

'Yes, of course. Those two. Wretched shame for George Caspar. So disappointing.'

'Tell us about them.'

'Nothing much to tell, really. Nothing out of the ordinary, except that they were both so good as two-year-olds. Probably that was the cause of their troubles, if the truth were told.'

'How do you mean?' I said.

His nervous tensions escaped in small jerks of his head as he brought forth some unflattering opinions. 'Well, one hesitates to say so, of course, to top trainers like Caspar, but it is all too easy to strain a two-year-old's heart, and if they are good two-year-olds they run in top races, and the pressure to win may be terrific, because of stud values and everything, and a jockey, riding strictly to orders, mind you, may press a game youngster so hard that although it wins it is also more or less ruined for the future.'

'Gleaner won the Doncaster Futurity in the mud,' I said thoughtfully. 'I saw it. It was a very hard race.'

'That's right,' Brothersmith said. 'I checked him thoroughly afterwards, though. The trouble didn't start at once. In fact, it didn't show at all, until he ran in the Guineas. He came in from that in a state of complete exhaustion. First of all we thought it was the virus but then after a few days we got this very irregular heart beat, and then it was obvious what was the matter.'

'What virus?' I said.

'Let's see . . . The evening of the Guineas he had a very slight fever, as if he were in for equine flu, or some such. But it didn't develop. So it wasn't that. It was his heart, all right. But we couldn't have foreseen it.'

'What percentage of horses develop bad hearts?' I said.

Some of the chronic anxiety state diminished as he moved confidently on to neutral ground.

'Perhaps ten per cent have irregular heart beats. It doesn't always mean anything. Owners don't like to buy horses which have them, but look at Night Nurse which won the Champion Hurdle, that had a heart murmur.'

'But how often do you get horses having to stop racing because of bad hearts?'

He shrugged. 'Perhaps two or three in a hundred.'

George Caspar, I reflected, trained upwards of a hundred and thirty horses, year after year.

'On average,' I said, 'are George Caspar's horses more prone to bad hearts than any other trainer's?'

The anxiety state returned in full force. 'I don't know if I should answer that.'

'If it's "no",' I said, 'what's the hassle?'

'But your purpose in asking . . .'

'A client,' I said, lying with regrettable ease, 'wants to know if he should send George Caspar a sparkling yearling. He asked me to check on Gleaner and Zingaloo.'

'Oh, I see. Well, no, I don't suppose he has more. Nothing significant. Caspar's an excellent trainer, of course. If your client isn't too greedy when his horse is two, there shouldn't be any risk at all.'

'Thanks, then.' I stood up and shook hands with him. 'I suppose there's no heart trouble with Tri-Nitro?'

'None at all. Sound, through and through. His heart bangs away like a gong, loud and clear.'

CHAPTER SIX

'That's that, then,' Chico said over a pint and pie in the White Hart Hotel. 'End of case. Mrs Caspar's off her tiny rocker, and no one's been getting at George Caspar's youngsters except George Caspar himself.'

'She won't be pleased to hear it,' I said.

'Will you tell her?'

'Straight away. If she's convinced, she might calm down.'

So I telephoned to George Caspar's house, and asked for Rosemary, saying I was a Mr Barnes. She came on the line and said hello in the questioning voice one uses to unknown callers.

'Mr . . . Barnes?'

'It's Sid Halley.'

The alarm came instantly. 'I can't talk to you.'

'Can you meet me, then?'

'Of course not. I've no reason for going to London.'

'I'm just down the road, in the town,' I said. 'I've things to tell you. And I don't honestly think there's any need for disguises and so on.'

'I'm not being seen with you in Newmarket.'

She agreed, however, to drive out in her car, pick Chico up, and go where he directed: and Chico and I worked out a place on the map which looked a tranquillizing spot for paranoiacs. The churchyard at Barton Mills, eight miles towards Norwich.

We parked the cars side by side at the gate and Rosemary walked with me among the graves. She was wearing again the fawn raincoat and a scarf, but not this time the false curls. The wind blew wisps of her own chestnut hair across her eyes, and she pulled them away impatiently: not with quite as much tension as when she had come to my flat, but still with more force than was needed.

I told her I had been to see Tom Garvey and Henry Thrace at their stud farms. I told her I had talked to Brothersmith; and I told her what they'd all said. She listened, and shook her head.

'The horses were nobbled,' she said obstinately. 'I'm sure they were.'

'How?'

'I don't know how.' Her voice rose sharply, the agitation showing in spasms of the muscles round her mouth. 'But I told you. I told you, they'll get at Tri-Nitro. A week today, it's the Guineas. You've got to keep him safe for a week.'

We walked along the path beside the quiet mounds and the grey weatherbeaten headstones. The grass was mown, but there were no flowers, and no mourners. The dead there were long gone, long forgotten. Raw grief and tears now in the municipal plot outside the town; brown heaps of earth and brilliant wreaths and desolation in tidy rows.

'George has doubled the security on Tri-Nitro,' I said.

'I know that. Don't be stupid.'

I said reluctantly, 'In the normal course of events he'll be giving Tri-Nitro some strong work before the Guineas. Probably on Saturday morning.'

'I suppose so. What do you mean? Why do you ask?'

'Well . . .' I paused, wondering if indeed it would be sensible to suggest a way-out theory without testing it, and thinking that there was no way of testing it anyway.

'Go on,' she said sharply. 'What do you mean?'

'You could . . . er . . . make sure he takes all sorts of precautions when he gives Tri-Nitro that last gallop.' I paused. 'Inspect the saddle . . . that sort of thing.'

Rosemary said fiercely, 'What are you saying? Spell it out, for God's sake. Don't pussyfoot round it.'

'Lots of races have been lost because of too-hard training gallops too soon beforehand.'

'Of course,' she said impatiently. 'Everyone knows that. But George would never do it.'

'What if the saddle was packed with lead? What if a three-year-old was given a strong gallop carrying fifty pounds dead weight? And then ran under severe pressure a few days later in the Guineas? And strained his heart?'

'My God,' she said. 'My God.'

'I'm not saying that it did happen to Zingaloo and Gleaner, or anything like it. Only that it's a distant possibility. And if it's something like that . . . it must involve someone inside the stable.'

She had begun trembling again.

'You must go on,' she said. 'Please go on trying. I brought some money for you.' She plunged a hand into her raincoat pocket and brought out a smallish brown envelope. 'It's cash. I can't give you a cheque.'

'I haven't earned it,' I said.

'Yes, yes. Take it.' She was insistent, and finally I put it in my pocket, unopened.

'Let me consult George,' I said.

'No. He'd be furious. I'll do it . . . I mean, I'll warn him about the gallops. He thinks I'm crazy, but if I go on about it long enough he'll take notice.' She looked at her watch and her agitation increased. 'I'll have to go back now. I said I was going for a walk on the Heath. I never do that. I'll have to get back, or they'll be wondering.'

'Who'll be wondering?'

'George, of course.'

'Does he know where you are every minute of the day?'

We were retracing our steps with some speed towards the churchyard gates. Rosemary looked as if she would soon be running.

'We always talk. He asks where I've been. He's not suspicious . . . it's just a habit. We're always together.

101

Well, you know what it's like in a racing household. Owners come at odd times. George likes me to be there.'

We reached the cars. She said goodbye uncertainly, and drove off homewards in a great hurry. Chico, waiting in the Scimitar, said, 'Quiet here, isn't it? Even the ghosts must find it boring.'

I got into the car and tossed Rosemary's envelope on to his lap. 'Count that,' I said, starting the engine. 'See how we're doing.'

He tore it open, pulled out a neat wad of expensive-coloured banknotes, and licked his fingers.

'Phew,' he said, coming to the end. 'She's bonkers.'

'She wants us to go on.'

'Then you know what this is, Sid,' he said, flicking the stack. 'Guilt money. To spur you on when you want to stop.'

'Well, it works.'

We spent some of Rosemary's incentive in staying overnight in Newmarket and going round the bars, Chico where the lads hung out and I with the trainers. It was Tuesday evening and very quiet everywhere. I heard nothing of any interest and drank more than enough whisky, and Chico came back with hiccups and not much else.

'Ever heard of Inky Poole?' he said.

'Is that a song?'

'No, it's a work jockey. What's a work jockey? Chico my son, a work jockey is a lad who rides work on the gallops.'

'You're drunk,' I said.

'Certainly not. What's a work jockey?'

'What you just said. Not much good in races but can gallop the best at home.'

'Inky Poole,' he said, 'is George Caspar's work jockey. Inky Poole rides Tri-Nitro his strong work at home on the gallops. Did you ask me to find out who rides Tri-Nitro's gallops?'

'Yes, I did,' I said. 'And you're drunk.'

'Inky Poole, Inky Poole,' he said.

'Did you talk to him?'

'Never met him. Bunch of the lads, they told me. George Caspar's work jockey. Inky Poole.'

Armed with raceglasses on a strap round my neck I walked along to Warren Hill at seven-thirty in the morning to watch the strings out at morning exercise. A long time, it seemed, since I'd been one of the tucked-up figures in sweaters and skull cap, with three horses to muck out and care for, and a bed in a hostel with rain-soaked breeches for ever drying on an airer in the kitchen. Frozen fingers and not enough baths, ears full of four-letter words and no chance of being alone.

I had enjoyed it all well enough, when I was sixteen, on account of the horses. Beautiful, marvellous creatures whose responses and instincts worked on a plane as different from humans' as water and oil, not mingling even where they touched. Insight into their senses and consciousness had been like an opening door, a foreign language glimpsed and half learned, full comprehension maddeningly baulked by not having the right sort of hearing or sense of smell, nor sufficient skill in telepathy.

The feeling of oneness with horses I'd sometimes had in the heat of a race had been their gift to an inferior being; and maybe my passion for winning had been my gift to them. The urge to get to the front was born in them; all they needed was to be shown where and when to go. It could fairly be said that like most jump jockeys I had aided and abetted horses beyond the bounds of common sense.

The smell and sight of them on the Heath was like a sea breeze to a sailor. I filled my lungs and eyes, and felt content.

Each exercise string was accompanied and shepherded by its watchful trainer, some of them arriving in cars, some on horseback, some on foot. I collected a lot of 'Good morning, Sid's. Several smiling faces seemed genuinely pleased to see me; and some that weren't in a hurry stopped to talk.

'Sid!' exclaimed one I'd ridden for on the flat in the years before my weight caught up with my height, 'Sid, we don't see you up here much these days.'

'My loss,' I said, smiling.

'Why don't you come and ride out for me? Next time you're here, give me a ring, and we'll fix it.'

'Do you mean it?'

'Of course I mean it. If you'd like to, that is.'

'I'd love it.'

'Right. That's great. Don't forget, now.' He wheeled away, waving, to shout to a lad earning his disfavour by slopping in the saddle like a disorganized jellyfish. 'How the bloody hell d'you expect your horse to pay attention if you don't?' The boy sat decently for all of twenty seconds. He'd go far, I thought, starting from New-market station.

Wednesday being a morning for full training gallops, there was the usual scattering of interested watchers: owners, Pressmen, and assorted bookmakers' touts. Binoculars sprouted like an extra growth of eyes, and notes went down in private shorthand. Though the morning was cold the new season was warming up. There was a feeling overall of purpose, and the bustle of things happening. An industry flexing its muscles. Money, profit, and tax revenue making their proper circle under the wide Suffolk sky. I was still a part of it, even if not in the old way. And Jenny was right. I'd die in an office.

'Morning, Sid.'

I looked round. George Caspar, on a horse, his eyes on a distant string walking down the side of the Heath from his stable in Bury Road.

'Morning, George.'

'You staying up here?'

'Just for a night or two.'

'You should've let us know. We've always a bed. Give Rosemary a ring.' His eyes were on his string: the invitation a politeness, not meant to be accepted. Rosemary, I thought, would have fainted if she'd heard.

'Is Tri-Nitro in that lot?' I said.

'Yes, he is. Sixth from the front.' He looked round at the interested spectators. 'Have you seen Trevor Deansgate anywhere? He said he was coming up here this morning from London. Setting off early.'

'Haven't seen him.' I shook my head.

'He's got two in the string. He was coming to see them work.' He shrugged. 'He'll miss them if he isn't here soon.'

I smiled to myself. Some trainers might delay working the horses until the owner did arrive, but not George. Owners queued up for his favours and treasured his comments, and Trevor Deansgate for all his power was just one of a crowd. I lifted my raceglasses and watched while the string, forty strong, approached and began circling, waiting for their turn on the uphill gallop. The stable before George's had nearly finished, and George would be next.

The lad on Tri-Nitro wore a red scarf in the neck of his olive-green husky jacket. I lowered the glasses and kept my eye on him as he circled, and looked at his mount with the same curiosity as everyone else. A good-looking bay colt, well grown, with strong shoulders and a lot of heart room; but nothing about him to shout from the housetops that here was the wildly backed winter favourite for the Guineas and the Derby. If you hadn't known, you wouldn't have known, as they say.

'Do you mind photographs, George?' I said.

'Help yourself, Sid.'

'Thanks.'

I seldom went anywhere these days without a camera in my pocket. Sixteen millimetre, automatic light meter, all the expense in its lens. I brought it out and showed it to him, and he nodded. 'Take what you like.'

He shook up his patient hack and went away, across to his string, to begin the morning's business. The lad who rode a horse down from the stables wasn't necessarily the same one who rode it in fast work, and as usual there was a good deal of swapping around, to put the best lads up where it mattered. The boy with the red scarf dismounted from Tri-Nitro and held him, and presently a much older lad swung up on to his back.

I walked across to be close to the string, and took three or four photographs of the wonder horse and a couple of closer shots of his rider.

'Inky Poole?' I said to him at one point, as he rode by six feet away.

'That's right,' he said. 'Mind your back. You're in the way.'

A right touch of surliness. If he hadn't seen me talking to George first, he would have objected to my being there at all. I wondered if his grudging against-the-world manner was the cause or the result of his not getting on as a jockey, and felt sympathy for him, on the whole.

George began detailing his lads into the small bunches that would go up the gallops together, and I walked back to the fringes of things, to watch.

A car arrived very fast and pulled up with a jerk, alarming some horses alongside and sending them skittering, with the lads' voices rising high in alarm and protest.

Trevor Deansgate climbed out of his Jaguar and for good measure slammed the door. He was dressed in a city suit, in contrast to everyone else there, and looked ready for the boardroom. Black hair rigorously brushed, chin smoothly shaven, shoes polished like glass. Not the sort of man I would have sought as a friend, because I didn't on the whole like to sit at the feet of power, picking up crumbs of patronage with nervous laughter, but a force to be reckoned with on the racing scene.

Big-scale bookmakers could be and often were a positive influence for good, a stance I thought sardonically that they had been pushed into, to survive the lobby that knew that a Tote monopoly (and a less greedy tax climate) would put back into racing what bookmakers took out. Trevor Deansgate personified the new breed; urbane, a man of the world, seeking top company, becoming a name in the City, the sycophant of earls.

'Hello,' he said, seeing me. 'I met you at Kempton . . . Do you know where George's horses are?'

'Right there,' I said, pointing. 'You're just in time.'

'Bloody traffic.'

He strode across the grass towards George, race-glasses swinging from his hand, and George said hallo briefly and apparently told him to watch the gallops with me, because he came straight back, heavy and confident, and stopped at my side.

'George says my two both go in the first bunch. He said you'd tell me how they're doing, insolent bugger. Got eyes, haven't I? He's going on up the hill.'

I nodded. Trainers often went up halfway and watched from there, the better to see their horses' action as they galloped past.

Four horses were wheeling into position at the starting point. Trevor Deansgate applied his binoculars, twisting them to focus. Navy suiting with faint red pin-stripes. The well-kept hands, gold cuff links, onyx ring, as before.

'Which are yours?' I said.

'The two chestnuts. That one with the white socks is Pinafore. The other's nothing much.'

The nothing much had short cannon bones and a rounded rump. Might make a 'chaser one day, I thought. I liked the look of him better than the whippet-shaped Pinafore. They set off together up the gallop at

George's signal, and the sprinting blood showed all the way to the top. Pinafore romped it and the nothing much lived up to his owner's assessment. Trevor Deansgate lowered his binoculars with a sigh.

'That's that, then. Are you coming to George's for breakfast?'

'No. Not today.'

He raised the glasses again and focused them on the much nearer target of the circling string, and, from the angle, he was looking at the riders, not the horses. The search came to an end on Inky Poole: he lowered the glasses and followed Tri-Nitro with the naked eye.

'A week today,' I said.

'Looks a picture.'

I supposed that he, like all bookmakers, would be happy to see the hot favourite lose the Guineas, but there was nothing in his voice except admiration for a great horse. Tri-Nitro lined up in his turn and at a signal from George set off with two companions at a deceptively fast pace. Inky Poole, I was interested to see, sat as quiet as patience and rode with a skill worth ten times what he would be paid. Good work jockeys were undervalued. Bad ones could ruin a horse's mouth and temperament and whole career. It figured that for the stableful he'd got, George Caspar would employ only the best.

It was not the flat-out searching gallop they would hold on the following Saturday morning over a long smooth surface like the Limekilns. Up the incline of

Warren Hill a fast canter was testing enough. Tri-Nitro took the whole thing without a hint of effort, and breasted the top as if he could go up there six times more without noticing.

Impressive, I thought. The Press, clearly agreeing, were scribbling in their notebooks. Trevor Deansgate looked thoughtful, as well he might, and George Caspar, coming down the hill and reining in near us, looked almost smugly satisfied. The Guineas, one felt, were in the bag.

After they had done their work the horses walked down the hill to join the still circling string where the work riders changed on to fresh mounts and set off again up to the top. Tri-Nitro got back his lad with the olive-green husky and the red scarf, and eventually the whole lot of them set off home.

'That's that, then,' George said. 'All set, Trevor? Breakfast?'

They nodded farewells to me and set off, one in the car, one on the horse. I had eyes mostly, however, for Inky Poole, who had been four times up the hill and was walking off a shade morosely to a parked car.

'Inky,' I said, coming up behind him, 'the gallop on Tri-Nitro . . . that was great.'

He looked at me sourly. 'I've got nothing to say.'

'I'm not from the Press.'

'I know who you are. Saw you racing. Who hasn't?' Unfriendly: almost a sneer. 'What do you want?'

111

'How does Tri-Nitro compare with Gleaner, this time last year?'

He fished the car keys out of a zipper pocket in his anorak, and fitted one into the lock. What I could see of his face looked obstinately unhelpful.

'Did Gleaner, a week before the Guineas, give you the same sort of feel?' I said.

'I'm not talking to you.'

'How about Zingaloo?' I said. 'Or Bethesda?'

He opened his car door and slid down into the driving seat, taking out time to give me a hostile glare.

'Piss off,' he said. Slammed the door. Stabbed the ignition key into the dashboard and forcefully drove away.

Chico had arisen to breakfast but was sitting in the pub's dining room holding his head.

'Don't look so healthy,' he said when I joined him.

'Bacon and eggs,' I said. 'That's what I'll have. Or kippers, perhaps. And strawberry jam.'

He groaned.

'I'm going back to London,' I said. 'But would you mind staying here?' I brought the camera out of my pocket. 'Take the film out of that and get it developed. Overnight if possible. There's some pictures of Tri-Nitro and Inky Poole on there. We might find them helpful, you never know.'

'OK, then,' he said. 'But you'll have to ring up the

Comprehensive and tell them that my black belt's at the cleaners.'

I laughed. 'There were some girls riding in George Caspar's string this morning,' I said. 'See what you can do.'

'That's beyond the call of duty.' But his eye seemed suddenly brighter. 'What am I asking?'

'Things like who saddles Tri-Nitro for exercise gallops, and what's the routine from now until next Wednesday, and whether anything nasty is stirring in the jungle.'

'What about you, then?'

'I'll be back Friday night,' I said. 'In time for the gallops on Saturday. They're bound to gallop Tri-Nitro on Saturday. A strong work-out, to bring him to a peak.'

'Do you really think anything dodgy's going on?' Chico said.

'A toss-up. I just don't know. I'd better ring Rosemary.'

I went through the Mr Barnes routine again and Rosemary came on the line sounding as agitated as ever.

'I can't talk. We've people here for breakfast.'

'Just listen, then,' I said. 'Try to persuade George to vary his routine, when he gallops Tri-Nitro on Saturday. Put up a different jockey, for instance. Not Inky Poole.'

'You don't think . . .' Her voice was high, and broke off.

'I don't know at all,' I said. 'But if George changed

everything about, there'd be less chance of skulduggery. Routine is the robber's best friend.'

'What? Oh yes. All right. I'll try. What about you?'

'I'll be out watching the gallop. After that, I'll stick around, until after the Guineas is safely over. But I wish you'd let me talk to George.'

'No. He'd be livid. I'll have to go now.' The receiver went down with a rattle which spoke of still unsteady hands, and I feared that George might be right about his wife being neurotic.

Charles and I met as usual at the Cavendish the following day, and sat in the upstairs bar's armchairs.

'You look happier,' he said, 'than I've seen you since . . .' he gestured to my arm, with his glass. 'Released in spirit. Not your usual stoical self.'

'I've been in Newmarket,' I said. 'Watched the gallops, yesterday morning.'

'I would have thought . . .' he stopped.

'That I'd be eaten by jealousy?' I said. 'So would I. But I enjoyed it.'

'Good.'

'I'm going up again tomorrow night and staying until after the Guineas next Wednesday.'

'And lunch, next Thursday?'

I smiled and bought him a large pink gin. 'I'll be back for that.'

In due course we ate scallops one-handedly in a wine and cheese sauce, and he gave me the news of Jenny.

'Oliver Quayle sent the address you asked for, for the polish.' He took a paper from his breast pocket and handed it over. 'Oliver is worried. He says the police are actively pursuing their enquiries, and Jenny is almost certain to be charged.'

'When?'

'I don't know. Oliver doesn't know. Sometimes these things take weeks, but not always. And when they charge her, Oliver says, she will have to appear in a magistrates' court, and they are certain to refer the case to the Crown Court, as so much money is involved. They'll give her bail, or course.'

'Bail!'

'Oliver says she is unfortunately very likely to be convicted, but that if it is stressed that she acted as she did under the influence of Nicholas Ashe, she'll probably get some sympathy from the judge and a conditional discharge.'

'Even if he isn't found?'

'Yes. But of course if he *is* found, and charged, and found guilty, Jenny would with luck escape a conviction altogether.'

I took a deep breath that was half a sigh.

'Have to find him then, won't we?' I said.

'How?'

'Well . . . I spent a lot of Monday, and all of this morning, looking through a box of letters. They came from the people who sent money, and ordered wax. Eighteen hundred of them, or thereabouts.'

'How do they help?'

'I've started sorting them into alphabetical order, and making a list.' He frowned sceptically, but I went on. 'The interesting thing is that all the surnames start with the letters L, M, N, and O. None from A to K, and none from P to Z.'

'I don't see . . .'

'They might be part of a mailing list,' I said. 'Like for a catalogue. Or even for a charity. There must be thousands of mailing lists, but this one certainly did produce the required results, so it wasn't a mailing list for dog licence reminders, for example.'

'That seems reasonable,' he said drily.

'I thought I'd get all the names into order and then see if anyone, like Christie's or Sotheby's, say – because of the polish angle – has a mailing list which matches. A long shot, I know, but there's just a chance.'

'I could help you,' he said.

'It's a boring job.'

'She's my daughter.'

'All right then. I'd like it.'

I finished the scallops and sat back in my chair, and drank Charles's good cold white wine.

He said he would stay overnight in his club and come to my flat in the morning to help with the sorting, and I gave him a spare key to get in with, in case I should be out for a newspaper or cigarettes when he came. He lit a cigar and watched me through the smoke. 'What did Jenny say to you upstairs after lunch on Sunday?'

I looked at him briefly. 'Nothing much.'

'She was moody all day, afterwards. She even snapped at Toby.' He smiled. 'Toby protested, and Jenny said, "At least Sid didn't whine."' He paused. 'I gathered that she'd been giving you a particularly rough mauling, and was feeling guilty.'

'It wouldn't be guilt. With luck, it was misgivings about Ashe.'

'And not before time.'

From the Cavendish I went to the Portman Square headquarters of the Jockey Club, to keep an appointment made that morning on the telephone by Lucas Wainwright. Unofficial my task for him might be, but official enough for him to ask me to his office. Ex-Superintendent Eddy Keith, it transpired, had gone to Yorkshire to look into a positive doping test, and no one else was going to wonder much at my visit.

'I've got all the files for you,' Lucas said. 'Eddy's reports on the syndicates, and some notes on the rogues he OK'd.'

'I'll make a start then,' I said. 'Can I take them away, or do you want me to look at them here?'

'Here, if you would,' he said. 'I don't want to draw my secretary's attention to them by letting them out or getting them xeroxed, as she works for Eddy too, and I know she admires him. She would tell him. You'd better copy down what you need.'

'Right,' I said.

He gave me a table to one side of his room, and a comfortable chair, and a bright light, and for an hour or so I read and made notes. At his own desk he did some desultory pen-pushing and rustled a few papers, but in the end it was clear that it was only a pretence of being busy. He wasn't so much waiting for me to finish as generally uneasy.

I looked up from my writing. 'What's the matter?' I said.

'The . . . matter?'

'Something's troubling you.'

He hesitated. 'Have you done all you want?' he said, nodding at my work.

'Only about half,' I said. 'Can you give me another hour?'

'Yes, but . . . Look, I'll have to be fair with you. There's something you'll have to know.'

'What sort of thing?'

Lucas, who was normally urbane even when in a hurry, and whose naval habits of thought I understood from long practice with my Admiral father-in-law, was showing signs of embarrassment. The things that acutely embarrassed naval officers were collisions between warships and quaysides, ladies visiting the crew's mess deck with the crew present and at ease, and dishonourable conduct among gentlemen. It couldn't be the first two; so where were we with the third?

'I have not perhaps given you all the facts,' he said.

'Go on, then.'

'I did send someone else to check on two of the syndicates, some time ago. Six months ago.' He fiddled with some paper-clips, no longer looking in my direction. 'Before Eddy checked them.'

'With what result?'

'Ah. Yes.' He cleared his throat. 'The man I sent – his name's Mason – we never received his report because he was attacked in the street before he could write it.'

Attacked in the street . . . 'What sort of attack?' I said. 'And who attacked him?'

He shook his head. 'Nobody knows who attacked him. He was found on the pavement by some passer-by, who called the police.'

'Well . . . have you asked him – Mason?' But I guessed at something of the answer, if not all of it.

'He's, er, never really recovered,' Lucas said regretfully. 'His head, it seemed, had been repeatedly kicked, as well as his body. There was a good deal of brain damage. He's still in an institution. He always will be. He's a vegetable . . . and he's blind.'

I bit the end of the pencil with which I'd been making notes. 'Was he robbed?' I said.

'His wallet was missing. But not his watch.' His face was worried.

'So it might have been a straightforward mugging?'

119

'Yes . . . except that the police treated it as intended homicide, because of the number and target of the boot marks.'

He sat back in his chair as if he'd got rid of an unwelcome burden. Honour among gentlemen . . . honour satisfied.

'All right,' I said. 'Which two syndicates was he checking?'

'The first two that you have there.'

'And do you think any of the people on them – the undesirables – are the sort to kick their way out of trouble?'

He said unhappily, 'They might be.'

'And am I,' I said carefully, 'investigating the possible corruption of Eddy Keith, or Mason's semi-murder?'

After a pause, he said, 'Perhaps both.'

There was a long silence. Finally I said, 'You do realize that by sending me notes at the races and meeting me in the tea room and bringing me here, you haven't left much doubt that I'm working for you?'

'But it could be at anything.'

I said gloomily, 'Not when I turn up on the syndicates' doorsteps.'

'I'd quite understand,' he said, 'if, in view of what I've said, you wanted to . . . er . . .'

So would I, I thought. I would understand that I didn't want my head kicked in. But then what I'd told Jenny was true: one never thought it would happen. And you're always wrong, she'd said.

I sighed. 'You'd better tell me about Mason. Where he went, and who he saw. Anything you can think of.'

'It's practically nothing. He went off in the ordinary way and the next we heard was he'd been attacked. The police couldn't trace where he'd been, and all the syndicate people swore they'd never seen him. The case isn't closed, of course, but after six months it's got no sort of priority.'

We talked it over for a while, and I spent another hour after that writing notes. I left the Jockey Club premises at a quarter to six, to go back to the flat; and I didn't get there.

CHAPTER SEVEN

I went home in a taxi and paid it off outside the entrance to the flats, yet not exactly outside, because a dark car was squarely parked there on the double yellow lines, which was a towing-away place.

I scarcely looked at the car, which was my mistake, because as I reached it and turned away towards the entrance its nearside doors opened and spilled out the worst sort of trouble.

Two men in dark clothes grabbed me. One hit me dizzyingly on the head with something hard and the other flung what I later found was a kind of lasso of thick rope over my arms and chest and pulled it tight. They both bundled me into the back of the car where one of them for good measure tied a dark piece of cloth over my dazed half-shut eyes.

'Keys,' a voice said. 'Quick. No one saw us.'

I felt them fumbling in my pockets. There was a clink as they found what they were looking for. I began to come back into focus, so to speak, and to struggle, which was a reflex action but all the same another mistake.

The cloth over my eyes was reinforced by a sickly smelling wad over my nose and mouth. Anaesthetic fumes made a nonsense of consciousness, and the last thing I thought was that if I was going the way of Mason they hadn't wasted any time.

I was aware, first of all, that I was lying on straw.

Straw, as in stable. Rustling when I tried to move. Hearing, as always, had returned first.

I had been concussed a few times over the years, in racing falls. I thought for a while that I must have come off a horse, though I couldn't remember which, or where I'd been riding.

Funny.

The unwelcome news came back with a rush. I had not been racing. I had one hand. I had been abducted in daylight from a London street. I was lying on my back on some straw, blindfolded, with a rope tied tight round my chest, above the elbows, fastening my upper arms against my body. I was lying on the knot. I didn't know why I was there . . . and had no great faith in the future.

Damn, damn, *damn*.

My feet were tethered to some immovable object. It was black dark, even round the edges of the blindfold. I sat up and tried to get some part of me disentangled; a lot of effort and no results.

Ages later there was a tramp of footsteps outside on

a gritty surface, and the creak of a wooden door, and sudden light on the sides of my nose.

'Stop trying, Mr Halley,' a voice said. 'You won't undo those knots with one hand.'

I stopped trying. There was no point in going on.

'A spot of overkill,' he said, enjoying himself. 'Ropes *and* anaesthetic *and* blackjack *and* blindfold. Well, I did tell them of course, to be careful, and not to get within hitting distance of that thin arm. A villain I know has very nasty things to say about you hitting him with what he didn't expect.'

I knew the voice. Undertones of Manchester, overtones of all the way up the social ladder. The confidence of power.

Trevor Deansgate.

Last seen on the gallops at Newmarket, looking for Tri-Nitro in the string, and identifying him because he knew the work jockey, which most people didn't. Deansgate, going to George Caspar's for breakfast. Bookmaker Trevor Deansgate had been a question mark, a possibility, someone to be assessed, looked into. Something I would have done, and hadn't done yet.

'Take the blindfold off,' he said. 'I want him to see me.'

Fingers took their time over untying the tight piece of cloth. When it fell away, the light was temporarily dazzling; but the first thing I saw was the double barrel of a shotgun pointing my way.

'Guns too,' I said sourly.

It was a storage barn, not a stable. There was a stack of several tons of straw bales to my left, and on the right, a few yards away, a tractor. My feet were fastened to the trailer bar of a farm roller. The barn had a high roof, with beams; and one meagre electric light, which shone on Trevor Deansgate.

'You're too bloody clever for your own good,' he said. 'You know what they say? If Halley's after you, watch out. He'll sneak up on you when you think he doesn't know you exist, and they'll be slamming the cell doors on you before you've worked it out.'

I didn't say anything. What could one say? Especially sitting trussed up like a fool at the wrong end of a shotgun.

'Well, I'm not waiting for you, do you see?' he said. 'I know how bloody close you are to getting me nicked. Just laying your snares, weren't you? Just waiting for me to fall into your hands, like you've caught so many others.' He stopped and reconsidered what he'd said. 'Into your hand,' he said, 'and that fancy hook.'

He had a way of speaking to me that acknowledged mutual origins, that we'd both come a long way from where we'd started. It was not a matter of accent, but of manner. There was no need for social pretence. The message was raw, and between equals, and would be understood.

He was dressed, as before, in a City suit. Navy; chalk pinstripe this time; Gucci tie. The well-manicured hands held the shotgun with the expertise of many a weekend on country estates. What did it matter, I thought, if the finger that pulled the trigger was clean and cared for. What did it matter if his shoes were polished ... I looked at the silly details because I didn't want to think about death.

He stood for a while without speaking: simply watching. I sat without moving, as best I could, and thought about a nice safe job in a stockbroker's office.

'No bloody nerves, have you?' he said. 'None at all.'

I didn't answer.

The other two men were behind me to the right, out of my sight. I could hear their feet as they occasionally shuffled on the straw. Far too far away for me to reach.

I was wearing what I had put on for lunch with Charles. Grey trousers, socks, dark brown shoes; rope extra. Shirt, tie, and a recently bought blazer, quite expensive. What did that matter? If he killed me, Jenny would get the rest. I hadn't changed my will.

Trevor Deansgate switched his attention to the men behind me.

'Now listen,' he said, 'and don't snarl it up. Get these two pieces of rope and tie one to his left arm and one to the right. And watch out for any tricks.'

He lifted the gun a fraction until I could see down the barrels. If he shot from there, I thought, he would hit his chums. It didn't after all look like straight execution. The chums were busy tying bits of rope to both of my wrists.

'Not the left wrist, you stupid bugger,' Trevor

Deansgate said. 'That one comes right off. Use your bloody head. Tie it high, above his elbow.'

The chum in question did as he said and pulled the knots tight, and almost casually picked up a stout metal bar, like a crowbar, standing there gripping it as if he thought that somehow I could liberate myself like Superman and still attack him.

Crowbar . . . Nasty shivers of apprehension suddenly crawled all over my scalp. There had been another villain, before, who had known where to hurt me most, the one who had hit my already useless left hand with a poker, and turned it from a ruin into a total loss. I had had regrets enough since, and all sorts of private agonies, but I hadn't realized, until that sickening moment, how much I valued what remained. The muscles that worked the electrodes, they at least gave me the semblance of a working hand. If they were injured again I wouldn't have even that. As for the elbow itself . . . if he wanted to put me out of effective action for a long time, he had only to use that crowbar.

'You don't like that, do you, Mr Halley?' Trevor Deansgate said.

I turned my head back to him. His voice and face were suddenly full of a mixture of triumph and satisfaction, and what seemed like relief.

I said nothing.

'You're sweating,' he said.

He had another order for the chums. 'Untie that rope

round his chest. And do it carefully. Hold on to the ropes on his arms.'

They untied the knot, and pulled the constricting rope away from round my chest. It didn't make much difference to my chances of escape. They were wildly exaggerating my ability in a fight.

'Lie down,' he said to me; and when I didn't at once comply, he said, 'Push him down,' to the chums. One way or another, I ended on my back.

'I don't want to kill you,' he said. 'I could dump your body somewhere, but there would be too many questions. I can't risk it. But if I don't kill you, I've got to shut you up. Once and for all. Permanently.'

Short of killing me I didn't see how he could do it; and I was stupid.

'Pull his arm sideways, away from his body,' he said.

The pull on my left arm had a man's weight behind it and was stronger than I was. I rolled my head that way and tried not to beg, not to weep.

'Not that one, you bloody fool,' Trevor Deansgate said. 'The other one. The right one. Pull it out, to this side.'

The chum on my right used all his strength on the rope and hauled so that my arm finished straight out sideways, at right angles to my body, palm upwards.

Trevor Deansgate stepped towards me and lowered the gun until the black holes of the barrel were pointing straight at my stretched right wrist. Then he carefully lowered the barrel another inch, making direct contact on my skin, pressing down against the straw-covered floor. I could feel the metal rims hard across the bones and nerves and sinews. Across the bridge to a healthy hand.

I heard the click as he cocked the firing mechanism. One blast from a twelve bore would take off most of the arm.

A dizzy wave of faintness drenched all my limbs with sweat.

Whatever anyone said, I intimately knew about fear. Not fear of any horse, or of racing, or falling, or of ordinary physical pain. But of humiliation and rejection and helplessness and failure . . . all of those.

All the fear I'd ever felt in all my life was as nothing compared with the liquefying, mind-shattering disintegration of that appalling minute. It broke me in pieces. Swamped me. Brought me down to a morass of terror, to a whimper in the soul. And instinctively, hopelessly, I tried not to let it show.

He watched motionlessly through uncountable intensifying silent seconds. Making me wait. Making it worse.

At length he took a deep breath and said, 'As you see, I could shoot off your hand. Nothing easier. But I'm probably not going to. Not today.' He paused. 'Are you listening?'

I nodded the merest fraction. My eyes were full of gun.

His voice came quietly, seriously, giving weight to

every sentence. 'You can give me your assurance that you'll back off. You'll do nothing more which is directed against me, in any way, ever. You'll go to France tomorrow morning, and you'll stay there until after the Guineas. After that, you can do what you like. But if you break your assurance . . . well, you're easy to find. I'll find you, and I'll blow your right hand off. I mean it, and you'd better believe it. Some time or other. You'd never escape it. Do you understand?'

I nodded, as before. I could feel the gun as if it were hot. Don't let him, I thought. Dear God, don't let him.

'Give me your assurance. Say it.'

I swallowed painfully. Dredged up a voice. Low and hoarse. 'I give it.'

'You'll back off.'

'Yes.'

'You'll not come after me again, ever.'

'No.'

'You'll go to France and stay there until after the Guineas.'

'Yes.'

Another silence lengthened for what seemed a hundred years, while I stared beyond my undamaged wrist to the dark side of the moon.

He took the gun away, in the end. Broke it open. Removed the cartridges. I felt physically, almost uncontrollably, sick.

He knelt on his pin-striped knees beside me and looked closely at whatever defence I could put into an unmoving face and expressionless eyes. I could feel the treacherous sweat trickling down my cheek. He nodded, with grim satisfaction.

'I knew you couldn't face that. Not the other one as well. No one could. There's no need to kill you.'

He stood up again and stretched his body, as if relaxing a wound-up inner tension. Then he put his hands into various pockets, and produced things.

'Here are your keys. Your passport. Your cheque book. Credit cards.' He put them on a straw bale. To the chums, he said, 'Untie him, and drive him to the airport. To Heathrow.'

131

CHAPTER EIGHT

I flew to Paris and stayed right there where I landed, in
an airport hotel, with no impetus or heart to go further.
I stayed for six days, not leaving my room, spending
most of the time by the window, watching the aeroplanes come and go.

I felt stunned. I felt ill. Disorientated and overthrown
and severed from my own roots. Crushed into an abject
state of mental misery, knowing that this time I really
had run away.

It was easy to convince myself that logically I had had
no choice but to give Deansgate his assurance, when he
asked for it. If I hadn't, he would have killed me
anyway. I could tell myself, as I continually did, that
sticking to his instructions had been merely common
sense; but the fact remained that when the chums
decanted me at Heathrow they had driven off at once,
and it had been of my own free will that I'd bought my
ticket, waited in the departure lounge, and walked to
the aircraft.

There had been no one there with guns to make me

do it. Only the fact that as Deansgate had truly said, I couldn't face losing the other hand. I couldn't face even the risk of it. The thought of it, like a conditioned response, brought out the sweat.

As the days passed, the feeling I had had of disintegration seemed not to fade but to deepen.

The automatic part of me still went on working: walking, talking, ordering coffee, going to the bathroom. In the part that mattered there was turmoil and anguish and a feeling that my whole self had been literally smashed in those few cataclysmic minutes on the straw.

Part of the trouble was that I knew my weaknesses too well. Knew that if I hadn't had so much pride it wouldn't have destroyed me so much to have lost it.

To have been forced to realize that my basic view of myself had been an illusion was proving a psychic upheaval like an earthquake, and perhaps it wasn't surprising that I felt I had, I really had, come to pieces.

I didn't know that I could face that, either.

I wished I could sleep properly, and get some peace.

When Wednesday came I thought of Newmarket and of all the brave hopes for the Guineas.

Thought of George Caspar, taking Tri-Nitro to the test, producing him proudly in peak condition and swearing to himself that this time nothing could go wrong. Thought of Rosemary, jangling with nerves, willing the horse to win and knowing it wouldn't. Thought of Trevor Deansgate, unsuspected, moving like a mole to vandalize, somehow, the best colt in the kingdom.

I could have stopped him, if I'd tried.

Wednesday for me was the worst day of all, the day I learned about despair and desolation and guilt.

On the sixth day, Thursday morning, I went down to the lobby and bought an English newspaper.

They had run the Two Thousand Guineas, as scheduled.

Tri-Nitro had started hot favourite at even money; and he had finished last.

I paid my bill and went to the airport. There were aeroplanes to everywhere, to escape in. The urge to escape was very strong. But wherever one went, one took oneself along. From oneself there was no escape. Wherever I went, in the end I would have to go back.

If I went back in my split-apart state I'd have to live all the time on two levels. I'd have to behave in the old way, which everyone would expect. Have to think and drive and talk and get on with life. Going back meant all that. It also meant doing all that, and proving to myself that I could do it, when I wasn't the same inside.

I thought that what I had lost might be worse than a

hand. For a hand there were substitutes which could grip and look passable. But if the core of oneself had crumbled, how could one manage at all?

If I went back, I would have to try.

If I couldn't try, why go back?

It took me a long, lonely time to buy a ticket to Heathrow.

I landed at midday, made a brief telephone call to the Cavendish, to ask them to apologize to the Admiral because I couldn't keep our date, and took a taxi home.

Everything, in the lobby, on the stairs, and along the landing looking the same and yet completely different. It was I who was different. I put the key in the lock and turned it, and went into the flat.

I had expected it to be empty but before I'd even shut the door I heard a rustle in the sitting room, and then Chico's voice. 'Is that you, Admiral?'

I simply didn't answer. In a brief moment his head appeared, questioning, and after that, his whole self.

'About time too,' he said. He looked, on the whole, relieved to see me.

'I sent you a telegram.'

'Oh sure. I've got it here, propped on the shelf. *Leave Newmarket and go home stop shall be away for a few days will telephone.* What sort of telegram's that? Sent from Heathrow, early Friday. You been on holiday?'

'Yeah.'

I walked past him, into the sitting room. In there, it didn't look at all the same. There were files and papers everywhere, on every surface, with coffee-marked cups and saucers holding them down.

'You went away without the charger,' Chico said. 'You never do that, even overnight. The spare batteries are all here. You haven't been able to move that hand for six days.'

'Let's have some coffee.'

'You didn't take any clothes, or your razor.'

'I stayed in a hotel. They had throwaway razors, if you asked. What's all this mess?'

'The polish letters.'

'What?'

'You know. The polish letters. Your wife's spot of trouble.'

'Oh . . .'

I stared at it blankly.

'Look,' Chico said. 'Cheese on toast? I'm starving.'

'That would be nice.' It was unreal. It was all unreal.

He went into the kitchen and started banging about. I took the dead battery out of my arm and put in a charged one. The fingers opened and closed, like old times. I had missed them more than I would have imagined.

Chico brought the cheese on toast. He ate his, and I looked at mine. I'd better eat it, I thought, and didn't have the energy. There was the sound of the door of the flat being opened with a key, and after that, my father-in-law's voice from the hall.

'He didn't turn up at the Cavendish, but he did at least leave a message.' He came into the room from behind where I sat and saw Chico nodding his head in my direction.

'He's back,' Chico said. 'The boy himself.'

'Hello, Charles,' I said.

He took a long slow look. Very controlled, very civilized. 'We have, you know, been worried.' It was a reproach.

'I'm sorry.'

'Where have you been?' he said.

I found I couldn't tell him. If I told him where, I would have to tell him why, and I shrank from why. I just didn't say anything at all.

Chico gave him a cheerful grin. 'Sid's got a bad attack of the brick walls.' He looked at his watch. 'Seeing that you're here, Admiral, I might as well get along and teach the little bleeders at the Comprehensive how to throw their grannies over their shoulders. And, Sid, before I go, there's about fifty messages on the phone pad. There's two new insurance investigations waiting to be done, and a guard job. Lucas Wainwright wants you, he's rung four times. And Rosemary Caspar has been screeching fit to blast the eardrums. It's all there, written down. See you, then. I'll come back here later.'

I almost asked him not to, but he'd gone.

'You've lost weight,' Charles said.

It wasn't surprising. I looked again at the toasted cheese and decided that coming back also had to include things like eating.

'Want some?' I said.

He eyed the congealing square. 'No, thank you.'

Nor did I. I pushed it away. Sat and stared into space.

'What's happened to you?' he said.

'Nothing.'

'Last week you came into the Cavendish like a spring,' he said. 'Bursting with life. Eyes actually sparkling. And now look at you.'

'Well, don't,' I said. 'Don't look at me. How are you doing with the letters?'

'Sid . . .'

'Admiral.' I stood up restlessly, to escape his probing gaze. 'Leave me alone.'

He paused, considering, then said, 'You've been speculating in commodities, recently. Have you lost your money, is that it?'

I was surprised almost to the point of amusement.

'No,' I said.

He said, 'You went dead like this before, when you lost your career and my daughter. So what have you lost this time, if it isn't money? What could be as bad . . . or worse?'

I knew the answer. I'd learned it in Paris, in torment and shame. My whole mind formed the word *courage* with such violent intensity that I was afraid it would leap out of its own accord from my brain to his.

He showed no sign of receiving it. He was still waiting for a reply.

I swallowed. 'Six days,' I said neutrally. 'I've lost six days. Let's go on with tracing Nicholas Ashe.'

He shook his head in disapproval and frustration, but began to explain what he'd been doing.

'This thick pile is from people with names beginning with M. I've put them into strictly alphabetical order, and typed out a list. It seemed to me that we might get results from one letter only ... are you paying attention?'

'Yes.'

'I took the list to Christie's and Sotheby's, as you suggested, and persuaded them to help. But the M section of their catalogue mailing list is not the same as this one. And I found that there may be difficulties with this matching, as so many envelopes are addressed nowadays by computers.'

'You've worked hard,' I said.

'Chico and I have been sitting here in shifts, answering your telephone, and trying to find out where you'd gone. Your car was still here, in the garage, and Chico said you would never have gone anywhere of your own accord without the battery charger for your arm.'

'Well ... I did.'

'Sid ...'

'No,' I said. 'What we need now is a list of periodicals

and magazines dealing with antique furniture. We'll try those first with the M people.'

'It's an awfully big project,' Charles said doubtfully. 'And even if we do find it, what then? I mean, as the man at Christie's pointed out, even if we find whose mailing list was being used, where does it get us? The firm or magazine wouldn't be able to tell us which of the many people who had access to the list was Nicholas Ashe, particularly as he is almost certain not to have used that name if he had any dealings with them.'

'Mm,' I said. 'But there's a chance he's started operating again somewhere else, and is still using the same list. He took it with him, when he went. If we can find out whose list it is, we might go and call on some people who are on it, whose names start with A to K, and P to Z, and find out if they've received any of those begging letters recently. Because if they have, the letters will have the address on, to which the money is to be sent. And there, at that address, we might find Mr Ashe.'

Charles put his mouth into the shape of a whistle, but what came out was more like a sigh.

'You've come back with your brains intact, anyway,' he said.

Oh God, I thought, I'm making myself think to shut out the abyss. I'm in splinters . . . I'm never going to be right again. The analytical reasoning part of my mind might be marching straight on, but what had to be called the soul was sick and dying.

'And there's the polish,' I said. I still had in my

pocket the paper he'd given me the week before. I took it out and put it on the table. 'If the idea of special polish is closely geared to the mailing list, then to get maximum results the polish is necessary. There can't be many private individuals ordering so much wax in unprinted tins packed in little white boxes. We could ask the polish firm to let us know if another lot is ordered. It's just faintly possible that Ashe will use the same firm again, even if not at once. He ought to see the danger . . . but he might be a fool.'

I turned away wearily. Thought about whisky. Went over and poured myself a large one.

'Drinking heavily, are you?' Charles said from behind me, in his most offensive drawl.

I shut my teeth hard, and said, 'No.' Apart from coffee and water, it was my first drink for a week.

'Your first alcoholic black-out, was it, these last few days?'

I left the glass untouched on the drinks tray and turned round. His eyes were at their coldest, as unkind as in the days when we'd first met.

'Don't be so bloody stupid,' I said.

He lifted his chin a fraction. 'A spark,' he said sarcastically. 'Still got your pride, I see.'

I compressed my lips and turned my back on him, and drank a lot of the Scotch. After a bit I deliberately loosened a few tensed-up muscles, and said, 'You won't find out that way. I know you too well. You use insults as a lever, to sting people into opening up. You've done it to me in the past. But not this time.'

'If I find the right sting,' he said, 'I'll use it.'

'Do you want a drink?' I said.

'Since you ask, yes.'

We sat opposite each other in armchairs in unchanged companionship, and I thought vaguely of this and that and shied away from the crucifying bits.

'You know,' I said. 'We don't have to go trailing that mailing list around to see whose it is. All we do is ask the people themselves. Those . . .' I nodded towards the M stack. 'We just ask some of them what mailing lists they themselves are on. We'd only need to ask a few . . . the common denominator would be certain to turn up.'

When Charles had gone home to Aynsford I wandered aimlessly round the flat, tie off and in shirtsleeves, trying to be sensible. I told myself that nothing much had happened, only that Trevor Deansgate had used a lot of horrible threats to get me to stop doing something that I hadn't yet started. But I couldn't dodge the guilt. Once he'd revealed himself, once I knew he would do *something*, I could have stopped him, and I hadn't.

If he hadn't got me so effectively out of Newmarket I would very likely have still been prodding unproductively away, unsure even if there was anything to discover, right up to the moment in the Guineas when Tri-Nitro tottered in last. But I would also be up there now, I thought, certain and inquisitive; and because of his threat, I wasn't.

I could call my absence prudence, common sense, the only possible course in the circumstances. I could rationalize and excuse. I could say I wouldn't have been doing anything that wasn't already being done by the Jockey Club. I came back, all the time, to the swingeing truth, that I wasn't there now because I was afraid to be.

Chico came back from his judo class and set to again to find out where I'd been; and for the same reasons I didn't tell him, even though I knew he wouldn't despise me as I despised myself.

'All right,' he said finally. 'You just keep it all bottled up and see where it gets you. Wherever you've been, it was bad. You've only got to look at you. It's not going to do you any good to shut it all up inside.'

Shutting it all up inside, however, was a lifelong habit, a defence learned in childhood, a wall against the world, impossible to change.

I raised at least half a smile. 'You setting up in Harley Street?'

'That's better,' he said. 'You missed all the fun, did you know? Tri-Nitro got stuffed after all in the Guineas yesterday, and they're turning George Caspar's yard inside out. It's all here, somewhere, in the *Sporting Life*. The Admiral brought it. Have you read it?'

I shook my head.

'Our Rosemary, she wasn't bonkers after all, was she? How do you think they managed it?'

'They?' I said.

'Whoever did it.'

'I don't know.'

'I went along to see the gallop on Saturday morning,' he said. 'Yeah, yeah, I know you sent the telegram about leaving, but I'd got a real little dolly lined up for a bit of the other on Friday night, so I stayed. One more night wasn't going to make any difference, and besides, she was George Caspar's typist.'

'She was . . .'

'Does the typing. Rides the horses sometimes. Into everything, she is, and talkative with it.'

The new scared Sid Halley didn't even want to listen.

'There was a right old rumpus all day Wednesday in George Caspar's house,' Chico said. 'It started at breakfast when that Inky Poole turned up and said Sid Halley had been asking questions that he, Inky Poole, didn't like.'

He paused for effect. I simply stared.

'Are you listening?' he said.

'Yes.'

'You got your stone face act on again.'

'Sorry.'

'Then Brothersmith the vet turned up and heard Inky Poole letting off, and he said funny, Sid Halley had been around him asking questions too. About bad hearts, he said. Same horses as Inky Poole was talking about. Bethesda, Gleaner and Zingaloo. And how was Tri-Nitro's heart, for good measure. My little dolly

144

typist said you could've heard George Caspar blowing up all the way to Cambridge. He's really touchy about those horses.'

Trevor Deansgate, I thought coldly, had been at George Caspar's for breakfast, and had heard every word.

'Of course,' Chico said, 'some time later they checked the studs, Garvey's and Thrace's, and found you'd been there too. My dolly says your name is mud.'

I rubbed my hand over my face. 'Does your dolly know you were working with me?'

'Do us a favour. Of course not.'

'Did she say anything else?' What the hell am I asking for, I thought.

'Yeah. Well, she said Rosemary got on to George Caspar to change all the routine for the Saturday morning gallop, nagged him all day Thursday and all day Friday and George Caspar was climbing the walls. And at the yard they had so much security they were tripping over their own alarm bells.' He paused for breath. 'After that she didn't say much else on account of three martinis and time for tickle.'

I sat on the arm of the sofa and stared at the carpet.

'Next morning,' Chico said, 'I watched the gallop, like I said. Your photos came in very handy. Hundreds of ruddy horses . . . Someone told me which were Caspar's, and there was Inky Poole, scowling like in the pictures, so I just zeroed in on him and hung about. There was a lot of fuss when it came to Tri-Nitro. They took the saddle off and put a little one on, and Inky Poole rode on that.'

'It was Inky Poole, then, who rode Tri-Nitro, same as usual?'

'They looked just like your pictures,' Chico said. 'Can't swear to it more than that.'

I stared some more at the carpet.

'So what do we do next?' he said.

'Nothing . . . We give Rosemary her money back and draw a line.'

'But hey,' Chico said in protest. 'Someone got at the horse. You know they did.'

'Not our business, any more.'

I wished that he, too, would stop looking at me. I felt a distinct need to crawl into a hole and hide.

The doorbell rang with the long peal of a determined thumb. 'We're out,' I said; but Chico went and answered it.

Rosemary Caspar swept past him, through the hall and into the sitting room, advancing in the old fawn raincoat and a fulminating rage. No scarf, no false curls, and no loving kindness.

'So there you are,' she said forcefully. 'I knew you'd be here, skulking out of sight. Your friend kept telling me when I telephoned that you weren't here, but I knew he was lying.'

'I wasn't here,' I said. As well try damming the St Lawrence with a twig.

'You weren't where I paid you to be, which was up in

Newmarket. And I told you from the beginning that George wasn't to find out you were asking questions, and he did, and we've been having one God-awful bloody row ever since, and now Tri-Nitro has disgraced us unbearably and it's all your bloody fault.'

Chico raised his eyebrows comically. 'Sid didn't ride it . . . or train it.'

She glared at him with transferred hatred. 'And he didn't keep him safe, either.'

'Er, no,' Chico said. 'Granted.'

'As for you,' she said, swinging back to me. 'You're a useless bloody humbug. It's all rubbish, this detecting. Why don't you grow up and stop playing games? All you did was stir up trouble, and I want my money back.'

'Will a cheque do?' I said.

'You're not arguing, then?'

'No,' I said.

'Do you mean you admit that you failed?'

After a small pause, I said, 'Yes.'

'Oh.' She sounded as if I had unexpectedly deprived her of a good deal of what she had come to say, but while I wrote out a cheque for her she went on complaining sharply enough.

'All your ideas about changing the routine, they were useless. I've been on and on at George about security and taking care, and he says he couldn't have done any more, no one could, and he's in absolute despair – and I'd hoped, I'd really hoped, what a laugh, that somehow or other you would work a miracle, and that Tri-Nitro would win, because I was so sure, so sure . . . and I was right.'

I finished writing. 'Why were you always so sure?' I said.

'I don't know. I just *knew*. I've been afraid of it for weeks . . . otherwise I would not have been so desperate as to try you, in the first place. And I might as well not have bothered . . . it's caused so much trouble, and I can't bear it. I can't bear it. Yesterday was terrible. He should have won . . . I knew he wouldn't. I felt ill. I still feel ill.'

She was trembling again. The pain in her face was acute. So many hopes, so much work had gone into Tri-Nitro, such anxiety and such care. Winning races was to a trainer like a film to a film maker. If you got it right, they applauded; wrong, and they booed. And either way you'd poured your soul into it, and your thoughts and your skill and weeks of worry. I understood what the lost race meant to George, and to Rosemary equally, because she cared so much.

'Rosemary . . .' I said, in useless sympathy.

'It's pointless Brothersmith saying he must have had an infection,' she said. 'He's always saying things like that. He's so wet, I can't stand him, always looking over his shoulder, I've never liked him. And it was his job anyway to cheek Tri-Nitro and he did, over and over, and there was nothing wrong with him, nothing. He went down to the post looking beautiful, and in the parade ring before that, there was nothing wrong, nothing. And then in the race, he just went backwards, and he finished . . . he came back . . . exhausted.' There was a glitter of tears for a moment, but she visibly willed them from overwhelming her.

'They've done dope tests, I suppose,' Chico said.

It angered her again. 'Dope tests! Of course they have. What do you expect? Blood tests, urine tests, saliva tests, dozens of bloody tests. They gave George duplicate samples, and that's why we're down here, he's trying to fix up with some private lab . . . but they won't be positive. It will be like before . . . absolutely nothing.'

I tore out the cheque and gave it to her, and she glanced at it blindly.

'I wish I'd never come here. My God, I wish I hadn't. You're only a jockey. I should have known better. I don't want to talk to you again. Don't talk to me at the races, do you understand.'

I nodded. I did understand. She turned abruptly to go away. 'And for God's sake don't speak to George, either.' She went alone out of the room, and out of the flat, and slammed the door.

Chico clicked his tongue and shrugged. 'You can't win them all,' he said. 'What could you do that her husband couldn't, not to mention a private police force and half a dozen guard dogs?' He was excusing me, and we both knew it.

I didn't answer.

'Sid?'

'I don't know that I'm going on with it,' I said. 'This sort of job.'

'You don't want to take any notice of what she said,' he protested. 'You can't give it up. You're too good at it. Look at the awful messes you've put right. Just because of one that's gone wrong . . .'

I stared hollowly at a lot of unseen things.

'You're a big boy now,' he said. And he was seven years younger than I, near enough. 'You want to cry on Daddy's shoulder?' He paused. 'Look, Sid mate, you've got to snap out of it. Whatever's happened it can't be as bad as when that horse sliced your hand up, nothing could. This is no time to die inside, we've got about five other jobs lined up. The insurance, and the guard job, and Lucas Wainwright's syndicates . . .'

'No,' I said. I felt leaden and useless. 'Not now, honestly, Chico.'

I got up and went into the bedroom. Shut the door. Went purposelessly to the window and looked out at the scenery of roofs and chimney pots, glistening in the beginnings of rain. The pots were still there, though the chimneys underneath were blocked off and the fires long dead. I felt at one with the chimney pots. When fires went out, one froze.

The door opened.

'Sid,' Chico said.

I said resignedly, 'Remind me to put a lock on that door.'

'You've got another visitor.'

'Tell him to go away.'

'It's a girl. Louise somebody.'

I rubbed my hand over my face and head and down to the back of my neck. Eased the muscles. Turned from the window.

'Louise McInnes?'

'That's right.'

'She shares the flat with Jenny,' I said.

'Oh, that one. Well then, Sid, if that's all for today I'll be off. And . . . er . . . be here tomorrow, won't you?'

'Yeah.'

He nodded. We left everything else unsaid. The amusement, mockery, friendship and stifled anxiety were all there in his face and his voice . . . Maybe he read the same in mine. At any rate he gave me a widening grin as he departed, and I went into the sitting room thinking that some debts couldn't be paid.

Louise was standing in the middle of things, looking around her in the way I had, in Jenny's flat. Through her eyes I saw my own room afresh: its irregular shape, high-ceilinged, not modern; and the tan leather sofa, the table with drinks by the window, the shelves with books, the prints framed and hung, and on the door, leaning against the wall, the big painting of racing horses which I'd somehow never bothered to hang up. There were coffee cups and glasses scattered about, and full ash-trays, and the piles of letters on the coffee table and everywhere else.

Louise herself looked different: the full production,

not the Sunday morning tumble out of bed. A brown velvet jacket, a blazing white sweater, a soft mottled brown skirt with a wide leather belt round an untroubled waist. Fair hair washed and shining, rose-petal make-up on the English-rose skin. A detachment in the eyes which said that all this honey was not chiefly there for the attracting of bees.

'Mr Halley.'

'You could try Sid,' I said. 'You know me quite well, by proxy.'

Her smile reached halfway. 'Sid.'

'Louise.'

'Jenny says Sid is a plumber's mate's sort of name.'

'Very good people, plumbers' mates.'

'Did you know,' she said, looking away and continuing the visual tour of inspection, 'that in Arabic "Sid" means "lord"?'

'No, I didn't.'

'Well, it does.'

'You could tell Jenny,' I said.

Her gaze came back fast to my face. 'She gets to you, doesn't she?'

I smiled. 'Like some coffee? Or a drink?'

'Tea?'

'Sure.'

She came into the kitchen with me and watched me make it, and made no funny remarks about bionic hands, which was a nice change from most new acquaintances, who tended to be fascinated, and to say so, at length. Instead she looked around with inoffensive curiosity, and finally fastened her attention on the calendar which hung from the knob on the pine cupboard door. Photographs of horses, a Christmas hand-out from a bookmaking firm. She flipped up the pages, looking at the pictures of the future months, and stopped at December, where a horse and jockey jumping the Chair at Aintree were silhouetted spectacularly against the sky.

'That's good,' she said, and then, in surprise, reading the caption, 'That's *you*.'

'He's a good photographer.'

'Did you win that race?'

'Yes,' I said mildly. 'Do you take sugar?'

'No thanks.' She let the pages fall back. 'How odd to find oneself on a calendar.'

To me, it wasn't odd. How odd, I thought, to have seen one's picture in print so much that one scarcely noticed.

I carried the tray into the sitting room and put it on top of the letters on the coffee table. 'Sit down,' I said, and we sat.

'All these,' I said, nodding to them, 'are the letters which came with the cheques for the wax.'

She looked doubtful. 'Are they of any use?'

'I hope so,' I said, and explained about the mailing list.

'Good heavens.' She hesitated, 'Well, perhaps you won't need what I brought.' She picked up her brown leather handbag, and opened it. 'I didn't come all this way specially,' she said. 'I've an aunt near here whom I visit. Anyway, I thought you might like to have this, as I was here, near your flat.'

She pulled out a paperback book. She could have posted it, I thought; but I was quite glad she hadn't.

'I was trying to put a bit of order into the chaos in my bedroom,' she said. 'I've a lot of books. They tend to pile up.'

I didn't tell her I'd seen them. 'Books do,' I said.

'Well, this was among them. It's Nicky's.'

She gave me the paperback. I glanced at the cover and put it down, in order to pour out the tea. *Navigation for Beginners*. I handed her the cup and saucer. 'Was he interested in navigation?'

'I've no idea. But I was. I borrowed it out of his room. I don't think he even knew I'd borrowed it. He had a box with some things in – like a tuck box that boys take to public school – and one day when I went into his room the things were all on the chest of drawers, as if he was tidying. Anyway, he was out, and I borrowed the book ... He wouldn't have minded, he was terribly easy-going ... and I suppose I put it down in my room, and put something else on top, and just forgot it.'

'Did you read it?' I said.

'No. Never got round to it. It was weeks ago.'

I picked up the book and opened it. On the fly-leaf

someone had written 'John Viking' in a firm legible signature in black felt-tip.

'I don't know,' Louise said, anticipating my question, 'whether that is Nicky's writing or not.'

'Does Jenny know?'

'She hasn't seen this. She's staying with Toby in Yorkshire.'

Jenny with Toby. Jenny with Ashe. For God's sake, I thought, what do you expect? She's gone, she's gone, she's not yours, you're divorced. And I hadn't been alone, not entirely.

'You look very tired,' Louise said doubtfully.

I was disconcerted. 'Of course not.' I turned the pages, letting them flick over from under my thumb. It was, as it promised to be, a book about navigation, sea and air, with line drawings and diagrams. Dead reckoning, sextants, magnetism and drift. Nothing of any note except a single line of letters and figures, written with the same black ink, on the inside of the back cover.

$$\text{Lift} = 22.024 \times V \times P \times (1/T_1 - 1/T_2)$$

I handed it over to Louise.

'Does this mean anything to you? Charles said you've a degree in mathematics.'

She frowned at it faintly. 'Nicky needed a calculator for two plus two.'

155

He had done all right at two plus ten thousand, I thought.

'Um,' she said. 'Lift equals 22.024 times volume times pressure, times . . . I should think this is something to do with temperature change. Not my subject, really. This is physics.'

'Something to do with navigation?' I said.

She concentrated. I watched the way her face grew taut while she did the internal scan. A fast brain, I thought, under the pretty hair.

'It's funny,' she said finally, 'but I think it's just possibly something to do with how much you can lift with a gas-bag.'

'Airship?' I said, thinking.

'It depends what 22.024 is,' she said. 'That's a constant. Which means,' she added, 'it is special to whatever this equation is all about.'

'I'm better at what's likely to win the three-thirty.'

She looked at her watch. 'You're three hours too late.'

'It'll come round again tomorrow.'

She relaxed into the armchair, handing back the book. 'I don't suppose it will help,' she said, 'but you seemed to want anything of Nicky's.'

'It might help a lot. You never know.'

'But how?'

'It's John Viking's book. John Viking might know Nicky Ashe.'

'But . . . you don't know John Viking.'

'No,' I said, 'but he knows gas-bags. And I know someone who knows gas-bags. And I bet gas-bags are a small world, like racing.'

She looked at the heaps of letters, and then at the book. She said slowly, 'I guess you'll find him, one way or another.'

I looked away from her, and at nothing in particular.

'Jenny says you never give up.'

I smiled faintly. 'Her exact words?'

'No.' I felt her amusement. 'Obstinate, selfish, and determined to get his own way.'

'Not far off.' I tapped the book. 'Can I keep this?'

'Of course.'

'Thanks.'

We looked at each other as people do, especially if they're youngish and male and female, and sitting in a quiet flat at the end of an April day.

She read my expression and answered the unspoken thought. 'Some other time,' she said drily.

'How long will you be staying with Jenny?'

'Would that matter to you?' she said.

'Mm.'

'She says you're as hard as flint. She says steel's a pushover, beside you.'

I thought of terror and misery and self-loathing. I shook my head.

'What I see,' she said slowly, 'is a man who looks ill being polite to an unwanted visitor.'

'You're wanted,' I said. 'And I'm fine.'

She stood up, however, and I also, after her.

'I hope,' I said, 'that you're fond of your aunt?'

'Devoted.'

She gave me a cool, half ironic smile in which there was also surprise.

'Goodbye . . . Sid.'

'Goodbye, Louise.'

When she'd gone I switched on a table light or two against the slow dusk, and poured a whisky, and looked at a pale bunch of sausages in the fridge and didn't cook them.

No one else would come, I thought. They had all in their way held off the shadows, particularly Louise. No one else real would come, but he would be with me, as he'd been in Paris . . . Trevor Deansgate. Inescapable. Reminding me inexorably of what I would rather forget.

After a while I stepped out of trousers and shirt and put on a short blue bathrobe, and took off the arm. It was one of the times when taking it off really hurt. It didn't seem to matter, after the rest.

I went back to the sitting room to do something about the clutter, but there was simply too much to bother with, so I stood looking at it, and held my weaker upper arm with my strong, whole, agile right hand, as I often did, for support, and I wondered which crippled one worse, amputation without or within.

Humiliation and rejection and helplessness and failure . . .

After all these years I would *not*, I thought wretchedly, I would damned well *not* be defeated by fear.

CHAPTER NINE

Lucas Wainwright telephoned the next morning while I was stacking cups in the dishwasher.

'Any progress?' he said, sounding very Commander-ish.

'I'm afraid,' I said regretfully, 'that I've lost all those notes. I'll have to do them again.'

'For heaven's sake.' He wasn't pleased. I didn't tell him that I'd lost the notes on account of being bashed on the head and dropping the large brown envelope that contained them in the gutter. 'Come right away, then. Eddy won't be in until this afternoon.'

Slowly, absentmindedly, I finished tidying up, while I thought about Lucas Wainwright, and what he could do for me, if he would. Then I sat at the table and wrote down what I wanted. Then I looked at what I'd written, and at my fingers holding the pen, and shivered. Then I folded the paper and put it in my pocket, and went to Portman Square deciding not to give it to Lucas, after all.

He had the files ready in his office, and I sat at the same table as before and re-copied all I needed.

'You won't let it drag on much longer, will you, Sid?'

'Full attention,' I said. 'Starting tomorrow. I'll go to Kent tomorrow afternoon.'

'Good.' He stood up as I put the new notes into a fresh envelope and waited for me to go, not through impatience with me particularly, but because he was that sort of man. Brisk. One task finished, get on with the next, don't hang about.

I hesitated cravenly and found myself speaking before I had consciously decided whether to or not. 'Commander. Do you remember that you said you might pay me for this job not with money, but with help, if I should want it?'

I got a reasonable smile and a postponement of the goodbyes.

'Of course I remember. You haven't done the job yet. What help?'

'Er . . . it's nothing much. Very little.' I took the paper out and handed it to him. Waited while he read the brief contents. Felt as if I had planted a landmine and would presently step on it.

'I don't see why not,' he said. 'If that's what you want. But are you on to something that we should know about?'

I gestured to the paper, 'You'll know about it as soon as I do, if you do that.' It wasn't a satisfactory answer, but he didn't press it. 'The only thing I beg of you, though, is that you won't mention my name at all. Don't say it was my idea, not to *anyone*. I . . . er . . . you might get me killed, Commander, and I'm not being funny.'

He looked from me to the paper and back again, and frowned. 'This doesn't look like a killing matter, Sid.'

'You never know what is until you're dead.'

He smiled. 'All right. I'll write the letter as from the Jockey Club, and I'll take you seriously about the death risk. Will that do?'

'It will indeed.'

We shook hands, and I left his office carrying the brown envelope, and at the Portman Square entrance, going out, I met Eddy Keith coming in. We both paused, as one does. I hoped he couldn't see the dismay in my face at his early return, or guess that I was perhaps carrying the seeds of his downfall.

'Eddy,' I said, smiling and feeling a traitor.

'Hello, Sid,' he said cheerfully, twinkling at me from above rounded cheeks. 'What are you doing here?' A good-natured normal enquiry. No suspicions. No tremor.

'Looking for crumbs,' I said.

He chuckled fatly. 'From what I hear, it's us picking up yours. Have us all out of work, you will, soon.'

'Not a chance.'

'Don't step on our toes, Sid.'

The smile was still there, the voice devoid of threat. The fuzzy hair, the big moustache, the big broad fleshy face still exuded good will: but the arctic had briefly come and gone in his eyes, and I was in no doubt that I'd received a serious warning off.

'Never, Eddy,' I said insincerely.

'See you, fella,' he said, preparing to go indoors, nodding, smiling widely, and giving me the usual hearty buffet on the shoulder. 'Take care.'

'You too, Eddy,' I said to his departing back; and under my breath, again, in a sort of sorrow, 'You too.'

I carried the notes safely back to the flat, and thought a bit, and telephoned my man in gas-bags.

He said hello and great to hear from you and how about a jar sometime, and no, he had never heard of anyone called John Viking. I read out the equation and asked if it meant anything to him, and he laughed and said it sounded like a formula for taking a hot-air balloon to the moon.

'Thanks very much,' I said sarcastically.

'No, seriously, Sid. It's a calculation for maximum height. Try a balloonist. They're always after records . . . the highest, the furthest, that sort of thing.'

I asked if he knew any balloonists but he said sorry, no he didn't, he was only into airships, and we disconnected with another vague resolution to meet somewhere, sometime, one of these days. Idly, and certain it was useless, I leafed through the telephone directory, and there, incredibly, the words stood out

163

bold and clear: The Hot Air Balloon Company, offices in London, number provided.

I got through. A pleasant male voice at the other end said that of course he knew John Viking, everyone in ballooning knew John Viking, he was a madman of the first order.

Madman?

John Viking, the voice explained, took risks which no sensible balloonist would dream of. If I wanted to talk to him, the voice said, I would undoubtedly find him at the balloon race on Monday afternoon.

Where was the balloon race on Monday afternoon?

Horse show, balloon race, swings and roundabouts, you name it, all part of the May Day holiday junketings at Highalane Park in Wiltshire. John Viking would be there. Sure to be.

I thanked the voice for his help and rang off, reflecting that I had forgotten about the May Day holiday. National holidays had always been work days for me, as for everyone in racing; providing the entertainment for the public's leisure. I tended not to notice them come and go.

Chico arrived with fish and chips for two in the sort of hygienic greaseproof wrappings which kept the steam in and made the chips go soggy.

'Did you know it's the May Day holiday on Monday?' I said.

'Running a judo tournament for the little bleeders, aren't I?'

He tipped the lunch on to two plates, and we ate it, mostly with fingers.

'You've come to life again, I see,' he said.

'It's temporary.'

'We'd better get some work done, then, while you're still with us.'

'The syndicates,' I said.

Chico shook salt on his chips. 'We'll have to be careful.'

'Start this afternoon?'

'Sure.' He paused reflectively, licking his fingers. 'We're not getting paid for this, didn't you say?'

'Not directly.'

'Why don't we do these insurance enquiries, then? Nice quiet questions with a guaranteed fee.'

'I promised Lucas Wainwright I'd do the syndicates first.'

He shrugged. 'You're the boss. But that makes three in a row, counting your wife and Rosemary getting her cash back, that we've worked on for nothing.'

'We'll make up for it later.'

'You are going on, then?'

I didn't answer at once. Apart from not knowing whether I wanted to, I didn't know if I could. Over the past months Chico and I had tended to get somewhat battered by bully boys trying to stop us in our tracks. We didn't have the protection of being either in the Racecourse Security Service or the police. No one to defend us but ourselves. We had looked upon the bruises as part of the job, as racing falls had been to me, and bad judo falls to Chico. What if Trevor Deansgate had changed all that . . . Not just for one terrible week, but for much longer; for always?

'Sid,' Chico said sharply. 'Come back.'

I swallowed. 'Well . . . er . . . we'll do the syndicates. Then we'll see.' Then I'll know, I thought. I'll know inside me, one way or the other. If I couldn't walk into tigers' cages any more, we were done. One of us wasn't enough: it had to be both.

If I couldn't . . . I'd as soon be dead.

The first syndicate on Lucas's list had been formed by eight people, of whom three were registered owners, headed by Philip Friarly. Registered owners were those acceptable to the racing authorities, owners who paid their dues and kept the rules, were no trouble to anybody, and represented the source and mainspring of the whole industry.

Syndicates were a way of involving more people directly in racing, which was good for the sport, and dividing the training costs into smaller fractions, which was good for the owners. There were syndicates of millionaires, coal miners, groups of rock guitarists, the clientele of pubs. Anyone from Aunty Flo to the under-taker could join a syndicate, and all Eddy Keith should have done was check that everyone on the list was who they said they were.

'It's not the registered owners we're looking at,' I said. 'It's all the others.'

We were driving through Kent on our way to Tunbridge Wells. Ultra-respectable place, Tunbridge Wells. Resort of retired colonels and ladies who played bridge. Low on the national crime league. Hometown, all the same, of a certain Peter Rammileese, who was, so Lucas Wainwright's informant had said, in fact the instigating member of all four of the doubtful syndicates, although his own name nowhere appeared.

'Mason,' I said, conversationally, 'was attacked and left for dead in the streets of Tunbridge Wells.'

'Now he tells me.'

'Chico,' I said. 'Do you want to turn back?'

'You got a premonition, or something?'

After a pause, I said, 'No,' and drove a shade too fast round a sharpish bend.

'Look, Sid,' he said. 'We don't have to go to Tunbridge Wells. We're on a hiding to nothing, with this lark.'

'What do you think, then?'

He was silent.

'We do have to go,' I said.

'Yeah.'

'So we have to work out what it was that Mason asked, and not ask it.'

'This Rammileese,' Chico said. 'What's he like?'

'I haven't met him, myself, but I've heard of him. He's a farmer who's made a packet out of crooked dealings in horses. The Jockey Club won't have him as a registered owner, and most racecourses don't let him through the gates. He'll try to bribe anyone from the Senior Steward to the scrubbers, and where he can't bribe, he threatens.'

'Oh, jolly.'

'Two jockeys and a trainer, not so long ago, lost their licences for taking his bribes. One of the jockeys got the sack from his stable and he's so broke he's hanging around outside the racecourse gates begging for handouts.'

'Is that the one I saw you talking to, a while ago?'

'That's right.'

'And how much did you give him?'

'Never you mind.'

'You're a pushover, Sid.'

'A case of "but-for-the-grace-of-God",' I said.

'Oh, sure. I could see you taking bribes from a crooked horse dealer. Most likely thing on earth.'

'Anyway,' I said, 'what we're trying to find out is not whether Peter Rammileese is manipulating four race-horses, which he is, but whether Eddy Keith knows it, and is keeping quiet.'

'Right.' We sped deeper into rural Kent, and then he said, 'You know why we've had such good results, on the whole, since we've been together on this job?'

'Why, then?'

'It's because all the villains know you. I mean, they know you by sight, most of them. So when they see you poking around on their patch, they get the heebies, and start doing silly things like setting the heavies on us, and then we see them loud and clear, and what they're up to, which we wouldn't have done if they'd sat tight.'

I sighed and said, 'I guess so,' and thought about Trevor Deansgate; thought and tried not to. Without any hands one couldn't drive a car . . . Just don't think about it, I told myself. Just keep your mind off it, it's a one-way trip into jellyfish.

I swung round another corner too fast and collected a sideways look from Chico, but no comment.

'Look at the map,' I said. 'Do something useful.'

We found the house of Peter Rammileese without much trouble, and pulled into the yard of a small farm that looked as if the outskirts of Tunbridge Wells had rolled round it like a sea, leaving it isolated and incongruous. There was a large white farmhouse, three storeys high, and a modern wooden stable block, and a long, extra-large barn. Nothing significantly prosperous about the place, but no nettles either.

No one about. I put the brake on as we rolled to a stop, and we got out of the car.

'Front door?' Chico said.

'Back door, for farms.'

We had taken only five or six steps in that direction, however, when a small boy ran into the yard from a doorway in the barn, and came over to us, breathlessly.

'Did you bring the ambulance?'

His eyes looked past me, to my car, and his face

puckered into agitation and disappointment. He was about seven, dressed in jodhpurs and T-shirt, and he had been crying.

'What's the matter?' I said.

'I rang for the ambulance . . . A long time ago.'

'We might help,' I said.

'It's Mum,' he said. 'She's lying in there, and she won't wake up.'

'Come on, you show us.'

He was a sturdy little boy, brown-haired and brown-eyed and very frightened. He ran towards the barn, and we followed without wasting time. Once through the door we could see that it wasn't an ordinary barn, but an indoor riding school, a totally enclosed area of about twenty metres wide by thirty-five long, lit by windows in the roof. The floor, wall to wall, was covered with a thick layer of tan-coloured wood chippings, springy and quiet for horses to work on.

There was a pony and a horse careering about; and, in danger from their hooves, a crumpled female figure lying on the ground.

Chico and I went over to her fast. She was young, on her side, face half downwards; unconscious, but not, I thought, deeply. Her breathing was shallow and her skin had whitened in a mottled fashion under her make-up, but the pulse in her wrist was strong and regular. The crash helmet which hadn't saved her lay several feet away on the floor.

'Go and ring again,' I said to Chico.

'Shouldn't we move her?'

'No . . . in case she's broken anything. You can do a lot of damage moving people too much when they're unconscious.'

'You should know.' He turned away and ran off towards the house.

'Is she all right?' the boy said anxiously. 'Bingo started bucking and she fell off, and I think he kicked her head.'

'Bingo is the horse?'

'His saddle slipped,' he said; and Bingo, with the saddle down under his belly, was still bucking and kicking like a rodeo.

'What's your name?' I said.

'Mark.'

'Well, Mark, as far as I can see, your mum is going to be all right, and you're a brave little boy.'

'I'm six,' he said, as if that wasn't so little.

The worst of the fright had died out of his eyes, now that he had help. I knelt on the ground beside his mother and smoothed the brown hair away from her forehead. She made a small moaning sound, and her eyelids fluttered. She was perceptibly nearer the surface, even in the short time we'd been there.

'I thought she was dying,' the boy said. 'We had a rabbit a little time ago . . . he panted and shut his eyes, and we couldn't wake him up again, and he died.'

'Your mum will wake up again.'

'Are you sure?'

'Yes, Mark, I'm sure.'

He seemed deeply reassured, and told me readily that the pony was called Sooty, and was his own, and that his dad was away until tomorrow morning, and there was only his mum there, and him, and she'd been schooling Bingo because she was selling him to a girl for show-jumping.

Chico came back and said the ambulance was on its way. The boy, cheering up enormously, said we ought to catch the horses because they were cantering about and the reins were all loose, and if the saddles and bridles got broken his dad would be bloody angry.

Both Chico and I laughed at the adult words, seriously spoken. While he and Mark stood guard over the patient, I caught the horses one by one, with the aid of a few horse-nuts which Mark produced from his pockets, and tied their reins to tethering rings in the walls. Bingo, once the agitating girths were undone and the saddle off, stood quietly enough, and Mark darted briefly away from his mother to give his own pony some brisk encouraging slaps and some more horse-nuts.

Chico said the emergency service had indeed had a call from a child fifteen minutes earlier, but he'd hung up before they could ask him where he lived.

'Don't tell him,' I said.

'You're a softie.'

'He's a brave little kid.'

'Not bad for a little bleeder. While you were catching the bucking bronco he told me his dad gets bloody

angry pretty often.' He looked down at the still unconscious girl. 'You really reckon she's OK, do you?'

'She'll come out of it. It's a matter of waiting.'

The ambulance came in due course, but Mark's
anxiety reappeared, strongly, when the men loaded his
mother into the van and prepared to depart. He wanted
to go with her, and the men wouldn't take him on his
own. She was stirring and mumbling, and it distressed
him.

I said to Chico, 'Drive him to the hospital . . . Follow
the ambulance. He needs to see her wide awake and
speaking to him. I'll take a look round in the house. His
dad's away until tomorrow.'

'Convenient,' he said sardonically. He collected
Mark into the Scimitar, and drove away down the road,
and I could see their heads talking to each other,
through the rear window.

I went through the open back door with the confidence of the invited. Nothing difficult about entering a
tiger's cage while the tiger was out.

It was an old house filled with brash new opulent
furnishings, which I found overpowering. Lush loud
carpets, huge stereo equipment, a lamp standard of a
golden nymph and deep armchairs covered in black and
khaki zigzags. Sitting and dining rooms shining and tidy,
with no sign that a small boy lived there. Kitchen unclut-
tered, hygienic surfaces wiped clean. Study . . .

The positively aggressive tidiness of the study made
me pause and consider. No horse trader that I'd ever

come across had kept his books and papers in such neat rectangular stacks; and the ledgers themselves, when I opened them, contained up-to-the-minute entries.

I looked into drawers and filing cabinets, being extremely careful to leave everything squared up after me, but there was nothing there except the outward show of honesty. Not a single drawer or cupboard was locked. It was almost, I thought with cynicism, as if the whole thing were stage dressing, orchestrated to confound any invasion of tax snoopers. The real records, if he kept any, were probably somewhere outside, in a biscuit tin, in a hole in the ground.

I went upstairs. Mark's room was unmistakable, but all the toys were in boxes, and all the clothes in drawers. There were three unoccupied bedrooms with the outlines of folded blankets showing under covers, and a suite of bedroom, dressing room and bathroom furnished with the same expense and tidiness as downstairs.

An oval dark red bath with taps like gilt dolphins. A huge bed with a bright brocade cover clashing with wall-to-wall jazz on the floor. No clutter on the curvaceous cream and gold dressing table, no brushes on any surface in the dressing room.

Mark's mum's clothes were fur and glitter and breeches and jackets. Mark's dad's clothes, thorn-proof tweeds, vicuna overcoat, a dozen or more suits, none of them handmade, all seemingly bought because they were expensive. Handfuls of illicit cash, I thought, and nothing much to do with it. Peter Rammileese, it seemed, was crooked by nature and not by necessity.

The same incredible tidiness extended through every drawer and every shelf, and even into the soiled linen basket, where a pair of pyjamas were neatly folded.

I went through the pockets of his suits, but he had left nothing at all in them. There were no pieces of paper of any sort anywhere in the dressing room.

Frustrated, I went up to the third floor, where there were six rooms, one containing a variety of empty suit-cases, and the others, nothing at all.

No one, I thought on the way down again, lived so excessively carefully if they had nothing to hide; which was scarcely evidence to offer in court. The present life of the Rammileese family was an expensive vacuum, and of the past there was no sign at all. No souvenirs, no old books, not even any photographs except a recent one of Mark on his pony, taken outside in the yard.

I was looking round the outbuildings when Chico came back. There were no animals except seven horses in the stable and the two in the covered school. No sign of farming in progress. No rosettes in the tack room, just a lot more tidiness and the smell of saddle-soap. I went out to meet Chico and ask what he had done with Mark.

'The nurses are stuffing him with jam butties and trying to ring his dad. Mum is awake and talking. How did you get on? Do you want to drive?'

'No, you drive.' I sat in beside him. 'That house is the most suspicious case of no history I've ever seen.'

'Like that, eh?'

'Mm. And not a chance of finding any link with Eddy Keith.'

'Wasted journey, then,' he said.

'Lucky for Mark.'

'Yeah. Good little bleeder, that. Told me he's going to be a furniture-moving man when he grows up.' Chico looked across at me and grinned. 'Seems he's moved house three times that he can remember.'

CHAPTER TEN

Chico and I spent most of Saturday separately traipsing around all the London addresses on the M list of wax names, and met at six o'clock, footsore and thirsty, at a pub we both knew in Fulham.

'We never ought to have done it on a Saturday, and a holiday weekend at that,' Chico said.

'No.' I agreed.

Chico watched the beer sliding mouth-wateringly into the glass. 'More than half of them were out.'

'Mine too. Nearly all.'

'And the ones that were in were watching the racing or the wrestling or groping their girlfriends, and didn't want to know.'

We carried his beer and my whisky over to a small table, drank deeply, and compared notes. Chico had finally pinned down four people, and I only two, but the results were there, all the same.

All six, whatever other mailing lists they had confessed to, had been in regular happy receipt of *Antiques for All*.

'That's it, then,' Chico said. 'Conclusive.' He leaned back against the wall, luxuriously relaxing. 'We can't do any more until Tuesday. Everything's shut.'

'Are you busy tomorrow?'

'Have a heart. The girl in Wembley.' He looked at his watch and swallowed the rest of the beer. 'And so long, Sid boy, or I'll be late. She doesn't like me sweaty.'

He grinned and departed, and I more slowly finished my drink and went home.

Wandered about. Changed the batteries. Ate some cornflakes. Got out the form books and looked up the syndicated horses. Highly variable form: races lost at short odds and won at long. All the signs of steady and expert fixing. I yawned. It went on all the time.

I pottered some more, restlessly, sorely missing the peace that usually filled me in that place, when I was alone. Undressed, put on a bathrobe, pulled off the arm. Tried to watch the television: couldn't concentrate. Switched it off.

I usually pulled the arm off after I'd put the bathrobe on because that way I didn't have to look at the bit of me that remained below the left elbow. I could come to terms with the fact of it but still not really the sight, though it was neat enough and not horrific, as the messed up hand had been. I dare say it was senseless to be faintly repelled, but I was. I hated anyone except the limb man to see it; even Chico. I was ashamed of it, and that too was illogical. People without handicaps never understood that ashamed feeling, and nor had I, until the day soon after the original injury when I'd blushed crimson because I'd had to ask someone to cut up my food. There had been many times after that when I'd gone hungry rather than ask. Not having to ask, ever, since I'd had the electronic hand, had been a psychological release of soul-saving proportions.

The new hand had meant, too, a return to full normal human status. No one treated me as an idiot, or with the pity which in the past had made me cringe. No one made allowances any more, or got themselves tongue-tied with trying not to say the wrong thing. The days of the useless deformity seemed in retrospect an unbearable nightmare. I was often quite grateful to the villain who had set me free.

With one hand, I was a self-sufficient man.

Without any . . .

Oh God, I thought. Don't think about it. *There is nothing either good or bad, but thinking makes it so.* Hamlet, however, didn't have the same problems.

I got through the night, and the next morning, and the afternoon, but at around six I gave up and got in the car, and drove to Aynsford.

If Jenny was there, I thought, easing up the back drive and stopping quietly in the yard outside the kitchen, I would just turn right round and go back to London, and at least the driving would have occupied the time. But no one seemed to be about, and I walked in through the side door which had a long passage into the house.

179

Charles was in the small sitting room that he called the wardroom, sitting alone, sorting out his much-loved collection of fishing flies.

He looked up. No surprise. No effusive welcome. No fuss. Yet I'd never gone there before without invitation.

'Hello,' he said.

'Hello.'

I stood there, and he looked at me, and waited.

'I wanted some company,' I said.

He squinted at a dry fly. 'Did you bring an overnight bag?'

I nodded.

He pointed to the drinks tray. 'Help yourself. And pour me a pink gin, will you? Ice in the kitchen.'

I fetched him his drink, and my own, and sat in an armchair.

'Come to tell me?' he said.

'No.'

He smiled. 'Supper then? And chess?'

We ate, and played two games. He won the first easily, and told me to pay attention. The second, after an hour and a half, was a draw. 'That's better,' he said.

The peace I hadn't been able to find on my own came slowly back with Charles, even though I knew it had more to do with the ease I felt with him personally, and the timelessness of his vast old house, than with a real resolution of the destruction within. In any case, for the first time in ten days, I slept soundly for hours.

At breakfast we discussed the day ahead. He himself

was going to the steeplechase meeting at Towcester, forty-five minutes northwards, to act as a steward, an honorary job that he enjoyed. I told him about John Viking and the balloon race, and also about the visits to the M people, and *Antiques for All*, and he smiled with his own familiar mixture of satisfaction and amusement, as if I were some creation of his that was coming up to expectations. It was he who had originally driven me to becoming an investigator. Whenever I got anything right he took the credit for it himself.

'Did Mrs Cross tell you about the telephone call?' he said, buttering toast. Mrs Cross was his housekeeper, quiet, effective and kind.

'What telephone call?'

'Someone rang here about seven this morning, asking if you were here. Mrs Cross said you were asleep and could she take a message, but whoever it was said he would ring later.'

'Was it Chico? He might guess I'd come here, if he couldn't get me in the flat.'

'Mrs Cross said he didn't give a name.'

I shrugged and reached for the coffee pot. 'It can't have been urgent, or he'd have told her to wake me up.'

Charles smiled. 'Mrs Cross sleeps in curlers and face cream. She'd never have let you see her at seven o'clock in the morning, short of an earthquake. She thinks you're a lovely young man. She tells me so, every time you come.'

'For God's sakes.'

'Will you be back here, tonight?' he said.

'I don't know yet.'

He folded his napkin, looking down at it. 'I'm glad that you came, yesterday.'

I looked at him. 'Yeah,' I said. 'Well, you want me to say it, so I'll say it. And I mean it.' I paused a fraction, searching for the simplest words that would tell him what I felt for him. Found some. Said them. 'This is my home.'

He looked up quickly, and I smiled twistedly, mocking myself, mocking him, mocking the whole damned world.

Highalane Park was a stately home uneasily coming to terms with the plastic age. The house itself opened to the public like an agitated virgin only half a dozen times a year, but the parkland was always out for rent for game fairs and circuses, and things like the May Day jamboree.

They had made little enough effort on the roadside to attract the passing crowd. No bunting, no razzamatazz, no posters with print large enough to read at ten paces; everything slightly coy and apologetic. Considering all that, the numbers pouring on to the showground were impressive. I paid at the gate in my turn and bumped over some grass to park the car obediently in a row in the roped-off parking area. Other cars followed, neatly alongside.

There were a few people on horses cantering busily about in haphazard directions, but the roundabouts on the fairground to one side were silent and motionless, and there was no sight of any balloons.

I got out of the car and locked the door, and thought that one-thirty was probably too early for much in the way of action.

One can be so wrong.

A voice behind me said, 'Is this the man?'

I turned and found two people advancing into the small space between my car and the one next to it: a man I didn't know, and a little boy, whom I did.

'Yes,' the boy said, pleased. 'Hello.'

'Hallo, Mark,' I said. 'How's your mum?'

'I told Dad about you coming.' He looked up at the man beside him.

'Did you now?' I thought his being at Highalane was only an extraordinary coincidence, but it wasn't.

'He described you,' the man said. 'That hand, and the way you could handle horses . . . I knew who he meant, right enough.' His face and voice were hard and wary, with a quality that I by now recognized on sight: guilty knowledge faced by trouble. 'I don't take kindly to you poking your nose around my place.'

'You were out,' I said mildly.

'Aye, I was out. And this nipper, here, he left you there all alone.'

He was about forty, a wiry man with evil intentions stamped clearly all over him.

183

'I knew your car, too,' Mark said proudly. 'Dad says I'm clever.'

'Kids are observant,' his father said, with nasty relish.

'We waited for you to come out of a big house,' Mark said. 'And then we followed you all the way here.' He beamed, inviting me to enjoy the game. 'This is our car, next to yours.' He patted the maroon Daimler alongside.

The telephone call, I thought fleetingly. Not Chico. Peter Rammileese, checking around.

'Dad says,' Mark chatted on happily, 'that he'll take me to see those roundabouts while our friends take you for a ride in our car.'

His father looked down at him sharply, not having expected so much repeated truth, but Mark, oblivious, was looking at a point behind my back.

I glanced round. Between the Scimitar and the Daimler stood two more people. Large unsmiling men from a muscular brotherhood. Brass knuckles and toecaps.

'Get into the car,' Rammileese said, nodding to his, not to mine. 'Rear door.'

Oh sure, I thought. Did he think I was mad? I stooped slightly as if to obey and then instead of opening the door scooped Mark up bodily, with my right arm, and ran.

Rammileese turned with a shout. Mark's face, next to mine, was astonished but laughing. I ran about twenty paces with him, and set him down in the path of his furiously advancing father, and then kept on going, away from the cars and towards the crowds in the centre part of the showground.

Bloody hell, I thought. Chico was right. These days we only had to twitch an eyelid for them to wheel out the heavies. It was getting too much.

It had been the sort of ambush that might have orked if Mark hadn't been there: one kidney-punch and into the car before I'd got my breath. But they'd needed Mark, I supposed, to identify me, because although they knew me by name, they didn't by sight. They weren't going to catch me on the open showground, that was for sure, and when I went back to my car it would be with a load of protectors. Maybe, I thought hopefully, they would see it was useless, and just go away.

I reached the outskirts of the show-jumping arena, and looked back from over the head of a small girl sucking an ice-cream cornet. No one had called off the heavies. They were still doggedly in pursuit. I decided not to see what would happen if I simply stood my ground and requested the assorted families round about to save me from being frogmarched to oblivion and waking up with my head kicked in in the streets of Tunbridge Wells. The assorted families, with dogs and grannies and prams and picnics, were more likely to dither with their mouths open and wonder what it had all been about, once it was over.

I went on, deeper into the show, circling the ring,

bumping into children as I looked over my shoulder, and seeing the two men always behind me.

The arena itself was on my left, with show-jumping in progress inside, and ring-side cars encircling it outside. Behind the cars there was the broad grass walkway along which I was going, and, on my right, the outer ring of the stalls one always gets at horse-shows. Tented shops selling saddlery, riding clothes, pictures, toys, hot dogs, fruit, more saddles, hardware, tweeds, sheepskin slippers . . . an endless circle of small traders.

Among the tents, the vans: ice-cream vans, riding associations' caravans, a display of crafts, a fortune teller, a charity jumble shop, a mobile cinema showing films of sheepdogs, a drop-sided juggernaut spilling out kitchen equipment in orange and yellow and green. Crowds along the fronts of all of them and no depth of shelter inside.

'Do you know where the balloons are?' I asked someone, and he pointed, and it was to a stall selling gas balloons of brilliant colours: children buying them and tying them to their wrists.

Not those, I thought. Surely not those. I didn't stop to explain, but asked again, further on.

'The balloon race? In the next field, I think, but it isn't time yet.'

'Thanks,' I said. The posters had announced a three o'clock start, but I'd have to talk to John Viking well before that, while he was willing to listen.

What was a balloon race, I wondered? Surely all balloons went at the same speed, the speed of the wind.

My trackers wouldn't give up. They weren't running, and nor was I. They just followed me steadily, as if locked on to a target by a radio beam; minds taking literally an order to stick to my heels. I'd have to get lost, I thought, and stay lost until after I'd found John Viking, and maybe then I'd go in search of helpful defences like show secretaries and first-aid ladies, and the single policeman out on the road directing traffic.

I was on the far side of the arena by that time, crossing the collecting ring area with children on ponies buzzing around like bees, looking strained as they went in to jump, and tearful or triumphant as they came out.

Past them, past the commentating box ... 'Jane Smith had a clear round, the next to jump is Robin Daly on Traddles' ... past the little private grandstand for the organizers and bigwigs – rows of empty folding seats – past an open-sided refreshment tent, full, and so back to the stalls.

I did a bit of dodging in and out of those, and round the backs, ducking under guy ropes and round dumps of cardboard boxes. From inside the depths of a stall hung thickly outside with riding jackets I watched the two of them go past, hurrying, looking about them, distinctly anxious.

They weren't like the two Trevor Deansgate had sent, I thought. His had been clumsier, smaller, and less professional. These two looked as if this sort of work was their daily bread; and for all the comparative safety of the showground, where as a last resort I could get into the arena itself and scream for help, there was something daunting about them. Rent-a-thugs usually came at so much per hour. These two looked salaried, if not actually on the Board.

I left the riding jackets and dodged into the film about sheepdogs, which I dare say would have been riveting but for the shepherding going on outside, with me as the sheep.

I looked at my watch. After two o'clock. Too much time was passing. I had to try another sortie outside and find my way to the balloons.

I couldn't see them. I slithered among the crowd, asking for directions.

'Up at the end, mate,' a decisive man told me, pointing. 'Past the hot dogs, turn right, there's a gate in the fence. You can't miss it.'

I nodded my thanks and turned to go that way, and saw one of my trackers coming towards me, searching the stalls with his eyes and looking worried.

In a second he would see me . . . I looked around in a hurry and found I was outside the caravan of the fortune-teller. There was a curtain of plastic streamers, black and white, over the open doorway, and behind that a shadowy figure. I took four quick strides, brushed through the plastic strips, and stepped up into the van.

It was quieter inside and darker, with daylight filtering dimly through lace-hung windows. A Victorian sort of decor; mock oil lamps and chenille tablecloths. Outside, the tracker went past, giving the fortune-teller no more than a flickering glance. His attention lay ahead. He hadn't seen me come in.

The fortune-teller, however, had, and to her I represented business.

'Do you want your whole life, dear, the past and everything, or just the future?'

'Er . . .' I said. 'I don't really know. How long does it take?'

'A quarter of an hour, dear, for the whole thing.'

'Let's just have the future.'

I looked out of the window. A part of my future was searching among the ring-side cars, asking questions and getting a lot of shaken heads.

'Sit on the sofa beside me here, dear, and give me your left hand.'

'It'll have to be the right,' I said absently.

'No, dear.' Her voice was quite sharp. 'Always the left.'

Amused, I sat down and gave her the left. She felt it, and looked at it, and raised her eyes to mine. She was short and plump, dark-haired, middle-aged, and in no way remarkable.

'Well, dear,' she said after a pause, 'it will have to be the right, though I'm not used to it, and we may not get such good results.'

'I'll risk it,' I said; so we changed places on the sofa,

and she held my right hand firmly in her two warm ones, and I watched the tracker move along the row of cars.

'You have suffered,' she said.

As she knew about my left hand, I didn't think much of that for a guess, and she seemed to sense it. She coughed apologetically.

'Do you mind if I use a crystal?' she said.

'Go ahead.'

I had vague visions of her peering into a large ball on a table, but she took a small one, the size of a tennis ball, and put it in the palm of my hand.

'You are a kind person,' she said. 'Gentle. People like you. People smile at you wherever you go.'

Outside, twenty yards away, the two heavies had met to consult. Not a smile, there, of any sort.

'You are respected by everyone.'

Regulation stuff, designed to please the customers.

Chico should hear it, I thought. Gentle, kind, respected . . . he'd laugh his head off.

She said doubtfully, 'I see a great many people, cheering and clapping. Shouting loudly, cheering you . . . does that mean anything to you, dear?'

I slowly turned my head. Her dark eyes watched me calmly.

'That's the past,' I said.

'It's recent,' she said. 'It's still there.'

I didn't believe it. I didn't believe in fortune-tellers. I wondered if she had seen me before, on a racecourse or talking on television. She must have.

She bent her head again over the crystal which she held on my hand, moving the glass gently over my skin.

'You have good health. You have vigour. You have great physical stamina . . . There is much to endure.'

Her voice broke off, and she raised her head a little, frowning. I had a strong impression that what she had said had surprised her.

After a pause, she said, 'I can't tell you any more.'

'Why not?'

'I'm not used to the right hand.'

'Tell me what you see,' I said.

She shook her head slightly and raised the calm dark eyes.

'You will live a long time.'

I glanced out through the plastic curtain. The trackers had moved off out of sight.

'How much do I owe you?' I asked. She told me, and I paid her, and went quietly over to the doorway.

'Take care, dear,' she said. 'Be careful.'

I looked back. Her face was still calm, but her voice had been urgent. I didn't want to believe in the conviction that looked out of her eyes. She might have felt the disturbance of my present problem with the trackers, but no more than that. I pushed the curtain gently aside and stepped from the dim world of hovering horrors into the bright May sunlight, where they might in truth lie in wait.

CHAPTER ELEVEN

There was no longer any need to ask where the balloons were. No one could miss them. They were beginning to rise like gaudy monstrous mushrooms, humped on the ground, spread all over an enormous area of grassland beyond the actual showground. I had thought vaguely that there would be two or three balloons, or at most six, but there must have been twenty.

Among a whole stream of people going the same way, I went down to the gate and through into the far field, and realized that I had absolutely underestimated the task of finding John Viking.

There was a rope, for a start, and marshals telling the crowd to stand behind it. I ducked those obstacles at least, but found myself in a forest of half-inflated balloons, which billowed immensely all around and cut off any length of sight.

The first clump of people I came to were busy with a pink and purple monster into whose mouth they were blowing air by means of a large engine-driven fan. The balloon was attached by four fine nylon ropes to the basket, which lay on its side, with a young man in a red crash helmet peering anxiously into its depth.

'Excuse me,' I said to a girl on the edge of the group. 'Do you know where I can find John Viking?'

'Sorry.'

The red crash helmet raised itself to reveal a pair of very blue eyes. 'He's here somewhere,' he said politely. 'Flies a Stormcloud balloon. Now would you mind getting the hell out, we're busy.'

I walked along the edge of things, trying to keep out of their way. Balloon races, it seemed, were a serious business and no occasion for light laughter and social chat. The intent faces leaned over ropes and equipment, testing, checking, worriedly frowning. No balloons looked much like stormclouds. I risked another question.

'John Viking? That bloody idiot. Yes, he's here. Flies a Stormcloud.' He turned away, busy and anxious.

'What colour is it?' I said.

'Yellow and green. Look, go away, will you?'

There were balloons advertising whisky and marmalade and towns, and even insurance companies. Balloons in brilliant primary colours and pink and white pastels, balloons in the sunshine rising from the green grass in glorious jumbled rainbows. On an ordinary day, a scene of delight, but to me, trying to get round them to ask fruitlessly at the next clump gathered anxiously by its basket, a frustrating silky maze.

I circled a soft billowing black and white monster and

went deeper into the centre. As if at a signal, there arose in a chorus from all around a series of deep-throated roars, caused by flames suddenly spurting from the large burners which were supported on frames above the baskets. The flames roared into the open mouths of the half-inflated balloons, heating and expanding the air already there and driving in more. The gleaming envelopes swelled and surged with quickening life, growing from mushrooms to toadstools, the tops rising slowly and magnificently towards the hazy blue sky.

'John Viking? Somewhere over there.' A girl swung her arm vaguely. 'But he'll be as busy as we are.'

As the balloons filled they began to heave off the ground and sway in great floating masses, bumping into each other, still billowing, still not full enough to live with the birds. Under each balloon the flames roared, scarlet and lusty, with the little clusters of helpers clinging to the baskets to prevent them escaping too soon.

With the balloons off the ground, I saw a yellow and green one quite easily; yellow and green in segments, like an orange, with a wide green band at the bottom. There was one man already in the basket, with about three people holding it down, and he, unlike everyone else in sight, wore not a crash helmet but a blue denim cap.

I ran in his direction, and even as I ran there was the sound of a starter's pistol. All around me the baskets were released, and began dragging and bumping over the ground; and a great cheer went up from the watching crowd.

I reached the bunch of people I was aiming for and put my hand on the basket.

'John Viking?'

No one listened. They were deep in a quarrel. A girl in a crash helmet, skiing jacket, jeans and boots stood on the ground, with the two helpers beside her looking glum and embarrassed.

'I'm not coming. You're a bloody madman.'

'Get in, get in dammit. The race has started.'

He was very tall, very thin, very agitated.

'I'm not coming.'

'You must.' He made a grab at her and held her wrist in a sinewy grip. It looked almost as if he were going to haul her wholesale into the basket, and she certainly believed it. She tugged and panted and screamed at him. 'Let go, John. Let go. I'm not coming.'

'Are you John Viking?' I said loudly.

He swung his head and kept hold of the girl.

'Yes, I am, what do you want? I'm starting this race as soon as my passenger gets in.'

'I'm not *going*,' she screamed.

I looked around. The other baskets were mostly airborne, sweeping gently across the area a foot or two above the surface, and rising in a smooth, glorious crowd. Every basket, I saw, carried two people.

'If you want a passenger,' I said, 'I'll come.'

He let go of the girl and looked me up and down.

'How much do you weigh?' And then, impatiently, as he saw the other balloons getting a head start, 'Oh, all right, get in. Get in.'

I gripped hold of a stay, and jumped, and wriggled, and ended standing inside a rather small hamper under a very large cloud of balloon.

'Leave go,' commanded the captain of this ship, and the helpers somewhat helplessly obeyed.

The basket momentarily stayed exactly where it was. Then John Viking reached above his head and flipped a lever which operated the burners, and there at close quarters, right above our heads, was the flame and the ear-filling roar.

The girl's face was still on a level with mine. 'He's mad,' she yelled. 'And you're crazy.'

The basket moved away, bumped, and rose quite suddenly to a height of six feet. The girl ran after it and delivered a parting encouragement. 'And you haven't got a crash helmet.'

What I did have, though, was a marvellous escape route from two purposeful thugs, and a crash helmet at that moment seemed superfluous, particularly as my companion hadn't one either.

John Viking was staring about him in the remnants of fury, muttering under his breath, and operating the burner almost non-stop. His was the last balloon away. I looked down to where the applauding holiday crowd were watching the mass departure and a small boy darted suddenly from under the restraining rope, and

ran into the now empty starting area, shouting and pointing. Pointing at John Viking's balloon, pointing
excitedly at me.

My pal Mark, with his bright little eyes and his
truthful tongue. My pal Mark, whom I'd like to have
strangled.

John Viking started cursing. I switched my attention
from ground to air and saw that the reason for the
resounding and imaginative obscenities floating to
heaven was a belt of trees lying ahead which might
prevent us going in the same direction. One balloon
already lay in a tangle on the take-off side, and another,
scarlet and purple, seemed set on a collision course.

John Viking yelled at me over the continuing roar of
the burner, 'Hold on bloody tight with both hands. If the
basket hits the tops of the trees we don't want to be
spilled right out.'

The trees looked sixty feet high and a formidable
obstacle, but most of the balloons had cleared them
easily and were drifting away skywards, great bright
pear-shaped fantasies hanging on the wind.

John Viking's basket closed with a rush towards the
treetops with the burner roaring over our heads like a
demented dragon. The lift it should have provided
seemed totally lacking.

'Turbulence,' John Viking shrieked. 'Bloody wind
turbulence. Hold on. It's a long way down.'

Frightfully jolly, I thought, being tipped out of a
hamper sixty feet from the ground without a crash

helmet. I grinned at him, and he caught the expression and looked startled.

The basket hit the treetops, and tipped on its side, tumbling me from the vertical to the horizontal with no trouble at all. I grabbed right-handed at whatever I could to stop myself falling right out, and I felt as much as saw that the majestically swelling envelope above us was carrying on with its journey regardless. It tugged the basket after it, crashing and bumping through the tops of the trees, flinging me about like a rag doll with at times most of my body hanging out in space. My host, made of sterner stuff, had one arm clamped like a vice round one of the metal struts which supported the burner, and the other twined into a black rubber strap. His legs were braced against the side of the basket, which was now the floor, and he changed his footholds as necessary, at one point planting one foot firmly on my stomach.

With a last sickening jolt and wrench the basket tore itself free, and we swung to and fro under the wobbling balloon like a pendulum. I was by this manoeuvre wedged into a disorganized heap in the bottom of the basket, but John Viking still stood rather splendidly on his feet.

There really wasn't much room, I thought, disentangling myself and straightening upwards. The basket, still swaying and shaking, was only four feet square, and reached no higher than one's waist. Along two opposite sides stood eight gas cylinders, four each side, fastened to the wickerwork with rubber straps. The oblong space left was big enough for two men to stand in, but not overgenerous even for that: about two feet by two feet per person.

John Viking gave the burner a rest at last, and into the sudden silence said forcefully, 'Why the hell didn't you hold on like I told you to? Don't you know you damned nearly fell out, and got me into trouble?'

'Sorry,' I said, amused. 'Is it usual to go on burning, when you're stuck on a tree?'

'It got us clear, didn't it?' he demanded.

'It sure did.'

'Don't complain, then. I didn't ask you to come.'

He was of about my own age; perhaps a year or two younger. His face under his blue denim yachting cap was craggy with a bone structure that might one day give him distinction, and his blue eyes shone with the brilliance of the true fanatic. John Viking the madman, I thought, and warmed to him.

'Check round the outsides, will you,' he said. 'See if anything's come adrift.'

It seemed he meant the outside of the basket, as he was himself looking outwards, over the edge. I discovered that on my side, too, there were bundles on the outside of the basket, either strapped to it tight, or swinging on ropes.

One short rope, attached to the basket, had nothing on the end of it. I pulled it up and showed it to him.

'Damnation,' he said explosively. 'Lost in the trees, I

suppose. Plastic water container. Hope you're not thirsty.' He stretched up and gave the burner another long burst, and I listened in my mind to the echo of his Etonian drawl and totally understood why he was as he was.

'Do you have to finish first, to win a balloon race?' I said.

He looked surprised. 'Not this one. This is a two-and-a-half-hour race. The one who gets furthest in that time is the winner.' He frowned. 'Haven't you ever been in a balloon before?'

'No.'

'My God,' he said. 'What chance have I got?'

'None at all, if I hadn't come,' I said mildly.

'That's true.' He looked down from somewhere like six feet four. 'What's your name?'

'Sid,' I said.

He looked as if Sid wasn't exactly the sort of name his friends had, but faced the fact manfully.

'Why wouldn't your girl come with you?' I said.

'Who? Oh, you mean Popsy. She's not my girl. I don't really know her. She was going to come because my usual passenger broke his leg, silly bugger, when we made a bit of a rough landing last week. Popsy wanted to bring some ruddy big handbag. Wouldn't come without it, wouldn't be parted from it. I ask you! Where is the room for a handbag? And it was heavy, as well. Every pound counts. Carry a pound less, you can go a mile further.'

'Where do you expect to come down?' I said.

'It depends on the wind.' He looked up at the sky. 'We're going roughly north-east at the moment, but I'm going higher. There's a front forecast from the west, and I guess there'll be some pretty useful activity high up. We might make it to Brighton.'

'*Brighton*.' I had thought in terms of perhaps twenty miles, not a hundred. And he must be wrong. I thought: one couldn't go a hundred miles in a balloon in two and a half hours.

'If the wind's more from the north-west we might reach the Isle of Wight. Or France. Depends how much gas is left. We don't want to come down in the sea, not in this. Can you swim?'

I nodded. I supposed I still could: hadn't tried it one-handed. 'I'd rather not,' I said.

He laughed. 'Don't worry. The balloon's too darned expensive for me to want to sink it.'

Once free of the trees we had risen very fast, and now floated across country at a height from which cars on the roads looked like toys, though still recognizable as to size and colour.

Noises came up clearly. One could hear the cars' engines, and dogs barking, and an occasional human shout. People looked up and waved to us as we passed. A world removed, I thought. I was in a child's world, idyllically drifting with the wind, sloughing off the dreary earthbound millstones, free and rising and filled with intense delight.

John Viking flipped the lever and the flame roared, shooting up into the green-and-yellow cavern, a scarlet and gold tongue of dragon fire. The burn endured for twenty seconds and we rose perceptibly in the sudden ensuing silence.

'What gas do you use?' I said.

'Propane.'

He was looking over the side of the basket and around at the countryside, as if judging his position. 'Look, get the map out, will you. It's in a pouch thing, on your side. And for God's sake don't let it blow away.'

I looked over the side, and found what he meant. A satchel-like object strapped on through the wickerwork, its outward-facing flap fastened shut with a buckle. I undid the buckle, looked inside, took a fair grip of the large folded map, and delivered it safely to the captain.

He was looking fixedly at my left hand, which I'd used as a sort of counterweight on the edge of the basket while I leaned over. I let it fall by my side, and his gaze swept upwards to my face.

'You're missing a hand,' he said incredulously.

'That's right.'

He waved his own two arms in a fierce gesture of frustration. 'How the *hell* am I going to win this race?'

I laughed.

He glanced at me. 'It's not damned funny.'

'Oh yes it is. And I like winning races . . . you won't lose it because of me.'

He frowned disgustedly. 'I suppose you can't be

202

much more useless than Popsy,' he said. 'But at least they say she can read a map.' He unfolded the sheet I'd given him, which proved to be a map designed for the navigation of aircraft, its surface covered with a plastic film, for writing on. 'Look,' he said. 'We started from here.' He pointed. 'We're travelling roughly north-east. You take the map, and find out where we are.' He paused. 'Do you know the first bloody thing about using your watch as a compass, or about dead reckoning?'

I had a book about dead reckoning, which I hadn't read, in a pocket of the light cotton anorak I was wearing; and also, I thanked God, in another zippered compartment, a spare fully charged battery. 'Give me the map,' I said. 'And let's see.'

He handed it over with no confidence and started another burn. I worked out roughly where we should be, and looked over the side, and discovered straight away that the ground didn't look like the map. Where villages and roads were marked clearly on the map, they faded into the brown and green carpet of earth like patches of camouflage, the sunlight mottling them with shadows and dissolving them into ragged edges. The spread-out vistas all around looked all the same, defying me to recognize anything special, proving conclusively I was less use than Popsy.

Dammit, I thought. Start again.

We had set off at three o'clock, give a minute or two. We had been airborne for twelve minutes. On the ground the wind had been gentle and from the south, but we were now travelling slightly faster, and north-east. Say . . . fifteen knots. Twelve minutes at fifteen knots . . . about three nautical miles. I had been looking too far ahead. There should be, I thought, a river to cross; and in spite of gazing earnestly down I nearly missed it, because it was a firm blue line on the map and in reality a silvery reflecting thread that wound unobtrusively between a meadow and a wood. To the right of it, half hidden by a hill, lay a village, with beyond it, a railway line.

'We're there,' I said, pointing to the map.

He squinted at the print and searched the ground beneath us.

'Fair enough,' he said. 'So we are. Right. You keep the map. We might as well know where we are, all the way.'

He flipped the lever and gave it a long burn. The balloons ahead of us were also lower. We were definitely looking down on their tops. During the next patch of silence he consulted two instruments which were strapped on to the outside of the basket at his end, and grunted.

'What are those?' I said, nodding at the dials.

'Altimeter and rate-of-climb meter,' he said. 'We're at five thousand feet now, and rising at eight hundred feet a minute.'

'Rising?'

'Yeah.' He gave a sudden, wolfish grin in which I read unmistakably the fierce unholy glee of the mischievous child. 'That's why Popsy wouldn't come. Someone told her I would go high. She didn't want to.'

'How high?' I said.

'I don't mess about,' he said. 'When I race, I race to win. They all know I'll win. They don't like it. They think you should never take risks. They're all safety-conscious these days and getting softer. Hah!' His scorn was absolute. 'In the old days, at the beginning of the century, when they had the Gordon Bennet races, they would fly for two days and do a thousand miles or more. But nowadays . . . safety bloody first.' He glared at me. 'And if I didn't have to have a passenger, I wouldn't. Passengers always argue and complain.'

He pulled a packet of cigarettes out of his pocket and lit one with a flick of a lighter. We were surrounded by cylinders of liquid gas. I thought about all the embargoes against naked flames near any sort of stored fuel, and kept my mouth shut.

The flock of balloons below us seemed to be veering away to the left; but then I realized that it was we who were going to the right. John Viking watched the changing direction with great satisfaction and started another long burn. We rose perceptibly faster, and the sun, instead of shining full on our backs, appeared on our starboard side.

In spite of the sunshine it was getting pretty cold. A look over the side showed the earth very far beneath, and one could now see a very long way in all directions.

I checked with the map, and kept an eye on where we were.

'What are you wearing?' he said.

'What you see, more or less.'

'Huh.'

During the burns, the flame over one's head was almost too hot, and there was always a certain amount of hot air escaping from the bottom of the balloon. There was no wind factor, as of course the balloon was travelling with the wind, at the wind's speed. It was sheer altitude that was making us cold.

'How high are we now?' I said.

He glanced at his instruments. 'Eleven thousand feet.'

'And still rising?'

He nodded. The other balloons, far below and to the left, were a cluster of distant bright blobs against the green earth.

'All that lot,' he said, 'will stay down at five thousand feet, because of staying under the airways.' He gave me a sideways look. 'You'll see on the map. The airways that the airlines use are marked, and so are the heights at which one is not allowed to fly through them.'

'And one is not allowed to fly through an airway at eleven thousand feet in a balloon?'

'Sid,' he said, grinning, 'you're not bad.'

He flicked the lever, and the burner roared, cutting off chat. I checked the ground against the map and nearly lost our position entirely, because we seemed suddenly to have travelled much faster, and quite definitely to the south-east. The other balloons, when I next looked, were out of sight.

In the next silence John Viking told me that the helpers of the other balloons would follow them on the ground, in cars, ready to retrieve them when they came down.

'What about you?' I asked. 'Do we have someone following?'

Did we indeed have Peter Rammileese following, complete with thugs, ready to pounce again at the further end? We were even, I thought fleetingly, doing him a favour with the general direction, taking him south-eastwards, home to Kent.

John Viking gave his wolfish smile, and said, 'No car on earth could keep up with us today.'

'Do you mean it?' I exclaimed.

He looked at the altimeter. 'Fifteen thousand feet,' he said. 'We'll stay at that. I got a forecast from the air boys for this trip. Fifty-knot wind from two nine zero at fifteen thousand feet, that's what they said. You hang on, Sid, pal, and we'll get to Brighton.'

I thought about the two of us standing in a waist-high four-foot-square wicker basket, supported by Terylene and hot air, fifteen thousand feet above the solid ground, travelling without any feeling of speed at fifty-seven miles an hour. Quite mad, I thought.

From the ground, we would be a black speck. On the ground, no car could keep up. I grinned back at John

Viking with a satisfaction as great as his own, and he laughed aloud.

'Would you believe it?' he said. 'At last I've got someone up here who's not puking with fright.'

He lit another cigarette, and then he changed the supply line to the burner from one cylinder to the next. This involved switching off the empty tank, unscrewing the connecting nut, screwing it into the next cylinder, and switching on the new supply. There were two lines to the double burner, one for each set of four cylinders. He held the cigarette in his mouth throughout, and squinted through the smoke.

I had seen from the map that we were flying straight towards the airway which led in and out of Gatwick, where large aeroplanes thundered up and down not expecting to meet squashy balloons illegally in their path.

His appetite for taking risks was way out of my class. He made sitting on a horse over fences on the ground seem rather tame. Except, I thought with a jerk, that I no longer did it, I fooled around instead with men who threatened to shoot hands off ... and I was safer up here with John Viking the madman, propane and cigarettes, mid-air collisions and all.

'Right,' he said. 'We just stay as we are for an hour and a half and let the wind take us. If you feel odd, it's lack of oxygen.' He took a pair of wool gloves from his pocket and put them on. 'Are you cold?'

'Yes, a bit.'

He grinned. 'I've got long johns under my jeans, and two sweaters under my anorak. You'll just have to freeze.'

'Thanks very much.' I stood on the map and put my real hand deep into the pocket of my cotton anorak and he said at least the false hand couldn't get frostbite.

He operated the burner and looked at his watch and the ground and the altimeter, and seemed pleased with the way things were. Then he looked at me in slight puzzlement and I knew he was wondering, now that there was time, how I happened to be where I was.

'I came to Highalane Park to see you,' I said. 'I mean, you, John Viking, particularly.'

He looked startled. 'Do you read minds?'

'All the time.' I pulled my hand out of one pocket and dipped into another, and brought out the paperback on navigation. 'I came to ask you about this. It's got your name on the flyleaf.'

He frowned at it, and opened the front cover. 'Good Lord. I wondered where this had got to. How did you have it?'

'Did you lend it to anyone?'

'I don't think so.'

'Um . . .' I said. 'If I describe someone to you, will you say if you know him?'

'Fire away.'

'A man of about twenty-eight,' I said. 'Dark hair,

good looks, full of fun and jokes, easy-going, likes girls, great company, has a habit of carrying a knife strapped to his leg under his sock, and is very likely a crook.'

'Oh yes,' he said, nodding. 'He's my cousin.'

CHAPTER TWELVE

His cousin, Norris Abbott. What had he done this time, he demanded, and I asked, what had he done before?

'A trail of bouncing cheques that his mother paid for.'

Where did he live, I asked. John Viking didn't know. He saw him only when Norris turned up occasionally on his doorstep, usually broke and looking for free meals.

'A laugh a minute for a day or two. Then he's gone.'

'Where does his mother live?'

'She's dead. He's alone now. No parents or brothers or sisters. No relatives except me.' He peered at me, frowning. 'Why do you ask all this?'

'A girl I know wants to find him.' I shrugged. 'It's nothing much.'

He lost interest at once and flicked the lever for another burn. 'We use twice the fuel up here as near the ground,' he said afterwards. 'That's why I brought so much. That's how some nosey parker told Popsy I was planning to go high, and through the airways.'

By my reckoning the airway was not that far off.

'Won't you get into trouble?' I said.

The wolf grin came and went. 'They've got to see us, first. We won't show up on radar. We're too small for the equipment they use. With a bit of luck, we'll sneak across and no one will be any the wiser.'

I picked up the map and studied it. At fifteen thousand feet we would be illegal from when we entered controlled airspace until we landed, all but the last two hundred feet. The airway over Brighton began at a thousand feet above sea level and the hills to the north were eight hundred feet high. Did John Viking know all that? Yes, he did.

When we had been flying for one hour and fifty minutes he made a fuel line change from cylinder to cylinder that resulted in a thin jet of liquid gas spurting out from the connection like water out of a badly joined hose. The jet shot across the corner of the basket and hit a patch of wickerwork about six inches below the top rail.

John Viking was smoking at the time.

Liquid propane began trickling down the inside of the basket in a stream. John Viking cursed and fiddled with the faulty connection, bending over it; and his glowing cigarette ignited the gas.

There was no ultimate and final explosion. The jet burnt as jets do, and directed its flame in an organized manner at the patch of basket it was hitting. John Viking threw his cigarette over the side and snatched off his denim cap, and beat at the burning basket with great flailing motions of his arm, while I managed to stifle the jet at source by turning off the main switch on the cylinder.

When the flames and smoke and cursing died down, we had a hole six inches in diameter right through the basket, but no other damage.

'Baskets don't burn easily,' he said calmly, as if nothing had happened. 'Never known one burn much more than this.' He inspected his cap, which was scorched into black-edged lace, and gave me a maniacal four seconds from the bright blue eyes. 'You can't put out a fire with a crash helmet,' he said.

I laughed quite a lot.

It was the altitude, I thought, which was making me giggle.

'Want some chocolate?' he said.

There were no signposts in the sky to tell us when we crossed the boundary of the airway. We saw an aeroplane or two some way off, but nothing near us. No one came buzzing around to direct us downward. We simply sailed straight on, blowing across the sky as fast as a train.

At ten past five he said it was time to go down, because if we didn't touch ground by five-thirty exactly he would be disqualified, and he didn't want that; he wanted to win. Winning was what it was all about.

'How would anyone know exactly when we touched down?' I said.

He gave me a pitying look and gently directed his toe

at a small box strapped to the floor beside one of the corner cylinders.

'In here is a barograph, all stuck about with pompous red seals. The judges seal it, before the start. It shows variations in air pressure. Highly sensitive. All our journey shows up like a row of peaks. When you're on the ground, the trace is flat and steady. It tells the judges just when you took off and when you landed. Right?'

'Right.'

'OK. Down we go, then.'

He reached up and untied a red cord which was knotted to the burner frame, and pulled it. 'It opens a panel at the top of the balloon,' he said. 'Lets the hot air out.'

His idea of descent was all of a piece. The altimeter unwound like a broken clock and the rate-of-climb meter was pointing to a thousand feet a minute, downwards. He seemed to be quite unaffected, but it made me queasy and hurt my eardrums. Swallowing made things a bit better, but not much. I concentrated, as an antidote, on checking with the map to see where we were going.

The Channel lay like a broad grey carpet to our right, and it was incredible but, whichever way I looked at it, it seemed that we were on a collision course with Beachy Head.

'Yeah,' John Viking casually confirmed. 'Guess we'll try not to get blown off those cliffs. Might be better to land on the beach further on . . .' He checked his watch.

'Ten minutes to go. We're still at six thousand feet . . . that's all right . . . might be the edge of the sea . . .'

'Not the sea,' I said positively.

'Why not? We might have to.'

'Well,' I said, 'this . . .' I lifted my left arm. 'Inside this hand-shaped plastic there's actually a lot of fine engineering. Strong pincers inside the thumb and first two fingers. A lot of fine precision gears and transistors and printed electrical circuits. Dunking it in the sea would be like dunking a radio. A total ruin. And it would cost me two thousand quid to get a new one.'

He was astonished. 'You're joking.'

'No.'

'Better keep you dry, then. And anyway, now we're down here, I don't think we'll get as far south as Beachy Head. Probably further east.' He paused and looked at my left hand doubtfully. 'It'll be a rough landing. The fuel's cold from being so high . . . the burner doesn't function well on cold fuel. It takes time to heat enough air to give us a softer touch-down.'

A softer touch-down took time . . . too much time.

'Win the race,' I said.

His face lit into sheer happiness. 'Right,' he said decisively. 'What's that town just ahead?'

I studied the map. 'Eastbourne.'

He looked at his watch. 'Five minutes.' He looked at the altimeter and at Eastbourne, upon which we were rapidly descending. 'Two thousand feet. Bit dicey, hitting the roofs. There isn't much wind down here, is

215

there . . . But if I burn, we might not get down in time. No, no burn.'

A thousand feet a minute, I reckoned, was eleven or twelve miles an hour. I had been used for years to hitting the ground at more than twice that speed . . . though not in a basket, and not when the ground might turn out to be fully inhabited by brick walls.

We were travelling sideways over the town, with houses below us. Descent was very fast. 'Three minutes,' he said.

The sea lay ahead again, fringing the far side of the town, and for a moment it looked as if it was there we would have to come down after all. John Viking, however, knew better.

'Hang on,' he said. 'This is it.'

He hauled strongly on the red cord he held, which led upwards into the balloon. Somewhere above, the vent for the hot air widened dramatically, the lifting power of the balloon fell away, and the solid edge of Eastbourne came up with a rush.

We scraped the eaves of grey slate roofs, made a sharp diagonal descent over a road and a patch of grass, and smashed down on a broad concrete walk twenty yards from the waves.

'Don't get out. Don't get out,' he yelled. The basket tipped on its side and began to slither along the concrete, dragged by the still half-inflated silken mass. 'Without our weight, it could still fly away.'

As I was again wedged among the cylinders, it was

superfluous advice. The basket rocked and tumbled a few more times and I with it, and John Viking cursed and hauled at his red cord and finally let out enough air for us to be still.

He looked at his watch, and his blue eyes blazed with triumph.

'We've made it. Five twenty-nine. That was a bloody good race. The best ever. What are you doing next Saturday?'

I went back to Aynsford by train, which took for ever, with Charles picking me up from Oxford station not far short of midnight.

'You went on the balloon race,' he repeated disbelievingly. 'Did you enjoy it?'

'Very much.'

'And your car's still at Highalane Park?'

'It can stay there until morning,' I yawned. 'Nicholas Ashe now has a name, by the way. He's someone called Norris Abbott. Same initials, silly man.'

'Will you tell the police?'

'See if we can find him, first.'

He glanced at me sideways. 'Jenny came back this evening, after you'd telephoned.'

'Oh no.'

'I didn't know she was going to.'

I supposed I believed him. I hoped she would have gone to bed before I arrived, but she hadn't. She was

217

sitting on the gold brocade sofa in the drawing room, looking belligerent.

'I don't like you coming here so much,' she said.

A knife to the heart of things from my pretty wife.

Charles said smoothly, 'Sid is welcome here always.'

'Discarded husbands should have more pride than to fawn on their fathers-in-law, who put up with it because they're sorry for them.'

'You're jealous,' I said, surprised.

She stood up fast, as angry as I'd ever seen her.

'How dare you!' she said. 'He always takes your side. He thinks you're bloody marvellous. He doesn't know you like I do, all your stubborn little ways and your meanness and thinking you're always *right*.'

'I'm going to bed,' I said.

'And you're a coward as well,' she said furiously. 'Running away from a few straight truths.'

'Good night, Charles,' I said. 'Good night, Jenny. Sleep well, my love, and pleasant dreams.'

'You . . .' she said. 'You . . . I hate you, Sid.'

I went out of the drawing room without fuss and upstairs to the bedroom I thought of as mine; the one I always slept in nowadays at Aynsford.

You don't have to hate me, Jenny, I thought miserably; I hate myself.

Charles drove me to Wiltshire in the morning to collect my car, which still stood where I'd left it, though surrounded now by acres of empty grass. There was no Peter Rammileese in sight, and no thugs waiting in ambush. All clear for an uneventful return to London.

'Sid,' Charles said, as I unlocked the car door. 'Don't pay any attention to Jenny.'

'No.'

'Come to Aynsford whenever you want.'

I nodded.

'I mean it, Sid.'

'Yeah.'

'Damn Jenny,' he said explosively.

'Oh no. She's unhappy. She . . .' I paused. 'I guess she needs comforting. A shoulder to cry on, and all that.'

He said austerely, 'I don't care for tears.'

'No.' I sighed and got into the car, waved goodbye, and drove over the bumpy grass to the gate. The help that Jenny needed, she wouldn't take from me; and her father didn't know how to give it. Just another of life's bloody muddles, another irony in the general mess.

I drove into the city and around in a few small circles, and ended up in the publishing offices of *Antiques for All*, which proved to be only one of a number of specialist magazines put out by a newspaper company. To the *Antiques* editor, a fair-haired earnest young man in heavy-framed specs, I explained both the position and the need.

'Our mailing list?' he said doubtfully. 'Mailing lists are strictly private, you know.'

I explained all over again, and threw in a lot of

pathos. My wife behind bars if I didn't find the con man, that sort of thing.

'Oh very well,' he said. 'But it will be stored in a computer. You'll have to wait for a print-out.'

I waited patiently, and received in the end a stack of paper setting out fifty-three thousand names and addresses, give or take a few dead ones.

'And we want it back,' he said severely. 'Unmarked and complete.'

'How did Norris Abbott get hold of it?' I asked.

He didn't know, and neither the name nor the description of Abbott/Ashe brought any glimmer of recognition.

'How about a copy of the magazine, for good measure?'

I got that too, and disappeared before he could regret all his generosity. Back in the car, I telephoned to Chico and got him to come to the flat. Meet me outside, I said. Carry my bag upstairs and earn your salary.

He was there when I pulled up at a vacant parking meter and we went upstairs together. The flat was empty, and quiet, and safe.

'A lot of leg work, my son,' I said, taking the mailing list out of the package I had transported it in, and putting it on the table. 'All your own.'

He eyed it unenthusiastically. 'And what about you?'

'Chester races,' I said. 'One of the syndicate horses runs there tomorrow. Meet me back here Thursday morning, ten o'clock. OK?'

'Yeah.' He thought. 'Suppose our Nicky hasn't got himself organized yet, and sends out his begging letters next week, after we've drawn a blank?'

'Mm ... Better take some sticky labels with this address on, and ask them to send the letters here, if they get them.'

'We'll be lucky.'

'You never know. No one likes being conned.'

'May as well get started, then.' He picked up the folder containing the magazine and mailing list, and looked ready to leave.

'Chico ... Stay until I've repacked my bag. I think I'll start northwards right now. Stay until I go.'

He was puzzled. 'If you like, but what for?'

'Er ...'

'Come on, Sid. Out with it.'

'Peter Rammileese and a couple of guys came looking for me yesterday at Highalane Park. So I'd just like you around, while I'm here.'

'What sort of guys?' he said suspiciously.

I nodded. 'Those sort. Hard eyes and boots.'

'Guys who kick people half to death in Tunbridge Wells?'

'Maybe,' I said.

'You dodged them, I see.'

'In a balloon.' I told him about the race while I put some things in a suitcase. He laughed at the story but afterwards came quite seriously back to business.

'Those guys of yours don't sound like your ordinary

run-of-the-mill rent-a-thug,' he said. 'Here, let me fold that jacket, you'll turn up at Chester all creased.' He took my packing out of my hands and did it for me, quickly and neatly. 'Got all the spare batteries? There's one in the bathroom.' I fetched it. 'Look, Sid, I don't like these syndicates.' He snapped the locks shut and carried the case into the hall. 'Let's tell Lucas Wainwright we're not doing them.'

'And who tells Peter Rammileese?'

'We do. We ring him up and tell him.'

'You do it,' I said. 'Right now.'

We stood and looked at each other. Then he shrugged and picked up the suitcase. 'Got everything?' he said. 'Raincoat?' We went down to the car and stowed my case in the boot. 'Look, Sid, you just take care, will you? I don't like hospital visiting, you know that.'

'Don't lose that mailing list,' I said. 'Or the editor of *Antiques* will be cross.'

I booked unmolested into a motel and spent the evening watching television, and the following afternoon arrived without trouble at Chester races.

All the usual crowd were there, standing around, making the usual conversations. It was my first time on a racecourse since the dreary week in Paris, and it seemed to me when I walked in that the change in me must be clearly visible. But no one, of course, noticed the blistering sense of shame I felt at the sight of George Caspar outside the weighing room, or treated me any differently from usual. It was I alone who knew I didn't deserve the smiles and the welcome. I was a fraud. I shrank inside. I hadn't known I would feel so bad.

The trainer from Newmarket who had offered me a ride with his string was there, and repeated his offer.

'Sid, do come. Come this Friday, stay the night with us, and ride work on Saturday morning.'

There wasn't much, I reflected, that anyone could give me that I'd rather accept: and besides, Peter Rammileese and his merry men would have a job finding me there.

'Martin . . . Yes, I'd love to.'

'Great.' He seemed pleased. 'Come for evening stables, Friday night.'

He went on into the weighing room, and I wondered if he would have asked me if he'd known how I'd spent Guineas day.

Bobby Unwin buttonholed me with inquisitive eyes. 'Where have you been?' he said. 'I didn't see you at the Guineas.'

'I didn't go.'

'I thought you'd be bound to, after all your interest in Tri-Nitro.'

'No.'

'I reckon you had the smell of something going on there, Sid. All that interest in the Caspars, and about

Gleaner and Zingaloo. Come clean, now, what do you know?'

'Nothing, Bobby.'

'I don't believe you.' He gave me a hard unforgiving stare and steered his beaky nose towards more fruitful copy in the shape of a top trainer enduring a losing streak. I would have trouble persuading him, I thought, if I should ever ask for his help again.

Rosemary Caspar, walking with a woman friend to whom she was chatting, almost bumped into me before either of us was aware of the other being there. The look in her eyes made Bobby Unwin seem loving.

'Go away,' she said violently. 'Why are you here?'

The woman friend looked very surprised. I stepped out of the way without saying a word, which surprised her still further. Rosemary impatiently twitched her onwards, and I heard her voice rising, 'But surely, Rosemary, that was Sid Halley . . .'

My face felt stiff. It's too bloody much, I thought. I couldn't have made their horse win if I'd stayed. *I couldn't* . . . but I might have. I would always think I might have, if I'd tried. If I hadn't been scared out of my mind.

'Hello, Sid,' a voice said at my side. 'Lovely day, isn't it?'

'Oh, lovely.'

Philip Friarly smiled and watched Rosemary's retreating back. 'She's been snapping at everyone since that disaster last week. Poor Rosemary. Takes things so much to heart.'

'You can't blame her,' I said. 'She said it would happen, and no one believed her.'

'Did she tell you?' he said curiously.

I nodded.

'Ah,' he said, in understanding. 'Galling for you.'

I took a deep loosening breath and made myself concentrate on something different.

'That horse of yours, today,' I said. 'Are you just giving it a sharpener, running it here on the flat?'

'Yes,' he said briefly. 'And if you ask me how it will run, I'll have to tell you that it depends on who's giving the orders, and who's taking them.'

'That's cynical.'

'Have you found out anything for me?'

'Not very much. It's why I came here.' I paused. 'Do you know the name and address of the person who formed your syndicates?'

'Not offhand,' he said. 'I didn't deal with him myself, do you see? The syndicates were already well advanced when I was asked to join. The horses had already been bought, and most of the shares were sold.'

'They used you,' I said. 'Used your name. A respectable front.'

He nodded unhappily. 'I'm afraid so.'

'Do you know Peter Rammileese?'

'Who?' He shook his head. 'Never heard of him.'

'He buys and sells horses,' I said. 'Lucas Wainwright

thinks it was he who formed your syndicates, and he who is operating them, and he's bad news to the Jockey Club and barred from most racecourses.'

'Oh dear.' He sounded distressed. 'If Lucas is looking into them . . . What do you think I should do, Sid?'

'From your own point of view,' I said, 'I think you should sell your shares, or dissolve the syndicates entirely, and get your name out of them as fast as possible.'

'All right, I will. And Sid . . . next time I'm tempted, I'll get you to check on the other people in the syndicate. The security section are supposed to have done these, and look at them!'

'Who's riding your horse today?' I said.

'Larry Server.'

He waited for an opinion, but I didn't give it. Larry Server was middle-ability, middle-employed, rode mostly on the flat and sometimes over hurdles, and was to my mind in the market for unlawful bargains.

'Who chooses the jockey?' I said. 'Larry Server doesn't ride all that often for your horse's trainer.'

'I don't know,' he said doubtfully. 'I leave all that to the trainer, of course.'

I made a small grimace.

'Don't you approve?' he said.

'If you like,' I said, 'I'll give you a list of jockeys for your jumpers that you can at least trust to be trying to win. Can't guarantee their ability, but you can't have everything.'

'Now who's a cynic?' He smiled, and said with patent and piercing regret, 'I wish you were still riding them, Sid.'

'Yeah.' I said it with a smile, but he saw the flicker I hadn't managed to keep out of my eyes.

With a compassion I definitely didn't want, he said, 'I'm so sorry.'

'It was great while it lasted,' I said lightly. 'That's all that matters.'

He shook his head, annoyed with himself for his clumsiness.

'Look,' I said, 'if you were *glad* I'm not still riding them I'd feel a whole lot worse.'

'We had some grand times, didn't we? Some exceptional days.'

'Yes, we did.'

There could be an understanding between an owner and a jockey, I thought, that was intensely intimate. In the small area where their lives touched, where the speed and the winning were all that mattered, there could be a privately shared joy, like a secret, that endured like cement. I hadn't felt it often, nor with many of the people I had ridden for, but with Philip Friarly, nearly always.

A man detached himself from another group near us, and came towards us with a smiling face.

'Philip. Sid. Nice to see you.'

We made the polite noises back, but with genuine pleasure, as Sir Thomas Ullaston, the reigning Senior

Steward, head of the Jockey Club, head, more or less, of the whole racing industry, was a sensible man and a fair and open-minded administrator. A little severe at times, some thought, but it wasn't a job for a soft man. In the short time since he'd been put in charge of things there had been some good new rules and a clearing out of injustices, and he was as decisive as his predecessor had been weak.

'How's it going, Sid?' he said. 'Caught any good crooks lately?'

'Not lately,' I said ruefully.

He smiled to Philip Friarly, 'Our Sid's putting the security section's nose out of joint, did you know? I had Eddy Keith along in my office on Monday complaining that we give Sid too free a hand, and asking that we shouldn't let him operate on the racecourse.'

'Eddy Keith?' I said.

'Don't look so shocked, Sid,' Sir Thomas said teasingly. 'I told him that racing owed you a great deal, starting with the saving of Seabury racecourse itself and going right on from there, and that in no way would the Jockey Club ever interfere with you, unless you did something absolutely diabolical, which on past form I can't see you doing.'

'Thank you,' I said faintly.

'And you may take it,' he said firmly, 'that that is the official Jockey Club view, as well as my own.'

'Why,' I said slowly, 'does Eddy Keith want me stopped?'

He shrugged. 'Something about access to the Jockey Club files. Apparently you saw some, and he resented it. I told him he'd have to live with it, because I was certainly not in any way going to put restraints on what I consider a positive force for good in racing.'

I felt grindingly undeserving of all that, but he gave me no time to protest.

'Why don't both of you come upstairs for a drink and a sandwich? Come along, Sid, Philip . . .' He turned, gesturing us to follow, leading the way.

We went up those stairs marked 'Private' which on most racecourses lead to the civilized luxuries of the Stewards' box, and into a carpeted glass-fronted room looking out to the white-railed track. There were several groups of people there already, and a man-servant handing around drinks on a tray.

'I expect you know most people,' Sir Thomas said, hospitably making introductions. 'Madelaine, my dear . . .' to his wife, ' . . . do you know Lord Friarly, and Sid Halley?' We shook her hand. 'And oh yes, Sid,' he said, touching my arm to bring me around face to face with another of his guests . . .

'Have you met Trevor Deansgate?'

CHAPTER THIRTEEN

We stared at each other, probably equally stunned.

I thought of how he had last seen me, on my back in the straw barn, spilling my guts out with fear. He'll see it still in my face, I thought. He knows what he's made of me. I can't just stand here without moving a muscle . . . and yet I must.

My head seemed to be floating somewhere above the rest of my body, and an awful lot of awfulness got condensed into four seconds.

'Do you know each other?' Sir Thomas said, slightly puzzled.

Trevor Deansgate said, 'Yes. We've met.'

There was at least no sneer either in his eyes or his voice. If it hadn't been impossible, I would have thought that what he looked was *wary*.

'Drink, Sid?' said Sir Thomas; and I found the man with the tray at my elbow. I took a tumbler with whisky-coloured contents and tried to stop my fingers trembling.

Sir Thomas said conversationally, 'I've just been

telling Sid how much the Jockey Club appreciates his successes, and it seems to have silenced him completely.'

Neither Trevor Deansgate nor I said anything. Sir Thomas raised his eyebrows a fraction and tried again. 'Well, Sid, tell us a good thing for the big race.'

I dragged my scattered wits back into at least a pretence of life going uneventfully on.

'Oh . . . Winetaster, I should think.'

My voice sounded strained, to me, but Sir Thomas seemed not to notice. Trevor Deansgate looked down to the glass in his own well-manicured hand and swivelled the ice cubes round in the golden liquid. Another of the guests spoke to Sir Thomas, and he turned away, and Trevor Deansgate's gaze came immediately back to my face filled with naked savage threat. His voice, quick and hard, spoke straight from the primitive underbelly, the world of violence and vengeance and no pity at all.

'If you break your assurance, I'll do what I said.'

He held my eyes until he was sure I had received the message, and then he too turned away, and I could see the heavy muscles of his shoulders bunching formidably inside his coat.

'Sid,' Philip Friarly said, appearing once more at my side. 'Lady Ullaston wants to know . . . I say, are you feeling all right?'

I nodded a bit faintly.

'My dear chap, you look frightfully pale.'

'I . . . er . . .' I took a vague grip on things. 'What did you say?'

'Lady Ullaston wants to know . . .' He went on at some length, and I listened and answered with a feeling of complete unreality. One could literally be torn apart in spirit while standing with a glass in one's hand making social chit-chat to the Senior Steward's lady. I couldn't remember, five minutes later, a word that was said. I couldn't feel my feet on the carpet. I'm a mess, I thought.

The afternoon went on. Winetaster got beaten in the big race by a glossy dark filly called Mrs Hillman, and in the race after that Larry Server took Philip Friarly's syndicate horse to the back of the field, and stayed there. Nothing improved internally, and after the fifth I decided it was pointless staying any longer, since I couldn't even think effectively.

Outside the gate there was the usual gaggle of chauffeurs leaning against cars, waiting for their employers; and also, with them, one of the jump jockeys whose licence had been lost through taking bribes from Rammileese.

I nodded to him, as I passed. 'Jacksy.'

'Sid.'

I walked on to the car, and unlocked it, and slung my raceglasses on to the back seat. Got in. Started the engine. Paused for a bit, and reversed all the way back to the gate.

'Jacksy?' I said. 'Get in. I'm buying.'

'Buying what?' He came over and opened the passenger door, and sat in beside me. I fished my wallet out of my rear trouser pocket and tossed it into his lap.

'Take all the money,' I said. I drove forward through the car park and out through the distant gate on to the public road.

'But you dropped me quite a lot, not long ago,' he said.

I gave him a fleeting sideways smile. 'Yeah. Well . . . this is for services about to be rendered.'

He counted the notes. 'All of it?' he said doubtfully.

'I want to know about Peter Rammileese.'

'Oh no.' He made as if to open the door, but the car by then was going too fast.

'Jacksy,' I said, 'no one's listening but me, and I'm not telling anyone else. Just say how much he paid you and what for, and anything else you can think of.'

He was silent for a bit. Then he said, 'It's more than my life's worth, Sid. There's a whisper out that he's brought two pros down from Glasgow for a special job and anyone who gets in his way just now is liable to be stamped on.'

'Have you seen these pros?' I said, thinking that I had.

'No. It just come through on the grapevine, like.'

'Does the grapevine know what the special job is?'

He shook his head.

'Anything to do with syndicates?'

'Be your age, Sid. Everything to do with Rammileese

is always to do with syndicates. He runs about twenty. Maybe more.'

Twenty, I thought, frowning. I said, 'What's his rate for the job of doing a Larry Server, like today?'

'Sid,' he protested.

'How does he get someone like Larry Server on to a horse he wouldn't normally ride?'

'He asks the trainer nicely, with a fistful of dollars.'

'He bribes the *trainers*?'

'It doesn't take much, sometimes.' He looked thoughtful for a while. 'Don't you quote me, but there were races run last autumn where Rammileese was behind every horse in the field. He just carved them up as he liked.'

'It's impossible,' I said.

'No. All that dry weather we had, remember? Fields of four, five or six runners, sometimes, because the ground was so hard? I know of three races for sure when all the runners were his. The poor sodding bookies didn't know what had hit them.'

Jacksy counted the money again. 'Do you know how much you've got here?' he said.

'Just about.'

I glanced at him briefly. He was twenty-five, an ex-apprentice grown too heavy for the flat and known to resent it. Jump jockeys on the whole earned less than the Flat boys, and there were the bruises besides, and it wasn't everyone who like me found steeplechasing double the fun. Jacksy didn't; but he could ride pretty

well, and I'd raced alongside him often enough to know
he wouldn't put you over the rails for nothing at all. For
a consideration, yes, but for nothing, no.

The money was troubling him. For ten or twenty he
would have lied to me easily; but we had a host of
shared memories of changing rooms and horses and wet
days and mud and falls and trudging back over sodden
turf in paper-thin racing boots, and it isn't so easy, if
you're not a real villain, to rob someone you know as
well as that.

'Funny,' he said, 'you taking to this detecting lark.'

'Riotous.'

'No, straight up. I mean, you don't come after the
lads for little things.'

'No,' I agreed. Little things like taking bribes. My
business, on the whole, was with the people who offered
them.

'I kept all the newspapers,' he said. 'After that trial.'

I shook my head resignedly. Too many people in the
racing world had kept those papers, and the trial had
been a trial for me in more ways than one. Defence
counsel had revelled in deeply embarrassing the victim;
and the prisoner, charged with causing grievous bodily
harm with intent, contrary to section 18 of the Offences
Against the Person Act 1861 (or in other words,
bopping an ex-jockey's left hand with a poker), had
been rewarded by four years in clink. It would be difficult to say who had enjoyed the proceedings less, the
one in the witness box or the one in the dock.

Jacksy kept up his disconnected remarks, which I gathered were a form of time-filling while he sorted himself out underneath.

'I'll get my licence back for next season,' he said.

'Great.'

'Seabury's a good track. I'll be riding there in August. All the lads think it's fine the course is still going, even if . . .' He glanced at my hand. 'Well . . . you couldn't race with it anyway, could you, as it was?'

'Jacksy,' I said, exasperated. 'Will you or won't you?'

He flipped through the notes again, and folded them, and put them in his pocket.

'Yes. All right. Here's your wallet.'

'Put it in the glove box.'

He did that, and looked out of the window. 'Where are we going?' he said.

'Anywhere you like.'

'I got a lift to Chester. He'll have gone without me by now. Can you take me south, like, and I'll hitch the rest.'

So I drove towards London, and Jacksy talked.

'Rammileese gave me ten times the regular fee, for riding a loser. Now listen, Sid, you swear this won't get back to him?'

'Not through me.'

'Yeah. Well, I suppose I do trust you.'

'Get on, then.'

'He buys quite good horses. Horses that can win. Then he syndicates them. I reckon sometimes he makes five hundred per cent profit on them for a start. He bought one I knew of for six thousand and sold ten shares at three thousand each. He's got two pals who are OK registered owners, and he puts one of them in each syndicate, and they swing it so some fancy figurehead takes a share, so the whole thing looks right.'

'Who are the two pals?'

He gulped a lot, but told me. One name meant nothing, but the other had appeared on all of Philip Friarly's syndicates.

'Right,' I said. 'On you go.'

'The horses get trained by anyone who can turn them out looking nice for double the usual training fees and no questions asked. Then Rammileese works out what races they're going to run in, and they're all running way below their real class, see, so that when he says go, by Christ you're on a flyer.' He grinned. 'Twenty times the riding fee, for a winner.'

It sounded a lot more than it was.

'How often did you ride for him?'

'One or two, most weeks.'

'Will you do it again, when you get your licence back?'

He turned in his seat until his back was against the car's door and spent a long time studying the half of my face he could see. His silence itself was an answer, but when we had travelled fully three miles he sighed deeply and said, finally, 'Yes.'

As an act of trust, that was remarkable.

'Tell me about the horses,' I said, and he did, at

some length. The names of some of them were a great surprise, and the careers of all of them as straightforward as Nicholas Ashe.

'Tell me how you got your licence suspended,' I said.

He had been riding for one of the amenable trainers, he said, only the trainer hadn't had an amenable wife. 'She had a bit of a spite on, so she shopped him with the Jockey Club. Wrote to Thomas Ullaston personally, I ask you. Of course, the whole bleeding lot of Stewards believed her, and suspended the lot of us, me, him, and the other jock who rides for him, poor sod, who never got a penny from Rammileese and wouldn't know a backhander if it smacked him in the face.'

'How come,' I said casually, 'that no one in the Jockey Club has found out about all these syndicates and done something positive about Rammileese?'

'Good question.'

I glanced at him, hearing the doubt in his voice and seeing the frown. 'Go on,' I said.

'Yeah ... This is strictly a whisper, see, not even a rumour hardly, just something I heard ...' He paused, then he said, 'I don't reckon it's true.'

'Try me.'

'One of the bookies ... I was waiting about outside the gates at Kempton, see, and these two bookies came out, and one was saying that the bloke in the Security Service would smooth it over if the price was right.' He stopped again, and went on, 'One of the lads said I'd never have got suspended if that bitch of a trainer's wife had sent her letter to the Security Service and not to the big white chief himself.'

'Which of the lads said that?'

'Yeah. Well, I can't remember. And don't look like that, Sid, I really can't. It was months ago. I mean, I didn't even think about it until I heard the bookies at Kempton. I don't reckon there could be anyone that bent in the Security Service, do you? I mean, not in the Jockey Club.'

His faith was touching, I thought, considering his present troubles, but in days gone by I would have thought he was right. Once plant the doubt, though, and one could see there were a lot of dirty misdeeds that Eddy Keith might have ignored in return for a tax-free gain. He had passed the four Friarly syndicates, and he might have done all of the twenty or more. He might even have put Rammileese's two pals on the respectable owners' list, knowing they weren't. Somehow or other, I would have to find out.

'Sid,' Jacksy said. 'Don't you get me in bad with the brass. I'm not repeating what I just told you, not to no stewards.'

'I won't say you told me,' I assured him. 'Do you know those two bookies at Kempton?'

'Not a chance. I mean, I don't even know they were bookies. They just looked like them. I mean, I thought "bookies" when I saw them.'

So strong an impression was probably right, but not of much help; and Jacksy, altogether, had run dry. I dropped him where he wanted, at the outskirts of Watford, and the last thing he said was that if I was going after Rammileese to keep him, Jacksy, strictly out of it, like I'd promised.

I stayed in a hotel in London instead of the flat, and felt over-cautious. Chico, however, when I telephoned, said it made sense. Breakfast, I suggested, and he said he'd be there.

He came, but without much hooray. He had trudged around all day visiting the people on the mailing list, but no one had received a begging letter from Ashe within the last month.

'Tell you what, though,' he said. 'People beginning with A and B and right down to K have had wax in the past, so it'll be the Ps and Rs that get done next time, which narrows the legwork.'

'Great,' I said, meaning it.

'I left sticky labels everywhere with your address on, and some of them said they'd let us know, if it came. But whether they'll bother . . .'

'It would only take one,' I said.

'That's true.'

'Feel like a spot of breaking and entering?'

'Don't see why not.' He started on a huge order of scrambled eggs and sausages. 'Where and what for?'

'Er . . .' I said. 'This morning you do a recce. This

evening, after office hours but before it gets dark, we drift along to Portman Square.'

Chico stopped chewing in mid-mouthful, and then carefully swallowed before saying, 'By Portman Square, do you mean the Jockey Club?'

'That's right.'

'Haven't you noticed they let you in the front door?'

'I want a quiet look-see that they don't know about.'

He shrugged. 'All right then. Meet you back here after the recce?'

I nodded. 'The Admiral's coming here for lunch. He went down to the wax factory yesterday.'

'That should put a shine in his eyes.'

'Oh, very funny.'

While he finished the eggs and attacked the toast I told him most of what Jacksy had said about the syndicates, and also about rumours of kickbacks in high places.

'And that's what we're looking for? Turning out Eddy Keith's office to see what he didn't do when he should've?'

'You got it. Sir Thomas Ullaston – Senior Steward – says Eddy was along complaining to him about me seeing the files, and Lucas Wainwright can't let me see them without Eddy's secretary knowing, and she's loyal to Eddy. So if I want to look, it has to be quiet.' And would breaking into the Jockey Club, I wondered, be considered 'absolutely diabolical' if I were found out?

241

'OK,' he said. 'I got the judo today, don't forget.'

'The little bleeders,' I said, 'are welcome.'

Charles came at twelve, sniffing the air of the unfamiliar surroundings like an unsettled dog.

'I got your message from Mrs Cross,' he said. 'But why here? Why not the Cavendish, as usual?'

'There's someone I don't want to meet,' I said. 'He won't look for me here. Pink gin?'

'A double.'

I ordered the drinks. He said, 'Is that what it was, for those six days? Evasive action?'

I didn't reply.

He looked at me quizzically. 'I see it still hurts you, whatever it was.'

'Leave it, Charles.'

He sighed and lit a cigar, sucking in smoke and eyeing me through the flame of the match. 'So who don't you want to meet?'

'A man called Peter Rammileese. If anyone asks, you don't know where I am.'

'I seldom do.' He smoked with enjoyment, filling his lungs and inspecting the burning ash as if it were precious. 'Going off in balloons . . .'

I smiled. 'I got offered the post of regular co-pilot to a madman.'

'It doesn't surprise me,' he said drily.

'How did you get on with the wax?'

He wouldn't tell me until after the drinks had come, and then he wasted a lot of time asking why I was drinking Perrier water and not whisky.

'To keep a clear head for burglary,' I said truthfully, which he half believed and half didn't.

'The wax is made,' he said finally, 'in a sort of cottage industry flourishing next to a plant which processes honey.'

'Beeswax!' I said incredulously.

He nodded. 'Beeswax, paraffin wax, and turpentine, that's what's in that polish.' He smoked luxuriously, taking his time. 'A charming woman there was most obliging. We spent a long time going back over the order books. People seldom ordered as much at a time as Jenny had done, and very few stipulated that the tins should be packed in white boxes for posting.' His eyes gleamed over the cigar. 'Three people, all in the last year, to be exact.'

'Three . . . Do you think . . . it was Nicholas Ashe, three times?'

'Always about the same amount,' he said, enjoying himself. 'Different names and addresses, of course.'

'Which you did bring away with you?'

'Which I did.' He pulled a folded paper out of an inner pocket. 'There you are.'

'Got him,' I said, with intense satisfaction. 'He's a fool.'

'There was a policeman there on the same errand,' Charles said. 'He came just after I'd written out those names. It seems they really are looking for Ashe, themselves.'

'Good. Er . . . did you tell them about the mailing list?'

'No, I didn't.' He squinted at his glass, holding it up to the light, as if one pink gin were not the same as the next and he wanted to memorize the colour. 'I would like it to be you who finds him first.'

'Hm.' I thought about that. 'If you think Jenny will be grateful, you'll be disappointed.'

'But you'll have got her off the hook.'

'She would prefer it to be the police.' She might even be nicer to me, I thought, if she was sure I had failed; and it wasn't the sort of niceness I would want.

Chico telephoned during the afternoon.

'What are you doing in your bedroom at this time of day?' he demanded.

'Watching Chester races on television.'

'Stands to reason,' he said resignedly. 'Well, look, I've done the recce, and we can get in all right, but you'll have to be through the main doors before four o'clock. I've scrubbed the little bleeders. Look, this is what you do. You go in through the front door, right, as if you'd got pukka business. Now, in the hall there's two lifts. One that goes to a couple of businesses that are on the first and second floors, and as far as the third, which is all Jockey Club, as you know.'

'Yes,' I said.

'When all the little workers and Stewards and such have gone home, they leave that lift at the third floor with its doors open, so no one can use it. There's a night porter, but after he's seen to the lift he doesn't do any rounds, he just stays downstairs. And oh yes, when he's fixed the lift he goes down your actual stairs, locking a door across the stairway at each landing, which makes three in all. Got it?'

'Yes.'

'Right. Now there's another lift which goes to the top four floors of the building, and up there there's eight flats, two on each floor, with people living in them. And between those floors and the Jockey Club below, there's only one door locked across the stairway.'

'I'm with you,' I said.

'Right. Now I reckon the porter in the hall, or whatever you call him, he might just know you by sight, so he'd think it odd if you came after the offices were closed. So you'd better get there before, and go up in the lift to the flats, go right up to the top, and I'll meet you there. It's OK, there's a sort of seat by a window, read a book or something.'

'I'll see you,' I said.

I went in a taxi, armed with a plausible reason for my visit if I should meet anyone I knew in the hall: but in fact I saw no one, and stepped into the lift to the flats without any trouble. At the top, as Chico had said, there was a bench by a window, where I sat and thought unproductively for over an hour. No one came or went from either of the two flats. No one came up in the lift. The first time its doors opened, it brought Chico.

Chico was dressed in white overalls and carried a bag of tools. I gave him a sardonic head-to-foot inspection.

'Well, you got to look the part,' he said defensively. 'I came here like this earlier, and when I left I told the chap I'd be back with spare parts. He just nodded when I walked in just now. When we go, I'll keep him talking while you gumshoe out.'

'If it's the same chap.'

'He goes off at eight. We better be finished before then.'

'Was the Jockey Club lift still working?' I said.

'Yeah.'

'Let's go down there, then, so we can hear when the porter brings the lift up and leaves it.'

He nodded. We went through the door beside the lift, into the stair well, which was utilitarian, not plushy, and lit by electric lights, and just inside there dumped the clinking bag of tools. Four floors down we came to the locked door, and stood there, waiting.

The door was flat, made of some filling covered on the side on which we stood by a sheet of silvery metal. The keyhole proclaimed a mortice lock set into the depth of the door, the sort of barrier which took Chico about three minutes, usually, to negotiate.

As usual on these excursions, we had brought gloves. I thought back to one of the first times, when Chico had said, 'One good thing about that hand of yours, it can't leave any dabs.' I wore a glove over it anyway, as being a lot less noticeable if we were ever casually seen where we shouldn't be.

I had never got entirely used to breaking in, not to the point of not feeling my heart beat faster or my breath go shallow. Chico, for all his longer experience at the same game, gave himself away always by smoothing out the laughter lines round his eyes as the skin tautened over his cheekbones. We stood there waiting, the physical signs of stress with us, knowing the risks.

We heard the lift come up and stop. Held our breaths to see if it would go down again, but it didn't. Instead, we were electrified by the noise of someone unlocking the door we were standing behind. I caught a flash of Chico's alarmed eyes as he leapt away from the lock and joined me on the hinge side, our backs pressed hard against the wall.

The door opened until it was touching my chest. The porter coughed and sniffed on the other side of the barrier, looking, I thought, up the stairs, checking that all was as it should be.

The door swung shut again, and the key clicked in the lock. I let a long-held breath out in a slow soundless whistle, and Chico gave me the sickly grin that came from semi-released tension.

We felt the faint thud through the fabric of the building as the door on the floor below us was shut and locked. Chico raised his eyebrows and I nodded, and he applied his bunch of lock-pickers to the problem. There was a faint scraping noise as he sorted his way into the mechanism, and then the application of some muscle, and finally his clearing look of satisfaction as the metal tongue retracted into the door.

We went through, taking the keys but leaving the door unlocked, and found ourselves in the familiar headquarters of British racing. Acres of carpet, comfortable chairs, polished wood furniture, and the scent of extinct cigars.

The security section had its own corridor of smaller workaday offices, and down there without difficulty we eased into Eddy Keith's.

None of the internal doors seemed to be locked, and I supposed there was in fact little to steal, bar electric typewriters and other such trifles. Eddy Keith's filing cabinets all slid open easily, and so did the drawers in his desk.

In the strong evening sunlight we sat and read the reports on the extra syndicates that Jacksy had told me of. Eleven horses whose names I had written down, when he'd gone, so as not to forget them. Eleven syndicates apparently checked and accepted by Eddy, with Rammileese's two registered-owner pals appearing inexorably on all of them: and as with the previous four, headed by Philip Friarly, there was nothing in the files themselves to prove anything one way or the other. They were carefully, meticulously presented, openly ready for inspection.

There was one odd thing: the four Friarly files were all missing.

We looked through the desk. Eddy kept in it a few personal objects: a battery razor, indigestion tablets, a comb, and about sixteen packs of book matches, all from gambling clubs. Otherwise there was simple stationery, pens, a pocket calculator and a desk diary. His engagements, past and future, were merely down as the race meetings he was due to attend.

I looked at my watch. Seven forty-five. Chico nodded and began putting the files back neatly into their drawers. Frustrating, I thought. An absolute blank.

When we were ready to go I took a quick look into a filing cabinet marked 'Personnel' which contained slim factual files about everyone presently employed by the Jockey Club, and everyone receiving its pensions. I looked for a file marked 'Mason', but someone had taken that, too.

'Coming?' Chico said.

I nodded regretfully. We left Eddy's office as we'd found it and went back to the door to the stairway. Nothing stirred. The headquarters of British racing lay wide open to intruders, who were having to go away empty-handed.

CHAPTER FOURTEEN

On Friday afternoon, depressed on many accounts, I drove comparatively slowly to Newmarket.

The day itself was hot, the weather reportedly stoking up to the sort of intense heatwave one could get in May, promising a glorious summer that seldom materialized. I drove in shirtsleeves with the window open, and decided to go to Hawaii and lie on the beach for a while, like a thousand years.

Martin England was out in his stable yard when I got there, also in shirtsleeves and wiping his forehead with a handkerchief.

'Sid!' he said, seeming truly pleased. 'Great. I'm just starting evening stables. You couldn't have timed it better.'

We walked round the boxes together in the usual ritual, the trainer visiting every horse and checking its health, the guest admiring and complimenting and keeping his tongue off the flaws. Martin's horses were middling to good, like himself, like the majority of trainers, the sort that provided the bulk of all racing, and of all jockeys' incomes.

'A long time since you rode for me,' he said, catching my thought.

'Ten years or more.'

'What do you weigh, now, Sid?'

'About ten stone, stripped.' Thinner, in fact, than when I'd stopped racing.

'Pretty fit, are you?'

'Same as usual,' I said. 'I suppose.'

He nodded, and we went from the fillies' side of the yard to the colts. He had a good lot of two-year-olds, it seemed to me, and he was pleased when I said so.

'This is Flotilla,' he said, going to the next box. 'He's three. He runs in the Dante at York next Wednesday, and if that's OK he'll go for the Derby.'

'He looks well,' I said.

Martin gave a carrot to his hope of glory. There was pride in his kind, fiftyish face, not for himself but for the shining coat and quiet eye and waiting muscles of the splendid four-legged creature. I ran my hand down the glossy neck, and patted the dark bay shoulder, and felt the slender, rock-hard forelegs.

'He's in grand shape,' I said. 'Should do you proud.'

He nodded with the thoroughly normal hint of anxiety showing under the pride, and we continued down the line, patting and discussing, and feeling content. Perhaps this was what I really needed. I thought: forty horses and hard work and routine.

Planning and administering and paperwork. Pleasure enough in preparing a winner, sadness enough in seeing one lose. A busy, satisfying, out-of-doors lifestyle, a businessman on the back of a horse.

I thought of what Chico and I had been doing for months. Chasing villains, big and small. Wiping up a few messy bits of the racing industry. Getting knocked about, now and then. Taking our wits into minefields and fooling with people with shotguns.

It would be no public disgrace if I gave it up and decided to train. A much more normal life for an ex-jockey, everyone would think. A sensible, orderly decision, looking forward to middle and old age. I alone . . . and Trevor Deansgate . . . would know why I'd done it. I could live for a long time, knowing it.

I didn't want to.

In the morning at seven-thirty I went down to the yard in jodhpurs and boots and a pull-on jersey shirt. Early as it was, the air was warm, and with the sounds and bustle and smell of the stables all around my spirits rose from bedrock and hovered at somewhere about knee level.

Martin, standing with a list in his hand, shouted good morning, and I went down to join him to see what he'd given me to ride. There was a five-year-old, up to my weight, that he'd think just the job.

Flotilla's lad was leading him out of his box, and I watched him admiringly as I turned towards Martin.

'Go on, then,' he said. There was amusement in his face, enjoyment in his eyes.

'What?' I said.

'Ride Flotilla.'

I swung towards the horse, totally surprised. His best horse, his Derby hope, and I out of practice and with one hand.

'Don't you want to?' he said. 'He'd've been yours ten years ago as of right. And my jockey's gone to Ireland to race at the Curragh. It's either you or one of my lads, and to be honest, I'd rather have you.'

I didn't argue. One doesn't turn down a chunk of heaven. I thought he was a bit mad, but if that was what he wanted, so did I. He gave me a leg-up, and I pulled the stirrup leathers to my own length, and felt like an exile coming home.

'Do you want a helmet?' he said, looking around vaguely as if expecting one to materialize out of the tarmac.

'Not for this.'

He nodded. 'You never have.' And he himself was wearing his usual checked cloth cap, in spite of the heat. I had always preferred riding bareheaded except in races: something to do with liking the feel of lightness and moving air.

'What about a whip?' he said.

He knew that I'd always carried one automatically, because a jockey's whip was a great aid to keeping a horse balanced and running straight: a tap down the shoulder did the trick, and one pulled the stick through from hand to hand, as required. I looked at the two hands in front of me. I thought that if I took a whip and fumbled it, I might drop it: and I needed above all to be efficient.

I shook my head. 'Not today.'

'Right, then,' he said. 'Let's be off.'

With me in its midst the string pulled out of the yard and went right through Newmarket town on the horse-walks along the back roads, out to the wide sweeping Limekilns gallops to the north. Martin, himself riding the quiet five-year-old, pulled up there beside me.

'Give him a sharpish warm-up canter for three fur-longs, and then take him a mile up the trial ground, upsides with Gulliver. It's Flotilla's last work-out before the Dante, so make it a good one. OK?'

'Yes,' I said.

'Wait until I get up there,' he pointed, 'to watch.'

'Yep.'

He rode away happily towards a vantage point more than half a mile distant, from where he could see the whole gallop. I wound the left-hand rein round my plastic fingers and longed to be able to feel the pull from the horse's mouth. It would be easy to be clumsy, to upset the lie of the bit and the whole balance of the horse, if I got the tension wrong. In my right hand, the reins felt alive, carrying messages, telling Flotilla, and Flotilla telling me, where we were going, and how, and how fast. A private language, shared, understood.

Let me not make a mess of it, I thought. Let me just be able to do what I'd done thousands of times in the past, let the old skill be there, one hand or no. I could lose him the Dante and the Derby and any other race you cared to mention, if I got it really wrong.

The boy on Gulliver circled with me, waiting for the moment, answering my casual remarks in monosyllables and grunts. I wondered if he was the one who would have ridden Flotilla if I hadn't been there, and asked him, and he said, grumpily, yes. Too bad, I thought. Your turn will come.

Up the gallop, Martin waved. The boy on Gulliver kicked his mount into a fast pace at once, not waiting to start evenly together. You little sod, I thought. You do what you damned well like, but I'm going to take Flotilla along at the right speeds for the occasion and distance, and to hell with your tantrums.

It was absolutely great, going up there. It suddenly came right, as natural as if there had been no interval and no missing limb. I threaded the left rein through bad and good hands alike and felt the vibrations from both sides of the bit, and if it wasn't the most perfect style ever seen on the Heath, it at least got the job done.

Flotilla swept over the turf in a balanced working gallop and came upsides with Gulliver effortlessly. I stayed beside the other horse then for most of the way, but as Flotilla was easily the better I took him on from six furlongs and finished the mile at a good pace that was still short of strain. He was fit, I thought, pulling him back to a canter. He would do well in the Dante. He'd given me a good feel.

I said so to Martin, when I rejoined him, walking back. He was pleased, and laughed. 'You can still ride, can't you? You looked just the same.'

I sighed internally. I had been let back for a brief moment into the life I'd lost, but I wasn't just the same. I might have managed one working gallop without making an ass of myself, but it wasn't the Gold Cup at Cheltenham.

'Thanks,' I said, 'for a terrific morning.'

We walked back through the town to his stable and to breakfast, and afterwards I went with him in his Land Rover to see his second lot work on the racecourse side. When we got back from that we sat in his office and drank coffee and talked for a bit, and with some regret I said it was time I was going.

The telephone rang. Martin answered it, and held out the receiver to me.

'It's for you, Sid.'

I thought it would be Chico, but it wasn't. It was, surprisingly, Henry Thrace, calling from his stud farm just outside the town.

'My girl assistant says she saw you riding work on the Heath,' he said. 'I didn't really believe her, but she was sure. Your head, without a helmet, unmistakable. With Martin England's horses, she said, so I rang on the off-chance.'

'What can I do for you?' I said.

'Actually it's the other way round,' he said. 'Or at least, I think so. I had a letter from the Jockey Club earlier this week, all very official and everything, asking me to let them know at once if Gleaner or Zingaloo died, and not to get rid of the carcass. Well, when I got that letter I rang Lucas Wainwright, who signed it, to ask what the hell it was all about, and he said it was really *you* who wanted to know if either of those horses died. He was telling me that in confidence, he said.'

My mouth went as dry as vinegar.

'Are you still there?'

'Yes,' I said.

'Then I'd better tell you that Gleaner has, in fact, just died.'

'When?' I said, feeling stupid. 'Er . . . how?' My heart rate had gone up to at least double. Talk about over-reacting, I thought, and felt the fear stab through like toothache.

'A mare he was due to cover came into use, so we put him to her,' he said, 'this morning. An hour ago, maybe. He was sweating a lot, in this heat. It's hot in the breeding shed, with the sun on it. Anyway, he served her and got down all right, and then he just staggered and fell and died almost at once.'

I unstuck my tongue. 'Where is he now?'

'Still in the breeding shed. We're not using it again this morning so I've left him there. I've tried to ring the Jockey Club, but it's Saturday and Lucas Wainwright isn't there, and anyway, as my girl said that you yourself were actually here in Newmarket . . .'

'Yes,' I said. I took a shaky breath. 'A post-mortem. You would agree, wouldn't you?'

'Essential, I'd say. Insurance, and all that.'

'I'll try and get Ken Armadale,' I said. 'From the Equine Research Establishment. I know him . . . Would he do you?'

'Couldn't be better.'

'I'll ring you back.'

'Right,' he said, and disconnected.

I stood with Martin's telephone in my hand and looked into far dark spaces. It's too soon, I thought. Much too soon.

'What's the matter?' Martin said.

'A horse I've been enquiring about has died.' . . . Oh God Almighty . . . 'Can I use your phone?' I said.

'Help yourself.'

Ken Armadale said he was gardening and would much rather cut up a dead horse. I'll pick you up, I said, and he said he'd be waiting. My hand, I saw remotely, was actually shaking.

I rang back to Henry Thrace, to confirm. Thanked Martin for his tremendous hospitality. Put my suitcase and myself in the car, and picked up Ken Armadale from his large modern house on the southern edge of Newmarket.

'What am I looking for?' he said.

'Heart, I think.'

He nodded. He was a strong dark-haired research vet in his middle thirties, a man I'd dealt with on similar jaunts before, to the extent that I felt easy with him and trusted him, and as far as I could tell he felt the same about me. A professional friendship, extending to a drink in a pub but not to Christmas cards, the sort of relationship that remained unchanged and could be taken up and put down as need arose.

'Anything special?' he said.

'Yes . . . but I don't know what.'

'That's cryptic.'

'Let's see what you find.'

Gleaner, I thought. If there were three horses I should definitely be doing nothing about, they were Gleaner and Zingaloo and Tri-Nitro. I wished I hadn't asked Lucas Wainwright to write those letters, one to Henry Thrace, the other to George Caspar. If those horses died, let me know . . . but not so soon, so appallingly soon.

I drove into Henry Thrace's stud farm and pulled up with a jerk. He came out of his house to meet us, and we walked across to the breeding shed. As with most such structures, its walls swept up to a height of ten feet, unbroken except for double entrance doors. Above that there was a row of windows, and above those, a roof. Very like Peter Rammilecse's covered riding school, I thought, only smaller.

The day, which was hot outside, was very much hotter inside. The dead horse lay where he had fallen on the tan-covered floor, a sad brown hump with milky grey eyes.

'I rang the knackers,' Ken said. 'They'll be here pretty soon.'

Henry Thrace nodded. It was impossible to do the post-mortem where the horse lay, as the smell of blood would linger for days and upset any other horse that came in there. We waited for not very long until the lorry arrived with its winch, and when the horse was loaded, we followed it down to the knackers' yard where Newmarket's casualties were cut up for dog food. A small hygienic place; very clean.

Ken Armadale opened the bag he had brought and handed me a washable nylon boiler suit, like his own, to cover trousers and shirt. The horse lay in a square room with whitewashed walls and a concrete floor. In the floor, runnels and a drain. Ken turned on a tap so that water ran out of the hose beside the horse, and pulled on a pair of long rubber gloves.

'All set?' he said.

I nodded, and he made the first long incision. The smell, as on past occasions, was what I liked least about the next ten minutes, but Ken seemed not to notice it as he checked methodically through the contents. When the chest cavity had been opened he removed its whole heart-lung mass and carried it over to the table which stood under the single window.

'This is odd,' he said, after a pause.

'What is?'

'Take a look.'

I went over beside him and looked where he was pointing, but I hadn't his knowledge behind my eyes, and all I saw was a blood-covered lump of tissue with tough-looking ridges of gristle in it.

'His heart?' I said.

'That's right. Look at these valves . . .' He turned his head to me, frowning. 'He died of something horses don't get.' He thought it over. 'It's a great pity we couldn't have had a blood sample before he died.'

'There's another horse at Henry Thrace's with the same thing,' I said. 'You can get your blood sample from him.'

He straightened up from bending over the heart, and stared at me.

'Sid,' he said. 'You'd better tell me what's up. And outside, don't you think, in some fresh air.'

We went out, and it was a great deal better. He stood listening, with blood all over his gloves and down the front of his overalls, while I wrestled with the horrors in the back of my mind and spoke with flat lack of emotion from the front.

'There are . . . or were . . . four of them,' I said. 'Four that I know of. They were all top star horses, favourites all winter for the Guineas and the Derby. That class. The very top. They all came from the same stable. They all went out to race in Guineas week looking marvellous. They all started hot favourites, and they all totally flopped. They all suffered from a mild virus infection at about that time, but it didn't develop. They all were subsequently found to have heart murmurs.'

Ken frowned heavily. 'Go on.'

'There was Bethesda, who ran in the One Thousand Guineas two years ago. She went to stud, and she died of heart failure this spring, while she was foaling.'

Ken took a deep breath.

'There's this one,' I said, pointing. 'Gleaner. He was favourite for the Guineas last year. He then got a really bad heart, and also arthritis. The other horse at Henry Thrace's, Zingaloo, he went out fit to a race and afterwards could hardly stand from exhaustion.'

Ken nodded. 'And which is the fourth one?'

I looked up at the sky. Blue and clear. I'm killing myself, I thought. I looked back at him and said, 'Tri-Nitro.'

'Sid!' He was shocked. 'Only ten days ago.'

'So what is it?' I said. 'What's the matter with them?'

'I'd have to do some tests to be certain,' he said. 'But the symptoms you've described are typical, and those heart valves are unmistakable. That horse died from swine erysipelas, which is a disease you get only in pigs.'

Ken said, 'We need to keep that heart for evidence.'

'Yes,' I said.

Dear God . . .

'Get one of those bags, will you?' he said. 'Hold it open.' He put the heart inside. 'We'd better go along to the Research Centre, later. I've been thinking ... I know I've got some reference papers there about erysipelas in horses. We could look them up if you like.'

'Yes,' I said.

He peeled off his blood-spattered overalls. 'Heat and exertion,' he said. 'That's what did for this fellow. A deadly combination, with a heart in that state. He might have lived for years, otherwise.'

Ironic, I thought bitterly.

He packed everything away, and we went back to Henry Thrace. A blood sample from Zingaloo? No problem, he said.

Ken took enough blood to float a battleship, it seemed to me, but what was a litre to a horse which had gallons. We accepted reviving Scotches from Henry with gratitude, and afterwards took our trophies to the Equine Research Establishment along the Bury Road.

Ken's office was a small extension to a large laboratory, where he took the bag containing Gleaner's heart over to the sink and told me he was washing out the remaining blood.

'Now come and look,' he said.

This time I could see exactly what he meant. Along all the edges of the valves there were small knobbly growths, like baby cauliflowers, creamy white.

'That's vegetation,' he said. 'It prevents the valves from closing. Makes the heart as efficient as a leaking pump.'

'I can see it would.'

'I'll put this in the fridge, then we'll look through those veterinary journals for that paper.'

I sat on a hard chair in his utilitarian office while he searched for what he wanted. I looked at my fingers. Curled and uncurled them. This can't all be happening, I thought. It's only three days since I saw Trevor Deansgate at Chester. *If you break your assurance, I'll do what I said.*

'Here it is,' Ken exclaimed, flattening a paper open. 'Shall I read you the relevant bits?'

I nodded.

'Swine erysipelas – in 1938 – occurred in a horse, with vegetative endocarditis – the chronic form of the illness in pigs.' He looked up. 'That's those cauliflower growths. Right?'

'Yes.'

He read again from the paper. 'During 1944 a mutant strain of erysipelas rhusiopathiae appeared suddenly in a laboratory specializing in antisera production and produced acute endocarditis in the serum horses.'

'Translate,' I said.

He smiled. 'They used to use horses for producing vaccines. You inject the horse with pig disease, wait until it develops antibodies, draw off blood, and extract the serum. The serum, injected into healthy pigs, prevents them getting the disease. Same process as for all human vaccinations, smallpox and so on. Standard procedure.'

'OK,' I said. 'Go on.'

264

'What happened was that instead of growing antibodies as usual, the horses themselves got the disease.'

'How could that happen?'

'It doesn't say here. You'd have to ask the pharmaceutical firm concerned, which I see is the Tierson vaccine lab along at Cambridge. They'd tell you, I should think, if you asked. I know someone there, if you want an introduction.'

'It's a long time ago,' I said.

'My dear fellow, germs don't die. They can live like time-bombs, waiting for some fool to take stupid liberties. Some of these labs keep virulent strains around for decades. You'd be surprised.'

He looked down again at the paper, and said, 'You'd better read these next paragraphs yourself. They look pretty straightforward.' He pushed the journal across to me, and I read the page where he pointed.

1 24–48 hours after intra-muscular injection of the pure culture, inflammation of one or more of the heart valves commences. At this time, apart from a slight rise in temperature and occasional palpitations, no other symptoms are seen unless the horse is subjected to severe exertion, when auricular fibrillation or interference with the blood supply to the lungs occurs; both occasion severe distress which only resolves after 2–3 hours' rest.

2 Between the second and the sixth day pyrexia (temperature rise) increases and white cell count of the blood increases and the horse is listless and off food. This could easily be loosely diagnosed as 'the virus'. However, examination by stethoscope reveals a progressively increasing heart murmur. After about ten days the temperature returns to normal and, unless subjected to more than walk or trot, the horse may appear to have recovered. The murmur is still present and it then becomes necessary to retire the horse from fast work since this induces respiratory distress.

3 Over the next few months vegetations grow on the heart valves, and arthritis in some joints, particularly of the limbs, may or may not appear. The condition is permanent and progressive and death may occur suddenly following exertion or during very hot weather, sometimes years after the original infection.

I looked up. 'That's it, exactly, isn't it,' I said.

'Bang on the nose.'

I said slowly, 'Intra-muscular injection of the pure culture could absolutely not have occurred accidentally.'

'Absolutely not,' he agreed.

I said, 'George Caspar had his yard sewn up so tight this year with alarm bells and guards and dogs that no

one could have got within screaming distance of Tri-
Nitro with a syringeful of live germs.'

He smiled, 'You wouldn't need a syringeful. Come
into the lab, and I'll show you.'

I followed him, and we fetched up beside one of the
cupboards with sliding doors that lined the whole of
the wall. He opened the cupboard and pulled out a box,
which proved to contain a large number of smallish
plastic envelopes.

He tore open one of the envelopes and tipped the
contents on to his hand: a hypodermic needle attached
to a plastic capsule only the size of a pea. The whole
thing looked like a tiny dart with a small round balloon
at one end, about as long, altogether, as one's little
finger.

He picked up the capsule and squeezed it. 'Dip that
into liquid, you draw up half a teaspoonful. You don't
need that much pure culture to produce a disease.'

'You could hold that in your hand, out of sight,' I
said.

He nodded. 'Just slap the horse with it. Done in a
flash. I use these sometimes for horses that shy away
from a syringe.' He showed me how, holding the capsule
between thumb and index finger, so that the sharp end
pointed down from his palm. 'Shove the needle in and
squeeze,' he said.

'Could you spare one of these?'

'Sure,' he said, giving me an envelope. 'Anything you
like.'

I put it in my pocket. Dear God in heaven.

Ken said slowly, 'You know, we might just be able to do something about Tri-Nitro.'

'How do you mean?'

He pondered, looking at the large bottle of Zingaloo's blood, which stood on the draining board beside the sink.

'We might find an antibiotic which would cure the disease.'

'Isn't it too late?' I said.

'Too late for Zingaloo. But I don't think those vegetations would start growing at once. If Tri-Nitro was infected . . . say . . .'

'Say two weeks ago today, after his final working gallop.'

He looked at me with amusement. 'Say two weeks ago, then. His heart will be in trouble, but the vegetation won't have started. If he gets the right antibiotic soon, he might make a full recovery.'

'Do you mean . . . back to normal?'

'Don't see why not.'

'What are you waiting for?' I said.

CHAPTER FIFTEEN

I spent most of Sunday beside the sea, driving north-east from Newmarket to the wide deserted coast of Norfolk. Just for somewhere to go, something to do, to pass the time.

Even though the sun shone, the wind off the North Sea was keeping the beaches almost empty; small groups were huddled into the shelter of flimsy canvas screens, and a few intrepid children built castles.

I sat in the sun in a hollow in a sand dune which was covered with coarse tufts of grass, and watched the waves come and go. I walked along the shore, kicking the worm casts. I stood looking out to sea, holding up my left upper arm for support, aware of the weight of the machinery lower down, which was not so very heavy, but always there.

I had often felt released and restored by lonely places, but not on that day. The demons came with me. The cost of pride ... the price of safety. If you didn't expect so much of yourself, Charles had said once, you'd give yourself an easier time. It hadn't really made sense.

One was as one was. Or at least, one was as one was until someone came along and broke you all up.

If you sneezed on the Limekilns, they said in New-market, it was heard two miles away on the racecourse. The news of my attendance at Gleaner's post-mortem would be given to George Caspar within a day. Trevor Deansgate would hear of it: he was sure to.

I could still go away, I thought. It wasn't too late. Travel. Wander by other seas, under other skies. I could go away and keep very quiet. I could still escape from the terror he induced in me. I could still . . . run away.

I left the coast and drove numbly to Cambridge. Stayed in the University Arms Hotel and, in the morning, went along to Tierson Pharmaceuticals Vaccine Laboratories. I asked for, and got, a Mr Living-ston, who was maybe sixty and greyishly thin. He made small nibbling movements with his mouth when he spoke. He looks a dried-up old cuss, Ken Armadale had said, but he's got a mind like a monkey.

'Mr Halley, is it?' Livingston said, shaking hands in the entrance hall. 'Mr Armadale has been on the phone to me, explaining what you want. I think I can help you, yes I do indeed. Come along, come along, this way.'

He walked in small steps before me, looking back frequently to make sure I was following. It seemed to be a precaution born of losing people, because the place was a labyrinth of glass-walled passages with labora-tories and gardens apparently intermixed at random.

'The place just grew,' he said, when I remarked on it.

'But here we are.' He led the way into a large laboratory which looked through glass walls into the passage on one side, and a garden on another, and straight into another lab on the third.

'This is the experimental section,' he said, his gesture embracing both rooms. 'Most of the laboratories just manufacture the vaccines commercially, but in here we potter about inventing new ones.'

'And resurrecting old ones?' I said.

He looked at me sharply. 'Certainly not. I believe you came for information, not to accuse us of carelessness.'

'Sorry,' I said placatingly. 'That's quite right.'

'Well then. Ask your question.'

'Er, yes. How did the serum horses you were using in the 1940s get swine erysipelas?'

'Ah,' he said. 'Pertinent. Brief. To the point. We published a paper about it, didn't we? Before my time, of course. But I've heard about it. Yes. Well, it's possible. It's possible. It happened. But it shouldn't have done. Sheer carelessness, do you see? I hate carelessness. Hate it.'

Just as well, I thought. In his line of business, carelessness might be fatal.

'Do you know anything about the production of erysipelas antiserum?' he said.

'You could write it on a thumbnail.'

'Ah,' he said. 'Then I'll explain as to a child. Will that do?'

'Nicely,' I said.

He gave me another sharp glance in which there was this time amusement.

'You inject live erysipelas germs into a horse. Are you with me? I am talking about the past, now, when they did use horses. We haven't used horses since the early 1950s, and nor have Burroughs Wellcome, and Bayer in Germany. The past, do you see?'

'Yes,' I said.

'The horse's blood produces antibodies to fight the germ, but the horse does not develop the disease, because it is a disease pigs get and horses don't.'

'A child,' I assured him, 'would understand.'

'Very well. Now sometimes the standard strain of erysipelas becomes weakened, and in order to make it virulent again we pass it through pigeons.'

'Pigeons?' I said, very politely.

He raised his eyebrows. 'Customary practice. Pass a weak strain through pigeons to recover virulence.'

'Oh, of course,' I said.

He pounced on the satire in my voice. 'Mr Halley,' he said severely. 'Do you want to know all this or don't you?'

'Yes, please,' I said meekly.

'Very well, then. The virulent strain was removed from the pigeons and subcultured on to blood agar plates.' He broke off, looking at the blankness of my ignorance. 'Let me put it this way. The live virulent germs were transferred from the pigeons on to dishes containing blood, where they then multiplied, thus producing a useful quantity for injecting into the serum horses.'

'That's fine,' I said. 'I do understand.'

'All right.' He nodded. 'Now the blood on the dishes was bull's blood. Bovine blood.'

'Yes,' I said.

'But owing to someone's stupid carelessness, the blood agar plates were prepared one day with horse blood. This produced a mutant strain of the disease.' He paused. 'Mutants are changes which occur suddenly and for no apparent reason throughout nature.'

'Yes,' I said again.

'No one realized what had happened,' he said, 'until the mutant strain was injected into the serum horses and they all got erysipelas. The mutant strain proved remarkably constant. The incubation period was always 24–48 hours after inoculation, and endocarditis . . . that is, inflammation of the heart valves . . . was always the result.'

A youngish man in a white coat, unbuttoned down the front, came into the room next door, and I watched him vaguely as he began pottering about.

'What became of this mutant strain?' I said.

Livingston nibbled a good deal with the lips, but finally said, 'Wc would have kept some, I dare say, as a curiosity. But of course it would be weakened by now, and to restore it to full virulence, one would have to . . .'

'Yeah,' I said. 'Pass it through pigeons.'

He didn't think it was funny. 'Quite so,' he said.

'And all this passing through pigeons and subculture on agar plates, how much skill does this take?'

He blinked. 'I could do it, of course.'

I couldn't. Any injections I'd handled had come in neat little ampoules, packed in boxes.

The man in the next room was opening cupboards, looking for something.

I said, 'Would there be any of this mutant strain anywhere else in the world, besides here? I mean, did this laboratory send any of it out to anywhere else?'

The lips pursed and the eyebrows went up. 'I've no idea,' he said. He looked through the glass and gestured towards the man in the next room. 'You could ask Barry Shummuck. He would know. Mutant strains are his speciality.'

He pronounced 'Shummuck' to rhyme with 'hummock'. I know the name, I thought. I . . . *oh my God*.

The shock of it fizzed through my brain and left me half breathless. I knew someone too well whose real name was Shummuck.

I swallowed and felt shivery. 'Tell me more about your Mr Shummuck,' I said.

Livingston was a natural chatterer and saw no harm in it. He shrugged. 'He came up the hard way. Still talks like it. He used to have a terrible chip on his shoulder. The world owed him a living, that sort of thing. Shades of student demos. He's settled down recently. He's good at his job.'

'You don't care for him?' I said.

Livingston was startled. 'I didn't say that.'

He had, plainly, in his face and in his voice. I said only, 'What sort of accent?'

'Northern. I don't know exactly. What does it matter?'

Barry Shummuck looked like no one I knew. I said slowly, hesitantly, 'Do you know if he has . . . a brother?'

Livingston's face showed surprise. 'Yes, he has. Funny thing, he's a bookmaker.' He pondered. 'Some name like Terry. Not Terry . . . Trevor, that's it. They come here together sometimes, the two of them . . . thick as thieves.'

Barry Shummuck gave up his search and moved towards the door.

'Would you like to meet him?' Mr Livingston said.

Speechlessly, I shook my head. The last thing I wanted, in a building full of virulent germs which he knew how to handle and I didn't, was to be introduced to the brother of Trevor Deansgate.

Shummuck went through the door and into the glass-walled corridor, and turned in our direction.

Oh no, I thought.

He walked purposefully along and pushed open the door of the lab we were in. Head and shoulders leaned forward.

'Morning, Mr Livingston,' he said. 'Have you seen my box of transparencies anywhere?'

The basic voice was the same, self-confident and slightly abrasive. Manchester accent, much stronger. I held my left arm out of sight half behind my back and willed him to go away.

'No,' said Mr Livingston, with just a shade of pleasure. 'But Barry, can you spare . . .'

Livingston and I were standing in front of a work bench which held various empty glass jars and a row of clamps. I turned leftwards, with my arm still hidden, and clumsily, with my right hand, knocked over a clamp and two glass jars.

More clatter than breakage. Livingston gave a quick nibble of surprised annoyance, and righted the rolling jars. I gripped the clamp, which was metal and heavy, and would have to do.

I turned back towards the door.

The door was shutting. The backview of Barry Shummuck was striding away along the corridor, the front edges of his white coat flapping.

I let a shuddering breath out through my nose and carefully put the clamp back at the end of the row.

'He's gone,' Mr Livingston said. 'What a pity.'

I drove back to Newmarket, to the Equine Research Establishment and Ken Armadale.

I wondered how long it would take chatty Mr Livingston to tell Barry Shummuck of the visit of a man called Halley who wanted to know about a pig disease in horses.

I felt faintly, and continuously, sick.

'It's been made resistant to all ordinary antibiotics,' Ken said. 'A real neat little job.'

'How do you mean?'

'If any old antibiotic would kill it, you couldn't be sure the horse wouldn't be given a shot as soon as he had a temperature, and never develop the disease.'

I sighed. 'So how do they make it resistant?'

'Feed it tiny doses of antibiotic until it becomes immune.'

'All this is technically difficult, isn't it?'

'Yes, fairly.'

'Have you ever heard of Barry Shummuck?'

He frowned. 'No, I don't think so.'

The craven inner voice told me urgently to shut up, to escape, to fly to safety . . . to Australia . . . to a desert.

'Do you have a cassette recorder here?' I said.

'Yes. I use it for making notes while I'm operating.' He went out and fetched it and set it up for me on his desk, loaded with a new tape. 'Just talk,' he said. 'It has a built-in microphone.'

'Stay and listen,' I said. 'I want . . . a witness.'

He regarded me slowly. 'You look so strained . . . It's no gentle game, is it, what you do?'

277

'Not always.'

I switched on the recorder, and for introduction spoke my name, the place, and the date. Then I switched off again and sat looking at the fingers I needed for pressing the buttons.

'What is it, Sid?' Ken said.

I glanced at him and down again. 'Nothing.'

I had got to do it, I thought. I had absolutely got to. I was never in any way going to be whole again, if I didn't.

If I had to choose, and it seemed to me that I did have to choose, I would have to settle for wholeness of mind, and put up with what it cost. Perhaps I could deal with physical fear. Perhaps I could deal with anything that happened to my body, and even with helplessness. What I could not for ever deal with . . . and I saw it finally with clarity and certainty . . . was despising myself.

I pressed the 'play' and 'record' buttons together, and irrevocably broke my assurance to Trevor Deansgate.

CHAPTER SIXTEEN

I telephoned Chico at lunchtime and told him what I'd found out about Rosemary's horses.

'What it amounts to,' I said, 'is that those four horses had bad hearts because they'd been given a pig disease. There's a lot of complicated info about how it was done, but that's now the Stewards' headache.'

'Pig disease?' Chico said disbelievingly.

'Yeah. That big bookmaker Trevor Deansgate has a brother who works in a place that produces vaccines for inoculating people against smallpox and diphtheria and so on, and they cooked up a plan to squirt pig germs into those red-hot favourites.'

'Which duly lost,' Chico said, 'while the bookmaker raked in the lolly.'

'Right,' I said.

It felt very odd to put Trevor Deansgate's scheme into casual words and to be talking about him as if he were just one of our customary puzzles.

'How did you find out?' Chico said.

'Gleaner died at Henry Thrace's, and the pig disease

turned up at the post-mortem. When I went to the vaccine lab I saw a man called Shummuck who deals in odd germs, and I remembered that Shummuck was Trevor Deansgate's real name. And Trevor Deansgate is very thick with George Caspar . . . and all the affected horses, that we know of, have come from George Caspar's stable.'

'Circumstantial, isn't it?' Chico said.

'A bit, yes. But the Security Service can take it from there.'

'Eddy Keith?' he said sceptically.

'He can't hush this one up, don't you worry.'

'Have you told Rosemary?'

'Not yet.'

'Bit of a laugh,' Chico said.

'Mm.'

'Well, Sid mate,' he said. 'This is results day all round. We got a fix on Nicky Ashe.'

Nicky Ashe with a knife in his sock. A pushover, compared with . . . compared with . . .

'Hey,' Chico's voice said aggrievedly through the receiver. 'Aren't you pleased?'

'Yes, of course. What sort of fix?'

'He's been sending out some of those damn fool letters. I went to your place this morning, just to see, like, and there were two great envelopes there with our sticky labels on.'

'Great,' I said.

'I opened them. They'd both been sent to us by

280

people whose names started with P. All that legwork
paid off.'

'So we've got the begging letter?'

'We sure have. It's exactly the same as the ones your
wife had, except for the address to send the money to, of
course. Got a pencil?'

'Yeah.'

He read the address, which was in Clifton, Bristol. I
looked at it thoughtfully. I could either give it straight to
the police, or I could check it first myself. Checking it, in
one certain way, had persuasive attractions.

'Chico,' I said. 'Ring Jenny's flat in Oxford and ask
for Louise McInnes. Ask her to ring me here at the
Rutland Hotel in Newmarket.'

'Scared of your missus, are you?'

'Will you do it?'

'Oh, sure.' He laughed, and rang off. When the bell
rang again, however, it was not Louise at the other end,
but still Chico.

'She's left the flat,' he said. 'Your wife gave me her
new number.' He read it out. 'Anything else?'

'Can you bring your cassette player to the Jockey
Club, Portman Square, tomorrow afternoon at, say, four
o'clock?'

'Like last time?'

'No,' I said. 'Front door, all the way.'

*

Louise, to my relief, answered her telephone. When I told her what I wanted, she was incredulous.

'You actually *found* him?'

'Well,' I said. 'Probably. Will you come, then, and identify him?'

'Yes.' No hesitation. 'Where and when?'

'Some place in Bristol.' I paused, and said diffidently, 'I'm in Newmarket now. I could pick you up in Oxford this afternoon, and we could go straight on. We might spot him this evening . . . or tomorrow morning.'

There was a silence at the other end. Then she said, 'I've moved out of Jenny's flat.'

'Yes.'

Another silence, and then her voice, quiet, and committed.

'All right.'

She was waiting for me in Oxford, and she had brought an overnight bag.

'Hello,' I said, getting out of the car.

'Hello.'

We looked at each other. I kissed her cheek. She smiled with what I had to believe was enjoyment, and slung her case in the boot beside mine.

'You can always retreat,' I said.

'So can you.'

We sat in the car, however, and I drove to Bristol feeling contented and carefree. Trevor Deansgate wouldn't yet have started looking for me, and Peter Rammileese and his boys hadn't been in sight for a week, and no one except Chico knew where I was going. The shadowy future, I thought, was not going to spoil the satisfactory present. I decided not even to think of it, and for most of the time, I didn't.

We went first to the country house hotel which someone had once told me of, high on the cliffs overlooking the Avon gorge, and geared to rich-American-tourist comfort.

'We'll never get in here,' Louise said, eyeing the opulence.

'I telephoned.'

'How organized! One room or two?'

'One.'

She smiled as if that suited her well, and we were shown into a large wood-panelled room with stretches of carpet, antique polished furniture, and a huge four-poster bed decked with American-style white muslin frills.

'My God,' Louise said. 'And I expected a motel.'

'I didn't know about the fourposter,' I said a little weakly.

'Wow,' she said, laughing. 'This is more *fun*.'

We parked the suitcases and freshened up in the modern bathroom tucked discreetly behind the panelling, and went back to the car; and Louise smiled to herself all the way to the new address of Nicholas Ashe.

It was a prosperous looking house in a prosperous-looking street. A solid five-or-six-bedroomed affair, mellowed and white-painted and uninformative in the early evening sun.

I stopped the car on the same side of the road, pretty close, at a place from where we could see both the front door and the gate into the driveway. Nicky, Louise had said on the way down, often used to go out for a walk at about seven o'clock, after a hard day's typing. Maybe he would again, if he was there.

Maybe he wouldn't.

We had the car's windows open because of the warm air. I lit a cigarette, and the smoke floated in a quiet curl through lack of wind. Very peaceful, I thought, waiting there.

'Where do you come from?' Louise said.

I blew a smoke ring. 'I'm the posthumous illegitimate son of a twenty-year-old window cleaner who fell off his ladder just before his wedding.'

She laughed. 'Very elegantly put.'

'And you?'

'The legitimate daughter of the manager of a glass factory and a magistrate, both alive and living in Essex.'

We consulted about brothers and sisters, of which I had none and she had two, one of each. About education, of which I'd had some and she a lot. About life in general, of which she'd seen a little, and I a bit more.

An hour passed in the quiet street. A few birds sang. Sporadic cars drove by. Men came home from work and turned into the driveways. Distant doors slammed. No one moved in the house we were watching.

'You're patient,' Louise said.

'I spend hours doing this, sometimes.'

'Pretty unexciting.'

I looked at her clear intelligent eyes. 'Not this evening.'

Seven o'clock came and went; and Nicky didn't.

'How long will we stay?'

'Until dark.'

'I'm hungry.'

Half an hour drifted by. I learned that she liked curry and paella and hated rhubarb. I learned that the thesis she was writing was giving her hell.

'I'm so far behind schedule,' she said, 'and . . . oh my goodness, *there he is*.'

Her eyes had opened very wide. I looked where she looked, and saw Nicholas Ashe.

Coming not from the front door, but from the side of the house. My age, or a bit younger. Taller, but of my own thin build. My colouring. Dark hair, slightly curly. Dark eyes. Narrow jaw. All the same.

He looked sufficiently like me for it to be a shock, but was nevertheless quite different. I took my baby camera out of my trouser pocket and pulled it open with my teeth as usual, and took his picture.

When he reached the gate he paused and looked back, and a woman ran after him calling, 'Ned, Ned, wait for me.'

'Ned!' Louise said, sliding down in her seat. 'If he comes this way, won't he see me?'

'Not if I kiss you.'

'Well, do it,' she said.

I took, however, another photograph.

The woman looked older, about forty; slim, pleasant, excited. She tucked her arm into his and looked up at his eyes, her own clearly, even from twenty feet away, full of adoration. He looked down and laughed delightfully, then he kissed her forehead and swung her round in a little circle on to the pavement, and put his arm round her waist, and walked towards us with vivid gaiety and a bounce in his step.

I risked one more photograph from the shadows of the car, and leaned across and kissed Louise with enthusiasm.

Their footsteps went past. Abreast of us they must have seen us, or at least my back, for they both suddenly giggled lightheartedly, lovers sharing their secret with lovers. They almost paused, then went on, their steps growing softer until they had gone.

I sat up reluctantly.

Louise said, 'Whew!' but whether it was the result of the kiss, or the proximity of Ashe, I wasn't quite sure.

'He's just the same,' she said.

'Casanova himself,' I said drily.

She glanced at me swiftly and I guessed she was wondering whether I was jealous of his success with Jenny, but in fact I was wondering whether Jenny had been attracted to him because he resembled me, or whether she had been attracted to me in the first place, and also to him, because we matched some internal picture she had of a sexually interesting male. I was more disturbed than I liked by the physical appearance of Nicholas Ashe.

'Well,' I said, 'that's that. Let's find some dinner.'

I drove back to the hotel, and we went upstairs before we ate, Louise saying she wanted to change out of the blouse and skirt she had worn all day.

I took the battery charger out of my suitcase and plugged it in: took a spent battery from my pocket, and rolled up my shirtsleeve and snapped out the one from my arm, and put them both in the charger. Then I took a charged battery from my suitcase and inserted it in the empty socket in the arm. And Louise watched.

I said, 'Are you . . . revolted?'

'No, of course not.'

I pulled my sleeve down and buttoned the cuff.

'How long does a battery last?' she said.

'Six hours, if I use it a lot. About eight, usually.'

She merely nodded, as if people with electric arms were as normal as people with blue eyes. We went down to dinner and ate sole and afterwards strawberries, and if they'd tasted of seaweed I wouldn't have cared. It wasn't only because of Louise, but also because since that morning I had stopped tearing myself apart, and had slowly been growing back towards peace. I could feel it happening, and it was marvellous.

We sat side by side on a sofa in the hotel lounge, drinking small cups of coffee.

'Of course,' she said, 'now that we have seen Nicky, we don't really need to stay until tomorrow.'

'Are you thinking of leaving?' I said.

'About as much as you are.'

'Who is seducing whom?' I said.

'Mm,' she said, smiling. 'This whole thing is so unexpected.'

She looked calmly at my left hand, which rested on the sofa between us. I couldn't tell what she was thinking, but I said on impulse, 'Touch it.'

She looked up at me quickly. 'What?'

'Touch it. Feel it.'

She tentatively moved her right hand until her fingers were touching the tough, lifeless plastic skin. There was no drawing back, no flicker of revulsion in her face.

'It's metal, inside there,' I said. 'Gears and levers and electric circuits. Press harder, and you'll feel them.'

She did as I said, and I saw her surprise as she discovered the shape of the inner realities.

'There's a switch inside there too,' I said. 'You can't see it from the outside, but it's just below the thumb. One can switch the hand off, if one wants.'

'Why would you want to?'

'Very useful for carrying things, like a briefcase. You shut the fingers round the handle, and switch the current off, and the hand just stays shut without you having to do it all yourself.'

I put my right hand over and pushed the switch off and on, to show her.

'It's like the push-through switch on a table lamp,' I said. 'Feel it. Push it.'

She fumbled a bit because it wasn't all that easy to find if one didn't know, but in the end pushed it both ways, off and on. Nothing in her expression but concentration.

She felt some sort of tension relax in me, and looked up, accusingly.

'You were testing me,' she said.

I smiled. 'I suppose so.'

'You're a pig.'

I felt an unaccustomed uprush of mischief. 'As a matter of fact,' I said, holding my left hand in my right, 'if I unscrew it firmly round this way several times the whole hand will come right off at the wrist.'

'Don't do it,' she said, horrified.

I laughed with absolute enjoyment. I wouldn't have thought I would ever feel that way about that hand.

'Why does it come right off?' she said.

'Oh . . . servicing. Stuff like that.'

'You look so different,' she said.

I nodded. She was right. I said, 'Let's go to bed.'

'What a world of surprises,' she said, a good while later. 'Almost the last thing I would have expected you to be as a lover is gentle.'

'Too gentle?'

'No. I liked it.'

We lay in the dark, drowsily. She herself had been warmly receptive and generous, and had made it for me an intense sunburst of pleasure. It was a shame, I thought hazily, that the act of sex had got so cluttered up with taboos and techniques and therapists and sin and voyeurs and the whole commercial ballyhoo. Two people fitting together in the old design should be a private matter, and if you didn't expect too much, you'd get on better. One was as one was. Even if a girl wanted it, I could never have put on a pretence of being a rough, aggressive bull of a lover, because, I thought sardonically, I would have laughed at myself in the middle. And it had been all right, I thought, as it was.

'Louise,' I said.

No reply.

I shifted a little for deeper comfort, and drifted, like her, to sleep.

A while later, awake early as usual, I watched the daylight strengthen on her sleeping face. The fair hair lay tangled round her head in the way I had seen it first, and her skin looked soft and fresh. When she woke, even before she opened her eyes, she was smiling.

'Good morning,' I said.

'Morning.'

She moved towards me in the big bed, the white

muslin frills on the canopy overhead surrounding us like a frame.

'Like sleeping in clouds,' she said.

She came up against the hard shell of my left arm, and blinked from the awareness of it.

'You don't sleep in this when you're alone, do you?' she said.

'No.'

'Take it off, then.'

I said with a smile, 'No.'

She gave me a long considering inspection.

'Jenny's right about you being like flint,' she said.

'Well, I'm not.'

'She told me that at the exact moment some chap was smashing up your arm you were calmly working out how to defeat him.'

I made a face.

'Is it true?' she said.

'In a way.'

'Jenny said . . .'

'To be honest,' I said, 'I'd rather talk about you.'

'I'm not interesting.'

'That's a right come-on, that is,' I said.

'What are you waiting for, then?'

'I do so like your retreating maidenly blushes.'

I touched her lightly on her breast and it seemed to do for her what it did for me. Instant arousal, mutually pleasing.

'Clouds,' she said contentedly. 'What do you think of when you're doing it?'

'Sex?'

She nodded.

'I feel. It isn't thought.'

'Sometimes I see roses ... on trellises ... scarlet and pink and gold. Sometimes spiky stars. This time it will be white frilly muslin clouds.'

I asked her, after.

'No. All bright sunlight. Quite blinding.'

The sunlight, in truth, had flooded into the room, making the whole white canopy translucent and shimmering.

'Why didn't you want the curtains drawn, last night?' she said. 'Don't you like the dark?'

'I don't like sleeping when my enemies are up and about.'

I said it without thinking. The actual truth of it followed after, like a freezing shower.

'Like an animal,' she said, and then, 'what's the matter?'

Remember me, I thought, as I am. And I said, 'Like some breakfast?'

We went back to Oxford. I took the film to be developed, and we had lunch at *Les Quat' Saisons,* where the delectable *pâté de turbot* and the superb *quenelle de brochet soufflée* kept the shadows at bay a while longer. With the coffee, though, came the unavoidable minute.

'I have to be in London at four o'clock,' I said.

Louise said, 'When are you going to the police about Nicky?'

'I'll come back here on Thursday, day after tomorrow, to pick up the photos. I'll do it then.' I reflected. 'Give that lady in Bristol two more happy days.'

'Poor thing.'

'Will I see you, Thursday?' I said.

'Unless you're blind.'

Chico was propping up the Portman Square building with a look of resignation, as if he'd been there for hours. He shifted his shoulder off the stonework at my on-foot approach and said 'Took your time, didn't you?'

'The car park was full.'

From one hand he dangled the black cassette recorder we used occasionally, and he was otherwise wearing jeans and a sports shirt and no jacket. The hot weather, far from vanishing, had settled in on an almost stationary high-pressure system, and I was also in shirt-sleeves, though with a tie on, and a jacket over my arm. On the third floor all the windows were open, the street noises coming up sharply, and Sir Thomas Ullaston, sitting behind his big desk, had dealt with the day in pale blue shirting with white stripes.

'Come in, Sid,' he said, seeing me appear in his open doorway. 'I've been waiting for you.'

'I'm sorry I'm late,' I said, shaking hands. 'This is Chico Barnes, who works with me.'

He shook Chico's hand. 'Right,' he said. 'Now you're here, we'll get Lucas Wainwright and the others along.' He pressed an intercom button and spoke to his secretary. 'And bring some more chairs, would you?'

The office slowly filled up with more people than I'd expected, but all of whom I knew at least to talk to. The top administrative brass in full force, about six of them, all urbane worldly men, the people who really ran racing. Chico looked at them slightly nervously as if at an alien breed, and seemed to be relieved when a table was provided for him to put the recorder on. He sat with the table between himself and the room, like a barrier. I fished into my jacket for the cassette I'd brought, and gave it to him.

Lucas Wainwright came with Eddy Keith on his heels: Eddy looking coldly out of the genial face; big bluff Eddy whose warmth for me was slowly dying.

'Well, Sid,' Sir Thomas said. 'Here we all are. Now, on the telephone yesterday you told me you had discovered how Tri-Nitro had been nobbled for the Guineas, and as you see . . . we are all very interested.' He smiled. 'So fire away.'

I made my own manner match theirs: calm and dispassionate, as if Trevor Deansgate's threat wasn't anywhere in my mind, instead of continually flashing through it like stabs.

'I've . . . er . . . put it all on to tape,' I said. 'You'll hear two voices. The other is Ken Armadale, from the Equine Research. I asked him to clarify the veterinary details, which are his province, not mine.'

The well-brushed heads nodded. Eddy Keith merely stared. I glanced at Chico, who pressed the start button, and my own voice, disembodied, spoke loudly into a wholly attentive silence.

'This is Sid Halley, at the Equine Research Establishment, on Monday, May fourteenth . . .'

I listened to the flat sentences, spelling it out. The identical symptoms in four horses, the lost races, the bad hearts. My request, via Lucas Wainwright, to be informed if any of the three still alive should die. The post-mortem on Gleaner, with Ken Armadale repeating in greater detail my own simpler account. His voice explaining, again after me, how horses had come to be infected by a disease of pigs. His voice saying, 'I found active live germs in the lesions on Gleaner's heart valves, and also in the blood taken from Zingaloo . . .' and my voice continuing, 'A mutant strain of the disease was produced at the Tierson Vaccine Laboratory at Cambridge in the following manner . . .'

It wasn't the easiest of procedures to understand, but I watched the faces and saw that they did, particularly by the time Ken Armadale had gone through it all again, confirming what I'd said.

'As to motive and opportunity,' my voice said, 'we come to a man called Trevor Deansgate . . .'

Sir Thomas's head snapped back from its forward, listening posture, and he stared at me bleakly from across the room. Remembering, no doubt, that he had entertained Trevor Deansgate in the Stewards' box at Chester. Remembering perhaps that he had brought me and Trevor Deansgate there face to face.

Among the other listeners the name had created an almost equal stir. All of them either knew him or knew of him: the big up-and-coming influence among the bookmakers, the powerful man shouldering his way into top-rank social acceptance. They knew Trevor Deansgate, and their faces were shocked.

'The real name of Trevor Deansgate is Trevor Shummuck,' my voice said. 'There is a research worker at the vaccine laboratory called Barry Shummuck, who is his brother. The two brothers, on friendly terms, have been seen together at the laboratories on several occasions . . .'

Oh God, I thought. My voice went on, and I listened in snatches. I've really done it. There's no going back.

' . . . This is the laboratory where the mutant strain originally arose . . . unlikely after all this time for there to be any of it anywhere else . . .

'Trevor Deansgate owns a horse which George Caspar trains. Trevor Deansgate is on good terms with Caspar . . . watches the morning gallops and goes to breakfast. Trevor Deansgate stood to make a fortune if he knew in advance that the over-winter favourites for the Guineas and the Derby couldn't win. Trevor Deansgate had the means – the disease; the motive – money; and the opportunity – entry into Caspar's well-guarded stable. It would seem, therefore, that there are grounds for investigating his activities further.'

My voice stopped, and after a minute or two Chico switched off the recorder. Looking slightly dazed himself, he ejected the cassette and laid it carefully on the table.

'It's incredible,' Sir Thomas said, but not as if he didn't believe it. 'What do you think, Lucas?'

Lucas Wainwright cleared his throat. 'I think we should congratulate Sid on an exceptional piece of work.'

Except for Eddy Keith, they agreed with him and did so, to my embarrassment, and I thought it generous of him to have said it at all, considering the Security themselves had done negative dope tests and left it at that. But then the Security, I reflected, hadn't had Rosemary Caspar visiting them in false curls and hysteria; and they hadn't had the benefit of Trevor Deansgate revealing himself to them as a villain before they even positively suspected him, threatening vile things if they didn't leave him alone.

As Chico had said, our successes had stirred up the enemy to the point where they were likely to clobber us before we knew why.

Eddy Keith sat with his head very still, watching me.

I looked back at him, probably with much the same deceptively blank outer expression. Whatever he was thinking, I couldn't read. What I thought about was breaking into his office, and if he could read that he was clairvoyant.

Sir Thomas and the administrators, consulting among themselves, raised their heads to listen when Lucas Wainwright asked a question.

'Do you really think, Sid, that Deansgate infected those horses himself?' He seemed to think it unlikely. 'Surely he couldn't produce a syringe anywhere near any of those horses, let alone all four.'

'I did think,' I said, 'that it might have been someone else . . . like a work jockey, or even a vet . . .' Inky Poole and Brothersmith, I thought, would have had me for slander if they could have heard. ' . . . But there's a way almost anyone could do it.'

I dipped again into my jacket and produced the packet containing the needle attached to the pea-sized bladder. I gave the packet to Sir Thomas, who opened it, tipping the contents on to his desk.

They all looked. Understood. Were convinced.

'He'd be more likely to do it himself if he could,' I said. 'He wouldn't want to risk anyone else knowing, and perhaps having a hold over him.'

'It amazes me,' Sir Thomas said with apparent genuineness, 'how you work these things out, Sid.'

'But I . . .'

'Yes,' he said, smiling. 'We all know what you're going to say. At heart you're still a jockey.'

There seemed to be a long pause. Then I said, 'Sir, you're wrong. This . . .' I pointed to the cassette, 'is what I am now. And from now on.'

His face sobered into a long frowning look in which it seemed that he was reassessing his whole view of me, as so many others had recently done. It was to him, as to Rosemary, that I still appeared as a jockey, but to myself, no longer. When he spoke again his voice was an octave lower, and thoughtful.

'We've taken you too lightly.' He paused. 'I did mean what I said to you at Chester about being a positive force for good in racing, but I also see that I thought of it as something of an unexpected joke.' He shook his head slowly. 'I'm sorry.'

Lucas Wainwright said briskly. 'It's been increasingly clear what Sid has become.' He was tired of the subject and waiting as usual to spur on to the next thing. 'Do you have any plans, Sid, as to what to do next?'

'Talk to the Caspars,' I said. 'I thought I might drive up there tomorrow.'

'Good idea,' Lucas said. 'You won't mind if I come? It's a matter for the Security Service now, of course.'

'And for the police, in due course,' said Sir Thomas, with a touch of gloom. He saw all public prosecutions for racing-based crimes as sources of disgrace to the whole industry, and was inclined to let people get away with things, if prosecuting them would involve a damaging scandal. I tended to agree with him, to the point of doing the same myself, but only if privately one could fix it so that the offence wouldn't be repeated.

'If you're coming, Commander,' I said to Lucas Wainwright, 'perhaps you could make an appointment with them. They may be going to York. I was simply going to turn up at Newmarket early and trust to luck, but you won't want to do that.'

'Definitely not,' he said crisply. 'I'll telephone straight away.'

He bustled off to his own office, and I put the cassette into its small plastic box and handed it to Sir Thomas.

'I put it on tape because it's complicated, and you might want to hear it again.'

'You're so right, Sid,' said one of the administrators, ruefully. 'All that about pigeons . . .!'

Lucas Wainwright came back. 'The Caspars are at York, but went by air-taxi and are returning tonight. George Caspar wants to see his horses work, in the morning, before flying back to York. I told his secretary chap that it was of the utmost importance I see Caspar, so we're due there at eleven. Suit you, Sid?'

'Yes, fine.'

'Pick me up here, then, at nine?'

I nodded. 'OK.'

'I'll be in my office, checking the mail.'

Eddy Keith gave me a final blank stare and without a word removed himself from the room.

Sir Thomas and all the administrators shook my hand

and also Chico's; and going down in the lift Chico said, 'They'll be kissing you next.'

'It won't last.'

We walked back to where I had left the Scimitar, which was where I shouldn't have. There was a parking ticket under the wiper blade. There would be.

'Are you going back to the flat?' Chico said, folding himself into the passenger's seat.

'No.'

'You still think those boot men . . .?'

'Trevor Deansgate,' I said.

Chico's face melted into half-mocking comprehension.

'Afraid he'll duff you up?'

'He'll know by now . . . from his brother.' I shivered internally from a strong flash of the persistent horrors.

'Yeah, I suppose so.' It didn't worry him. 'Look, I brought that begging letter for you . . .' He dug into a trouser pocket and produced a much-folded and slightly grubby sheet of paper. I eyed it disgustedly, reading it through. Exactly the same as the ones Jenny had sent, except signed with a flourish 'Elizabeth More', and headed with the Clifton address.

'Do you realize they may have to produce this filthy bit of paper in court?'

'Been in my pocket, hasn't it?' he said defensively.

'What else've you got in there? Potting compost?'

He took the letter from me and put it in the glove box, and let down the window.

'Hot, isn't it?'

'Mm.'

I wound down my own side window, and started the car, and drove him back to his place in Finchley Road.

'I'll stay in the same hotel,' I said. 'And look . . . come to Newmarket with me tomorrow.'

'Sure, if you want. What for?'

I shrugged, making light of it. 'Bodyguard.'

He was surprised. He said wonderingly, 'You can't really be afraid of him . . . this Deansgate . . . are you?'

I shifted in my seat a bit, and sighed.

'I guess so,' I said.

CHAPTER SEVENTEEN

I talked to Ken Armadale in the early evening. He wanted to know how my session with the Jockey Club had gone, but more than that he sounded smugly self-satisfied, and not without reason.

'That erysipelas strain has been made immune to practically every antibiotic in the book,' he said. 'Very thorough. But I reckon there's an obscure little bunch he won't have bothered with, because no one would think of pumping them into horses. Rare, they are, and expensive. All the signs I have here are that they would work. Anyway, I've tracked some down.'

'Great,' I said. 'Where?'

'In London, at one of the teaching hospitals. I've talked with the pharmacist there, and he's promised to pack some in a box and leave it at the reception desk for you to collect. It will have Halley on it.'

'Ken, you're terrific.'

'I've had to mortgage my soul, to get it.'

*

I picked up the parcel in the morning and arrived at Portman Square to find Chico again waiting on the doorstep. Lucas Wainwright came down from his office and said he would drive us in his car, if we liked, and I thought of all the touring around I'd been doing for the past fortnight, and accepted gratefully. We left the Scimitar in the car park which had been full the day before, a temporary open-air affair in a cleared building site, and set off to Newmarket in a large, air-conditioned Mercedes.

'It's too darned hot,' Lucas said, switching on the refrigeration. 'Wrong time of year.'

He had come tidily dressed in a suit, which Chico and I hadn't: jeans and sports shirts and not a jacket between us.

'Nice car, this,' Chico said admiringly.

'You used to have a Merc, Sid, didn't you?' Lucas said.

I said yes, and we talked about cars half the way to Suffolk. Lucas drove well but as impatiently as he did everything else. A pepper and salt man, I thought, sitting beside him. Brown and grey speckled hair, brownish grey eyes, with flecks in the iris. Brown and grey checked shirt, with a nondescript tie. Pepper and salt in his manner, in his speech patterns, in all his behaviour.

He said, as in the end he was bound to, 'How are you getting on with the syndicates?'

Chico, sitting in the back seat, made a noise between a laugh and a snort.

'Er . . .' I said. 'Pity you asked, really.'

'Like that, is it?' Lucas said, frowning.

'Well,' I said. 'There is very clearly something going on, but we haven't come up with much more than rumour and hearsay.' I paused. 'Any chance of us collecting expenses?'

He was grimly amused. 'I suppose I could put it under the heading of general assistance to the Jockey Club. Can't see the administrators quibbling after yesterday.'

Chico gave me a thumbs-up sign from behind Lucas's head, and I thought I would pile it on a bit while the climate was favourable, and recover what I'd paid to Jacksy.

'Do you want us to go on trying?' I said.

'Definitely.' He nodded positively. 'Very much so.'

We reached Newmarket in good time and came to a smooth halt in George Caspar's well-tended driveway.

There were no other cars there: certainly not Trevor Deansgate's Jaguar. On that day he should be in the normal course of things at York, attending to his book-making business. I had no faith that he was.

George, expecting Lucas, was not at all pleased to see me, and Rosemary, coming downstairs and spotting me in the hall, charged across the parquet and rugs with shrill disapproval.

'Get out,' she said. 'How dare you come here?'

Two spots of colour flamed in her cheeks, and she looked almost as if she was going to try to throw me out bodily.

'No, no, I say,' Lucas Wainwright said, writhing as usual with naval embarrassment in the face of immodest female behaviour. 'George, make your wife *listen* to what we've come to tell you.'

Rosemary was persuaded, with a ramrod stiff back, to perch on a chair in her elegant drawing room, while Chico and I sat lazily in armchairs, and Lucas Wainwright did the talking, this time, about pig disease and bad hearts.

The Caspars listened in growing bewilderment and dismay, and when Lucas mentioned 'Trevor Deansgate' George stood up and began striding about in agitation.

'It isn't possible,' he said. 'Not Trevor. He's a friend.'

'Did you let him near Tri-Nitro, after that last training gallop?' I said.

George's face gave the answer.

'Sunday morning,' Rosemary said, in a hard cold voice. 'He came on the Sunday. He often does. He and George walked round the yard.' She paused. 'Trevor likes slapping horses. Slaps their rumps. Some people do that. Some people pat necks. Some people pull ears. Trevor slaps rumps.'

Lucas said, 'In due course, George, you'll have to give evidence in court.'

'I'm going to look a damned fool, aren't I?' he said

sourly. 'Filling my yard with guards and taking Deansgate in myself.'

Rosemary looked at me stonily, unforgiving.

'I told you they were being nobbled. I told you. You didn't believe me.'

Lucas looked surprised. 'But I thought you understood, Mrs Caspar. Sid did believe you. It was Sid who did all this investigating, not the Jockey Club.'

Her mouth opened, and stayed open, speechlessly.

'Look,' I said awkwardly, 'I've brought you a present. Ken Armadale along at the Equine Research has done a lot of work for you, and he thinks Tri-Nitro can be cured, by a course of some rather rare antibiotics. I've brought them with me from London.'

I stood up and took the box to Rosemary: put it into her hands, and kissed her cheek.

'I'm sorry, Rosemary love, that it wasn't in time for the Guineas. Maybe the Derby . . . but anyway the Irish Derby and the Diamond Stakes, and the Arc de Triomphe. Tri-Nitro will be fine for those.'

Rosemary Caspar, that tough lady, burst into tears.

We didn't get back to London until nearly five, owing to Lucas insisting on going to see Ken Armadale and Henry Thrace himself, face to face. The Director of Security to the Jockey Club was busy making everything official.

He was visibly relieved when Ken absolved the

people who'd done blood tests on the horses after their disaster races.

'The germ makes straight for the heart valves, and in the acute stage you'd never find it loose in the blood, even if you were thinking of illness and not merely looking for dope. It's only later, sometimes, that it gets freed into the blood, as it had in Zingaloo, when we took that sample.'

'Do you mean,' Lucas demanded, 'that if you did a blood test on Tri-Nitro at this minute you couldn't prove he had the disease?'

Ken said, 'You would only find antibodies.'

Lucas wasn't happy. 'Then how can we prove in court that he has got it?'

'Well,' Ken said, 'you could do an erysipelas antibody count today and another in a week's time. There would be a sharp rise in the number present, which would prove the horse must have the disease, because he's fighting it.'

Lucas shook his head mournfully. 'Juries won't like this.'

'Stick to Gleaner,' I said, and Ken agreed.

At one point Lucas disappeared into the Jockey Club rooms in the High Street and Chico and I drank in the White Hart and felt hot.

I changed the batteries. Routine. The day crawled.

'Let's go to Spain,' I said.

'Spain?'

'Anywhere.'

'I could just fancy a señorita.'

'You're disgusting.'

'Look who's talking.'

We reordered and drank and still felt hot.

'How much do you reckon we'll get?' Chico said.

'More or less what we ask.'

George Caspar had promised, if Tri-Nitro recovered, that the horse's owner would give us the earth.

'A fee will do,' I said drily.

Chico said, 'What will you ask, then?'

'I don't know. Perhaps five per cent of his prize money.'

'He couldn't complain.'

We set off southwards, finally, in the cooling car, and listened on the radio to the Dante Stakes at York.

Flotilla, to my intense pleasure, won it.

Chico, in the back seat, went to sleep. Lucas drove as impatiently as on the way up; and I sat and thought of Rosemary and Trevor Deansgate, and Nicholas Ashe, and Trevor Deansgate, and Louise, and Trevor Deansgate.

Stab. Stab. *'I'll do what I said.'*

Lucas dropped us at the entrance to the car park where I'd left the Scimitar. It would be like a furnace inside, I thought, sitting there all day in the sun. Chico and I walked over to it across the uneven stone-strewn ground.

Chico yawned.

A bath, I though. A long drink. Dinner. Find a hotel room again . . . not the flat.

There was a Land Rover with a two-horse trailer parked beside my car. Odd, I thought idly, to see them in central London. Chico, still yawning, walked between the trailer and my car to wait for me to unlock the doors.

'It'll be baking.' I said, fishing down into my pocket for the keys, and looking downwards into the car.

Chico made a choking sort of noise. I looked up, and thought confusedly how fast, how very fast a slightly boring hot afternoon could turn to stone cold disaster.

A large man stood in the space between the trailer and my car with his left arm clamped around Chico, who was facing me. The man was more or less supporting Chico's weight, because Chico's head lolled forward.

In his right hand the man held a small pear-shaped black truncheon.

The second man was letting down the ramp at the rear of the trailer.

I had no difficulty in recognizing them. The last time I'd seen them I'd been with a fortune-teller who hadn't liked my chances.

'Get in the trailer, laddie,' the one holding Chico said to me. 'The right-hand stall, laddie. Nice and quick. Otherwise I'll give your friend another tap or two. On the eyes, laddie. Or the base of the brain.'

Chico, on the far side of the Scimitar, mumbled vaguely and moved his head. The big man raised his truncheon and produced another short burst of uncompromising Scottish accent.

'Get in the trailer,' he said. 'Go right in, to the back.'

Seething with fury, I walked round the back of my car and up the ramp into the trailer. The right-hand stall, as he'd said. To the back. The second man stood carefully out of hitting distance, and there was no one else in the car park.

I found I was still holding my car keys, and put them back automatically into my pocket. Keys, handkerchief, money . . . and in the left-hand pocket, only a discharged battery. No weapon of any sort. A knife in the sock, I thought. I should have learned from Nicholas Ashe.

The man holding Chico came round to the back of the trailer and half dragged, half carried Chico into the left-hand stall.

'You make a noise, laddie,' he said, putting his head round to my side of the central partition, 'and I'll hit your friend here. On the eyes, laddie, and the mouth. You try and get help by shouting, laddie, and your friend won't have much face to speak of. Get it?'

I thought of Mason in Tunbridge Wells. A vegetable, and blind.

I said nothing at all.

'I'm travelling in here with your friend, all the way,' he said. 'Just remember that, laddie.'

The second man closed the ramp, shutting out the

sunlight, creating instant night. Where many trailers were open at the top at the back, this one was not.

Numb, I suppose, is how I felt.

The engine of the Land Rover started, and the trailer moved, backing out of the parking slot. The motion was enough to rock me against the trailer's side, enough to show I wasn't going very far standing up.

My eyes slowly adjusted to a darkness which wasn't totally black owing to various points where the ramp fitted less closely than others against the back of the trailer. In the end I could see clearly, as if it mattered, the variations that had been done to turn an ordinary trailer into an escape-proof transport. The extra piece at the back, closing the gap usually left open for air, and the extra piece inside, lengthways, raising the central partition from head height to the roof.

Basically, it was still a box built to withstand the weight and kicks of horses. I sat helplessly on the floor, which was bare of everything except muddy dust, and thought absolutely murderous thoughts.

After all that unpredictable travelling around I had agreed to go with Lucas and had stupidly left my car in plain vulnerable view all day. They must have picked me up at the Jockey Club, I thought. Either yesterday, or this morning. Yesterday, I thought, there had been no room in the car park, and I'd left my car in the street and got a ticket . . .

I hadn't been to my flat. I hadn't been back to Aynsford. I hadn't been to the Cavendish, or to any routine place.

I had, in the end, gone to the Jockey Club.

I sat and cursed and thought about Trevor Deansgate.

The journey lasted for well over an hour: a hot, jolting, depressing time which I spent mostly in consciously not wondering what lay at the end of it. After a while I could hear Chico talking, through the partition, though not the words. The flat, heavy, Glaswegian voice made shorter replies, rumbling like thunder.

A couple of pros from Glasgow, Jacksy had said. The one in with Chico, I thought, was certainly that. Not an average bashing mindless thug, but a hard man with brain power; and so much the worse.

Eventually the jolting stopped, and there were noises of the trailer being unhitched from the coupling; the Land Rover drove away, and in the sudden quiet I could hear Chico plainly.

'What's happening?' he said, and sounded still groggy.

'You'll find out soon enough, laddie.'

'Where's Sid?' he said.

'Be quiet, laddie.'

There was no sound of a blow, but Chico was quiet.

The man who had raised the ramp came and lowered

it, and six-thirty, Wednesday evening, flooded into the trailer.

'Out,' he said.

He was backing away from the trailer as I got to my feet, and he held a pitchfork at the ready, the sharp tines pointing my way.

From deep in the trailer I looked out and saw where we were. The trailer itself, disconnected from the Land Rover, was inside a building, and the building was the indoor riding school on Peter Rammileese's farm.

Timber-lined walls, windows in the roof, open because of the heat. No way that anyone could see in, casually, from outside.

'Out,' he said again, jerking the fork.

'Do what he says, laddie,' said the threatening voice of the man with Chico. 'At once.'

I did what he said.

Walked down the ramp on to the quiet tan-coloured riding-school floor.

'Over there.' He jerked the fork. 'Against the wall.' His voice was rougher, the accent stronger, than the man with Chico. For sheer bullying power, there wasn't much to choose.

I walked, feeling that my feet didn't belong to me.

'Back to the wall. Face his way.'

I turned with my shoulders lightly touching the wood.

Behind the man with the pitchfork, standing where from in the trailer I hadn't been able to see him, was

Peter Rammileese. His face bore a nasty mixture of satisfaction, sneer, and anticipation, quite unlike the careful intentness of the two Scots. He had driven the Land Rover, I supposed; out of my sight.

The man with Chico brought Chico to the top of the ramp and held him there. Chico half stood and half lay against him, smiling slightly and hopelessly disorientated.

'Hello, Sid,' he said.

The man holding him lifted the hand holding the truncheon, and spoke to me.

'Now listen, laddie. You stand quite still. Don't move. I'll finish your friend so quick you won't see it happen, if you move. Get it?'

I made no response of any kind, but after a moment he nodded sharply to the one with the pitchfork.

He came towards me slowly; warily. Showing me the prongs.

I looked at Chico. At the truncheon. At damage I couldn't risk.

I stood . . . quite still.

The man with the pitchfork raised it from pointing at my stomach to pointing at my heart, and from there, still higher. Slowly, carefully, one step at a time, he came forward until one of the prongs brushed my throat.

'Stand still,' said the man with Chico, warningly.

I stood.

The prongs of the pitchfork slid past my neck, one each side, below my chin, until they came to rest on

315

the wooden surface behind me. Pushing my head back. Pinning me by the neck against the wall, unharmed. Better than through the skin, I thought dimly, but hardly a ball for one's self-respect.

When he'd got the fork aligned as he wanted it, he gave the handle a strong thrusting jerk, digging the sharp tines into the wood. After that he put his weight into pushing against the handle, so that I shouldn't dislodge what he'd done, and get myself free. I had seldom felt more futile or more foolish.

The man holding Chico moved suddenly as if relaxed, carrying Chico bodily down the ramp and giving him a rough over-balancing shove at the bottom. As weak as a rag doll, Chico sprawled on the soft wood shavings, and the man strode over to me to feel for himself the force being applied in keeping me where I was.

He nodded to his partner. 'And you keep your mind on your business,' he said to him. 'Never mind yon other laddie. I'll see to him.'

I looked at their faces, remembering them for ever.

The hard callous lines of cheekbone and mouth. The cold eyes, observant and unfeeling. The black hair and pale skins. The set of a small head on a thick neck, the ears flat. The heavy shape of a jaw blue with beard. Late thirties, I guessed. Both much alike, and both giving forth at great magnitude the methodical brutality of the experienced mercenary.

Peter Rammileese, approaching, seemed in com-

parison a matter of sponge. Despite his chums'
disapproval he too put a hand on the pitchfork handle
and tried to give it a shake. It seemed to surprise him
that he couldn't.

He said to me, 'You'll keep your snotty nose out,
after this.'

I didn't bother to answer. Behind them, Chico got to
his feet, and for one surging moment I thought that he'd
been fooling them a bit with the concussed act, and was
awake and on the point of some effective judo.

It was only a moment. The kick he aimed at the man
who had been holding him wouldn't have knocked over
a house of cards. In sick and helpless fury I watched
the truncheon land again on Chico's head, sending him
down on to his knees, deepening the haze in his brain.

The man with the pitchfork was doing what he'd
been told and concentrating on keeping up the pressure
on the handle. I tugged and wrenched at it with desper-
ation to get free, and altogether failed, and the big man
with Chico unfastened his belt.

I saw with incredulity that what he'd worn round his
waist was not a leather strap but a length of chain, thin
and supple, like the stuff in grandfather clocks. At one
end he had fixed some sort of handle, which he grasped;
and he swung his arm so that the free end fizzed through
the air and wrapped itself around Chico.

Chico's head snapped up and his eyes and mouth
opened wide with astonishment, as if the new pain had
cleared away the mists like a flamethrower. The man

317

swung his arm again and the chain landed on Chico, and I could hear myself shouting, 'Bastards, bloody bastards . . .' and it made no difference at all.

Chico swayed to his feet and took some stumbling steps to get away, and the man followed him, hitting him all over with unvarying ferocity, taking a pride in his work.

I yelled incoherently . . . unconnected words, screaming at him to stop . . . feeling anger and grief and an agony of responsibility. If I hadn't taken Chico to Newmarket . . . if I hadn't been afraid of Trevor Deansgate . . . it was because of my fear that Chico was there . . . on that day . . . God . . . Bastard. Stop it . . . Stop . . . Wrenched at the pitchfork and couldn't get free.

Chico lurched and stumbled and finally crawled in a wandering circle round the riding school, and ended lying on his stomach not far away from me. The thin cotton of his shirt twitched when the chain landed, and I saw dotted red streaks of blood in the fabric here and there.

Chico . . . God . . .

It wasn't until he lay entirely still that the torment stopped. The man stood over him, looking down judiciously, holding his chain in a relaxed grasp.

Peter Rammileese looked if anything disconcerted and scared, and it was he who had got us there, he who had arranged it.

The man holding the pitchfork stopped looking at me

for the first time and switched his attention to where Chico lay. It was only a partial shift of his balance, but it made all the difference to the pressure on my neck. I wrenched at the handle with a force he wasn't ready for, and finally got myself away and off the wall; and it wasn't the man with Chico I sprang at in bloodlusting rage, but Peter Rammileese himself, who was nearer.

I hit him on the side of the face with all my strength, and I hit him with my hard left arm, two thousand quid's worth of delicate technology packed into a built-in club.

He screeched and raised his arms round his head, and I said 'Bastard' with savage intensity and hit him again, on the ribs.

The man with Chico turned his attention to me, and I discovered, as Chico had, that one's first feeling was of astonishment. The sting was incredible; and after the lacerating impact, a continuing fire.

I turned on the man in a rage I wouldn't have thought I could feel, and it was he who backed away from me.

I caught the next swing of his chain on my unfeeling arm. The free end wrapped itself round the forearm, and I tugged with such fierceness that he lost his grip on the handle. It swung down towards me, a stitched piece of leather; and if there had been just the two of us I would have avenged Chico and fought our way out of there, because there was nothing about cold blood in the way I went for him.

I grasped the leather handle, and as the supple links unwound and fell off my arm I swung the chain in a circle above my head and hit him an almighty crack around the shoulders. From his wide opening eyes and the outraged Scottish roar I guessed that he was learning for the first time what he had inflicted on others.

The man with the pitchfork at that point brought up the reserves, and although I might perhaps have managed one, it was hopeless against two.

He came charging straight at me with the wicked prongs and although I dodged them like a bullfighter the first man grabbed my right arm with both of his, intent on getting his chain back.

I swung round towards him in a sort of leap, and with the inside of my metal wrist hit him so hard on the ear and side of the head that the jolt shuddered up through my elbow and upper arm into my shoulder.

For a brief second I saw into his eyes at very close quarters; saw the measure of a hard fighting man, and knew he wasn't going to sit on the ramp of the trailer and wail, as Peter Rammileese was doing.

The crash on the head all the same loosened his grasp enough for me to wrench myself free, and I lunged away from him, still clutching his chain, and turned to look for the pitchfork. The pitchfork man, however, had thrown the fork away and was unfastening his own belt. I jumped towards him while he had both his hands at his waist and delivered to him too the realities of their chosen warfare.

In the half-second in which both of the Scots were

frozen with shock I turned and ran for the door, where, somewhere outside, there had to be people and safety and help.

Running on wood shavings felt like running through treacle, and although I got to the door I didn't get through it, because it was a large affair like a chunk of wall which pushed to one side on rollers, and it was fastened shut by a bolt which let down into the floor.

The pitchfork man reached me there before I even got the bolt up, and I found that his belt wasn't leather either, nor grandfather clock innards, but more like the chain for tethering guard dogs. Less sting. More thud.

I still had the stinger, and I swung round low from trying to undo the bolt and wrapped it round his legs. He grunted and rushed at me, and I found the other man right at my back, both of them clutching, and unfortunately I did them no more damage after that, though not for want of trying.

He got his chain back because he was stronger than I was and banged my hand against the wall to loosen my grasp, the other one holding on to me at the same time, and I thought well I'm damned well not going to make it easy for you and you'll have to work for what you want; and I ran round that place, and made them run, round the trailer, and round by the walls and down again to the door at the end.

I picked up the pitchfork and for a while held them off, and threw it at one of them, and missed; and because one can convert pain into many other things so as not to feel it, I felt little except rage and fury and anger, and concentrated on those feelings to make them a shield.

I ended as Chico had done, stumbling and swaying and crawling and finally lying motionless on the soft floor. Not so far from the door . . . but a long way from help.

They'll stop now I'm still, I thought: they'll stop in a minute: and they did.

CHAPTER EIGHTEEN

I lay with my face in the wood shavings and listened to them panting as they stood over me, both of them taking great gulps of breath after their exertions.

Peter Rammileese apparently came across to them, because I heard his voice from quite close, loaded with spite, mumbling and indistinct.

'Kill him,' he said. 'Don't stop there. Kill him.'

'Kill *him*?' said the man who'd been with Chico. 'Are you crazy?' He coughed, dragging in air. 'Yon laddie . . .'

'He's broken my jaw.'

'Kill him yourself then. We're not doing it.'

'Why not? He's cut your ear half off.'

'Grow up, mon.' He coughed again. 'We'd be grassed inside five minutes. We've been down here too long. Too many people've seen us. And this laddie, he's won money for every punter in Scotland. We'd be inside in a week.'

'I want you to kill him,' Peter Rammileese said, insisting.

'You're not paying,' said the Scot, flatly, still breathing heavily. 'We've done what was ordered, and that's that. We'll go into your house now for a beer, and after dark we'll dump these two, as arranged, and then we're finished. And we'll go straight up north tonight, we've been down here too long.'

They went away, and rolled the door open, and stepped out. I heard their feet on the gritty yard, and the door closing, and the metal grate of the outside bolt, which was to keep horses in, and would do for men.

I moved my head a bit to get my nose clear of the shavings, and looked idly at the colour of them so close to my eyes, and simply lay where I was, feeling shapeless, feeling pulped, and stupid, and defeated.

Jelly. A living jelly. Red. On fire. Burning, in a furnace.

There was a lot of romantic rubbish written about fainting from pain, I thought. One absolutely tended not to because there was no provision for it in nature. The mechanics were missing. There were no fail-safe cut-offs on sensory nerves: they went right on passing the message for as long as the message was there to pass. No other system had evolved, because through millennia it had been unnecessary. It was only man, the most savage of animals, who inflicted pain for its own sake on his fellows.

I thought: I did manage it once, for a short time, after very much too long. I thought: this isn't as bad as that, so I'm going to stay here awake, so I may as well find something to think about. If one couldn't stop the message passing, one could distract the receptors from paying much attention, as in acupuncture; and over the years I'd had a lot of practice.

I thought about a night I'd spent once where I could see a hospital clock. To distract myself from a high state of awfulness I'd spent the time counting. If I shut my eyes and counted for five minutes, five minutes would be gone; and every time I opened my eyes to check, it was only four minutes; and it had been a very long night. I could do better than that, nowadays.

I thought about John Viking in his balloon, and imagined him scudding across the sky, his eyes blazing with the glee of breaking safety regulations like bubbles. I thought about Flotilla on the gallops at Newmarket, and winning the Dante Stakes at York. I thought about races I'd ridden in, and won, and lost; and I thought about Louise, a good deal about Louise and fourposter beds.

Afterwards I reckoned that Chico and I had lain there without moving for over an hour, though I hadn't any clear idea of it at the time. The first sharp intrusion of the uncomfortable present was the noise of the bolt clicking open on the outside of the door, and the grinding noise as the door itself rolled partially open. They were going to dump us, they'd said, after dark; but it wasn't yet dark.

Footsteps made no sound on that soft surface, so that the first thing I heard was a voice.

'Are you asleep?'

'No,' I said.

I shifted my head back a bit and saw little Mark squatting there on his heels, in his pyjamas, studying me with six-year-old concern. Beyond him, the door, open enough to let his small body through. On the other side of the door, out in the yard, the Land Rover.

'Go and see if my friend's awake,' I said.

'OK.'

He straightened his legs and went over to Chico, and I'd got myself up from flat to kneeling by the time he returned with his report.

'He's asleep,' he said, looking at me anxiously. 'Your face is all wet. Are you hot?'

'Does your dad know you're down here?' I said.

'No, he doesn't. I had to go to bed early, but I heard a lot of shouting. I was frightened, I think.'

'Where's your dad now?' I said.

'He's in the sitting room with those friends. He's hurt his face and he's bloody angry.'

I practically smiled. 'Anything else?'

'Mum was saying what did he expect, and they were all having drinks.' He thought a bit. 'One of the friends said his eardrum was burst.'

'If I were you,' I said, 'I'd go straight back to bed and not let them catch you out here. Otherwise your dad might be bloody angry with you too, and that wouldn't be much fun, I shouldn't think.'

He shook his head.

'Good night, then,' I said.

'Good night.'

'And leave the door open,' I said. 'I'll shut it.'

'All right.'

He gave me a trusting and slightly conspiratorial smile, and crept out of the doorway to sneak back to bed.

I got to my feet and staggered around a bit, and made it to the door.

The Land Rover stood there about ten feet away. If the keys were in it, I thought, why wait to be dumped? Ten steps. Leant against the grey-green bodywork, and looked through the glass.

Keys. In the ignition.

I went back into the riding school and over to Chico, and knelt beside him because it was a lot less demanding than bending.

'Come on,' I said. 'Wake up. Time to go.'

He groaned.

'Chico, you've got to walk. I can't carry you.'

He opened his eyes. Still confused, I thought, but a great deal better.

'Get up,' I said urgently. 'We can get out, if you'll try.'

'Sid . . .'

'Yeah,' I said. 'Come on.'

'Go away. I can't.'

'Yes, you damned well can. You just say, "Sod the buggers," and it comes easy.'

It came harder than I'd thought, but I half lugged him

to his feet, and put my arm round his waist, and we meandered waveringly to the door like a pair of drunken lovers.

Through the door, and across to the Land Rover. No furious yells of discovery from the house; and as the sitting room was at the far end of it, with a bit of luck they wouldn't even hear the engine start.

I shovelled Chico on to the front seat and shut the door quietly, and went round to the driving side.

Land Rovers, I thought disgustedly, were made for left-handed people. All the controls, except the indicators, were on that side: and whether it was because I myself was weak, or the battery was flat, or I'd damaged the machinery by using it as a club, the fingers of my left hand would scarcely move.

I swore to myself and did everything with my right hand, which meant twisting, which would have hurt if I hadn't been in such a hurry.

Started the engine. Released the brake. Shoved the gear lever into first. Did the rest thankfully with my feet, and set off. Not the smoothest start ever, but enough. The Land Rover rolled to the gate, and I turned out in the opposite direction from London, thinking instinctively that if they found we'd gone and chased after us, it would be towards London that they would go in pursuit.

The 'sod the buggers' mentality lasted me well for two or three miles and through some dicey one-handed gear changing, but suffered a severe set-back when I looked at the petrol gauge and found it pointing to nearly empty.

The question of where we were going had to be sorted out, and immediately; and before I'd decided, we came round a bend and found in front of us a large garage, still open, with attendants by the pumps. Hardly believing it, I swerved untidily into the forecourt, and came to a jerking halt by the two-star.

Money in right-hand pocket, along with car keys and handkerchief. I pulled all of them out in a handful and separated the crumpled notes. Opened the window beside me. Gave the attendant who appeared the money and said I'd have that much petrol.

He was young, a school-kid, and he looked at me curiously.

'You all right?'

'It's hot,' I said, and wiped my face with the handkerchief. Some wood shavings fell out of my hair. I must indeed have looked odd.

The boy merely nodded, however, and stuck the petrol nozzle into the Land Rover's filling place, which was right beside the driver's door. He looked across me to Chico, who was half lying on the front seats with his eyes open.

'What's wrong with him, then?'

'Drunk,' I said.

He looked as if he thought we both were, but he simply finished the filling, and replaced the cap, and turned away to attend to the next customer. I went again through the tedious business of starting right-handedly, and pulled out on to the road. After a mile I turned off the main road into a side road, and went round a bend or two, and stopped.

'What's happening?' Chico said.

I looked at his still woozy eyes. Decide where to go, I thought. Decide for Chico. For myself, I already knew. I'd decided when I found I could drive without hitting things, and at the garage which had turned up so luckily, and when I'd had enough money for the petrol, and when I hadn't asked the boy to get us help in the shape of policemen and doctors.

Hospitals and bureaucracy and questions and being prodded about; all the things I most hated. I wasn't going near any of them, unless I had to for Chico.

'Where did we go, today?' I said.

After a while he said, 'Newmarket.'

'What's twice eight?'

Pause. 'Sixteen.'

I sat in a weak sort of gratitude for his returning wits, waiting for strength to go on. The impetus which had got me into the Land Rover and as far as that spot had ebbed away and left room for a return of fire and jelly. Power would come back, I thought, if I waited. Stamina and energy always came in cycles, so that what one couldn't do one minute, one could the next.

'I'm burning,' Chico said.

'Mm.'

'That was too much.'

I didn't answer. He moved on the seat and tried to sit upright, and I saw the full awareness flood into his face. He shut his eyes tight and said '*Jesus*', and after a while he looked at me through slits, and said, 'You too?'

'Mm.'

The long hot day was drawing to dusk. If I didn't get started, I thought vaguely, I wouldn't get anywhere.

The chief practical difficulty was that driving a Land Rover with one hand was risky, if not downright dangerous, as I had to leave go of the steering wheel and lean to the left every time I changed gear: and the answer to that was to get the left-hand fingers to grip the knob just once, and tightly, so that I could switch off the current, and the hand would stay there on the gear lever, unmoving, until further notice.

I did that. Then I switched on the side-lights, and the head-lights, dipped. Then the engine. I'd give anything for a drink, I thought, and set off on the long drive home.

'Where are we going?' Chico said.

'To the Admiral's.'

I had taken the southern route round Sevenoaks and Kingston and Colnbrook, and there was the M4 motorway stretch to do, and the cross at Maidenhead to the M40 motorway just north of Marlow, and then round the north Oxford ring road and the last leg to Aynsford.

Land Rovers weren't built for comfort and jolted the passengers at the best of times. Chico groaned now and then, and cursed, and said he wasn't getting into a mess like that again, ever. I stopped twice briefly on the way from weakness and general misery, but there wasn't much traffic, and we rolled into Charles's drive in three and a half hours, not too bad for the course.

I switched the Land Rover off and my left hand on, and couldn't get the fingers to move. That was all it needed, I thought despairingly, the final humiliation of that bloody evening, if I had to detach myself from the socket end and leave the electric part of me stuck to the gears. Why, *why*, couldn't I have two hands, like everyone else.

'Don't struggle,' Chico said, 'and you'll do it easy.'

I gave a cough that was somewhere between a laugh and a sob, and the fingers opened a fraction, and the hand fell off the knob.

'Told you,' he said.

I laid my right arm across the steering wheel and put my head down on that, and felt spent and depressed . . . and punished. And someone, somehow, had got to raise the strength to go in to tell Charles we were there.

He solved that himself by coming out to us in his dressing gown, the light streaming out behind him from his open front door. The first I knew, he was standing by the window of the Land Rover, looking in.

'Sid?' he said incredulously. 'Is it you?'

I dragged my head off the steering wheel and opened my eyes, and said, 'Yeah.'

'It's after midnight,' he said.

I got a smile at least into my voice. 'You said I could come any time.'

An hour later, Chico was upstairs in bed and I sat sideways on the gold sofa, shoes off, feet up, as I often did.

Charles came into the drawing room and said the doctor had finished with Chico and was ready for me, and I said no thanks very much and tell him to go home.

'He'll give you some knock-out stuff, like Chico.'

'Yes, and that's exactly what I don't want, and I hope he was careful about Chico's concussion, with those drugs.'

'You told him yourself about six times, when he came.' He paused. 'He's waiting for you.'

'I mean it, Charles,' I said. 'I want to think. I want just to sit here and think, so would you please say goodbye to the doctor and go to bed.'

'No,' he said. 'You can't.'

'I certainly can. In fact, I have to, while I still feel . . .' I stopped. While I still feel *flayed*, I thought; but one couldn't say that.

'It's not sensible.'

'No. The whole thing isn't sensible. That's the point. So go away and let me work it out.'

I had noticed before that sometimes when the body

was injured the mind cleared sharply and worked for a while with acute perception. It was a time to use, if one wanted to; not to waste.

'Have you seen Chico's skin?' he said.

'Often,' I said flippantly.

'Is yours in the same state?'

'I haven't looked.'

'You're exasperating.'

'Yeah,' I said. 'Go to bed.'

When he'd gone I sat there deliberately and vividly remembering in mind and body the biting horror I'd worked so hard to blank out.

It had been too much, as Chico said.

Too much.

Why?

Charles came downstairs again at six o'clock, in his dressing gown, and with his most impassive expression.

'You're still there, then,' he said.

'Yuh.'

'Coffee?'

'Tea,' I said.

He went and made it, and brought two big steaming mugs, naval fashion. He put mine on the table which stood along the back of the sofa, and sat with his in an armchair. The empty-looking eyes were switched steadily my way.

'Well?' he said.

I rubbed my forehead. 'When you look at me,' I said, hesitatingly. 'Usually, I mean. Not now. When you look at me, what do you see?'

'You know what I see.'

'Do you see a lot of fears and self-doubts, and feelings of shame and uselessness and inadequacy?'

'Of course not.' He seemed to find the question amusing, and then sipped the scalding tea, and said more seriously, 'You never show feelings like that.'

'No one does,' I said. 'Everyone has an outside and an inside, and the two can be quite different.'

'Is that just a general observation?'

'No.' I picked up the mug of tea, and blew across the steaming surface. 'To myself, I'm a jumble of uncertainty and fear and stupidity. And to others ... well, what happened to Chico and me last evening was because of the way others see us.' I took a tentative taste. As always when Charles made it, the tea was strong enough to rasp the fur off your tongue. I quite liked it, sometimes. I said, 'We've been lucky, since we started this investigating thing. In other words, the jobs we've done have been comparatively easy, and we've been getting a reputation for being successful, and the reputation has been getting bigger than the reality.'

'Which is, of course,' Charles said drily, 'that you're a pair of dim-witted layabouts.'

'You know what I mean.'

'Yes, I do. Tom Ullaston rang me here yesterday morning, to arrange about stewards for Epsom, he said, but I gathered it was mostly to tell me what he thought about you, which was, roughly speaking, that if you had still been a jockey it would be a pity.'

'It would be great,' I said, sighing.

'So someone lammed into you and Chico yesterday to stop you chalking up another success?'

'Not exactly,' I said.

I told him what I had spent the night sorting out; and his tea got cold.

When I'd finished he sat for quite a while in silence, simply staring at me in best give-away-nothing manner.

Then he said, 'It sounds as if yesterday evening was . . . terrible.'

'Well, yes, it was.'

More silence. Then, 'So what next?'

'I was wondering,' I said diffidently, 'if you'd do one or two jobs for me today, because I . . . er . . .'

'Of course,' he said. 'What?'

'It's your day for London. Thursday. So could you bear to drive the Land Rover up instead of the Rolls, and swap it for my car?'

'If you like,' he said, not looking enchanted.

'The battery charger's in it, in my suitcase,' I said.

'Of course I'll go.'

'Before that, in Oxford, could you pick up some photographs? They're of Nicholas Ashe.'

'Sid!'

I nodded. 'We found him. There's a letter in my car, too, with his new address on. A begging letter, same as before.'

He shook his head at the foolishness of Nicholas Ashe. 'Any more jobs?'

'Two, I'm afraid. The first's in London, and easy. But as for the other . . . Would you go to Tunbridge Wells?'

When I told him why, he said he would, even though it meant cancelling his afternoon's board meeting.

'And would you lend me your camera, because mine's in the car . . . and a clean shirt?'

'In that order?'

'Yes, please.'

Wishing I didn't have to move for a couple of thousand years I slowly unstuck myself from the sofa some time later and went upstairs, with Charles's camera, to see Chico.

He was lying on his side, his eyes dull and staring vaguely into space, the effect of the drugs wearing off. Sore enough to protest wearily when I told him what I wanted to photograph.

'Sod off.'

'Think about barmaids.'

I peeled back the blanket and sheet covering him and took pictures of the visible damage, front and back. Of the invisible damage there was no measure. I put the covers back again.

'Sorry,' I said.

He didn't answer, and I wondered whether I was really apologizing for disturbing him at that moment or more basically for having tangled his life in mine, with such dire results. A hiding to nothing was what he'd said we were on with those syndicates, and he'd been right.

I took the camera out on to the landing and gave it to Charles.

'Ask for blown-up prints by tomorrow morning,' I said. 'Tell him it's for a police case.'

'But you said no police . . .' Charles said.

'Yes, but if he thinks it's already for the police, he won't go trotting round to them when he sees what he's printing.'

'I suppose it's never occurred to you,' Charles said, handing over a clean shirt, 'that it's your view of you that's wrong, and Thomas Ullaston's that's right?'

I telephoned Louise and told her I couldn't make it that day, after all. Something's come up, I said, in the classic evasive excuse, and she answered with the disillusion it merited.

'Never mind, then.'

'I do mind, actually,' I said. 'So how about a week tomorrow? What are you doing after that for a few days?'

'Days?'

'And nights.'

Her voice cheered up considerably. 'Research for a thesis.'

'What subject?'

'Clouds and roses and stars, their variations and frequency in the life of your average liberated female.'

'Oh Louise,' I said, 'I'll . . . er . . . help you all I can.'

She laughed and hung up, and I went along to my room and took off my dusty, stained, sweaty shirt. Looked at my reflection briefly in the mirror and got no joy from it. Put on Charles's smooth sea island cotton and lay on the bed. I lay on one side, like Chico, and felt what Chico felt; and at one point or other, went to sleep.

In the evening I went down and sat on the sofa, as before, to wait for Charles, but the first person who came was Jenny.

She walked in, saw me, and was immediately annoyed. Then she took a second look, and said, 'Oh no, not again.'

I said merely, 'Hello.'

'What is it this time? Ribs, again?'

'Nothing.'

'I know you too well.' She sat at the other end of the sofa, beyond my feet. 'What are you doing here?'

'Waiting for your father.'

She looked at me moodily. 'I'm going to sell that flat in Oxford,' she said.

'Are you?'

'I don't like it any more. Louise McInnes has left, and it reminds me too much of Nicky . . .'

After a pause I said, 'Do I remind you of Nicky?'

With a flash of surprise she said, 'Of course not.' And then, more slowly, 'But he . . .' she stopped.

'I saw him,' I said. 'Three days ago, in Bristol. And he looks like me, a bit.'

She was stunned, and speechless.

'Didn't you realize?' I said.

She shook her head.

'You were trying to go back,' I said. 'To what we had, at the beginning.'

'It's not true.' But her voice said that she saw it was. She had even told me so, more or less, the evening I'd come to Aynsford to start finding Ashe.

'Where will you live?' I said.

'What do you care?'

I supposed I would always care, to some extent, which was my problem, not hers.

'How did you find him?' she said.

'He's a fool.'

She didn't like that. The look of enmity showed where her instinctive preference still lay.

'He's living with another girl,' I said.

She stood up furiously, and I remembered a bit late that I really didn't want her to touch me.

'Are you telling me that to be beastly?' she demanded.

'I'm telling you so you'll get him out of your system before he goes on trial and to jail. You're going to be damned unhappy if you don't.'

'I hate you,' she said.

'That's not hate, that's injured pride.'

'How dare you!'

'Jenny,' I said. 'I'll tell you plainly, I'd do a lot for you. I've loved you a long time, and I do care what happens to you. It's no good finding Ashe and getting him convicted of fraud instead of you, if you don't wake up and see him for what he is. I want to make you angry with him. For your own sake.'

'You won't manage it,' she said fiercely.

'Go away,' I said.

'What?'

'Go away. I'm tired.'

She stood there looking as much bewildered as annoyed, and at that moment Charles came back.

'Hello,' he said, taking a disapproving look at the general atmosphere. 'Hello, Jenny.'

She went over and kissed his cheek, from long habit.

'Has Sid told you he's found your friend Ashe?' he said.

'He couldn't wait.'

Charles was carrying a large brown envelope. He opened it, pulled out the contents, and handed them to me: the three photographs of Ashe, which had come out well, and the new begging letter.

Jenny took two jerky strides and looked down at the uppermost photograph.

'Her name is Elizabeth More,' I said slowly. 'His real name is Norris Abbott. She calls him Ned.'

The picture, the third one I'd taken, showed them laughing and entwined, looking into each other's eyes, the happiness in their faces sharply in focus.

Silently, I gave Jenny the letter. She opened it and looked at the signature at the bottom, and went very pale. I felt sorry for her, but she wouldn't have wanted me to say so.

She swallowed, and handed the letter to her father.

'All right,' she said after a pause. 'All right. Give it to the police.'

She sat down again on the sofa with a sort of emotional exhaustion slackening her limbs and curving her spine. Her eyes turned my way.

'Do you want me to thank you?' she said.

I shook my head.

'I suppose one day I will.'

'There's no need.'

With a flash of anger she said, 'You're doing it again.'

'Doing what?'

'Making me feel guilty. I know I'm pretty beastly to you sometimes. Because you make me feel guilty, and I want to get back at you for that.'

'Guilty for what?' I said.

'For leaving you. For our marriage going wrong.'

'But it wasn't your fault,' I protested.

'No, it was yours. Your selfishness, your pigheadedness. Your bloody determination to win. You'll do anything to win. You always have to win. You're so hard. Hard on yourself. Ruthless to yourself. I couldn't live with it. No one could live with it. Girls want men who'll come to them for comfort. Who say, I need you, help me, comfort me, kiss away my troubles. But you . . . you can't do that. You always build a wall and deal with your own troubles in silence, like you're doing now. And don't tell me you aren't hurt because I've seen it in you too often, and you can't disguise the way you hold your head, and this time it's very bad, I can see it. But you'd never say, would you, Jenny, hold me, help me, I want to cry?'

She stopped, and in the following silence made a sad little gesture with her hand.

'You see?' she said. 'You can't say it, can you?'

After another long pause I said, 'No.'

'Well,' she said, 'I need a husband who's not so rigidly in control of himself. I want someone who's not afraid of emotion, someone uninhibited, someone weaker. I can't live in the sort of purgatory you make of life for yourself. I want someone who can break down. I want . . . an ordinary man.'

She got up from the sofa and bent over and kissed my forehead.

'It's taken me a long time to see all that,' she said, 'and to say it. But I'm glad I have.' She turned to her father. 'Tell Mr Quayle I'm cured of Nicky, and I won't be obstructive from now on. I think I'll go back to the flat now. I feel a lot better.'

She went with Charles towards the door, and then paused and looked back, and said, 'Goodbye, Sid.'

'Goodbye,' I said: and I wanted to say, Jenny, hold me, help me, I want to cry: but I couldn't.

CHAPTER NINETEEN

Charles drove himself and me to London the following day in the Rolls with me still in a fairly droopy state and Charles saying we should put it off until Monday.

'No,' I said.

'But even for you this is daunting... and you're dreading it.'

Dread, I thought, was something I felt for Trevor Deansgate, who wasn't going to hold off just because I had other troubles. Dread was too strong a word for the purpose of the present journey; and reluctance too weak. Aversion, perhaps.

'It's better done today,' I said.

He didn't argue. He knew I was right, otherwise he wouldn't have been persuaded to drive me.

He dropped me at the door of the Jockey Club in Portman Square, and went and parked the car, and walked back again. I waited for him downstairs, and we went up in the lift together: he in his City suit, and I in trousers and a clean shirt, but no tie and no jacket. The weather was still hot. A whole week of it, we'd had, and it seemed that everyone except me was bronzed and healthy.

There was a looking glass in the lift. My face stared out of it, greyish and hollow-eyed, with a red streak of a healing cut slanting across near the hairline on my forehead, and a blackish bruise on the side of my jaw. Apart from that I looked calmer, less damaged and more normal than I felt, which was a relief. If I concentrated, I should be able to keep it that way.

We went straight to Sir Thomas Ullaston's office, where he was waiting for us. Shook hands, and all that.

To me he said, 'Your father-in-law told me on the telephone yesterday that you have something disturbing to tell me. He wouldn't say what it was.'

'No, not on the telephone,' I agreed.

'Sit down, then. Charles . . . Sid . . .' He offered chairs, and himself perched on the edge of his big desk. 'Very important, Charles said. So here I am, as requested. Fire away.'

'It's about syndicates,' I said. I began to tell him what I'd told Charles, but after a few minutes he stopped me.

'No. Look, Sid, this is not going to end here simply between me and you, is it? So I think we must have some of the others in, to hear what you're saying.'

I would have preferred him not to, but he summoned the whole heavy mob: the Controller of the Secretariat, the Head of Administration, the Secretary to the Stewards, the Licensing Officer, who dealt with the registration of owners, and the Head of Rules Department, whose province was disciplinary action. They came into the room and filled up the chairs, and for the second time in four days turned their serious civilized faces my way, to listen to the outcome of an investigation.

It was because of Tuesday, I thought, that they would listen to me now. Trevor Deansgate had given me an authority I wouldn't otherwise have had, in that company, in that room.

I said, 'I was asked by Lord Friarly, whom I used to ride for, to look into four syndicates, which he headed. The horses were running in his colours, and he wasn't happy about how they were doing. That wasn't surprising, as their starting prices were going up and down like yo-yos, with results to match. Lord Friarly felt he was being used as a front for some right wicked goings on, and he didn't like it.'

I paused, knowing I was using a light form of words because the next bit was going to fall like lead.

'On the same day, at Kempton, Commander Wainwright asked me to look into the same four syndicates, which I must say had been manipulated so thoroughly that it was a wonder they weren't a public scandal already.'

The smooth faces registered surprise. Sid Halley was not the natural person for Commander Wainwright to ask to look into syndicates, which were the normal business of the Security Section.

'Lucas Wainwright told me that all four syndicates

had been vetted and OK'd by Eddy Keith, and he asked me to find out if there was any unwelcome significance in that.'

For all that I put it at its least dramatic, the response from the cohorts was of considerable shock. Racing might suffer from its attraction for knaves and rogues, as it always had, but corruption within the headquarters itself? Never.

I said, 'I came here to Portman Square to make notes about the syndicates, which I took from Eddy Keith's files, without his knowledge. I wrote the notes in Lucas's office, and he told me about a man he'd sent out on the same errand as myself, six months ago. That man, Mason, had been attacked, and dumped in the streets of Tunbridge Wells, with appalling head injuries, caused by kicks. He was a vegetable, and blind. Lucas told me also that the man who had formed the syndicates, and who had been doing the manipulating, was a Peter Rammileese, who lived at Tunbridge Wells.'

The faces were all frowningly intent.

'After that I ... er ... went away for a week, and I also lost the notes, so I had to come back here and do them again, and Eddy Keith discovered I'd been seeing his files, and complained to you, Sir Thomas, if you remember?'

'That's right. I told him not to fuss.'

There were a few smiles all around, and a general loosening of tension. Inside me, a wilting fatigue.

'Go on, Sid,' Sir Thomas said.

Go on, I thought. I wished I felt less weak, less shaky, less continuously sore. Had to go on, now I'd started. Get on with it. Go on.

I said, 'Well, Chico Barnes, who was here with me on Tuesday . . .' They nodded. 'Chico and I, we went down to Tunbridge Wells, to see Peter Rammileese. He was away, as it happened. His wife and little son were there, but the wife had fallen off a horse and Chico went to the hospital with her, taking the little boy, which left me, and an open house. So I . . . er . . . looked around.'

Their faces said 'Tut tut', but none of their voices.

'I looked for any possible direct tie-in with Eddy, but actually the whole place was abnormally tidy and looked suspiciously prepared for any searches any tax men might make.'

They smiled slightly.

'Lucas warned me at the beginning that as what I was doing was unofficial, I couldn't be paid, but that he'd give me help instead, if I needed it. So I asked him to help me with the business of Trevor Deansgate, and he did.'

'In what way, Sid?'

'I asked him to write to Henry Thrace, to make sure that the Jockey Club would hear at once if Gleaner died, or Zingaloo, and to tell me, so that I could get a really thorough post-mortem done.'

They all nodded. They remembered.

'And then,' I said, 'I found Peter Rammileese on my heels with two very large men who looked just the sort to kick people's heads in and leave them blinded in Tunbridge Wells.'

No smiles.

'I dodged them that time, and I spent the next week rolling around England in unpredictable directions so that no one could really have known where to find me, and during that time, when I was chiefly learning about Gleaner and heart valves and so on, I was also told that the two big men had been imported especially from Scotland for some particular job with Peter Rammileese's syndicates. There was also some rumour of someone high up in the Security Service who would fix things for crooks, if properly paid.'

They were shocked again.

'Who told you that, Sid?' Sir Thomas asked.

'Someone reliable,' I said, thinking that maybe they wouldn't think a suspended jockey like Jacksy as reliable as I did.

'Go on.'

'I wasn't really making much progress with those syndicates, but Peter Rammileese apparently thought so, because he and his two men laid an ambush for Chico and me, the day before yesterday.'

Sir Thomas reflected. 'I thought that was the day you were going to Newmarket with Lucas to see the Caspars. The day after you were here telling us about Trevor Deansgate.'

'Yes, we did go to Newmarket. And I made the mistake of leaving my car in plain view near here all day.

The two men were waiting beside it when we got back. And ... er ... Chico and I got abducted, and where we landed up was at Peter Rammileese's place at Tunbridge Wells.'

Sir Thomas frowned. The others listened to the unemotional relating of what they must have realized had been a fairly violent occurrence with a calm understanding that such things could happen.

There had seldom been, I thought, a more silently attentive audience.

I said, 'They gave Chico and me a pretty rough time, but we did get out of there, owing to Peter Rammileese's little boy opening a door for us by chance, and we didn't end up in Tunbridge Wells streets, we got to my father-in-law's house near Oxford.'

They all looked at Charles, who nodded.

I took a deep breath. 'At about that point,' I said, 'I ... er ... began to see things the other way round.'

'How do you mean, Sid?'

'Until then, I thought the two Scotsmen were supposed to be preventing us from finding what we were looking for, in those syndicates.'

They nodded. Of course.

'But supposing it was exactly the reverse ... Supposing I'd been pointed at those syndicates in order to be led to the ambush. Suppose the ambush itself was the whole aim of the exercise.'

Silence.

I had come to the hard bit, and needed the reserves I

didn't have, of staying power, of will. I was aware of Charles sitting steadfastly beside me, trying to give me his strength.

I could feel myself shaking. I kept my voice flat and cold, saying the things I didn't like saying, that had to be said.

'I was shown an enemy, who was Peter Rammileese. I was given a reason for being beaten up, which was the syndicates. I was fed the expectation of it, through the man Mason. I was being given a background to what was going to happen; a background I would accept.'

Total silence and blank, uncomprehending expressions.

I said, 'If someone had savagely attacked me out of the blue, I wouldn't have been satisfied until I had found out who and why. So I thought, supposing someone wanted to attack me, but it was imperative that I didn't find out who or why. If I was given a false who, and a false why, I would believe in those, and not look any further.'

One or two very slight nods.

'I did believe in that who and that why for a while,' I said. 'But the attack, when it came, seemed out of all proportion . . . and from something one of our attackers said I gathered it was not Peter Rammileese himself who was paying them, but someone else.'

Silence.

'So, after we had reached the Admiral's house, I began thinking, and I thought, if the attack itself was the point, and it was not Peter Rammileese who had arranged it, then who had? Once I saw it that way, there was only one possible who. The person who had laid the trail for me to follow.'

The faces began to go stiff.

I said, 'It was Lucas himself who set us up.'

They broke up into loud, jumbled, collective protest, moving in their chairs with embarrassment, not meeting my eye, not wanting to look at someone who was so mistaken, so deluded, so pitiably ridiculous.

'No, Sid, really,' Sir Thomas said. 'We've a great regard for you . . .' the others looked as if the great regard was now definitely past tense, ' . . . but you can't say things like that.'

'As a matter of fact,' I said slowly, 'I would much rather have stayed away and not said it. I won't tell you any more, if you don't want to hear it.' I rubbed my fingers over my forehead from sheer lack of inner energy, and Charles half made, and then stopped himself making, a protective gesture of support.

Sir Thomas looked at Charles and then at me, and whatever he saw was enough to calm him from incredulity to puzzlement.

'All right,' he said soberly, 'we'll listen.'

The others all looked as if they didn't want to, but if the Senior Steward was willing, it was enough.

I said, with deep weariness and no satisfaction, 'To understand the *why* part, it's necessary to look at what's been happening during the past months. During the

353

time Chico and I have been doing . . . what we have. As you yourself said, Sir Thomas, we've been successful. Lucky . . . tackling pretty easy problems . . . but mostly sorting them out. To the extent that a few villains have tried to stop us dead as soon as we've appeared on the skyline.'

The disbelief still showed like snow in July, but at least they seemed to understand that too much success invited retaliation. The uncomfortable shiftings in the chairs grew gradually still.

'We've been prepared for it, more or less,' I said. 'In some cases it's even been useful, because it's shown us we're nearing the sensitive spot . . . But what we usually get is a couple of rent-a-thug bullies in or out of funny masks, giving us a warning bash or two and telling us to lay off. Which advice,' I added wryly, 'we have never taken.'

They had all begun looking at me again, even if sideways.

'So then people begin to stop thinking of me as a jockey, and gradually see that what Chico and I are doing isn't really the joke it seemed at first. And we get what you might call the Jockey Club Seal of Approval, and all of a sudden, to the really big crooks, we appear as a continuing, permanent menace.'

'Do you have proof of that, Sid?' Sir Thomas said.

Proof . . . Short of getting Trevor Deansgate in there to repeat his threat before witnesses, I had no proof. I said, 'I've had threats . . . only threats, before this.'

A pause. No one said anything, so I went on.

'I understand on good authority,' I said, with faint amusement, 'that there would be some reluctance to solve things by actually killing us, as people who had won money in the past on my winners would rise up in wrath and grass on the murderers.'

Some tentative half-smiles amid general dislike of such melodrama.

'Anyway, such a murder would tend to bring in its trail precisely the investigation it was designed to prevent.'

They were happier with that.

'So the next best thing is an ultimate deterrent. One that would so sicken Chico and me that we'd go and sell brushes instead. Something to stop us investigating anything else, ever again.'

It seemed all of a sudden as if they did understand what I was saying. The earlier, serious attention came right back. I thought it might be safe to mention Lucas again, and when I did there was none of the former vigorous reaction.

'If you could just imagine for a moment that there *is* someone in the Security Service who can be bribed, and that it is the Director himself, would you, if you were Lucas, be entirely pleased to see an independent investigator making progress in what had been exclusively your territory? Would you, if you were such a man, be pleased to see Sid Halley right here in the Jockey Club being congratulated by the Senior Steward and being given carte blanche to operate wherever he liked throughout racing?'

They stared.

'Would you, perhaps, be afraid that one of these days Sid Halley would stumble across something you couldn't afford for him to find out? And might you not, at that point, decide to remove the danger of it once and for all? Like putting weedkiller on a nettle, before it stings you.'

Charles cleared his throat. 'A pre-emptive strike,' he said smoothly, 'might appeal to a retired Commander.'

They remembered he had been an Admiral, and looked thoughtful.

'Lucas is only a man,' I said. 'The title of Director of Security sounds pretty grand, but the Security Service isn't that big, is it? I mean, there are only about thirty people in it full-time, aren't there, over the whole country?'

They nodded.

'I don't suppose the pay is a fortune. One hears about bent policemen from time to time, who've taken bribes from crooks. Well . . . Lucas is constantly in contact with people who might say, for instance, how about a quiet thousand in readies, Commander, to smother my little bit of trouble?'

The faces were shocked.

'It does happen, you know,' I said mildly. 'Back-handers are a flourishing industry. I agree that you wouldn't want the head of racing security to be shutting his eyes to skulduggery, but it's more a breach of trust than anything aggressively wicked.'

What he'd done to Chico and me was indeed aggressively wicked, but that wasn't the point I wanted to make.

'What I'm saying,' I said, 'is that in the wider context of the everyday immoral world, Lucas's dishonesty is no great shakes.'

They looked doubtful, but that was better than negative shakes of the head. If they could be persuaded to think of Lucas as a smallish-scale sinner they would believe more easily that he'd done what he had.

'If you start from the idea of a deterrent,' I said, 'you see everything from the other side.' I stopped. The inner exhaustion didn't. I'd like to sleep for a week, I thought.

'Go on, Sid.'

'Well . . .' I sighed. 'Lucas had to take the slight risk of pointing me at something he was involved in, because he needed a background he could control. He must have been badly shocked when Lord Friarly said he'd asked me to look into those syndicates, but if he had already toyed with the idea of getting rid of me, I'd guess he saw at that point how to do it.'

One or two of the heads nodded sharply in comprehension.

'Lucas must have been sure that a little surface digging wouldn't get me anywhere near him – which it didn't – but he minimized the risk by specifically directing my attention to Eddy Keith. It was safe to set me investigating Eddy's involvement with the shady side of the syndicates, because of course he wasn't involved. I could look for ever, and find nothing.' I paused. 'I don't think I was supposed to have much time to find out anything at all. I think that catching us took much longer than was intended in the original plan.'

Catching us . . . catching me. They'd have taken me alone, but both had been better for them . . . and far worse for me . . .

'Took much longer? How do you mean?' Sir Thomas said.

Concentrate, I thought. Get on with it.

'From Lucas's point of view, I was very slow,' I said. 'I was working on the Gleaner thing, and I didn't do anything at all about the syndicates for a week after he asked me. Then directly I'd been told about Peter Rammileese and Mason, and could have been expected to go down to Tunbridge Wells, I went away somewhere else entirely, for another week; during which time Lucas rang Chico four times to ask him where I was.'

Silent attention, as before.

'When I came back, I'd lost the notes, so I did them again in Lucas's office, and I told him Chico and I would go down to Peter Rammileese's place the following day, Saturday. I think it's likely that if we had done so the . . . er . . . deterring . . . would have been done then, but in fact we went the same afternoon that I'd been talking to Lucas, on the Friday, and Peter Rammileese wasn't there.'

Weren't they all thirsty, I wondered? Where was the coffee? My mouth was dry and a good deal of me hurt.

'It was on that Friday morning that I asked Lucas to write to Henry Thrace. I also asked him – entreated him, really – not to mention my name at all in connection with Gleaner, as it might get me killed.'

A lot of frowns awaited an explanation.

'Well . . . Trevor Deansgate had warned me in those sort of terms to stop investigating those horses.'

Sir Thomas managed to raise his eyebrows and imply a frown at one and the same time.

'Are those the threats you mentioned before?' he said.

'Yes, and he repeated them when you . . . er . . . introduced us, in your box at Chester.'

'Good God.'

'I wanted to get the investigation of Gleaner done by the Jockey Club so that Trevor Deansgate wouldn't know it had anything to do with me.'

'You did take those threats seriously,' Sir Thomas said thoughtfully.

I swallowed. 'They were . . . seriously given.'

'I see,' said Sir Thomas, although he didn't. 'Go on.'

'I didn't actually tell Lucas about the threats themselves,' I said. 'I just begged him not to tie me in with Gleaner. And within days, he had told Henry Thrace that it was I, not the Jockey Club, who really wanted to know if Gleaner died. At the time I reckoned that he had just been careless or forgetful, but now I think he did it on purpose. Anything which might get me killed was to him a bonus, even if he didn't see how it could do.'

They looked doubtful. Doubts were possible.

'So then Peter Rammileese – or Lucas – traced me to my father-in-law's house, and on the Monday Peter Rammileese and the two Scots followed me from there to a horse show, where they had a shot at abduction, which didn't come off. After that I kept out of their way for eight more days, which must have frustrated them no end.'

The faces waited attentively.

'During that time I learned that Peter Rammileese was manipulating not four, but nearer twenty syndicates, bribing trainers and jockeys wholesale. It was then also that I learned about the bribable top man in the Security Service who was turning a blind eye to the goings on, and I regret to say I thought it must be Eddy Keith.'

'I suppose,' Sir Thomas said, 'that that was understandable.'

'So, anyway, on Tuesday, Chico and I came here, and Lucas at last knew where I was. He asked to come to Newmarket with us on Wednesday, and he took us there in his own super four-litre air-conditioned highly expensive Mercedes, and although he's usually so keen to get on with the next thing, he wasted hours doing nothing in Newmarket, during which time I now think he was in fact arranging and waiting for the ambush to be properly set up, so that this time there should be no mistakes. Then he drove us to where the Scots were waiting for us, and we walked straight into it. The Scots did the special job they had been imported for, which was deterring Chico and me, and I heard one of them tell Peter Rammileese that now that they had done what was ordered they were going north straight away, they'd been in the south too long.'

Sir Thomas was looking slightly strained.

'Is that all, Sid?'

'No. There's the matter of Mason.'

Charles stirred beside me, uncrossing and recrossing his legs.

'I asked my father-in-law to go to Tunbridge Wells yesterday, to ask about Mason.'

Charles said, in his most impressive drawl, 'Sid asked me to see if Mason existed. I saw the police fellows in Tunbridge Wells. Very helpful, all of them. No one called Mason, or anything else for that matter, has ever been found kicked near to death and blinded in their streets, ever.'

'Lucas told me about Mason's case in great detail,' I said. 'He was very convincing, and of course I believed him. But have any of you ever heard of anyone called Mason who was employed by the Security Service, that was so badly injured?'

They silently, bleakly, shook their heads. I didn't tell them that I'd finally had doubts about Mason because there was no file for him in 'Personnel'. Even in a good cause, our breaking and entering wouldn't please them.

A certain amount of gloom had settled on their faces, but there were also questions they wanted to ask. Sir Thomas put their doubts into words.

'There's one obvious flaw in your reverse view of things, Sid, and that is that this deterrent . . . hasn't deterred you.'

After a pause I said, 'I don't know that it hasn't. Neither Chico nor I could go on, if it meant . . . if we thought . . . anything like that would happen again.'

'Like exactly what, Sid?'

I didn't reply. I could feel Charles glancing my way in his best noncommittal manner, and it was he, eventually, who got quietly to his feet, and walked across the room, and gave Sir Thomas the envelope which contained the pictures of Chico.

'It was a chain,' I said matter-of-factly.

They passed the photographs round in silence. I didn't particularly look to see what they were thinking. I was just hoping they wouldn't ask what I knew they would; and Sir Thomas said it baldly. 'Was this done to you as well?'

I reluctantly nodded.

'Will you take your shirt off, then, Sid?'

'Look,' I said. 'What does it matter? I'm not laying any charges of assault or grievous bodily harm, or anything like that. There's going to be no police, no court case, nothing. I've been through all that once, as you know, and I'm not, absolutely not, doing it again. This time there's to be no noise. All that's necessary is to tell Lucas I know what's been happening, and if you think it right, to get him to resign. There's nothing to be gained by anything else. You don't want any public scandal. It would be harmful to racing as a whole.'

'Yes, but . . .'

'There's Peter Rammileese,' I said. 'Perhaps Eddy Keith might really sort out those syndicates, now. It would only get Rammileese deeper in if he boasted that he'd bribed Lucas, so I shouldn't think he would. I doubt if he'd talk about Chico and me, either.'

Except perhaps, I thought sardonically, to complain that I'd hit him very hard.

'What about the two men from Glasgow?' Sir Thomas said. 'Are they just to get away with it?'

'I'd rather that than go to court again as a victim,' I said. I half smiled. 'You might say that the business over my hand successfully deterred me from that sort of thing for the rest of my life.'

A certain amount of urbane relief crept into both the faces and the general proceedings.

'However,' Sir Thomas said. 'The resignation of the Director of Security cannot be undertaken lightly. We must judge for ourselves whether or not what you have said is justified. The photographs of Mr Barnes aren't enough. So please . . . take off your shirt.'

Bugger it, I thought. I didn't want to. And from the distaste in their faces, they didn't want to see. I hated the whole damn thing. Hated what had happened to us. Detested it. I wished I hadn't come to Portman Square.

'Sid,' Sir Thomas said seriously. 'You must.'

I undid the buttons and stood up and slid the shirt off. The only pink bit of me was the plastic arm, the rest being mottled black with dark red criss-crossed streaks. It looked, by that time, with all the bruising coming out, a lot worse than it felt. It looked, as I knew, appalling. It also looked, on that day, the worst it would. It was because of that that I'd insisted on going to Portman Square on that day. I hadn't wanted to show them the damage, yet I'd known they would insist, and I would have to: and if I had to, that day was the most convincing. The human mind was deviously ambivalent, when it wanted to defeat its enemies.

In a week or so, most of the marks would have gone, and I doubted whether there would be a single permanent external scar. It had all been quite precisely a matter of outraging the sensitive nerves of the skin, transient, leaving no trace. With such a complete lack of lasting visible damage, the Scots would know that even if they were brought to trial, they would get off lightly. For a hand, all too visible, the sentence had been four years. The going rate for a few days' surface discomfort was probably three months. In long robbery-with-violence sentences it was always the robbery that stretched the time, not the violence.

'Turn round,' Sir Thomas said.

I turned round, and after a while I turned back. No

one said anything. Charles looked at his most unruffled. Sir Thomas stood up and walked over to me, and inspected the scenery more closely. Then he picked up my shirt from the chair, and held it for me to put on again.

I said, 'Thank you,' and did up the buttons. Pushed the tails untidily into the top of my trousers. Sat down.

It seemed quite a long time before Sir Thomas lifted the inter-office telephone and said to his secretary, 'Would you ask Commander Wainwright to come here, please?'

If the administrators still had any doubts, Lucas himself dispelled them. He walked briskly and unsuspectingly into a roomful of silence, and when he saw me sitting there he stopped moving suddenly, as if his brain had given up transmitting to his muscles.

The blood drained from his face, leaving the grey-brown eyes staring from a barren landscape. I had an idea that I must have looked like that to Trevor Deansgate, in the Stewards' box at Chester. I thought that quite likely, at that moment, Lucas couldn't feel his feet on the carpet.

'Lucas,' Sir Thomas said, pointing to a chair, 'sit down.'

Lucas fumbled his way into the chair with his gaze still fixedly on me, as if he couldn't believe I was there, as if by staring hard enough he could make me vanish.

Sir Thomas cleared his throat. 'Lucas, Sid Halley, here, has been telling us certain things which require explanation.'

Lucas was hardly listening. Lucas said to me, 'You can't be here.'

'Why not?' I said.

They waited for Lucas to answer, but he didn't.

Sir Thomas said eventually, 'Sid has made serious charges. I'll put them before you, Lucas, and you can answer as you will.'

He repeated more or less everything I'd told them, without emphasis and without mistake. The judicial mind, I thought, taking the heat out of things, reducing passion to probabilities. Lucas appeared to be listening, but he looked at me all the time.

'So you see,' Sir Thomas said finally, 'we are waiting for you to deny – or admit – that Sid's theories are true.'

Lucas turned his head away from me and looked vaguely round the room.

'It's all rubbish, of course,' he said.

'Carry on,' said Sir Thomas.

'He's making it all up.' He was thinking again, fast. The briskness in some measure returned to his manner. 'I certainly didn't tell him to investigate any syndicates. I certainly didn't tell him I had doubts about Eddy. I never talked to him about this imaginary Mason. He's invented it all.'

'With what purpose?' I said.

'How should I know?'

'I didn't invent coming here twice to copy down notes of the syndicates,' I said. 'I didn't invent Eddy complaining because I'd seen those files. I didn't invent you telephoning Chico at my flat four times. I didn't invent you dropping us at the car park. I didn't invent Peter Rammileese, who might be persuaded to . . . er . . . talk. I could also find those two Scots, if I tried.'

'How?' he said.

I'd ask young Mark, I thought. He would have learnt a lot about the friends in all that time: little Mark and his accurate ears.

I said, 'Don't you mean, I invented the Scots?'

He glared at me.

'I could also,' I said slowly, 'start looking for the real reasons behind all this. Trace the rumours of corruption to their source. Find out who, besides Peter Rammileese, is keeping you in Mercedes.'

Lucas Wainwright was silent. I didn't know that I could do all I'd said, but he wouldn't want to bet I couldn't. If he hadn't thought me capable he'd have seen no need to get rid of me in the first place. It was his own judgement I was invoking, not mine.

'Would you be prepared for that, Lucas?' Sir Thomas said.

Lucas stared my way some more, and didn't answer.

'On the other hand,' I said, 'I think if you resigned, it would be the end of it.'

He turned his head away from me and stared at the Senior Steward instead.

Sir Thomas nodded. 'That's all, Lucas. Just your resignation, now, in writing. If we had that, I would see no reason to proceed any further.'

It was the easiest let-off anyone could have had, but to Lucas, at that moment, it must have seemed bad enough. His face looked strained and pale, and there were tremors round his mouth.

Sir Thomas produced from his desk a sheet of paper, and from his pocket a gold ball-point pen.

'Sit here, Lucas.'

He rose and gestured to Lucas to sit by the desk.

Commander Wainwright walked over with stiff legs and shakily sat where he'd been told. He wrote a few words, which I read later. *I resign from the post of Director of Security to the Jockey Club. Lucas Wainwright.*

He looked around at the sober faces, at the people who had known him well, and trusted him, and had worked with him every day. He hadn't said a word, since he'd come into the office, of defence or appeal. I thought: how odd it must be for them all, facing such a shattering readjustment.

He stood up, the pepper and salt man, and walked towards the door.

As he came to where I sat he paused, and looked at me blankly, as if not understanding.

'What does it take,' he said, 'to stop you?'

I didn't answer.

What it took rested casually on my knee. Four strong fingers, and a thumb, and independence.

CHAPTER TWENTY

Charles drove us back to Aynsford.

'You'll get a bellyful of courtrooms anyway,' he said. 'With Nicholas Ashe, and Trevor Deansgate.'

'It's not so bad just being an ordinary witness.'

'You've done it a good few times, now.'

'Yes,' I said.

'What will Lucas Wainwright do after this, I wonder?'

'God knows.'

Charles glanced at me. 'Don't you feel the slightest desire to gloat?'

'Gloat?' I was astounded.

'Over the fallen enemy.'

'Oh yes?' I said. 'And in your war at sea, what did you do when you saw an enemy drowning? Gloat? Push him under?'

'Take him prisoner,' Charles said.

After a bit I said, 'His life from now on will be prison enough.'

Charles smiled his secret smile, and ten minutes further on he said, 'And do you forgive him, as well?'

'Don't ask such difficult questions.'

Love thine enemy. Forgive. Forget. I was no sort of Christian, I thought. I could manage not to hate Lucas himself. I didn't think I could forgive; and I would never forget.

We rolled on to Aynsford, where Mrs Cross, carrying a tray upstairs to her private sitting room, told me that Chico was up, and feeling better, and in the kitchen. I went along there and found him sitting alone at the table, looking at a mug of tea.

'Hello,' I said.

'Hello.'

There was no need, with him, to pretend anything. I filled a mug from the pot and sat opposite him.

'Bloody awful,' he said, 'wasn't it?'

'Yeah.'

'And I was dazed, like.'

'Mm.'

'You weren't. Made it worse.'

We sat for a while without talking. There was a sort of stark dullness in his eyes, and none of it, any longer, was concussion.

'Do you reckon,' he said, 'they let your head alone, for that?'

'Don't know.'

'They could've.'

I nodded. We drank the tea, bit by bit.

'What did they say, today?' he said. 'The brass.'

'They listened. Lucas resigned. End of story.'

'Not for us.'

'No.'

I moved stiffly on the chair.

'What'll we do?' he said.

'Have to see.'

'I couldn't . . .' He stopped. He looked tired and sore, and dispirited.

'No,' I said. 'Nor could I.'

'Sid . . . I reckon . . . I've had enough.'

'What, then?'

'Teach judo.'

And I could make a living. I suppose, from equities, commodities, insurance, and capital gains. Some sort of living . . . not much of a life.

In depression we finished the tea, feeling battered and weak and sorry for ourselves. I couldn't go on if he didn't, I thought. He'd made the job seem worthwhile. His naturalness, his good nature, his cheerfulness: I needed them around me. In many ways I couldn't function without him. In many ways, I wouldn't bother to function, if I didn't have him to consider.

After a while I said, 'You'd be bored.'

'What, with Wembley and not hurting, and the little bleeders?'

I rubbed my forehead, where the stray cut itched.

'Anyway,' he said, 'it was you, last week, who was going to give up.'

'Well . . . I don't like being . . .' I stopped.

'Beaten,' he said.

I took my hand away and looked at his eyes. There was the same thing there that had suddenly been in his voice. An awareness of the two meanings of the word. A glimmer of sardonic amusement. Life on its way back.

'Yeah.' I smiled twistedly. 'I don't like being beaten. Never did.'

'Sod the buggers, then?' he said.

I nodded. 'Sod 'em.'

'All right.'

We went on sitting there, but it was a lot better, after that.

Three days later, on Monday evening, we went back to London, and Chico, humouring the fears he didn't take seriously, came with me to the flat.

The hot weather had gone back to normal, or in other words, warm-front drizzle. Road surfaces were slippery with the oily patina left by hot dry tyres, and in West London every front garden was soggy with roses. Two weeks to the Derby ... and perhaps Tri-Nitro would run in it, if the infection cleared up. He was fit enough, apart from that.

The flat was empty and quiet.

'Told you,' Chico said, dumping my suitcase in the bedroom. 'Want me to look in the cupboards?'

'As you're here.'

He raised his eyebrows to heaven and did an inch by inch search.

'Only spiders,' he said. 'They've caught all the flies.'

We went down to where I'd parked at the front and I drove him to his place.

'Friday,' I said. 'I'm going away for a few days.'

'Oh yes? Dirty weekend?'

'You never know. I'll call you, when I get back.'

'Just the nice gentle crooks from now on, right?'

'Throw all the big ones back,' I said.

He grinned, waved, and went in, and I drove away with lights going on everywhere in the dusk. Back at the flats I went round to the lock-up garages to leave the car in the one I rented there, out of sight.

Unlocked the roll-up door, and pushed it high. Switched the light on. Drove the car in. Got out. Locked the car door. Put the keys in my pocket.

'Sid Halley,' a voice said.

A voice. *His* voice.

Trevor Deansgate.

I stood facing the door I'd just locked, as still as stone.

'Sid Halley.'

I had known it would happen, I supposed. Sometime, somewhere, like he'd said. He had made a serious threat. He had expected to be believed. I had believed him.

Oh God, I thought. It's too soon. It's always too soon. Let him not see the terror I feel. Let him not know. Dear God . . . give me courage.

I turned slowly towards him.

He stood a step inside the garage, in the light, the thin drizzle like a dark grey-silver sheet behind him.

He held the shotgun, with the barrels pointing my way.

I had a brick wall on my left and another behind me, and the car on my right; and there were never many people about at the back of the flats, by the garages. If anyone came, they'd hardly dawdle around, in the rain.

'I've been waiting for you,' he said.

He was dressed, as ever, in city pinstripes. He brought, as always, the aura of power.

With eyes and gun facing unwaveringly my way, he stretched up behind him quickly with his left hand and found the bottom edge of the roll-up door. He gave it a sharp downward tug, and it rolled down nearly to the ground behind him, closing us in. Both hands, clean, manicured, surrounded by white cuffs, were back on the gun.

'I've been waiting for you, on and off, for days. Since last Thursday.'

I didn't say anything.

'Last Thursday two policemen came to see me. George Caspar telephoned. The Jockey Club warned me they were going to take proceedings. My solicitor told me I'd lose my bookmaking licence. I would be warned off from racing, and might well go to jail. Since last Thursday, I've been waiting for you.'

His voice, as before, was a threat in itself, heavy with the raw realities of the urban jungle.

'The police have been to the lab. My brother is losing his job. His career. He worked hard for it.'

'Let's all cry,' I said. 'You both gambled. You've lost. Too bloody bad.'

His eyes narrowed and the gun barrels moved an inch or two as his body reacted.

'I came here to do what I said I would.'

Gambled . . . lost . . . so had I.

'I've been waiting in my car around these flats,' he said. 'I knew you'd come back, some time or other. I knew you would. All I had to do was wait. I've spent most of my time here, since last Thursday, waiting for you. So tonight you came back . . . with that friend. But I wanted you on your own . . . I went on waiting. And you came back. I knew you'd come, in the end.'

I said nothing.

'I came here to do what I promised. To blow your hand off.' He paused. 'Why don't you beg me not to? Why don't you go down on your bloody knees and beg me not to?'

I didn't answer. Didn't move.

He gave a short laugh that had no mirth in it at all. 'It didn't stop you, did it, that threat? Not for long. I thought it would. I thought no one could risk losing both their hands. Not just to get me busted. Not for something small, like that. You're a bloody fool, you are.'

I agreed with him, on the whole. I was also trembling inside, and concerned that he shouldn't see it.

'You don't turn a hair, do you?' he said.

He's playing with me, I thought. He must know I'm frightened. No one could possibly, in those circumstances, not be frightened to death. He's making me sweat . . . wanting me to beg him . . . and I'm not . . . *not* . . . going to.

'I came here to do it,' he said. 'I've been sitting here for days, thinking about it. Thinking of you with no hands . . . with just stumps . . . two plastic hooks.'

Sod you, I thought.

'Today,' he said, 'I started thinking about myself. I shoot off Sid Halley's right hand, and what happens to me?' He stared at me with increased intensity. 'I get the satisfaction of fixing you, making you a proper cripple instead of half a one. I get revenge . . . hideous delightful revenge. And what else do I get? I get ten years, perhaps. You can get life for GBH, if it's bad enough. Both hands . . . that might be bad enough. That's what I've been sitting here today thinking. And I've been thinking of the feeling there'd be against me in the slammer, for shooting your other hand off. Yours, of all people. I'd be better off killing you. That's what I thought.'

I thought numbly that I wasn't so sure either that I wouldn't rather be dead.

'This evening,' he said, 'after you'd come back for ten minutes, and gone away again, I thought of rotting away in jail year after year wishing I'd had the bloody sense to leave you alone. I reckoned it wasn't worth years in jail, just to know I'd fixed you. Fixed you alive, or fixed you dead. So I decided, just before you came back, not to do that, but just to get you down on the ground squealing for me not to. I'd have my revenge that way. I'd remind you of it, all your life. I'd tell people I'd had you crawling. Make them snigger.'

Jesus, I thought.

'I'd forgotten,' he said, 'what you're like. You've no bloody nerves. But I'm not going to shoot you. Like I said, it's not worth it.'

He turned abruptly, and stooped, putting one hand under the garage door. Heaved; rolled it upwards and open.

The warm drizzle in the dark outside fell like shoals of silver minnows. The gentle air came softly into the garage.

He stood there for a moment, brooding, holding his gun; and then he gave me back what in the straw barn he'd taken away.

'Isn't there *anything*,' he said bitterly, 'that you're afraid of?'

ODDS AGAINST

CHAPTER ONE

I was never particularly keen on my job before the day I got shot and nearly lost it, along with my life. But the .38 slug of lead which made a pepper-shaker out of my intestines left me with fire in my belly in more ways than one. Otherwise I should never have met Zanna Martin, and would still be held fast in the spider-threads of departed joys, of no use to anyone, least of all myself.

It was the first step to liberation, that bullet, though I wouldn't have said so at the time. I stopped it because I was careless. Careless because bored.

I woke up gradually in hospital, in a private room for which I got a whacking great bill a few days later. Even before I opened my eyes I began to regret I had not left the world completely. Someone had lit a bonfire under my navel.

A fierce conversation was being conducted in un-hushed voices over my head. With woolly wits, the anaesthetic still drifting inside my skull like puff-ball clouds in a summer sky, I tried unenthusiastically to make sense of what was being said.

'Can't you give him something to wake him more quickly?'

'No.'

'We can't do much until we have his story, you must see that. It's nearly seven hours since you finished operating. Surely . . .'

'And he was all of four hours on the table before that. Do you want to finish off what the shooting started?'

'Doctor . . .'

'I am sorry, but you'll have to wait.'

There's my pal, I thought. They'll have to wait. Who wants to hurry back into the dreary world? Why not go to sleep for a month and take things up again after they've put the bonfire out? I opened my eyes reluctantly.

It was night. A globe of electric light shone in the centre of the ceiling. That figured. It had been morning when Jones-boy found me still seeping gently on to the office linoleum and went to telephone, and it appeared that about twelve hours had passed since they stuck the first blessed needle into my arm. Would a twenty-four hour start, I wondered, be enough for a panic-stricken ineffectual little crook to get himself unde-tectably out of the country?

There were two policemen on my left, one in uni-form, one not. They were both sweating, because the

2

room was hot. The doctor stood on the right, fiddling with a tube which ran from a bottle into my elbow. Various other tubes sprouted disgustingly from my abdomen, partly covered by a light sheet. Drip and drainage, I thought sardonically. How absolutely charming.

Radnor was watching me from the foot of the bed, taking no part in the argument still in progress between medicine and the law. I wouldn't have thought I rated the boss himself attendant at the bedside, but then I suppose it wasn't every day that one of his employees got himself into such a spectacular mess.

He said, 'He's conscious again, and his eyes aren't so hazy. We might get some sense out of him this time.' He looked at his watch.

The doctor bent over me, felt my pulse, and nodded. 'Five minutes, then. Not a second more.'

The plain clothes policeman beat Radnor to it by a fraction of a second. 'Can you tell us who shot you?'

I still found it surprisingly difficult to speak, but not as impossible as it had been when they asked me the same question that morning. Then, I had been too far gone. Now, I was apparently on the way back. Even so, the policeman had plenty of time to repeat his question, and to wait some more, before I managed an answer.

'Andrews.'

It meant nothing to the policeman, but Radnor looked astonished and also disappointed.

'Thomas Andrews?' he asked.

'Yes.'

Radnor explained to the police. 'I told you that Halley here and another of my operatives set some sort of a trap intending to clear up an intimidation case we are investigating. I understand they were hoping for a big fish, but it seems now they caught a tiddler. Andrews is small stuff, a weak sort of youth used for running errands. I would never have thought he would carry a gun, much less that he would use it.'

Me neither. He had dragged the revolver clumsily out of his jacket pocket, pointed it shakily in my direction, and used both hands to pull the trigger. If I hadn't seen that it was only Andrews who had come to nibble at the bait I wouldn't have ambled unwarily out of the darkness of the washroom to tax him with breaking into the Cromwell Road premises of Hunt Radnor Associates at one o'clock in the morning. It simply hadn't occurred to me that he would attack me in any way.

By the time I realized that he really meant to use the gun and was not waving it about for effect, it was far too late. I had barely begun to turn to flip off the light switch when the bullet hit, in and out diagonally through my body. The force of it spun me on to my knees and then forward on to the floor.

As I went down he ran for the door, stiff-legged, crying out, with circles of white showing wild round his eyes. He was almost as horrified as I was at what he had done.

'At what time did the shooting take place?' asked the policeman formally.

After another pause I said, 'One o'clock, about.'

The doctor drew in a breath. He didn't need to say it; I knew I was lucky to be alive. In a progressively feeble state I'd lain on the floor through a chilly September night looking disgustedly at a telephone on which I couldn't summon help. The office telephones all worked through a switchboard. This might have been on the moon as far as I was concerned, instead of along the passage, down the curving stairs, and through the door to the reception desk, with the girl who worked the switches fast asleep in bed.

The policeman wrote in his notebook. 'Now sir, I can get a description of Thomas Andrews from someone else so as not to trouble you too much now, but I'd be glad if you can tell me what he was wearing.'

'Black jeans, very tight. Olive green jersey. Loose black jacket.' I paused. 'Black fur collar, black and white checked lining. All shabby . . . dirty.' I tried again. 'He had gun in jacket pocket right side . . . took it with him . . . no gloves . . . can't have a record.'

'Shoes?'

'Didn't see. Silent, though.'

'Anything else?'

I thought. 'He had some badges . . . place names, skull and crossbones, things like that . . . sewn on his jacket, left sleeve.'

'I see. Right. We'll get on with it then.' He snapped

5

shut his notebook, smiled briefly, turned, and walked to the door, followed by his uniformed ally, and by Radnor, presumably for Andrews' description.

The doctor took my pulse again, and slowly checked all the tubes. His face showed satisfaction.

He said cheerfully, 'You must have the constitution of a horse.'

'No,' said Radnor, coming in again and hearing him. 'Horses are really quite delicate creatures. Halley has the constitution of a jockey. A steeplechase jockey. He used to be one. He's got a body like a shock absorber . . . had to have to deal with all the fractures and injuries he got racing.'

'Is that what happened to his hand? A fall in a steeplechase?'

Radnor's glance flicked to my face and away again, uncomfortably. They never mentioned my hand to me in the office if they could help it. None of them, that is, except my fellow trapsetter Chico Barnes, who didn't care what he said to anyone.

'Yes,' Radnor said tersely. 'That's right.' He changed the subject. 'Well, Sid, come and see me when you are better. Take your time.' He nodded uncertainly to me, and he and the doctor, with a joint backward glance, ushered each other out of the door.

So Radnor was in no hurry to have me back. I would have smiled if I'd had the energy. When he first offered me a job I guessed that somewhere in the background my father-in-law was pulling strings; but I had been in a why-not mood at the time. Nothing mattered very much.

'Why not?' I said to Radnor, and he put me on his payroll as an investigator, Racing Section, ignoring my complete lack of experience and explaining to the rest of the staff that I was there in an advisory capacity, owing to my intimate knowledge of the game. They had taken it very well, on the whole. Perhaps they realized, as I did, that my employment was an act of pity. Perhaps they thought I should be too proud to accept that sort of pity. I wasn't. I didn't care one way or the other.

Radnor's agency ran Missing Persons, Guard, and Divorce departments, and also a section called Bona Fides, which was nearly as big as the others put together. Most of the work was routine painstaking inquiry stuff, sometimes leading to civil or divorce action, but oftener merely to a discreet report sent to the client. Criminal cases, though accepted, were rare. The Andrews business was the first for three months.

The Racing Section was Radnor's special baby. It hadn't existed, I'd been told, when he bought the agency with an Army gratuity after the war and developed it from a dingy three-roomed affair into something like a national institution. Radnor printed 'Speed, Results, and Secrecy' across the top of his stationery; promised them, and delivered them. A life-long addiction to racing, allied to six youthful rides in point-to-points, had led him not so much to ply for hire from the Jockey Club and the National Hunt Committee as to indicate that his agency was at their disposal. The Jockey Club and the National Hunt Committee tentatively wet their feet, found the water beneficial, and plunged right in. The Racing Section blossomed. Eventually private business outstripped the official, especially when Radnor began supplying pre-race guards for fancied horses.

By the time I joined the firm, 'Bona Fides: Racing' had proved so successful that it had spread from its own big office into the room next door. For a reasonable fee a trainer could check on the character and background of a prospective owner, a bookmaker on a client, a client on a bookmaker, anybody on anybody. The phrase 'OK'd by Radnor' had passed into racing slang. Genuine, it meant. Trustworthy. I had even heard it applied to a horse.

They had never given me a Bona Fides assignment. This work was done by a bunch of inconspicuous middle-aged retired policemen who took minimum time to get maximum results. I'd never been sent to sit all night outside the box of a hot favourite, though I would have done it willingly. I had never been put on a racecourse security patrol. If the Stewards asked for operators to keep tabs on undesirables at race meetings, I didn't go. If anyone had to watch for pickpockets in Tattersalls, it wasn't me. Radnor's two unvarying excuses for giving me nothing to do were first, that I was too well known to the whole racing world to be inconspicuous, and second, that even if I didn't seem to care, he was not going to be the one to give an ex-champion jockey tasks which meant a great loss of face.

As a result I spent most of my time kicking around the office reading other people's reports. When anyone asked me for the informed advice I was supposedly there to give, I gave it; if anyone asked what I would do in a certain set of circumstances, I told them. I got to know all the operators and gossiped with them when they came into the office. I always had the time. If I took a day off and went to the races, nobody complained. I sometimes wondered whether they even noticed.

At intervals I remarked to Radnor that he didn't have to keep me, as I so obviously did nothing to earn my salary. He replied each time that he was satisfied with the arrangement, if I was. I had the impression that he was waiting for something, but if it wasn't for me to leave, I didn't know what. On the day I walked into Andrews' bullet I had been with the agency in this fashion for exactly two years.

A nurse came in to check the tubes and take my blood pressure. She was starched and efficient. She smiled but didn't speak. I waited for her to say that my wife was outside asking about me anxiously. She didn't say it. My wife hadn't come. Wouldn't come. If I couldn't hold her when I was properly alive, why should my near-death bring her running? Jenny. My wife.

Still my wife in spite of three years' separation. Regret,
I think, held both of us back from the final step of
divorce: we had been through passion, delight, dissen-
sion, anger, and explosion. Only regret was left, and it
wouldn't be strong enough to bring her to the hospital.
She'd seen me in too many hospitals before. There was
no more drama, no more impact, in my form recum-
bent, even with tubes. She wouldn't come. Wouldn't
telephone. Wouldn't write. It was stupid of me to want
her to.

Time passed slowly and I didn't enjoy it, but eventually all the tubes except the one in my arm were
removed and I began to heal. The police didn't find
Andrews. Jenny didn't come, Radnor's typists sent me
a get-well card, and the hospital sent the bill.

Chico slouched in one evening, his hands in his
pockets and the usual derisive grin on his face. He
looked me over without haste and the grin, if anything,
widened.

'Rather you than me, mate,' he said.

'Go to bloody hell.'

He laughed. And well he might. I had been doing
his job for him because he had a date with a girl, and
Andrews' bullet should have been his bellyache, not
mine.

'Andrews,' he said musingly. 'Who'd have thought
it? Sodding little weasel. All the same, if you'd done
what I said and stayed in the washroom, and taken his
photo quiet like on the old infra-red, we'd have picked

10

him up later nice and easy and you'd have been lolling on your arse around the office as usual instead of sweating away in here.'

'You needn't rub it in,' I said. 'What would you have done?'

He grinned. 'The same as you, I expect. I'd have reckoned it would only take the old one-two for that little worm to come across with who sent him.'

'And now we don't know.'

'No.' He sighed. 'And the old man ain't too sweet about the whole thing. He did know I was using the office as a trap, but he didn't think it would work, and now this has happened he doesn't like it. He's leaning over backwards, hushing the whole thing up. They might have sent a bomb, not a sneak thief, he said. And of course Andrews bust a window getting in, which I've probably got to pay for. Trust the little sod not to know how to pick a lock.'

'I'll pay for the window,' I said.

'Yeah,' he grinned. 'I reckoned you would if I told you.'

He wandered round the room, looking at things. There wasn't much to see.

'What's in that bottle dripping into your arm?'

'Food of some sort, as far as I can gather. They never give me anything to eat.'

'Afraid you might bust out again, I expect.'

'I guess so,' I agreed.

He wandered on. 'Haven't you got a telly then?

11

Cheer you up a bit, wouldn't it, to see some other silly buggers getting shot?' He looked at the chart on the bottom of the bed. 'Your temperature was 102 this morning, did they tell you? Do you reckon you're going to kick it?'

'No.'

'Near thing, from what I've heard. Jones-boy said there was enough of your life's blood dirtying up the office floor to make a tidy few black puddings.'

I didn't appreciate Jones-boy's sense of humour.

Chico said, 'Are you coming back?'

'Perhaps.'

He began tying knots in the cord of the window blind. I watched him, a thin figure imbued with so much energy that it was difficult for him to keep still. He had spent two fruitless nights watching in the washroom before I took his place, and I knew that if he hadn't been dedicated to his job he couldn't have borne such inactivity. He was the youngest of Radnor's team. About twenty-four, he believed, though as he had been abandoned as a child on the steps of a police station in a pushchair, no one knew for certain.

If the police hadn't been so kind to him, Chico sometimes said, he would have taken advantage of his later opportunities and turned delinquent. He never grew tall enough to be a copper. Radnor's was the best he could do. And he did very well by Radnor. He put two and two together quickly and no one on the staff had faster physical reactions. Judo and wrestling were his hobbies, and along with the regular throws and holds he had been taught some strikingly dirty tricks. His smallness bore no relation whatever to his effectiveness in his job.

'How are you getting on with the case?' I asked.

'What case? Oh . . . that. Well since you got shot the heat's off, it seems. Brinton's had no threatening calls or letters since the other night. Whoever was leaning on him must have got the wind up. Anyway, he's feeling a bit safer all of a sudden and he's carping a lot to the old man about fees. Another day or two, I give it, and there won't be no one holding his hand at night. Anyway, I've been pulled off it. I'm flying from Newmarket to Ireland tomorrow, sharing a stall with a hundred thousand pounds' worth of stallion.'

Escort duty was another little job I never did. Chico liked it, and went often. As he had once thrown a fifteen stone would-be nobbler over a seven-foot wall, he was always much in demand.

'You ought to come back,' he said suddenly.

'Why?' I was surprised.

'I don't know . . .' he grinned. 'Silly, really, when you do sweet eff-all, but everybody seems to have got used to you being around. You're missed, kiddo, you'd be surprised.'

'You're joking, of course.'

'Yeah . . .' He undid the knots in the window cord, shrugged, and thrust his hands into his trouser pockets. 'God, this place gives you the willies. It reeks of warm

13

disinfectant. Creepy. How much longer are you going to lie here rotting?'

'Days,' I said mildly. 'Have a good trip.'

'See you.' He nodded, drifting in relief to the door. 'Do you want anything? I mean, books or anything?'

'Nothing, thanks.'

'Nothing... that's just your form, Sid, mate. You don't want nothing.' He grinned and went.

I wanted nothing. My form. My trouble. I'd had what I wanted most in the world and lost it irrevocably. I'd found nothing else to want. I stared at the ceiling, waiting for time to pass. All I wanted was to get back on my feet and stop feeling as though I had eaten a hundredweight of green apples.

Three weeks after the shooting I had a visit from my father-in-law. He came in the late afternoon, bringing with him a small parcel which he put without comment on the table beside the bed.

'Well, Sid, how are you?' He settled himself into an easy chair, crossed his legs, and lit a cigar.

'Cured, more or less. I'll be out of here soon.'

'Good. Good. And your plans are ...?'

'I haven't any.'

'You can't go back to the agency without some ... er ... convalescence,' he remarked.

'I suppose not.'

'You might prefer somewhere in the sun,' he said, studying the cigar. 'But I would like it if you could spend some time with me at Aynsford.'

I didn't answer immediately.

'Will . . .?' I began and stopped, wavering.

'No,' he said. 'She won't be there. She's gone out to Athens to stay with Jill and Tony. I saw her off yesterday. She sent you her regards.'

'Thanks,' I said dryly. As usual I did not know whether to be glad or sorry that I was not going to meet my wife. Nor was I sure that this trip to see her sister Jill was not as diplomatic as Tony's job in the Corps.

'You'll come, then? Mrs Cross will look after you splendidly.'

'Yes, Charles, thank you. I'd like to come for a little while.'

He gripped the cigar in his teeth, squinted through the smoke, and took out his diary.

'Let's see, suppose you leave here in, say, another week . . . No point in hurrying out before you're fit to go . . . that brings us to the twenty-sixth . . . hm . . . now, suppose you come down a week on Sunday, I'll be at home all that day. Will that suit you?'

'Yes, fine, if the doctors agree.'

'Right, then.' He wrote in the diary, put it away, and took the cigar carefully out of his mouth, smiling at me with the usual inscrutable blankness in his eyes. He sat easily in his dark city suit, Rear-Admiral Charles Roland, RN, retired, a man carrying his sixty-six years lightly. War photographs showed him tall, straight, bony almost, with a high forehead and thick dark hair. Time had greyed the hair, which in receding left his forehead higher than ever, and had added weight where it did no harm. His manner was ordinarily extremely charming and occasionally patronizingly offensive. I had been on the receiving end of both.

He relaxed in the armchair, talking unhurriedly about steeplechasing.

'What do you think of that new race at Sandown? I don't know about you, but I think it's framed rather awkwardly. They're bound to get a tiny field with those conditions and if Devil's Dyke doesn't run after all the whole thing will be a non-crowd puller *par excellence.*'

His interest in the game only dated back a few years, but recently to his pleasure he had been invited by one or two courses to act as a Steward. Listening to his easy familiarity with racing problems and racing jargon, I was in a quiet inward way amused. It was impossible to forget his reaction long ago to Jenny's engagement to a jockey, his unfriendly rejection of me as a future son-in-law, his absence from our wedding, the months afterwards of frigid disapproval, the way he had seldom spoken to or even looked at me.

I believed at the time that it was sheer snobbery, but it wasn't as simple as that. Certainly he didn't think me good enough, but not only, or even mainly, on a class distinction level; and probably we would never have understood each other, or come eventually to like each other, had it not been for a wet afternoon and a game of chess.

Jenny and I went to Aynsford for one of our rare, painful Sunday visits. We ate our roast beef in near silence, Jenny's father staring rudely out of the window and drumming his fingers on the table. I made up my mind that we wouldn't go again. I'd had enough. Jenny could visit him alone.

After lunch she said she wanted to sort out some of her books now that we had a new bookcase, and disappeared upstairs. Charles Roland and I looked at each other in dislike, the afternoon stretching drearily ahead and the downpour outside barring retreat into the garden and park beyond.

'Do you play chess?' he asked in a bored, expecting-the-answer-no voice.

'I know the moves,' I said.

He shrugged (it was more like a squirm), but clearly thinking that it would be less trouble than making conversation, he brought a chess set out and gestured to me to sit opposite him. He was normally a good player, but that afternoon he was bored and irritated and inattentive, and I beat him quite early in the game. He couldn't believe it. He sat staring at the board, fingering the bishop with which I'd got him in a classic discovered check.

'Where did you learn?' he said eventually, still looking down.

'Out of a book.'

'Have you played a great deal?'

'No, not much. Here and there.' But I'd played with some good players.

'Hm.' He paused. 'Will you play again?'

'Yes, if you like.'

We played. It was a long game and ended in a draw, with practically every piece off the board. A fortnight later he rang up and asked us, next time we came, to stay overnight. It was the first twig of the olive branch. We went more often and more willingly to Aynsford after that. Charles and I played chess occasionally and won a roughly equal number of games, and he began rather tentatively to go to the races. Ironically, from then on our mutual respect grew strong enough to survive even the crash of Jenny's and my marriage, and Charles's interest in racing expanded and deepened with every passing year.

'I went to Ascot yesterday,' he was saying, tapping ash off his cigar. 'It wasn't a bad crowd, considering the weather. I had a drink with that handicapper fellow, John Pagan. Nice chap. He was very pleased with himself because he got six abreast over the last in the handicap hurdle. There was an objection after the three mile chase – flagrant bit of crossing on the run-in. Carter swore blind he was leaning and couldn't help it, but you can never believe a word he says. Anyway, the Stewards took it away from him. The only thing they could do. Wally Gibbons rode a brilliant finish in the handicap hurdle and then made an almighty hash of the novice chase.'

18

'He's heavy-handed with novices,' I agreed.

'Wonderful course, that.'

'The tops.' A wave of weakness flowed outwards from my stomach. My legs trembled under the bedclothes. It was always happening. Infuriating.

'Good job it belongs to the Queen and is safe from the land-grabbers.' He smiled.

'Yes, I suppose so . . .'

'You're tired,' he said abruptly. 'I've stayed too long.'

'No,' I protested. 'Really, I'm fine.'

He put out the cigar, however, and stood up. 'I know you too well, Sid. Your idea of fine is not the same as anyone else's. If you're not well enough to come to Aynsford a week on Sunday you'll let me know. Otherwise I'll see you then.'

'Yes, OK.'

He went away, leaving me to reflect that I did still tire infernally easily. Must be old age, I grinned to myself, old age at thirty-one. Old tired battered Sid Halley, poor old chap. I grimaced at the ceiling.

A nurse came in for the evening jobs.

'You've got a parcel,' she said brightly, as if speaking to a retarded child. 'Aren't you going to open it?'

I had forgotten about Charles' parcel.

'Would you like me to open it for you? I mean, you can't find things like opening parcels very easy with a hand like yours.'

She was only being kind. 'Yes,' I said. 'Thank you.'

She snipped through the wrappings with scissors

19

from her pocket and looked dubiously at the slim dark book she found inside.

'I suppose it is meant for you? I mean somehow it doesn't seem like things people usually give patients.'

She put the book into my right hand and I read the title embossed in gold on the cover. *Outline of Company Law.*

'My father-in-law left it on purpose. He meant it for me.'

'Oh well, I suppose it's difficult to think of things for people who can't eat grapes and such.' She bustled around, efficient and slightly bullying, and finally left me alone again.

Outline of Company Law. I riffled through the pages. It was certainly a book about company law. Solidly legal. Not light entertainment for an invalid. I put the book on the table.

Charles Roland was a man of subtle mind, and subtlety gave him much pleasure. It hadn't been my parentage that he had objected to so much as what he took to be Jenny's rejection of his mental standards in choosing a jockey for a husband. He'd never met a jockey before, disliked the idea of racing, and took it for granted that everyone engaged in it was either a rogue or a moron. He'd wanted both his daughters to marry clever men, clever more than handsome or well-born or rich, so that he could enjoy their company. Jill had obliged him with Tony, Jenny disappointed him with me: that was how he saw it, until he found that at least I could play chess with him now and then.

Knowing his subtle habits, I took it for granted that he had not idly brought such a book and hadn't chosen it or left it by mistake. He meant me to read it for a purpose. Intended it to be useful to me – or to him – later on. Did he think he could manoeuvre me into business, now that I hadn't distinguished myself at the agency? A nudge, that book was. A nudge in some specific direction.

I thought back over what he had said, looking for a clue. He'd been insistent that I should go to Aynsford. He'd sent Jenny to Athens. He'd talked about racing, about the new race at Sandown, about Ascot, John Pagan, Carter, Wally Gibbons ... nothing there that I could see had the remotest connection with company law.

I sighed, shutting my eyes. I didn't feel too well. I didn't have to read the book, or go wherever Charles pointed. And yet ... why not? There was nothing I urgently wanted to do instead. I decided to do my stodgy homework. Tomorrow.

Perhaps.

CHAPTER TWO

Four days after my arrival at Aynsford I came downstairs from an afternoon's rest to find Charles delving into a large packing case in the centre of the hall. Strewn round on the half-acre of parquet was a vast amount of wood shavings, white and curly, and arranged carefully on a low table beside him were the first trophies out of the lucky dip, appearing to me to be dull chunks of rock.

I picked one of them up. One side had been ground into a smooth face and across the bottom of this was stuck a neat label. 'Porphyry' it said, and beneath, 'Carver Mineralogy Foundation'.

'I didn't know you had an obsessive interest in quartz.'

He gave me one of his blank stares, which I knew didn't mean that he hadn't heard or understood what I'd said, but that he didn't intend to explain.

'I'm going fishing,' he said, plunging his arms back into the box.

So the quartz was bait. I put down the porphyry and

picked up another piece. It was small, the size of a squared-off egg, and beautiful, as clear and translucent as glass. The label said simply 'Rock Crystal'.

'If you want something useful to do,' said Charles, 'you can write out what sort they all are on the plain labels you will find on my desk, and then soak the Foundation's label off and put the new ones on. Keep the old ones, though. We'll have to replace them when all this stuff goes back.'

'All right,' I agreed.

The next chunk I picked up was heavy with gold. 'Are these valuable?' I asked.

'Some are. There's a booklet somewhere. But I told the Foundation they'd be safe enough. I said I'd have a private detective in the house all the time guarding them.'

I laughed and began writing the new labels, working from the inventory. The lumps of quartz overflowed from the table on to the floor before the box was empty.

'There's another box outside,' Charles observed.

'Oh no!'

'I collect quartz,' said Charles with dignity, 'and don't you forget it. I've collected it for years. Years. Haven't I?'

'Years,' I agreed. 'You're an authority. Who wouldn't be an authority on rocks, after a life at sea.'

'I've got exactly one day to learn them in,' said Charles smiling. 'They've come later than I asked. I'll have to be word perfect by tomorrow night.'

He fetched the second lot, which was much smaller and was fastened with important looking seals. Inside were uncut gem quartz crystals, mounted on small individual black plinths. Their collective value was staggering. The Carver Foundation must have taken the private detective bit seriously. They'd have held tight to their rocks if they'd seen my state of health.

We worked for some time changing the labels while Charles muttered their names like incantations under his breath. 'Chrysoprase, Aventurine, Agate, Onyx, Chalcedony, Tiger-eye, Carnelian, Citrine, Rose, Plasma, Basanite, Bloodstone, Chert. Why the hell did I start this?'

'Well, why?'

I got the blank stare again. He wasn't telling. 'You can test me on them,' he said.

We carried them piece by piece into the dining-room, where I found the glass-doored bookshelves on each side of the fire had been cleared of their yards of leather-bound classics.

'They can go up there later,' said Charles, covering the huge dining-room table with a thick felt. 'Put them on the table for now.'

When they were all arranged he walked slowly round learning them. There were about fifty altogether. I tested him after a while, at his request, and he muddled up and forgot about half of them. They were difficult, because so many looked alike.

He sighed. 'It's time we had a noggin and you went

back to bed.' He led the way into the little sitting-room he occasionally referred to as the wardroom, and poured a couple of stiffish brandies. He raised his glass to me and appreciatively took a mouthful. There was a suppressed excitement in his expression, a glint in the unfathomable eyes. I sipped the brandy, wondering with more interest what he was up to.

'I have a few people coming for the weekend,' he said casually, squinting at his glass. 'A Mr and Mrs Rex van Dysart, a Mr and Mrs Howard Kraye, and my cousin Viola, who will act as hostess.'

'Old friends?' I murmured, having only ever heard of Viola.

'Not very,' he said smoothly. 'They'll be here in time for dinner tomorrow night. You'll meet them then.'

'But I'll make it an odd number . . . I'll go up before they come and stay out of your way for most of the weekend.'

'No,' he said sharply. Much too vehemently. I was surprised. Then it came to me suddenly that all he had been doing with his rocks and his offer of a place for my convalescence was to engineer a meeting between me and the weekend guests. He offered me rest. He offered Mr van Dysart, or perhaps Mr Kraye, rocks. Both of us had swallowed the hook. I decided to give the line a tug, to see just how determined was the fisherman.

'I'd be better upstairs. You know I can't eat normal meals.' My diet at that time consisted of brandy, beef juice, and some vacuum-packed pots of stuff which had been developed for feeding astronauts. Apparently none of these things affected the worst shot-up bits of my digestive tract.

'People loosen up over the dinner table ... they talk more, and you get to know them better.' He was carefully unpersuasive.

'They'll talk to you just as well if I'm not there – better in fact. And I couldn't stand watching you all tuck into steaks.'

He said musingly, 'You can stand anything, Sid. But I think you'd be interested. Not bored, I promise you. More brandy?'

I shook my head, and relented. 'All right, I'll be there at dinner, if you want it.'

He relaxed only a fraction. A controlled and subtle man. I smiled at him, and he guessed that I'd been playing him along.

'You're a bastard,' he said.

From him, it was a compliment.

The transistor beside my bed was busy with the morning news as I slowly ate my breakfast pot of astronaut paste.

'The race meeting scheduled for today and tomorrow at Seabury,' the announcer said, 'has had to be abandoned. A tanker carrying liquid chemical crashed and overturned at dusk yesterday afternoon on a road crossing the racecourse. There was considerable damage to the turf, and after an examination this morning the Stewards regretfully decided that it was not fit to be raced on. It is hoped to replace the affected turf in time for the next meeting in a fortnight's time, but an announcement will be made about this at a later date. And here is the weather forecast . . .'

Poor Seabury, I thought, always in the wars. It was only a year since their stable block had been burned down on the eve of a meeting. They had had to cancel then too, because temporary stables could not be erected overnight, and the National Hunt Committee in consultation with Radnor had decided that indiscriminate stabling in the surrounding district was too much of a security risk.

It was a nice track to ride on, a long circuit with no sharp bends, but there had been trouble with the surface in the spring; a drain of some sort had collapsed during a hurdle race. The forefeet of one unfortunate horse had gone right through into it to a depth of about eighteen inches and he had broken a leg. In the resulting pile-up two more horses had been ruinously injured and one jockey badly concussed. Maps of the course didn't even warn that the drain existed, and I'd heard trainers wondering whether there were any more antique waterways ready to collapse with as little notice. The executive, on their side, naturally swore there weren't.

For some time I lay day-dreaming, racing round Seabury again in my mind, and wishing uselessly, hopelessly, achingly, that I could do it again in fact.

Mrs Cross tapped on the door and came in. She was a quiet, unobtrusive mouse of a woman with soft brown hair and a slight outward cast in her grey-green eyes. Although she seemed to have no spirit whatever and seldom spoke, she ran the place like oiled machinery, helped by a largely invisible squad of 'dailies'. She had the great virtue to me of being fairly new in the job and impartial on the subject of Jenny and me. I wouldn't have trusted her predecessor, who had been fanatically fond of Jenny, not to have added cascara to my beef juice.

'The Admiral would like to know if you are feeling well today, Mr Halley,' said Mrs Cross primly, picking up my breakfast tray.

'Yes, I am, thank you.' More or less.

'He said, then, when you're ready would you join him in the dining-room?'

'The rocks?'

She gave me a small smile. 'He was up before me this morning, and had his breakfast on a tray in there. Shall I tell him you'll come down?'

'Please.'

When she had gone, and while I was slowly dressing, the telephone bell rang. Not long afterwards Charles himself came upstairs.

'That was the police,' he said abruptly, with a frown.

'Apparently they've found a body and they want you to go and identify it.'

'Whose body, for heaven's sake?'

'They didn't say. They said they would send a car for you immediately, though. I gathered they really rang here to locate you.'

'I haven't any relatives. It must be a mistake.'

He shrugged. 'We'll know soon, anyway. Come down now and test me on the quartz. I think I've got it taped at last.'

We went down to the dining-room, where I found he was right. He went round the whole lot without a mistake. I changed the order in which they stood, but it didn't throw him. He smiled, very pleased with himself.

'Word perfect,' he said. 'Let's put them up on the shelves now. At least, we'll put all the least valuable ones up there, and the gem stones in the bookcase in the drawing-room – that one with the curtains inside the glass doors.'

'They ought to be in a safe.' I had said it yesterday evening as well.

'They were quite all right on the dining-room table last night, in spite of your fears.'

'As the consultant private detective in the case I still advise a safe.'

He laughed. 'You know bloody well I haven't got a safe. But as consultant private detective you can guard the things properly tonight. You can put them under your pillow. How's that?'

29

'OK.' I nodded.

'You're not serious?'

'Well no . . . they'd be too hard under the pillow.'

'Damn it . . .'

'But upstairs, either with you or me, yes. Some of those stones really are valuable. You must have had to pay a big insurance premium on them.'

'Er . . . no,' admitted Charles. 'I guaranteed to replace anything which was damaged or lost.'

I goggled. 'I know you're rich, but . . . you're an absolute nut. Get them insured at once. Have you any idea what each specimen is worth?'

'No, as a matter of fact . . . no. I didn't ask.'

'Well, if you've got a collector coming to stay, he'll expect you to remember how much you paid for each.'

'I thought of that,' he interrupted. 'I inherited them all from a distant cousin. That covers a lot of ignorance, not only costs and values but about crystallography and distribution and rarity, and everything specialized. I found I couldn't possibly learn enough in one day. Just to be able to show some familiarity with the collection should be enough.'

'That's fair enough. But you ring the Carver Foundation at once and find out what the stones are worth just the same, and then get straight on to your broker. The trouble with you, Charles, is that you are too honest. Other people aren't. This is the bad rough world you're in now, not the Navy.'

30

'Very well,' he said amicably. 'I'll do as you say. Hand me that inventory.'

He went to telephone and I began putting the chunks of quartz on the empty bookshelves, but before I had done much the front door bell rang. Mrs Cross went to answer it and presently came to tell me that a policeman was asking for me.

I put my useless deformed left hand into my pocket, as I always did with strangers, and went into the hall. A tall heavy young man in uniform stood there, giving the impression of trying not to be overawed by his rather grand surroundings. I remembered how it felt.

'Is it about this body?' I asked.

'Yes, sir. I believe you are expecting us.'

'Whose body is it?'

'I don't know, sir. I was just asked to take you.'

'Well . . . where to?'

'Epping Forest, sir.'

'But that's miles away,' I protested.

'Yes, sir,' he agreed, with a touch of gloom.

'Are you sure it's me that's wanted?'

'Oh, positive, sir.'

'Well, all right. Sit down a minute while I get my coat and say where I'm going.'

The policeman drove on his gears, which I found tiring. It took two hours to go from Aynsford west of Oxford, to Epping Forest, and it was much too long. Finally, however, we were met at a crossroads by another policeman on a motor cycle, and followed him down a twisting secondary road. The forest stretched away all round, bare-branched and mournful in the grey damp day.

Round the bend we came on a row of two cars and a van, parked. The motor cyclist stopped and dismounted, and the policeman and I got out.

'ETA 12.15,' said the motor cyclist looking at his watch. 'You're late. The brass has been waiting here twenty minutes.'

'Traffic like caterpillars on the A40,' said my driver defensively.

'You should have used your bell,' the motor cyclist grinned. 'Come on. It's over this way.'

He led us down a barely perceptible track into the wood. We walked on dead brown leaves, rustling. After about half a mile we came to a group of men standing round a screen made of hessian. They were stamping their feet to keep warm and talking in quiet voices.

'Mr Halley?' One of them shook hands, a pleasant capable looking man in middle age who introduced himself as Chief-Inspector Cornish. 'We're sorry to bring you here all this way, but we want you to see the er . . . remains . . . before we move them. I'd better warn you, it's a perfectly horrible sight.' He gave a very human shudder.

'Who is it?' I asked.

'We're hoping you can tell us that, for sure. We think . . . but we'd like you to tell us without us putting it into your head. All right? Now?'

32

I nodded. He showed me round the screen.

It was Andrews. What was left of him. He had been dead a long time, and the Epping Forest scavengers seemed to have found him tasty. I could see why the police had wanted me to see him *in situ*. He was going to fall to pieces as soon as they moved him.

'Well?'

'Thomas Andrews,' I said.

They relaxed. 'Are you sure? Positive?'

'Yes.'

'It's not just the clothes?'

'No. The shape of the hair-line. Protruding ears. Exceptionally rounded helix, vestigial lobes. Very short eyebrows, thick near the nose. Spatulate thumbs, white marks across nails. Hair growing on backs of phalanges.'

'Good,' said Cornish. 'That's conclusive, I'd say. We made a preliminary identification fairly early because of the clothes – they were detailed on the wanted-for-questioning list, of course. But our first inquiries were negative. He seems to have no family and no one could remember that he had any distinguishing marks – no tattoos, no scars, no operations, and as far as we could find out he hadn't been to a dentist all his life.'

'It was intelligent of you to check all that before you gave him to the pathologist,' I remarked.

'It was the pathologist's idea, actually.' He smiled.

'Who found him?' I asked.

'Some boys. It's usually boys who find bodies.'

'When?'

'Three days ago. But obviously he's been here weeks, probably from very soon after he took a pot at you.'

'Yes. Is the gun still in his pocket?'

Cornish shook his head. 'No sign of it.'

'You don't know yet how he died?' I asked.

'No not yet. But now you've identified him we can get on with it.'

We went out from behind the screen and some of the other men went in with a stretcher. I didn't envy them.

Cornish turned to walk back to the road with me, the driver following at a short distance. We went fairly slowly, talking about Andrews, but it seemed more like eight miles than eight hundred yards. I wasn't quite ready for jolly country rambles.

As we reached the cars he asked me to lunch with him. I shook my head, explained about the diet, and suggested a drink instead.

'Fine,' he said. 'We could both do with one after that.' He jerked his head in the direction of Andrews. 'There's a good pub down the road this way. Your driver can follow us.'

He climbed into his car and we drove after him.

In the bar, equipped with a large brandy and water for me and a whisky and sandwiches for him, we sat at a black oak table, on chintzy chairs, surrounded by horse brasses, hunting horns, warming pans, and pewter pots.

'It's funny, meeting you like this,' said Cornish, in

between bites. 'I've watched you so often racing. You've won a tidy bit for me in your time. I hardly missed a meeting on the old Dunstable course, before they sold it for building. I don't get so much racing now, it's so far to a course. Nowhere now to slip along to for a couple of hours in an afternoon.' He grinned cheerfully and went on. 'You gave us some rare treats at Dunstable. Remember the day you rode that ding-dong finish on Brushwood?'

'I remember,' I said.

'You literally picked that horse up and carried him home.' He took another bite. 'I never heard such cheering. There's no mistake about it, you were something. Pity you had to give it up.'

'Yes . . .'

'Still, I suppose that's a risk you run, steeplechasing. There is always one crash too many.'

'That's right.'

'Where was it you finally bought it?'

'At Stratford on Avon, two years ago last May.'

He shook his head sympathetically. 'Rotten bad luck.'

I smiled. 'I'd had a pretty good run, though, before that.'

'I'll say you did.' He smacked his palm on the table. 'I took the Missus down to Kempton on Boxing Day, three or four years ago . . .' He went on talking with enjoyment about races he had watched, revealing himself as a true enthusiast, one of the people without whose interest all racing would collapse. Finally, regretfully, he finished his whisky and looked at his watch. 'I'll have to get back. I've enjoyed meeting you. It's odd how things turn out, isn't it? I don't suppose you ever thought when you were riding that you would be good at this sort of work.'

'What do you mean, good?' I asked, surprised.

'Hm? Oh, Andrews, of course. That description of his clothes you gave after he had shot you. And identifying him today. Most professional. Very efficient.' He grinned.

'Getting shot wasn't very efficient,' I pointed out.

He shrugged. 'That could happen to anyone, believe me ... I shouldn't worry about that.'

I smiled, as the driver jerked me back to Aynsford, at the thought that anyone could believe me good at detective work. There was a simple explanation of my being able to describe and identify – I had read so many of the Missing Persons and Divorce files. The band of ex-policemen who compiled them knew what to base identification on, the unchanging things like ears and hands, not hair colour or the wearing of spectacles or a moustache. One of them had told me without pride that wigs, beards, face-padding, and the wearing of or omission of cosmetics made no impression on him, because they were not what he looked at. 'Ears and fingers,' he said, 'they can't disguise those. They never think of trying. Stick to ears and fingers, and you don't go far wrong.'

Ears and fingers were just about all there was left of Andrews to identify. The unappetizing gristly bits.

The driver decanted me at Charles' back door and I walked along the passage to the hall. When I had one foot on the bottom tread of the staircase Charles himself appeared at the drawing-room door.

'Oh, hullo, I thought it might be you. Come in here and look at these.'

Reluctantly leaving the support of the banisters I followed him into the drawing-room.

'There,' he said, pointing. He had fixed up a strip of light inside his bookcase and it shone down on to the quartz gems, bringing them to sparkling life. The open doors with their red silk curtains made a softly glowing frame. It was an eye-catching and effective arrangement, and I told him so.

'Good. The light goes on automatically when the doors are open . . . nifty, don't you think?' He laughed. 'And you can set your mind at rest. They are now insured.'

'That's good.'

He shut the doors of the bookcase and the light inside went out. The red curtains discreetly hid their treasure. Turning to me more seriously, he said, 'Whose body?'

'Andrews.'

'The man who shot you? How extraordinary. Suicide?'

'No, I don't think so. The gun wasn't there, anyway.'

He made a quick gesture towards the chair. 'My dear Sid, sit down. You look like d . . . er . . . a bit worn out. You shouldn't have gone all that way. Put your feet up, I'll fetch you a drink.' He fussed over me like a mother hen, fetching me first water, then brandy, and finally a cup of warm beef juice from Mrs Cross, and sat opposite me watching while I dispatched it.

'Do you like that stuff?' he asked.

'Yes, luckily.'

'We used to have it when we were children. A ritual once a week. My father used to drain it out of the Sunday joint, propping the dish on the carving fork. We all loved it, but I haven't had any for years.'

'Try some?' I offered him the cup.

He took it and tasted it. 'Yes, it's good. Takes me back sixty years . . .' He smiled companionably, relaxing in his chair, and I told him about Andrews and the long-dead state he was in.

'It sounds,' he said slowly, 'as if he might have been murdered.'

'I wouldn't be surprised. He was young and healthy. He wouldn't just lie down and die of exposure in Essex.'

Charles laughed.

'What time are your guests expected?' I asked, glancing at the clock. It was just after five.

'About six.'

'I think I'll go up and lie on my bed for a while, then.'

38

'You are all right, Sid, aren't you? I mean, really all right?'

'Oh yes. Just tired.'

'Will you come down to dinner?' There was the faintest undercurrent of disappointment in his casual voice. I thought of all his hard work with the rocks and the amount of manoeuvring he had done. Besides, I was getting definitely curious myself about his intentions.

'Yes,' I nodded, getting up. 'Lay me a teaspoon.'

I made it upstairs and lay on my bed, sweating. And cursing. Although the bullet had missed everything vital in tearing holes through my gut, it had singed and upset a couple of nerves, and they had warned me in the hospital that it would be some time before I felt well. It didn't please me that so far they were right.

I heard the visitors arrive, heard their loud cheerful voices as they were shown up to their rooms, the doors shutting, the bath waters running, the various bumps and murmurs from the adjoining rooms; and eventually the diminishing chatter as they finished changing and went downstairs past my door. I heaved myself off the bed, took off the loose-waisted slacks and jersey shirt I felt most comfortable in, and put on a white cotton shirt and dark grey suit.

My face looked back at me, pale, gaunt, and dark-eyed as I brushed my hair. A bit of death's head at the feast. I grinned nastily at my reflection. It was only a slight improvement.

CHAPTER THREE

By the time I got to the foot of the stairs, Charles and his guests were coming across the hall from the drawing-room to the dining-room. The men all wore dinner jackets and the women, long dresses. Charles deliberately hadn't warned me, I reflected. He knew my convalescent kit didn't include a black tie.

He didn't stop and introduce me to his guests, but nodded slightly and went straight on into the dining-room, talking with charm to the rounded, fluffy little woman who walked beside him. Behind came Viola and a tall dark girl of striking good looks. Viola, Charles's elderly widowed cousin, gave me a passing half-smile, embarrassed and worried. I wondered what was the matter: normally she greeted me with affection, and it was only a short time since she had written warm wishes for my recovery. The girl beside her barely glanced in my direction, and the two men bringing up the rear didn't look at me at all.

Shrugging, I followed them into the dining-room. There was no mistaking the place laid for me: it consisted, in actual fact, of a spoon, a mat, a glass, and a fork, and it was situated in the centre of one of the sides. Opposite me was an empty gap. Charles seated his guests, himself in his usual place at the end of the table, with fluffy Mrs van Dysart on his right, and the striking Mrs Kraye on his left. I sat between Mrs Kraye and Rex van Dysart. It was only gradually that I sorted everyone out. Charles made no introductions whatsoever.

The groups at each end of the table fell into animated chat and paid me as much attention as a speed limit. I began to think I would go back to bed.

The manservant whom Charles engaged on these occasions served small individual tureens of turtle soup. My tureen, I found, contained more beef juice. Bread was passed, spoons clinked, salt and pepper were shaken, and the meal began. Still no one spoke to me, though the visitors were growing slightly curious. Mrs van Dysart flicked her sharp china blue eyes from Charles to me and back again, inviting an introduction. None came. He went on talking to the two women with almost overpowering charm, apparently oblivious.

Rex van Dysart on my left offered me bread with lifted eyebrows and a faint non-committal smile. He was a large man with a flat white face, heavy black rimmed spectacles and a domineering manner. When I refused the bread he put the basket down on the table, gave me the briefest of nods, and turned back to Viola.

Even before he brought quartz into his conversation I guessed it was for Howard Kraye that the show was being put on; and I disliked him on sight with a hackle-raising antipathy that disconcerted me. If Charles was planning that I should ever work for, or with, or near Mr Kraye, I thought, he could think again.

He was a substantial man of about forty-eight to fifty, with shoulders, waist and hips all knocking forty-four. The dinner jacket sat on him with the ease of a second skin, and when he shot his cuffs occasionally he did so without affectation, showing off noticeably well manicured hands.

He had tidy grey-brown hair, straight eyebrows, narrow nose, small firm mouth, rounded freshly shaven chin, and very high unwrinkled lower eyelids, which gave him a secret, shuttered look.

A neat enclosed face like a mask, with perhaps something rotten underneath. You could almost smell it across the dinner table. I guessed, rather fancifully, that he knew too much about too many vices. But on top he was smooth. Much too smooth. In my book, a nasty type of phony. I listened to him talking to Viola.

'. . . So when Doria and I got to New York I looked up those fellows in that fancy crystal palace on First Avenue and got them moving. You have to give the clothes-horse diplomats a lead, you know, they've absolutely no initiative of their own. Look, I told them, unilateral action is not only inadvisable, its impracticable. But they are so steeped in their own brand of pragmatism that informed opinion has as much chance of osmosing as mercury through rhyolite . . .'

Viola was nodding wisely while not understanding a word. The pretentious rigmarole floated comfortably over her sensible head and left her unmoved. But its flashiness seemed to me to be part of a gigantic confidence trick: one was meant to be enormously impressed. I couldn't believe that Charles had fallen under his spell. It was impossible. Not my subtle, clever, cool-headed father-in-law. Mr van Dysart, however, hung on every word.

By the end of the soup his wife at the other end of the table could contain her curiosity no longer. She put down her spoon, and with her eyes on me said to Charles in a low but clearly audible voice, 'Who is that?'

All the heads turned towards him, as if they had been waiting for the question. Charles lifted his chin and spoke distinctly, so that they should all hear the answer.

'That,' he said, 'is my son-in-law.' His tone was light, amused, and infinitely contemptuous; and it jabbed raw on a nerve I had thought long dead. I looked at him sharply, and his eyes met mine, blank and expressionless.

My gaze slid up over and past his head to the wall behind him. There for some years, and certainly that morning, had hung an oil painting of me on a horse going over a fence at Cheltenham. In its place there was

43

now an old-fashioned seascape, brown with Victorian varnish.

Charles was watching me. I looked back at him briefly and said nothing. I suppose he knew I wouldn't. My only defence against his insults long ago had been silence, and he was counting on my instant reaction being the same again.

Mrs van Dysart leaned forward a little, and with waking malice murmured, 'Do go on, Admiral.'

Without hesitation Charles obeyed her, in the same flaying voice. 'He was fathered, as far as he knows, by a window cleaner on a nineteen-year-old unmarried girl from the Liverpool slums. She later worked, I believe, as a packer in a biscuit factory.'

'Admiral, no!' exclaimed Mrs van Dysart breathlessly.

'Indeed yes,' nodded Charles. 'As you might guess, I did my best to stop my daughter making such an unsuitable match. He is small, as you see, and he has a crippled hand. Working class and undersized ... but my daughter was determined. You know what girls are.' He sighed.

'Perhaps she was sorry for him,' suggested Mrs van Dysart.

'Maybe,' said Charles. He hadn't finished, and wasn't to be deflected. 'If she had met him as a student of some sort, one might have understood it ... but he isn't even educated. He finished school at fifteen to be apprenticed to a trade. He has been unemployed now for some time. My daughter, I may say, has left him.'

I sat like stone, looking down at the congealed puddle at the bottom of my soup dish, trying to loosen the clamped muscles of my jaw, and to think straight. Not four hours ago he'd shown concern for me and had drunk from my cup. As far as I could ever be certain of anything, his affection for me was genuine and unchanged. So he must have a good reason for what he was doing to me now. At least I hoped so.

I glanced at Viola. She hadn't protested. She was looking unhappily down at her place. I remembered her embarrassment out in the hall, and I guessed that Charles had warned her what to expect. He might have warned me too, I thought grimly.

Not unexpectedly, they were all looking at me. The dark and beautiful Doria Kraye raised her lovely eyebrows and in a flat, nasal voice, remarked, 'You don't take offence, then.' It was halfway to a sneer. Clearly she thought I ought to take offence, if I had any guts.

'He is not offended,' said Charles easily. 'Why should the truth offend?'

'It is true then,' asked Doria down her flawless nose, 'that you are illegitimate, and all the rest?'

I took a deep breath and eased my muscles.

'Yes.'

There was an uncomfortable short silence. Doria said, 'Oh,' blankly, and began to crumble her bread.

On cue, and no doubt summoned by Charles' foot on the bell, the manservant came in to remove the

45

plates, and conversation trickled back to the party like cigarette smoke after a cancer scare.

I sat thinking of the details Charles had left out: the fact that my twenty-year-old father, working overtime for extra cash, had fallen from a high ladder and been killed three days before his wedding day, and that I had been born eight months later. The fact that my young mother, finding that she was dying from some obscure kidney ailment, had taken me from grammar school at fifteen, and because I was small for my age had apprenticed me to a racehorse trainer in Newmarket, so that I should have a home and someone to turn to when she had gone. They had been good enough people, both of them, and Charles knew that I thought so.

The next course was some sort of fish smothered in mushroom coloured sauce. My astronaut's delight, coming at the same time, didn't look noticeably different, as it was not in its pot, but out on a plate. Dear Mrs Cross, I thought fervently, I could kiss you. I could eat it this way with a fork, single-handed. The pots needed to be held; in my case inelegantly hugged between forearm and chest; and at that moment I would have starved rather than take my left hand out of my pocket.

Fluffy Mrs van Dysart was having a ball. Clearly she relished the idea of me sitting there practically isolated, dressed in the wrong clothes, and an object of open derision to her host. With her fair frizzy hair, her baby-blue eyes, and her rose pink silk dress embroidered with silver, she looked as sweet as sugar icing. What she said showed that she thoroughly understood the pleasures of keeping a whipping boy.

'Poor relations are such a problem, aren't they?' she said to Charles sympathetically, and intentionally loud enough for me to hear. 'You can't neglect them in our position, in case the Sunday papers get hold of them and pay them to make a smear. And it's especially difficult if one has to keep them in one's own house . . . one can't, I suppose, put them to eat in the kitchen, but there are so many occasions when one could do without them. Perhaps a tray upstairs is the best thing.'

'Ah, yes,' nodded Charles smoothly, 'but they won't always agree to that.'

I half choked on a mouthful, remembering the pressure he had exerted to get me downstairs. And immediately I felt not only reassured but deeply interested. This, then, was what he had been so industriously planning, the destruction of me as a man in the eyes of his guests. He would no doubt explain why in his own good time. Meanwhile I felt slightly less inclined to go back to bed.

I glanced at Kraye, and found his greenish-amber eyes steady on my face. It wasn't as overt as in Mrs van Dysart's case, but it was there: pleasure. My toes curled inside my shoes. Interested or not, it went hard to sit tight before that loathsome, taunting half-smile. I looked down, blotting him out.

He gave me a sound halfway between a cough and a laugh, turned his head, and began talking down the table to Charles about the collection of quartz.

'So sensible of you, my dear chap, to keep them all behind glass, though most tantalizing to me from here. Is that a geode, on the middle shelf? The reflection, you know . . . I can't quite see.'

'Er . . .' said Charles, not knowing any more than I did what a geode was. 'I'm looking forward to showing them to you. After dinner, perhaps? Or tomorrow?'

'Oh, tonight, I'd hate to postpone such a treat. Did you say that you had any felspar in your collection?'

'No,' said Charles uncertainly.

'No, well, I can see it is a small specialized collection. Perhaps you are wise in sticking to silicon dioxide.'

Charles glibly launched into the cousinly bequest alibi for ignorance, which Kraye accepted with courtesy and disappointment.

'A fascinating subject, though, my dear Roland. It repays study. The earth beneath our feet, the fundamental sediment from the Triassic and Jurassic epochs, is our priceless inheritance, the source of all our life and power . . . There is nothing which interests me so much as land.'

Doria on my right gave the tiniest of snorts, which her husband didn't hear. He was busy constructing another long, polysyllabic and largely unintelligible chat on the nature of the universe.

I sat unoccupied through the steaks, the meringue

pudding, the cheese, and the fruit. Conversations went on on either side of me and occasionally past me, but a deaf mute could have taken as much part as I did. Mrs van Dysart commented on the difficulties of feeding poor relations with delicate stomachs and choosy appetites. Charles neglected to tell her that I had been shot and wasn't poor, but agreed that a weak digestion in dependants was a moral fault. Mrs van Dysart loved it. Doria occasionally looked at me as if I were an interesting specimen of low life. Rex van Dysart again offered me the bread; and that was that. Finally Viola shepherded Doria and Mrs van Dysart out to have coffee in the drawing-room and Charles offered his guests port and brandy. He passed me the brandy bottle with an air of irritation and compressed his lips in disapproval when I took some. It wasn't lost on his guests.

After a while he rose, opened the glass bookcase doors, and showed the quartz to Kraye. Piece by piece the two discussed their way along the rows, with van Dysart standing beside them exhibiting polite interest and hiding his yawns of boredom. I stayed sitting down. I also helped myself to some more brandy.

Charles kept his end up very well and went through the whole lot without a mistake. He then transferred to the drawing-room, where his gem cabinet proved a great success. I tagged along, sat in an unobtrusive chair and listened to them all talking, but I came to no conclusions except that if I didn't soon go upstairs I wouldn't get there under my own steam. It was eleven o'clock and I had had a long day. Charles didn't look round when I left the room.

Half an hour later, when his guests had come murmuring up to their rooms, he came quietly through my door and over to the bed. I was still lying on top in my shirt and trousers, trying to summon some energy to finish undressing.

He stood looking down at me, smiling.

'Well?' he said.

'It is you,' I said, 'who is the dyed-in-the-wool, twenty-four carat, unmitigated bastard.'

He laughed. 'I thought you were going to spoil the whole thing when you saw your picture had gone.' He began taking off my shoes and socks. 'You looked as bleak as the Bering Strait in December. Pyjamas?'

'Under the pillow.'

He helped me undress in his quick, neat, naval fashion.

'Why did you do it?' I said.

He waited until I was lying between the sheets, then he perched on the edge of the bed.

'Did you mind?'

'Hell, Charles . . . of course. At first anyway.'

'I'm afraid it came out beastlier than I expected, but I'll tell you why I did it. Do you remember that first game of chess we had? When you beat me out of sight? You know why you won so easily?'

'You weren't paying enough attention.'

'Exactly. I wasn't paying enough attention, because I didn't think you were an opponent worth bothering about. A bad tactical error.' He grinned. 'An admiral should know better. If you underrate a strong opponent you are at a disadvantage. If you grossly underrate him, if you are convinced he is of absolutely no account, you prepare no defence and are certain to be defeated.' He paused for a moment, and went on. 'It is therefore good strategy to delude the enemy into believing you are too weak to be considered. And that is what I was doing tonight on your behalf.'

He looked at me gravely. After some seconds I said, 'At what game, exactly, do you expect me to play Howard Kraye?'

He sighed contentedly, and smiled. 'Do you remember what he said interested him most?'

I thought back. 'Land.'

Charles nodded. 'Land. That's right. He collects it. Chunks of it, yards of it, acres of it . . .' He hesitated.

'Well?'

'You can play him,' he said slowly, 'for Seabury Racecourse.'

The enormity of it took my breath away.

'What?' I said incredulously. 'Don't be silly. I'm only . . .'

'Shut up,' he interrupted. 'I don't want to hear what you think you are only. You're intelligent, aren't you? You work for a detective agency? You wouldn't want

51

Seabury to close down? Why shouldn't you do something about it?'

'But I imagine he's after some sort of take-over bid, from what you say. You want some powerful city chap or other to oppose him, not . . . me.'

'He is very much on his guard against powerful chaps in the city, but wide open to you.'

I stopped arguing because the implications were pushing into the background my inadequacy for such a task.

'Are you sure he is after Seabury?' I asked.

'Someone is,' said Charles. 'There has been a lot of buying and selling of the shares lately, and the price per share is up although they haven't paid a dividend this year. The Clerk of the Course told me about it. He said that the directors are very worried. On paper, there is no great concentration of shares in any one name, but there wasn't at Dunstable either. There, when it came to a vote on selling out to a land developer, they found that about twenty various nominees were in fact all agents for Kraye. He carried enough of the other shareholders with him, and the racecourse was lost to housing.'

'It was all legal, though?'

'A wangle; but legal, yes. And it looks like happening again.'

'But what's to stop him if it's legal?'

'You might try.'

I stared at him in silence. He stood up and straightened the bedcover neatly. 'It would be a pity if Seabury went the way of Dunstable.' He went towards the door.

'Where does van Dysart fit in?' I asked.

'Oh,' he said, turning, 'nowhere. I met them only a week or two ago. They're on a visit from South Africa, and I was sure they wouldn't know you. And it was Mrs van Dysart I wanted. She has a tongue like a rattlesnake. I knew she would help me tear you to pieces.' He grinned. 'She'll give you a terrible weekend, I'm glad to say.'

'Thanks very much,' I said sarcastically.

'I was a bit worried that Kraye would know you by sight,' he said thoughtfully. 'But he obviously doesn't, so that's all right. And I didn't mention your name tonight, as you probably noticed. I am being careful not to.' He smiled. 'And he doesn't know my daughter married Sid Halley ... I've given him several opportunities of mentioning it, because of course none of this would have been possible if he'd known, but he hasn't responded at all. As far as Kraye is concerned,' he finished with satisfaction, 'you are a pathetic cypher.'

I said, 'Why didn't you tell me all this before? When you so carefully left me that book on company law for instance? Or at least this evening when I came back from seeing Andrews, so that I could have been prepared, at dinner?'

He opened the door and smiled across the room, his eyes blank again.

'Sleep well,' he said. 'Goodnight, Sid.'

Charles took the two men out shooting the following morning, and Viola drove their wives into Oxford to do some shopping and visit an exhibition of Venetian glass. I took the opportunity of having a good look round the Krayes' bedroom.

It wasn't until I'd been there for more than ten minutes that it struck me that two years earlier I wouldn't have dreamed of doing such a thing. Now I had done it as a matter of course, without thinking twice. I grinned sardonically. Evidently even in just sitting around in a detective agency one caught an attitude of mind. I realized, moreover, that I had instinctively gone about my search methodically and with a careful touch. In an odd way it was extremely disconcerting.

I wasn't, of course, looking for anything special: just digging a little into the Krayes' characters. I wouldn't even concede in my own mind that I was interested in the challenge Charles had so elaborately thrown down. But all the same I searched, and thoroughly.

Howard Kraye slept in crimson pyjamas with his initials embroidered in white on the pocket. His dressing-gown was of crimson brocade with black quilted collar and black tassels on the belt. His washing things, neatly arranged in a large fitted toilet case in the adjoining bathroom, were numerous and ornate. He used pine scented after-shave lotion, cologne friction rub, lemon hand cream, and an oily hair dressing, all from gold-topped cut-glass bottles. There were also medicated soap tablets, special formula toothpaste, talcum powder in a gilt container, deodorant, and a supersonic looking electric razor. He wore false teeth and had a spare set. He had brought a half full tin of laxatives, some fruit salts, a bottle of mouth wash, some antiseptic foot powder, penicillin throat lozenges, a spot sealing stick, digestive tablets, and an eye bath. The body beautiful, in and out.

All his clothes, down to his vests and pants, had been made to measure, and he had brought enough to cover every possibility of a country weekend. I went through the pockets of his dinner-jacket and the three suits hanging beside it, but he was a tidy man and they were all empty, except for a nail file in each breast pocket. His six various pairs of shoes were hand-made and nearly new. I looked into each shoe separately, but except for trees they were all empty.

In a drawer I found neatly arranged his stock of ties, handkerchiefs, and socks: all expensive. A heavy chased silver box contained cuff links, studs, and tie pins; mostly of gold. He had avoided jewels, but one attractive pair of cuff links was made from pieces of what I now knew enough to identify as tiger-eye. The backs of his hair-brushes were beautiful slabs of the gem stone, smoky quartz. A few brown and grey hairs were lodged in between the bristles.

There remained only his luggage, four lavish suit-cases standing in a neat row beside the wardrobe. I opened each one. They were all empty except for the smallest, which contained a brown calf attaché case. I looked at it carefully before I touched it, but as Kraye didn't seem to have left any tell-tales like hairs or pieces of cotton attached, I lifted it out and put it on one of the beds. It was locked, but I had learnt how to deal with such drawbacks. A lugubrious ex-police sergeant on Radnor's pay-roll gave me progressively harder lessons in lock-picking every time he came into the office between jobs, moaning all the while about the damage the London soot did to his chrysanthemums. My one-handedness he had seen only as a challenge, and had invented a couple of new techniques and instruments entirely for my benefit. Recently he had presented me with a collection of fine delicate keys which he had once removed from a burglar, and had bullied me until I carried them with me everywhere. They were in my room. I went and fetched them and without much trouble opened the case.

It was as meticulously tidy as everything else, and I was particularly careful not to alter the position or order of any of the papers. There were several letters from a stockbroker, a bunch of share transfer certific-ates, various oddments, and a series of typed sheets, headed with the previous day's date, which were apparently an up to the minute analysis of his investments. He seemed to be a rich man and to do a good deal of buying and selling. He had money in oils, mines, property, and industrial stocks. There was also a sheet headed simply SR, on which every transaction was a purchase. Against each entry was a name and the address of a bank. Some names occurred three or four times, some only once.

Underneath the papers lay a large thick brown envelope inside which were two packets of new ten-pound notes. I didn't count, but there couldn't have been fewer than a hundred of them. The envelope was at the bottom of the case, except for a writing board with slightly used white blotting paper held by crocodile and gold corners. I pulled up the board and found underneath it two more sheets of paper, both covered with dates, initials, and sums of money.

I let the whole lot fall back into place, made sure that everything looked exactly as I had found it, relocked the case, and put it back into its covering suitcase.

The divine Doria, I found, was far from being as tidy as her husband. All her things were in a glorious jumble, which made leaving them undisturbed a difficult job, but also meant that she would be less likely than her husband to notice if anything were slightly out of place.

Her clothes though they looked and felt expensive, were bought ready-made and casually treated. Her washing things consisted of a plastic, zipped case, a flannel, a tooth brush, bath essence, and a puffing bottle of talc. Almost stark beside Howard's collection. No medicine. She appeared to wear nothing in bed, but a pretty white quilted dressing-gown hung half off a hanger behind the bathroom door.

She had not completely unpacked. Suitcases propped on chairs and stools still held stirred-up underclothes and various ultra-feminine equipment which I hadn't seen since Jenny left.

The top of the dressing-table, though the daily seemed to have done her best to dust it, was an expensive chaos. Pots of cosmetics, bottles of scent and hair spray stood on one side, a box of tissues, a scarf, and the cluttered tray out of the top of a dressing-case filled the other. The dressing-case itself, of crocodile with gold clips, stood on the floor. I picked it up and put it on the bed. It was locked. I unlocked it, and looked inside.

Doria was quite a girl. She possessed two sets of false eyelashes, spare fingernails, and a hair piece on a tortoiseshell headband. Her big jewel case, the one tidy thing in her whole luggage, contained on the top layer the sapphire and diamond earrings she had worn the previous evening, along with a diamond sunburst brooch and a sapphire ring; and on the lower layer a second necklace, bracelet, earrings, brooch, and ring all of gold, platinum, and citrine. The yellow jewels were uncommon, barbaric in design, and had no doubt been made especially for her.

Under the jewel case were four paperback novels so pornographic in content as to raise doubts about Kraye's ability as a lover. Jenny had held that a truly satisfied woman didn't need to read dirty sex. Doria clearly did.

Alongside the books was a thick leather covered diary to which the beautiful Mrs Kraye had confided the oddest thoughts. Her life seemed to be as untidy as her clothes, a mixture of ordinary social behaviour, dream fantasy, and a perverted marriage relationship. If the diary were to be believed, she and Howard obtained deeper pleasure, both of them, from him beating her, than from the normal act of love. Well, I reflected, at least they were well matched. Some of the divorces which Hunt Radnor Associates dealt with arose because one partner alone was pain fixated, the other being revolted.

At the bottom of the case were two other objects of interest. First, coiled in a brown velvet bag, the sort of leather strap used by schoolmasters, at whose purpose, in view of the diary, it was easy to guess; and second, in a chocolate box, a gun.

CHAPTER FOUR

Telephoning for the local taxi to come and fetch me, I went to Oxford and bought a camera. Although the shop was starting a busy Saturday afternoon, the boy who served me tackled the problem of a one-handed photographer with enthusiasm and as if he had all the time in the world. Between us we sorted out a miniature German sixteen millimetre camera, three inches long by one and a half wide, which I could hold, set, snap and wind with one hand with the greatest ease.

He gave me a thorough lesson in how to work it, added an inch to its length in the shape of a screwed-on photo-electric light meter, loaded it with film, and slid it into a black case so small that it made no bulge in my trouser pocket. He also offered to change the film later if I couldn't manage it. We parted on the best of terms.

When I got back everyone was sitting round a cosy fire in the drawing-room, eating crumpets. Very tantal-izing. I loved crumpets.

No one took much notice when I went in and sat down on the fringe of the circle except Mrs van Dysart, who began sharpening her claws. She got in a couple of quick digs about spongers marrying girls for their money, and Charles didn't say that I hadn't. Viola looked at me searchingly, worry opening her mouth. I winked, and she shut it again in relief.

I gathered that the morning's bag had been the usual mixture (two brace of pheasant, five wild duck, and a hare), because Charles preferred a rough shoot over his own land to organized affairs with beaters. The women had collected a poor opinion of Oxford shop assistants and a booklet on the manufacture of fifteenth-century Italian glass. All very normal for a country weekend. It was my snooping which seemed unreal. That, and the false position Charles had steered me into.

Kraye's gaze, and finally his hands, strayed back to the gem bookshelves. Again the door was opened, Charles' trick lighting working effectively, and one by one the gems were brought out, passed round and closely admired. Mrs van Dysart seemed much attached to a spectacular piece of rose quartz, playing with it to make light strike sparks from it, and smoothing her fingers over the glossy surface.

'Rex, you must collect some of this for me!' she ordered, her will showing like iron inside the fluff: and masterful looking Rex nodded his meek agreement.

Kraye was saying, 'You know, Roland, these are

really remarkably fine specimens. Among the best I've ever seen. Your cousin must have been extremely fortunate and influential to acquire so many fine crystals.'

'Oh, indeed he was,' agreed Charles equably.

'I should be interested if you ever think of realizing on them . . . a first option, perhaps?'

'You can have a first option by all means,' smiled Charles. 'But I shan't be selling them, I assure you.'

'Ah well, so you say now. But I don't give up easily . . . I shall try you later. But don't forget my first option?'

'Certainly,' said Charles. 'My word on it.'

Kraye smiled at the stone he held in his hands, a magnificent raw amethyst like a cluster of petrified violets.

'Don't let this fall into the fire,' he said. 'It would turn yellow.' He then treated everyone to a lecture on amethysts which would have been interesting had he made any attempt at simplicity: but blinding by words was with him either a habit or a policy. I wasn't certain which.

'. . . Manganese, of course occurring in geodes or agate nodules in South America or Russia, but with such a world-wide distribution it was only to be expected that elementary societies should ascribe to its supra-rational inherencies and attributes . . .'

I suddenly found him looking straight at me, and I knew my expression had not been one of impressed admiration. More like quizzical sarcasm. He didn't like it. There was a quick flash in his eyes.

'It is symptomatic of the slum mentality,' he remarked, 'to scoff at what it can't comprehend.'

'Sid,' said Charles sharply, unconsciously giving away half my name, 'I'm sure you must have something else to do. We can let you go until dinner.'

I stood up. The natural anger rose quickly, but only as far as my teeth. I swallowed. 'Very well,' I muttered.

'Before you go, Sid,' said Mrs van Dysart from the depths of a sofa, '... Sid, what a deliciously plebeian name, so suitable ... Put these down on the table for me.'

She held out both hands, one stone in each and another balanced between them. I couldn't manage them all, and dropped them.

'Oh dear,' said Mrs van Dysart, acidly sweet, as I knelt and picked them up, putting them one by one on the table, 'I forgot you were disabled, so silly of me.' She hadn't forgotten. 'Are you sure you can't get treatment for whatever is wrong with you? You ought to try some exercises, they'd do you the world of good. All you need is a little perseverance. You owe it to the Admiral, don't you think, to *try*?'

I didn't answer, and Charles at least had the grace to keep quiet.

'I know of a very good man over here,' went on Mrs van Dysart. 'He used to work for the army at home ... excellent at getting malingerers back into service. Now he's the sort of man who'd do you good. What do you think, Admiral, shall I fix up for your son-in-law to see him?'

'Er . . .' said Charles, 'I don't think it would work.'

'Nonsense.' She was brisk and full of smiles. 'You can't let him lounge about doing nothing for the rest of his life. A good bracing course of treatment, that's what he needs. Now,' she said turning to me, 'so that I know exactly what I'm talking about when I make an appointment, let's see this precious crippled hand of yours.'

There was a tiny pause. I could feel their probing eyes, their unfriendly curiosity.

'No,' I said calmly. 'Excuse me, but no.'

As I walked across the room and out of the door her voice floated after me. 'There you are, Admiral, he doesn't *want* to get better. They're all the same . . .'

I lay on my bed for a couple of hours re-reading the book on company law, especially now, the section on take-overs. It was no easier than it had been in the hospital, and now that I knew why I was reading it, it seemed more involved, not less. If the directors of Seabury were worried, they would surely have called in their own investigator. Someone who knew his way round the stock markets like I knew my way round the track. An expert. I wasn't at all the right sort of person to stop Kraye, even if indeed anyone could stop him. And yet . . . I stared at the ceiling, taking my lower lip between my teeth . . . and yet I did have a wild idea . . .

Viola came in, knocking as she opened the door.

'Sid, dear, are you all right? Can I do anything for you?' She shut the door, gentle, generous, and worried.

I sat up and swung my legs over the side of the bed. 'No thanks, I'm fine.'

She perched on the arm of an easy chair, looked at me with her kind, slightly mournful brown eyes, and said a little breathlessly, 'Sid, why are you letting Charles say such terrible things about you? It isn't only when you are there in the room, they've been, oh, almost sniggering about you behind your back. Charles and that frightful Mrs van Dysart ... What has happened between you and him? When you nearly died he couldn't have been more worried if you'd been his own son ... but now he is so cruel, and terribly unfair.'

'Dear Viola, don't worry. It's only some game that Charles is playing, and I go along with him.'

'Yes,' she said, nodding. 'He warned me. He said that you were both going to lay a smoke screen and that I was on no account to say a single word in your defence the whole weekend. But it wasn't true, was it? When I saw your face, when Charles said that about your poor mother, I knew you didn't know what he was going to do.'

'Was it so obvious?' I said ruefully. 'Well, I promise you I haven't quarrelled with him. Will you just be a dear and do exactly as he asked? Don't say a single word to any of them about ... um ... the more successful bits of my life history, or about my job at the agency, or about the shooting. You didn't today, did you, on the trip to Oxford?' I finished with some anxiety.

She shook her head. 'I thought I'd talk to you first.'

'Good,' I grinned.

'Oh dear,' she cried, partly in relief, partly in puzzlement. 'Well in that case, Charles asked me to pop in and make sure you would come down to dinner.'

'Oh he did, did he? Afraid I'll throw a boot at him, I should think, after sending me out of the room like that. Well, you just pop back to Charles and say that I'll come down to dinner on condition that he organizes some chemmy afterwards, and includes me out.'

Dinner was a bit of a trial: with their smoked salmon and pheasant the guests enjoyed another round of Sid-baiting. Both the Krayes, egged on by Charles and the fluffy harpy beside him, had developed a pricking skill at this novel weekend parlour game, and I heartily wished Charles had never thought of it. However, he kept his side of the bargain by digging out the chemmy shoe, and after the coffee, the brandy, and another inspection of the dining-room quartz, he settled his guests firmly round the table in the drawing-room.

Upstairs, once the shoe was clicking regularly and the players were well involved, I went and collected Kraye's attaché case and took it along to my room.

Because I was never going to get another chance and did not want to miss something I might regret later, I photographed every single paper in the case. All the stockbroker's letters and all the investment reports. All the share certificates, and also the two separate sheets under the writing board.

Although I had an ultra-bright light bulb and the exposure meter to help me to get the right setting, I took several pictures at different light values of the papers I considered the most important, in order to be sure of getting the sharpest possible result. The little camera handled beautifully, and I found I could change the films in their tiny cassettes without much difficulty. By the time I had finished I had used three whole films of twenty exposures on each. It took me a long time, as I had to put the camera down between each shot to move the next paper into my pool of light, and also had to be very careful not to alter the order in which the papers had lain in the case.

The envelope of ten-pound notes kept me hoping like crazy that Howard Kraye would not lose heavily and come upstairs for replacements. It seemed to me at the time a ridiculous thing to do, but I took the two flat blocks of tenners out of the envelope, and photographed them as well. Putting them back I flipped through them: the notes were new, consecutive, fifty to a packet. One thousand pounds to a penny.

When everything was back in the case I sat looking at the contents for a minute, checking their position against my visual memory of how they looked when I first saw them. At last satisfied, I shut the case, locked it, rubbed it over to remove any finger marks I might have left, and put it back where I had found it.

After that I went downstairs to the dining-room for the brandy I had refused at dinner. I needed it. Carrying the glass, I listened briefly outside the drawing-room door to the murmurs and clicks from within and went upstairs again, to bed.

Lying in the dark I reviewed the situation. Howard Kraye, drawn by the bait of a quartz collection, had accepted an invitation to a quiet weekend in the country with a retired admiral. With him he had brought a selection of private papers. As he had no possible reason to imagine that anyone in such innocent surroundings would spy on him, the papers might be very private indeed. So private that he felt safest when they were with him? Too private to leave at home? It would be nice to think so.

At that point, imperceptibly, I fell asleep.

The nerves in my abdomen wouldn't give up. After about five hours of fighting them unsuccessfully I decided that staying in bed all morning thinking about it was doing no good, and got up and dressed.

Drawn partly against my will, I walked along the passage to Jenny's room, and went in. It was the small sunny room she had had as a child. She had gone back to it when she left me and it was all hers alone. I had never slept there. The single bed, the relics of childhood, girlish muslin frills on curtains and dressing-table, everything shut me out. The photographs round the

68

room were of her father, her dead mother, her sister, brother-in-law, dogs and horses, but not of me. As far as she could, she had blotted out her marriage.

I walked slowly round touching her things, remembering how much I had loved her. Knowing, too, that there was no going back, and that if she walked through the door at that instant we would not fall into each other's arms in tearful reconciliation.

Removing a one-eyed teddy bear I sat down for a while on her pink armchair. It's difficult to say just where a marriage goes wrong, because the accepted reason often isn't the real one. The rows Jenny and I had had were all ostensibly caused by the same thing: my ambition. Grown finally too heavy for flat racing, I had switched entirely to steeplechasing the season before we married, and I wanted to be champion jumping jockey. To this end I was prepared to eat little, drink less, go to bed early, and not make love if I were racing the next day. It was unfortunate that she liked late-night parties and dancing more than anything else. At first she gave them up willingly, then less willingly, and finally in fury. After that, she started going on her own.

In the end she told me to choose between her and racing. But by then I was indeed champion jockey, and had been for some time, and I couldn't give it up. So Jenny left. It was just life's little irony that six months later I lost the racing as well. Gradually since then I had come to realize that a marriage didn't break up just because one half liked parties and the other didn't. I thought now that Jenny's insistence on a gay time was the result of my having failed her in some basic, deeply necessary way. Which did nothing whatsoever for my self-respect or my self-confidence.

I sighed, stood up, replaced the teddy bear, and went downstairs to the drawing-room. Eleven o'clock on a windy autumn morning.

Doria was alone in the big comfortable room, sitting on the window-seat and reading the Sunday papers, which lay around her on the floor in a haphazard mess.

'Hello,' she said, looking up. 'What hole did you crawl out of?'

I walked over to the fire and didn't answer.

'Poor little man, are his feelings hurt then?'

'I do have feelings, the same as anyone else.'

'So you actually can talk?' she said mockingly. 'I'd begun to wonder.'

'Yes, I can talk.'

'Well, now, tell me all your troubles, little man.'

'Life is just a bowl of cherries.'

She uncurled herself from the window seat and came across to the fire, looking remarkably out of place in skin-tight leopard printed pants and a black silk shirt.

She was the same height as Jenny, the same height as me, just touching five foot six. As my smallness had always been an asset for racing, I never looked on it as a handicap for life in general, either physical or social. Neither had I ever really understood why so many people thought that height for its own sake was important. But it would have been naïve not to take note of the widespread extraordinary assumption that the mind and heart could be measured by tallness. The little man with the big emotion was a stock comic figure. It was utterly irrational. What difference did three or four inches of leg bone make to a man's essential nature? Perhaps I had been fortunate in coming to terms early with the effect of poor nutrition in a difficult childhood; but it did not stop me understanding why other short men struck back in defensive aggression. There were the pinpricks, for instance, of girls like Doria calling one 'little' and intending it as an insult.

'You've dug yourself into a cushy berth here, haven't you?' she said, taking a cigarette from the silver box on the mantelpiece.

'I suppose so.'

'If I were the Admiral I'd kick you out.'

'Thank you,' I said, neglecting to offer her a light. With a mean look she found a box of matches and struck one for herself.

'Are you ill, or something?'

'No. Why?'

'You eat those faddy health foods, and you look such a sickly little creature . . . I just wondered.' She blew the smoke down her nose. 'The Admiral's daughter must have been pretty desperate for a wedding ring.'

'Give her her due,' I said mildly. 'At least she didn't pick a rich father-figure twice her age.'

I thought for a moment she meant to go into the corny routine of smacking my face, but as it happened she was holding the cigarette in the hand she needed.

'You little shit,' she said instead. A charming girl, altogether.

'I get along.'

'Not with me, you don't.' Her face was tight. I had struck very deep, it seemed.

'Where is everyone else?' I asked, gesturing around the empty room.

'Out with the Admiral somewhere. And you can take yourself off again too. You're not wanted in here.'

'I'm not going. I live here, remember?'

'You went quick enough last night,' she sneered. 'When the Admiral says jump, you jump. But fast, little man. And that I like to see.'

'The Admiral,' I pointed out, 'is the hand that feeds. I don't bite it.'

'Boot-licking little creep.'

I grinned at her nastily and sat down in an armchair. I still didn't feel too good. Pea green and clammy, to be exact. Nothing to be done though, but wait for it to clear off.

Doria tapped ash off her cigarette and looked at me down her nose, thinking up her next attack. Before she could launch it, however, the door opened and her husband came in.

'Doria,' he said happily, not immediately seeing me

in the armchair, 'where have you hidden my cigarette case? I shall punish you for it.'

She made a quick movement towards me with her hand and Howard saw me and stopped dead.

'What are you doing here?' he said brusquely, the fun-and-games dying abruptly out of his face and voice.

'Passing the time.'

'Clear out then. I want to talk to my wife.'

I shook my head and stayed put.

'Short of picking up and throwing him out bodily,' said Doria, 'you won't get rid of him. I've tried.'

Kraye shrugged. 'Roland puts up with him. I suppose we can too.' He picked up one of the newspapers and sat down in an armchair facing me. Doria wandered back to the window-seat, pouting. Kraye straightened up the paper and began to read the front page. Across the back page, the racing page, facing me across the fireplace, the black, bold headlines jumped out.

'ANOTHER HALLEY?'

Underneath, side by side, were two photographs; one of me, and the other of a boy who had won a big race the day before.

It was by then essential that Kraye should not discover how Charles had misrepresented me; it had gone much too far to be explained away as a joke. The photograph was clearly printed for once. I knew it well. It was an old one which the papers had used several times before, chiefly because it was a good likeness. Even if none of the guests read the racing column, as

73

Doria obviously hadn't, it might catch their eye in passing, through being in such a conspicuous place.

Kray finished reading the front page and began to turn the paper over.

'Mr Kraye,' I said. 'Do you have a very big quartz collection yourself?'

He lowered the paper a little and gave me an unenthusiastic glance.

'Yes, I have,' he said briefly.

'Then could you please tell me what would be a good thing to give the Admiral to add to his collection? And where would I get it, and how much would it cost?'

The paper folded over, hiding my picture. He cleared his throat and with strained politeness started to tell me about some obscure form of crystal which the Admiral didn't have. Press the right button, I thought . . . Doria spoilt it. She walked jerkily over to Kraye and said crossly, 'Howard, for God's sake. The little creep is buttering you up. I bet he wants something. You're a sucker for anyone who will talk about rocks.'

'People don't make a fool of me,' said Kraye flatly, his eyes narrowing in irritation.

'No. I only want to please the Admiral,' I explained.

'He's a sly little beast,' said Doria. 'I don't like him.'

Kraye shrugged, looked down at the newspaper and began to unfold it again.

'It's mutual,' I said casually. 'You Daddy's doll.'

Kraye stood up slowly and the paper slid to the floor, front page up.

'What did you say?'

'I said I didn't think much of your wife.'

He was outraged, as well he might be. He took a single step across the rug, and there was suddenly something more in the room than three guests sparring round a Sunday morning fire.

Even though I was as far as he knew an insignificant fly to swat, a clear quality of menace flowed out of him like a radio signal. The calm social mask had disappeared, along with the wordy, phony, surface personality. The vague suspicion I had gained from reading his papers, together with the antipathy I had felt for him all along, clarified into belated recognition: this was not just a smooth speculator operating near the legal borderline, but a full-blown, powerful, dangerous big-time crook.

Trust me, I thought, to prod an anthill and find a hornets' nest. Twist the tail of a grass snake and find a boa constrictor. What on earth would he be like, I wondered, if one did more to cross him than disparage his choice of wife.

'He's sweating,' said Doria, pleased. 'He's afraid of you.'

'Get up,' he said.

As I was sure that if I stood up he would simply knock me down again, I stayed where I was.

'I'll apologize,' I said.

'Oh no,' said Doria, 'that's much too easy.'

'Something subtle,' suggested Kraye, staring down.

'I know!' Doria was delighted with her idea. 'Let's get that hand out of his pocket.'

They both saw from my face that I would hate that more than anything. They both smiled. I thought of bolting, but it meant leaving the paper behind.

'That will do very nicely,' said Kraye. He leant down, twined one hand into the front of my jersey shirt and the other into my hair, and pulled me to my feet. The top of my head reached about to his chin. I wasn't in much physical shape for resisting, but I took a half-hearted swipe at him as I came up. Doria caught my swinging arm and twisted it up behind my back, using both of hers and an uncomfortable amount of pressure. She was a strong healthy girl with no inhibitions about hurting people.

'That'll teach you to be rude to me,' she said with satisfaction.

I thought of kicking her shins, but it would only have brought more retaliation. I also wished Charles would come back at once from wherever he was.

He didn't.

Kraye transferred his grip from my hair to my left forearm and began to pull. That arm was no longer much good, but I did my best. I tucked my elbow tight against my side, and my hand stayed in my pocket.

'Hold him harder,' he said to Doria. 'He's stronger than he looks.' She levered my arm up another inch and I started to roll round to get out of it. But Kraye still had his grasp on the front of my jersey, with his forearm leaning across under my throat, and between the two of them I was properly stuck. All the same, I found I couldn't just stand still and let them do what I so much didn't want them to.

'He squirms, doesn't he?' said Doria cheerfully.

I squirmed and struggled a good deal more; until they began getting savage with frustration, and I was panting. It was my wretched stomach which finished it. I began to feel too ill to go on. With a terrific jerk Kraye dragged my hand out.

'Now,' he said triumphantly.

He gripped my elbow fiercely and pulled the jersey sleeve up from my wrist. Doria let go of my right arm and came to look at their prize. I was shaking with rage, pain, humiliation . . . heaven knows what.

'Oh,' said Doria blankly. 'Oh.'

She was no longer smiling, and nor was her husband. They looked steadily at the wasted, flabby, twisted hand, and at the scars on my forearm, wrist, and palm, not only the terrible jagged marks of the original injury but the several tidier ones of the operations I had had since. It was a mess, a right and proper mess.

'So that's why the Admiral lets him stay, the nasty little beast,' said Doria, screwing up her face in distaste.

'It doesn't excuse his behaviour,' said Kraye. 'I'll make sure he keeps that tongue of his still, in future.'

He stiffened his free hand and chopped the edge of it across the worst part, the inside of my wrist. I jerked in his grasp.

'Ah . . .' I said. 'Don't.'

'He'll tell tales to the Admiral,' said Doria warningly, 'if you hurt him too much. It's a pity, but I should think that's about enough.'

'I don't agree, but . . .'

There was a scrunch on the gravel outside, and Charles' car swept past the window, coming back.

Kraye let go of my elbow with a shake. I went weakly down on my knees on the rug, and it wasn't all pretence.

'If you tell the Admiral about this, I'll deny it,' said Kraye, 'and we know who he'll believe.'

I did know who he'd believe, but I didn't say so. The newspaper which had caused the whole rumpus lay close beside me on the rug. The car doors slammed distantly. The Krayes turned away from me towards the window, listening. I picked up the paper, got to my feet, and set off for the door. They didn't try to stop me in any way. They didn't mention the newspaper either. I opened the door, went through, shut it, and steered a slightly crooked course across the hall to the wardroom. Upstairs was too far. I shut the wardroom door behind me, hid the newspaper, slid into Charles' favourite armchair, and waited for my various miseries, mental and physical, to subside.

Some time later Charles came in to fetch some fresh cartons of cigarettes.

'Hullo,' he said over his shoulder, opening the cupboard. 'I thought you were still in bed. Mrs Cross said you weren't very well this morning. It isn't at all warm in here. Why don't you come into the drawing-room?'

'The Krayes . . .' I stopped.

'They won't bite you.' He turned round, cigarettes in hand. He looked at my face. 'What's so funny?' and then more sharply, looking closer. 'What's the matter?'

'Oh, nothing. Have you seen today's *Sunday Hemisphere*?'

'No, not yet. Do you want it? I thought it was in the drawing-room with the other papers.'

'No, it's in the top drawer of your desk. Take a look.'

Puzzled, he opened the drawer, took out the paper, and unfolded it. He went to the racing section unerringly.

'My God!' he said, aghast. 'Today of all days.' His eyes skimmed down the page and he smiled. 'You've read this, of course?'

I shook my head. 'I just took it to hide it.'

He handed me the paper. 'Read it then. It'll be good for your ego. They won't let you die! "Young Finch", he quoted, "showed much of the judgement and miraculous precision of the great Sid". How about that? And that's just the start.'

'Yeah, how about it?' I grinned. 'Count me out for lunch, if you don't mind, Charles. You don't need me there any more.'

79

'All right, if you don't feel like it. They'll be gone by six at the latest, you'll be glad to hear.' He smiled and went back to his guests.

I read the newspaper before putting it away again. As Charles had said, it was good for the ego. I thought the columnist, whom I'd known for years, had somewhat exaggerated my erstwhile powers. A case of the myth growing bigger than the reality. But still, it was nice. Particularly in view of the galling, ignominious end to the rough-house in which the great Sid had so recently landed himself.

On the following morning Charles and I changed back the labels on the chunks of quartz and packed them up ready to return to the Carver Foundation. When we had finished we had one label left over.

'Are you sure we haven't put one stone in the box without changing the label?' said Charles.

'Positive.'

'I suppose we'd better check. I'm afraid that's what we've done.'

We took all the chunks out of the big box again. The gem collection, which Charles under protest had taken to bed with him each night, was complete; but we looked through them again too to make sure the missing rock had not got among them by mistake. It was nowhere to be found.

'St Luke's Stone,' I read from the label. 'I remember where that was, up on the top shelf on the right hand side.'

'Yes,' agreed Charles, 'a dull-looking lump about the size of a fist. I do hope we haven't lost it.'

'We have lost it,' I remarked. 'Kraye's pinched it.'

'Oh no,' Charles exclaimed. 'You can't be right.'

'Go and ring up the Foundation, and ask them what the stone is worth.'

He shook his head doubtfully, but went to the telephone, and came back frowning.,

'They say it hasn't any intrinsic value, but it's an extremely rare form of meteorite. It never turns up in mines or quarrying of course. You have to wait for it to fall from the heavens, and then find it. Very tricky.'

'A quartz which friend Kraye didn't have.'

'But he surely must know I'd suspect him?' Charles protested.

'You'd never have missed it, if it had really been part of your cousin's passed-on collection. There wasn't any gap on the shelf just now. He'd moved the others along. He couldn't know you would check carefully almost as soon as he had gone.'

Charles sighed. 'There isn't a chance of getting it back.'

'No,' I agreed.

'Well, it's a good thing you insisted on the insurance,' he said. 'Carver's valued that boring-looking lump more than all the rest put together. Only one other meteorite like it has ever been found: the St Mark's Stone.' He smiled suddenly. 'We seem to have mislaid the equivalent of the Penny Black.'

CHAPTER FIVE

Two days later I went back through the porticoed columned doorway of Hunt Radnor Associates, a lot more alive than when I last came out.

I got a big hullo from the girl on the switchboard, went up the curving staircase very nearly whistling, and was greeted by a barrage of ribald remarks from the Racing Section. What most surprised me was the feeling I had of coming home: I had never thought of myself as really belonging to the agency before, even though down at Aynsford I had realized that I very much didn't want to leave it. A bit late, that discovery. The skids were probably under me already.

Chico grinned widely. 'So you made it.'

'Well . . . Yes.'

'I mean, back here to the grindstone.'

'Yeah.'

'But,' he cast a rolling eye on the clock, 'late as usual.'

'Go stuff yourself,' I said.

Chico threw out an arm to the smiling department.

'Our Sid is back, his normal charming self. Work in the agency can now begin.'

'I see I still haven't got a desk,' I observed, looking round. No desk. No desk. No roots. No real job. As ever.

'Sit on Dolly's, she's kept it dusted for you.'

Dolly looked at Chico, smiling, the mother-hunger showing too vividly in her great blue eyes. She might be the second best head of department the agency possessed, with a cross-referencing filing-index mind like a computer, she might be a powerful, large, self-assured woman of forty-odd with a couple of marriages behind her and an ever hopeful old bachelor at her heels, but she still counted her life a wasteland because her body couldn't produce children. Dolly was a terrific worker, overflowing with intensely female vitality, excellent drinking company, and very, very sad.

Chico didn't want to be mothered. He was prickly about mothers. All of them in general, not just those who abandoned their tots in pushchairs at police stations near Barnes Bridge. He jollied Dolly along and deftly avoided her tentative maternal invitations.

I hitched a hip on to a long accustomed spot on the edge of Dolly's desk, and swung my leg.

'Well, Dolly my love, how's the sleuthing trade?' I said.

'What we need,' she said with mock tartness, 'is a bit more work from you and a lot less lip.'

'Give me a job, then.'

'Ah, now.' She pondered. 'You could . . .' she began,

then stopped. 'Well, no... perhaps not. And it had better be Chico who goes to Lambourn; some trainer there wants a doubtful lad checked on...'

'So there's nothing for me?'

'Er... well...' said Dolly. 'No.' She had said no a hundred times before. She had never once said yes.

I made a face at her, picked up her telephone, pressed the right button, and got through to Radnor's secretary.

'Joanie? This is Sid Halley. Yes... back from Beyond, that's it. Is the old man busy? I'd like a word with him.'

'Big deal,' said Chico.

Joanie's prim voice said, 'He's got a client with him just now. When she's gone I'll ask him, and ring you back.'

'OK.' I put down the receiver.

Dolly raised her eyebrows. As head of the department she was my immediate boss, and in asking direct for a session with Radnor I was blowing agency protocol a raspberry. But I was certain that her constant refusal to give me anything useful to do was a direct order from Radnor. If I wanted the drain unblocked I would have to go and pull out the plug. Or go on my knees to stay at all.

'Dolly, love, I'm tired of kicking my heels. Even against your well-worn desk, though the view from here is ravishing.' She was wearing, as she often did, a crossover cream silk shirt: it crossed over at a point which on a young girl would have caused a riot. On Dolly it still looked pretty potent, owing to the generosity of nature and the disposal of her arrangements.

'Are you chucking it in?' said Chico, coming to the point.

'It depends on the old man,' I said. 'He may be chucking me out.'

There was a brief, thoughtful silence in the department. They all knew very well how little I did. How little I had been content to do. Dolly looked blank, which wasn't helpful.

Jones-boy clattered in with a tray of impeccable unchipped tea mugs. He was sixteen; noisy, rude, anarchistic, callous, and probably the most efficient office boy in London. His hair grew robustly nearly down to his shoulders, wavy and fanatically clean, dipping slightly in an expensive styling at the back. From behind he looked like a girl, which never disconcerted him. From in front his bony, acned face proclaimed him unprepossessingly male. He spent half his pay packet and his Sundays in Carnaby Street and the other half on week nights chasing girls. According to him, he caught them. No girls had so far appeared in the office to corroborate his story.

Under the pink shirt beat a stony heart; inside the sprouting head hung a big 'So What?' Yet it was because this amusing, ambitious, unsocial creature invariably arrived well before his due hour to get his office arrangements ready for the day that he had found me before I died. There was a moral there, somewhere.

He gave me a look. 'The corpse has returned, I see.'

'Thanks to you,' I said idly, but he knew I meant it. He didn't care, though.

He said, 'Your blood and stuff ran through a crack in the linoleum and soaked the wood underneath. The old man was wondering if it would start dry rot or something.'

'Jones-boy,' protested Dolly, looking sick. 'Get the hell out of here, and shut up.'

The telephone rang on her desk. She picked it up and listened, said, 'All right,' and disconnected.

'The old man wants to see you. Right away.'

'Thanks.' I stood up.

'The flipping boot?' asked Jones-boy interestedly.

'Keep your snotty nose out,' said Chico.

'And balls to you . . .'

I went out smiling, hearing Dolly start to deal once again with the running dog fight Chico and Jones-boy never tired of. Downstairs, across the hall, into Joanie's little office and through into Radnor's.

He was standing by the window, watching the traffic doing its nut in the Cromwell Road. This room, where the clients poured out their troubles, was restfully painted a quiet grey, carpeted and curtained in crimson and furnished with comfortable armchairs, handy little tables with ashtrays, pictures on the walls, ornaments, and vases of flowers. Apart from Radnor's small desk in the corner, it looked like an ordinary sitting-room, and indeed everyone believed that he had bought the room intact with the lease, so much was it what one would expect to find in a graceful, six-storeyed, late Victorian town house. Radnor had a theory that people exaggerated and distorted facts less in such peaceful surroundings than in the formality of a more orthodox office.

'Come in, Sid.' He didn't move from the window, so I joined him there. He shook hands.

'Are you sure you're fit enough to be here? You haven't been as long as I expected. Even knowing you . . .' he smiled slightly, with watching eyes.

I said I was all right. He remarked on the weather, the rush-hour, and the political situation, and finally worked round to the point we both knew was at issue.

'So, Sid, I suppose you'll be looking around a bit now?'

Laid on the line, I thought.

'If I wanted to stay here . . .'

'If? Hm, I don't know.' He shook his head very slightly.

'Not on the same terms, I agree.'

'I'm sorry it hasn't worked out.' He sounded genuinely regretful, but he wasn't making it easy.

I said with careful calm, 'You've paid me for nothing for two years. Well, give me a chance now to earn what I've had. I don't really want to leave.'

He lifted his head slightly like a pointer to the scent, but he said nothing. I ploughed on.

'I'll work for you for nothing, to make up for it. But only if it's real, decent work. No more sitting around. It would drive me mad.'

He gave me a hard stare and let out a long breath like a sigh.

'Good God. At last,' he said. 'And it took a bullet to do it.'

'What do you mean?'

'Sid, have you ever seen a zombie wake up?'

'No,' I said ruefully, understanding him. 'It hasn't been as bad as that?'

He shrugged one shoulder. 'I saw you racing, don't forget. You notice when a fire goes out. We've had the pleasant, flippant ashes drifting round this office, that's all.' He smiled deprecatingly at his flight of fancy: he enjoyed making pictures of words. It wasted a lot of office time, on the whole.

'Consider me alight again, then,' I grinned. 'And I've brought a puzzle back with me. I want very much to sort it out.'

'A long story?'

'Fairly, yes.'

'We'd better sit down, then.'

He waved me to an armchair, sank into one himself, and prepared to listen with the stillness and concentration which sent him time and time again to the core of a problem.

I told him about Kraye's dealing in racecourses. Both what I knew and what I guessed. When at length I finished he said calmly, 'Where did you get hold of this?'

'My father-in-law, Charles Roland, tossed it at me while I was staying with him last weekend. He had Kraye as a house guest.' The subtle old fox, I thought, throwing me in at the deep end: making me wake up and swim.

'And Roland got it from where?'

'The Clerk of the Course at Seabury told him that the directors were worried about too much share movement, that it was Kraye who got control of Dunstable, and they were afraid he was at it again.'

'But the rest, what you've just told me, is your own supposition?'

'Yes.'

'Based on your appraisal of Kraye over one weekend?'

'Partly on what he showed me of his character, yes. Partly on what I read of his papers . . .' With some hesitation I told him about my snooping and the photography. '. . . The rest, I suppose, is a hunch.'

'Hmm. It needs checking . . . Have you brought the films with you?'

I nodded, took them out of my pocket, and put them on the little table beside me.

'I'll get them developed.' He drummed his fingers lightly on the arm of the chair, thinking. Then, as if having made a decision, said more briskly, 'Well, the first thing we need is a client.'

'A client?' I echoed absent-mindedly.

'Of course. What else? We are not the police. We work strictly for profit. Ratepayers don't pay the overheads and salaries in this agency. The clients do.'

'Oh . . . yes, of course.'

'The most likely client in this case is either Seabury Racecourse executive, or perhaps the National Hunt Committee. I think I should sound out the Senior Steward first, in either case. No harm in starting at the top.'

'He might prefer to try the police,' I said, 'free.'

'My dear Sid, the one thing people want when they employ private investigators is privacy. They pay for privacy. When the police investigate something, everyone knows about it. When we do, they don't. That's why we sometimes get criminal cases when it would undoubtedly be cheaper to go to the police.'

'I see. So you'll try the Senior Steward . . .'

'No,' he interrupted. 'You will.'

'I?'

'Naturally. It's your case.'

'But it's your agency . . . he is used to negotiating with you.'

'You know him too,' he pointed out.

'I used to ride for him, and that puts me on a bad footing for this sort of thing. I'm a jockey to him, an ex-jockey. He won't take me seriously.'

Radnor shrugged a shoulder. 'If you want to take on Kraye, you need a client. Go and get one.'

I knew very well that he never sent even senior operatives, let alone inexperienced ones, to arrange or angle for an assignment, so that for several moments I couldn't really believe that he intended me to go. But he said nothing else, and eventually I stood up and went towards the door.

'Sandown Races are on today,' I said tentatively. 'He's sure to be there.'

'A good opportunity.' He looked straight ahead, not at me.

'I'll try it, then.'

'Right.'

He wasn't letting me off. But then he hadn't kicked me out either. I went through the door and shut it behind me, and while I was still hesitating in disbelief I heard him inside the room give a sudden guffaw, a short, sharp, loud, triumphant snort of laughter.

I walked back to my flat, collected the car, and drove down to Sandown. It was a pleasant day, dry, sunny, and warm for November, just right for drawing a good crowd for steeplechasing.

I turned in through the racecourse gates, spirits lifting, parked the car (a Mercedes SL230 with automatic gears, power assisted steering, and a strap on the back saying NO HAND SIGNALS), and walked round to join the crowd outside the weighing room door. I could no longer go through it. It had been one of the hardest things to get used to, the fact that all the changing rooms and weighing rooms which had been my second homes for fourteen years were completely barred to me from the day I rode my last race. You didn't lose just a job when you handed in your jockey's licence, you lost a way of life.

There were a lot of people to talk to at Sandown, and as I hadn't been racing for six weeks I had a good deal of gossip to catch up on. No one seemed to know about the shooting, which was fine by me, and I didn't tell them. I immersed myself very happily in the race-course atmosphere and for an hour Kraye retreated slightly into the background.

Not that I didn't keep an eye on my purpose, but until the third race the Senior Steward, Viscount Hagbourne, was never out of a conversation long enough for me to catch him.

Although I had ridden for him for years and had found him understanding and fair, he was in most respects still a stranger. An aloof, distant man, he seemed to find it difficult to make ordinary human contacts, and unfortunately he had not proved a great success as Senior Steward. He gave the impression, not of power in himself, but of looking over his shoulder at power behind: I'd have said he was afraid of incurring the disapproval of the little knot of rigidly determined men who in fact ruled racing themselves, regardless of who might be in office at the time. Lord Hagbourne postponed making decisions until it was almost too late to make them, and there was still a danger after that that he would change his mind. But all the same he was the front man until his year of office ended, and with him I had to deal.

At length I fielded him neatly as he turned away from the Clerk of the Course and forestalled a trainer who was advancing upon him with a grievance. Lord Hagbourne, with one of his rare moments of humour, deliberately turned his back on the grievance and consequently greeted me with more warmth than usual.

'Sid, nice to see you. Where have you been lately?'

'Holidays,' I explained succinctly. 'Look, sir, can I have a talk with you after the races? There's something I want to discuss urgently.'

'No time like the present,' he said, one eye on the grievance. 'Fire away.'

'No, sir. It needs time and all your attention.'

'Hm?' The grievance was turning away. 'Not today, Sid, I have to get home. What is it? Tell me now.'

'I want to talk to you about the take-over bid for Seabury Racecourse.'

He looked at me, startled. 'You want . . .?'

'That's right. It can't be said out here where you will be needed at any moment by someone else. If you could just manage twenty minutes at the end of the afternoon . . .?'

'Er . . . what is your connection with Seabury?'

'None in particular, sir. I don't know if you remember, but I've been connected' (a precise way of putting it) 'with Hunt Radnor Associates for the last two years. Various . . . er . . . facts about Seabury have come our way and Mr Radnor thought you might be interested. I am here as his representative.'

'Oh, I see. Very well, Sid, come to the Stewards' tea room after the last. If I'm not there, wait for me. Right?'

'Yes. Thank you.'

I walked down the slope and then up the iron staircase to the jockeys' box in the stand, smiling at myself. Representative. A nice big important word. It covered anything from an ambassador down. Commercial travellers had rechristened themselves with its rolling syllables years ago ... they had done it because of the jokes, of course. It didn't sound the same, somehow, starting off with 'Did you hear the one about the representative who stopped at a lonely farmhouse ...?' Rodent officers, garbage disposal, and sanitary staff: pretty new names for rat-catchers, dustmen, and road sweepers. So why not for me?

'Only idiots laugh at nothing,' said a voice in my ear. 'What the hell are you looking so pleased about all of a sudden? And where the blazes have you been this last month?'

'Don't tell me you've missed me?' I grinned, not needing to look round. We went together through the door of the high-up jockeys' box, two of a kind, and stood looking out over the splendid racecourse.

'Best view in Europe.' He sighed. Mark Witney, thirty-eight years old, racehorse trainer. He had a face battered like a boxer's from too many racing falls and in the two years since he hung up his boots and stopped racing he had put on all of three stone. A fat, ugly man. We had a host of memories in common, a host of hard ridden races. I liked him a lot.

'How's things?' I said.

'Oh, fair, fair. They'll be a damn sight better if that animal of mine wins the fifth.'

'He must have a good chance.'

'He's a damn certainty, boy. A certainty. If he doesn't fall over his god-damned legs. Clumsiest sod this side of Hades.' He lifted his race glasses and looked at the number board. 'I see poor old Charlie can't do the weight again on that thing of Bob's ... That boy of Plumtree's is getting a lot of riding now. What do you think of him?'

'He takes too many risks,' I said. 'He'll break his neck.'

'Look who's talking ... No, seriously, I'm considering taking him on. What do you think?' He lowered his glasses. 'I need someone available regularly from now on and all the ones I'd choose are already tied up.'

'Well, you could do better, you could do worse, I suppose. He's a bit flashy for me, but he can ride, obviously. Will he do as he's told?'

He made a face. 'You've hit the bull's eye. That's the snag. He always knows best.'

'Pity.'

'Can you think of anyone else?'

'Um ... what about that boy Cotton? He's too young

95

really. But he's got the makings . . .' We drifted on in amiable chat, discussing his problem, while the box filled up around us and the horses went down to the start.

It was a three mile chase, and one of my ex-mounts was favourite. I watched the man who had my old job ride a very pretty race, and half my mind thought about housing estates.

Sandown itself had survived, some years ago, a bid to cover its green tempting acres with little boxes. Sandown had powerful friends. But Hurst Park, Manchester, and Birmingham racecourses had all gone under the rolling tide of mortar, lost to the double-barrelled persuasive arguments that shareholders liked capital gains and people needed houses. To defend itself from such a fate Cheltenham Racecourse had transformed itself from a private dividend-paying company into a non-profit-making Holdings Trust, and other racecourses had followed their lead.

But not Seabury. And Seabury was deep in a nasty situation. Not Dunstable, and Dunstable Racecourse was now a tidy dormitory for the Vauxhall workers of Luton.

Most British racecourses were, or had been, private companies, in which it was virtually impossible for an outsider to acquire shares against the will of the members. But four, Dunstable, Seabury, Sandown, and Chepstow, were public companies, and their shares could be bought on the open market, through the Stock Exchange.

Sandown had been played for in a straightforward and perfectly honourable way, and plans to turn it into suburban housing had been turned down by the local and county councils. Sandown flourished, made a good profit, paid a ten per cent dividend, and was probably now impregnable. Chepstow was surrounded by so much other open land that it was in little danger from the developers. But little Dunstable had been an oasis inside a growing industrial area.

Seabury was on the flat part of the south coast, flanked on every side by miles of warm little bungalows representing the dreams and savings of people in retirement. At twelve bungalows to the acre – elderly people liked tiny gardens – there must be room on the spacious racecourse for over three thousand more. Add six or seven hundred pounds to the building price of each bungalow for the plot it stood on, and you scooped something in the region of two million . . .

The favourite won and was duly cheered. I clattered down the iron staircase with Mark, and we went and had a drink together.

'Are you sending anything to Seabury next week?' I asked. Seabury was one of his nearest meetings.

'Perhaps. I don't know. It depends if they hold it at all, of course. But I've got mine entered at Lingfield as well, and I think I'll send them there instead. It's a much more prosperous looking place, and the owners like it better. Good lunch and all that. Seabury's so dingy these days. I had a hard job getting old Carmichael to agree to me running his horse there at the last meeting – and look what happened. The meeting was off and we'd missed the other engagement at Worcester too. It wasn't my fault, but I'd persuaded him that he stood more chance at Seabury, and he blamed me because in the end the horse stayed at home eating his head off for nothing. He says there's a jinx on Seabury, and I've a couple more owners who don't like me entering their horses there. I've told them that it's a super track from the horses' point of view, but it doesn't make much difference, they don't know it like we do.'

We finished our drinks and walked back towards the weighing room. His horse scrambled home in the fifth by a whisker and I saw him afterwards in the unsaddling enclosure beaming like a Hallowe'en turnip.

After the last race I went to the Stewards' tea room. There were several Stewards with their wives and friends having tea, but no Lord Hagbourne. The Stewards pulled out a chair, gave me a welcome, and talked, as ever, about the racing. Most of them had ridden as amateurs in their day, one against me in the not too distant past, and I knew them all well.

'Sid, what do you think of the new type hurdles?'

'Oh, much better. Far easier for a young horse to see.'

'Do you know of a good young chaser I could buy?'

'Didn't you think Hayward rode a splendid race?'

'I watched the third down at the Pond, and believe me that chestnut took off outside the wings . . .'

'. . . do you think we ought to have had him in, George?'

'. . . heard that Green bust his ribs again yesterday . . .'

'Don't like that breed, never did, not genuine . . .'

'Miffy can't seem to go wrong, he'd win with a carthorse . . .'

'Can you come and give a talk to our local pony club, Sid? I'll write you the details . . . what date would suit you?'

Gradually they finished their tea, said goodbye, and left for home. I waited. Eventually he came, hurrying, apologizing, explaining what had kept him.

'Now,' he said, biting into a sandwich. 'What's it all about, eh?'

'Seabury.'

'Ah yes, Seabury. Very worrying. Very worrying indeed.'

'A Mr Howard Kraye has acquired a large number of shares . . .'

'Now hold on a minute, Sid. That's only a guess, because of Dunstable. We've been trying to trace the buyer of Seabury shares through the Stock Exchange, and we find no definite lead to Kraye.'

'Hunt Radnor Associates do have that lead.'

He stared. 'Proof?'

'Yes.'

'What sort?'

'Photographs of share transfer certificates.' And heaven help me, I thought, if I've messed them up.

'Oh,' he said sombrely. 'While we weren't sure, there was some hope we were wrong. Where did you get these photographs?'

'I'm not at liberty to say, sir. But Hunt Radnor Associates would be prepared to make an attempt to forestall the takeover of Seabury.'

'For a fat fee, I suppose,' he said dubiously.

'I'm afraid so, sir, yes.'

'I don't connect you with this sort of thing, Sid.' He moved restlessly and looked at his watch.

'If you would forget about me being a jockey, and think of me as having come from Mr Radnor, it would make things a lot easier. How much is Seabury worth to National Hunt racing?'

He looked at me in surprise, but he answered the question, though not in the way I meant.

'Er . . . well you know it's an excellent course, good for horses and so on.'

'It didn't show a profit this year, though.'

'There was a great deal of bad luck.'

'Yes. Too much to be true, don't you think?'

'What do you mean?'

'Has it ever occurred to the National Hunt Committee that bad luck can be . . . well . . . arranged?'

'You aren't seriously suggesting that Kraye . . . I

100

mean that anyone would damage Seabury on purpose? In order to make it show a loss?'

'I am suggesting that it is a possibility. Yes.'

'Good God.' He sat down rather abruptly.

'Malicious damage,' I said. 'Sabotage, if you like. There's a great deal of industrial precedent. Hunt Radnor Associates investigated a case of it only last year in a small provincial brewery where the fermentation process kept going wrong. A prosecution resulted, and the brewery was able to remain in business.'

He shook his head. 'It is quite ridiculous to think that Kraye would be implicated in anything like that. He belongs to one of my clubs. He's a wealthy, respected man.'

'I know, I've met him,' I said.

'Well, then, you must be aware of what sort of person he is.'

'Yes.' Only too well.

'You can't seriously suggest . . .' he began.

'There would be no harm in finding out,' I interrupted. 'You'll have studied the figures. Seabury's quite a prize.'

'How do you see the figures, then?' It seemed he genuinely wanted to know, so I told him.

'Seabury Racecourses has an issued share capital of eighty thousand pounds in fully paid-up one pound shares. The land was bought when that part of the coast was more or less uninhabited, so that this sum bears absolutely no relation to the present value of the place. Any company in that position is just asking for a takeover.

'A buyer would in theory need fifty-one per cent of the shares to be certain of gaining control, but in practice, as was found in Dunstable, forty would be plenty. It would probably be swung on a good deal less, but from the point of view of the buyer, the more he got his hands on before declaring his intentions, the bigger would be his profit.

'The main difficulty in taking over a racecourse company – its only natural safeguard, in fact – is that the shares seldom come on the market. I understand that it isn't always by any means possible to buy even a few on the Stock Exchange, as people who own them tend to be fond of them, and as long as the shares pay any dividend, however small, they won't sell. But it's obvious that not everyone can afford to have bits of capital lying around unproductively, and once the racecourse starts showing a loss, the temptation grows to transfer to something else.

'Today's price of Seabury shares is thirty shillings, which is about four shillings higher than it was two years ago. If Kraye can manage to get hold of a forty per cent holding at an average price of thirty shillings, it will cost him only about forty-eight thousand pounds.

'With a holding that size, aided by other shareholders tempted by a very large capital gain, he can out-vote any opposition, and sell the whole company to a land developer. Planning permission would almost certainly be granted, as the land is not beautiful, and is surrounded already by houses. I estimate that a developer would pay roughly a million for it, as he could double that by selling off all those acres in tiny plots. There's the capital gains tax, of course, but Seabury shareholders stand to make eight hundred per cent on their original investment, if the scheme goes through. Four hundred thousand gross for Mr Kraye, perhaps. Did you ever find out how much he cleared at Dunstable?'

He didn't answer.

I went on. 'Seabury used to be a busy, lively, successful place, and now it isn't. It's a suspicious coincidence that as soon as a big buyer comes along the place goes downhill fast. They paid a dividend of only sixpence per share last year, a gross yield of under one and three-quarters per cent at today's price, and this year they showed a loss of three thousand, seven hundred and fourteen pounds. Unless something is done soon, there won't be a next year.'

He didn't reply at once. He stared at the floor for a long time with the half-eaten sandwich immobile in his hand.

Finally he said, 'Who did the arithmetic? Radnor?'

'No ... I did. It's very simple. I went to Company House in the City yesterday and looked up the Seabury balance sheets for the last few years, and I rang for a quotation of today's share price from a stockbroker this morning. You can easily check it.'

'Oh, I don't doubt you. I remember now, there was a rumour that you made a fortune on the Stock Exchange by the time you were twenty.'

'People exaggerate so,' I smiled. 'My old governor, where I was apprenticed, started me off investing, and I was a bit lucky.'

'Hm.'

There was another pause while he hesitated over his decision. I didn't interrupt him, but I was much relieved when finally he said, 'You have Radnor's authority for seeing me, and he knows what you have told me?'

'Yes.'

'Very well.' He got up stiffly and put down the unfinished sandwich. 'You can tell Radnor that I agree to an investigation being made, and I think I can vouch for my colleagues agreeing. You'll want to start at once, I suppose.'

I nodded.

'The usual terms?'

'I don't know,' I said. 'Perhaps you would get on to Mr Radnor about that.'

As I didn't know what the usual terms were, I didn't want to discuss them.

'Yes, all right. And Sid . . . it's understood that there is to be no leak about this? We can't afford to have Kraye slapping a libel or slander action on us.'

'The agency is always discreet,' I said, with an outward and an inward smile. Radnor was right. People paid for privacy. And why not?

CHAPTER SIX

The Racing Section was quiet when I went in next morning, mostly because Chico was out on an escort job. All the other heads were bent studiously over their desks, including Dolly's.

She looked up and said with a sigh, 'You're late again.' It was ten to ten. 'The old man wants to see you.'

I made a face at her and retraced my way down the staircase. Joanie looked pointedly at her watch.

'He's been asking for you for half an hour.'

I knocked and went in. Radnor was sitting behind his desk, reading some papers, pencil in hand. He looked at me and frowned.

'Why are you so late?'

'I had a pain in me tum,' I said flippantly.

'Don't be funny,' he said sharply, and then, more reasonably, 'Oh . . . I suppose you're not being funny.'

'No. But I'm sorry about being late.' I wasn't a bit sorry, however, that it had been noticed: before, no one would have said a thing if I hadn't turned up all day.

'How did you get on with Lord Hagbourne?' Radnor asked. 'Was he interested?'

'Yes. He agreed to an investigation. I said he should discuss terms with you.'

'I see.' He flicked a switch on the small box on his desk. 'Joanie, see if you can get hold of Lord Hagbourne. Try the London flat number first.'

'Yes, sir,' her voice came tinnily out of the speaker.

'Here,' said Radnor, picking up a shallow brown cardboard box. 'Look at these.'

The box contained a thick wad of large glossy photographs. I looked at them one by one and heaved a sigh of relief. They had all come out sharp and clear, except some of the ones I had duplicated at varying exposures.

The telephone on Radnor's desk rang once, quietly. He lifted the receiver.

'Oh, good morning Lord Hagbourne. Radnor here. Yes, that's right . . .' He gestured me to sit down, and I stayed there listening while he negotiated terms in a smooth, civilized, deceptively casual voice.

'And of course in a case like this, Lord Hagbourne, there's one other thing: we make a small surcharge if our operatives have to take out of the ordinary risks . . . Yes, as in the Canlas case, exactly. Right then, you shall have a preliminary report from us in a few days. Yes . . . goodbye.'

He put down the receiver, bit his thumb-nail thoughtfully for a few seconds, and said finally, 'Right, then, Sid. Get on with it.'

107

'But . . .' I began.

'But nothing,' he said. 'It's your case. Get on with it.'

I stood up, holding the packet of photographs. 'Can I . . . can I use Bona Fides and so on?'

He waved his hand permissively. 'Sid, use every resource in the agency you need. Keep an eye on expenses though, we don't want to price ourselves out of business. And if you want leg work done, arrange it through Dolly or the other department heads. Right?'

'Won't they think it odd? I mean . . . I don't amount to much around here.'

'And whose fault is that? If they won't do what you ask, refer them to me.' He looked at me expressionlessly.

'All right.' I walked to the door. 'Er . . . who . . . I said, turning the knob, 'gets the danger money? The operative or the agency?'

'You said you would work for nothing,' he observed dryly.

I laughed. 'Just so. Do I get expenses?'

'That car of yours drinks petrol.'

'It does twenty,' I protested.

'The agency rate is based on thirty. You can have that. And other expenses, yes. Put in a chit to accounts.'

'Thanks.'

He smiled suddenly, the rare sweet smile so incongruous to his military bearing, and launched into another elaborate metaphor.

'The tapes are up,' he said. 'What you do with the

race depends on your skill and timing, just as it always used to. I've backed you with the agency's reputation for getting results, and I can't afford to lose my stake. Remember that.'

'Yes,' I said soberly. 'I will.'

I thought, as I took my stupidly aching stomach up two storeys to Bona Fides, that it was time Radnor had a lift installed: and was glad I wasn't bound for Missing Persons away in the rarefied air of the fifth floor. There was a lot more character, I supposed, in the splendidly proportioned, solidly built town house that Radnor had chosen on a corner site in the Cromwell Road, but a flat half-acre of modern office block would have been easier on his staff. And about ten times as expensive, no doubt.

The basement, to start at the bottom, was – except for the kitchen – given over entirely to files and records. On the ground floor, besides Radnor himself and Joanie, there were two interview-cum-waiting rooms, and also the Divorce Section. On the first floor: the Racing Section, Accounts, another interview room, and the general secretarial department. Up one was Bona Fides, and above that, on the two smaller top floors, Guard and Missing Persons. Missing Persons alone had room to spare. Bona Fides, splitting at the seams, was encroaching on Guard. Guard was sticking in its toes.

Jones-boy, who acted as general messenger, must have had legs like iron from pounding up and down the stairs, though thanks to a tiny service lift used long ago to take nursery food to top-floor children, he could haul his tea trays up from landing to landing instead of carrying them.

In Bona Fides there was the usual chatter of six people talking on the telephone all at once. The department head, receiver glued to one ear and finger stuck in the other, was a large bald-headed man with half-moon spectacles sitting halfway down a prominent nose. As always, he was in his shirtsleeves, teamed with a frayed pullover and baggy grey flannels. No tie. He seemed to have an inexhaustible supply of old clothes but never any new ones, and Jones-boy had a theory that his wife dressed him from jumble sales.

I waited until he had finished a long conversation with a managing director about the character of the proposed production manager of a glass factory. The invaluable thing about Jack Copeland was his quick and comprehensive grasp of what dozens of jobs entailed. He was speaking to the glass manufacturer as if he had grown up in the industry: and in five minutes, I knew, he might be advising just as knowledgeably on the suitability of a town clerk. His summing up of a man went far beyond the basic list of honesty, conscientiousness, normality, and prudence, which was all that many employers wanted. He liked to discover his subject's reaction under stress, to find out what he disliked doing, and what he often forgot. The resulting footnotes to his reports were usually the most valuable part of them, and the faith large numbers of industrial firms had in him bore witness to his accuracy.

He wielded enormous power but did not seem conscious of it, which made him much liked. After Radnor, he was the most important person in the agency.

'Jack,' I said, as he put down the receiver. 'Can you check a man for me, please?'

'What's wrong with the Racing Section, pal?' he said, jerking his thumb towards the floor.

'He isn't a racing person.'

'Oh? Who is it?'

'A Howard Kraye. I don't know if he has a profession. He speculates on the stock market. He is a rabid collector of quartz.' I added Kraye's London address.

He scribbled it all down fast.

'OK, Sid. I'll put one of the boys on to it and let you have a prelim. Is it urgent?'

'Fairly.'

'Right.' He tore the sheet off the pad. 'George? You still doing that knitting wool client's report? When you've finished, here's your next one.'

'George,' I said. 'Be careful.'

They both looked at me, suddenly still.

'An unexploded bomb,' I observed. 'Don't set him off.'

George said cheerfully, 'Makes a nice change from knitting wool. Don't worry, Sid. I'll walk on eggs.'

Jack Copeland peered at me closely through the half specs.

'You've cleared it with the old man, I suppose?'

'Yes.' I nodded. 'It's a query fraud. He said to check with him if you wanted to.'

He smiled briefly. 'No need, I guess. Is that all then?'

'For the moment, yes, thanks.'

'Just for the record, is this your own show, or Dolly's, or whose?'

'I suppose . . . mine.'

'Uh-huh,' he said, accenting the second syllable. 'The wind of change, if I read it right?'

I laughed. 'You never know.'

Down in the Racing Section I found Dolly supervising the reshuffling of the furniture. I asked what was going on, and she gave me a flashing smile.

'It seems you're in, not out. The old man just rang to say you needed somewhere to work, and I've sent Jones-boy upstairs to pinch a table from Missing Persons. That'll do for now, won't it? There isn't a spare desk in the place.'

A series of bangs from outside heralded the return of Jones-boy, complete with a spindly plywood affair in a sickly lemon colour. 'How that lot ever find a missing person I'll never know. I bet they don't even find their missing junk.'

He disappeared and came back shortly with a chair.

'The things I do for you!' he said, setting it down in front of me. 'A dim little bird in the typing pool is now squatting on a stool. I chatted her up a bit.'

'What this place needs is some more equipment,' I murmured.

'Don't be funny,' said Dolly. 'Every time the old man buys one desk he takes on two assistants. When I first came here fifteen years ago we had a whole room each, believe it or not . . .'

The rearranged office settled down again, with my table wedged into a corner next to Dolly's desk. I sat behind it and spread out the photographs to sort them. The people who developed and printed all the agency's work had come up with their usual excellent job, and it amazed me that they had been able to enlarge the tiny negatives up to nine by seven inch prints, and get a clearly readable result.

I picked out all the fuzzy ones, the duplicates at the wrong exposures, tore them up, and put the pieces in Dolly's waste paper basket. That left me with fifty-one pictures of the contents of Kraye's attaché case. Innocent enough to the casual eye, but they turned out to be dynamite.

The two largest piles, when I had sorted them out, were Seabury share transfer certificates, and letters from Kraye's stockbroker. The paper headed SR revealed itself to be a summary in simple form of the share certificates, so I added it to that pile. I was left with the photographs of the bank notes, of share dealings which had nothing to do with Seabury, and the two sheets of figures I had found under the writing board at the bottom of the case.

I read through all the letters from the stockbroker, a man called Ellis Bolt, who belonged to a firm known as Charing, Street, and King. Bolt and Kraye were on friendly terms; the letters referred sometimes to social occasions on which they had met; but for the most part the typewritten sheets dealt with the availability and prospects of various shares (including Seabury), purchases made or proposed, and references to tax, stamp duty, and commission.

Two letters had been written in Bolt's own hand. The first, dated ten days ago, said briefly:

Dear H.
    Shall wait with interest for the news on Friday.

                                E

The second, which Kraye must have received on the morning he went to Aynsford, read:

Dear H.
    I have put the final draft in the hands of the printers, and the leaflets should be out by the end of next week, or the Tuesday following at the latest. Two or three days before the next meeting, anyway. That should do it, I think. There would be a lot of unrest should there be another hitch, but surely you will see to that.

                                E

114

'Dolly,' I said, 'may I borrow your phone?'

'Help yourself.'

I rang upstairs to Bona Fides. 'Jack? Can I have a rundown on another man as well? Ellis Bolt, stockbroker, works for a firm called Charing, Street, and King.' I gave him the address. 'He's a friend of Kraye's. Same care needed, I'm afraid.'

'Right. I'll let you know.'

I sat staring down at the two harmless looking letters.

'Shall wait with interest for the news on Friday.' It could mean any news, anything at all. It also could mean the News; and on the radio on Friday I had heard that Seabury Races were off because a lorry carrying chemicals had overturned and burned the turf.

The second letter was just as tricky. It could easily refer to a shareholders' meeting at which a hitch should be avoided at all costs. Or it could refer to a race meeting – at Seabury – where another hitch could affect the sale of shares yet again.

It was like looking at a conjuring trick: from one side you saw a normal object, but from the other, a sham.

If it were a sham, Mr Ellis Bolt was in a criminal career up to his eyebrows. If it was just my suspicious mind jumping to hasty conclusions I was doing an old-established respectable stockbroker a shocking injustice.

I picked up Dolly's telephone again and got an outside line.

'Charing, Street, and King, good morning,' said a quiet female voice.

'Oh, good morning. I would like to make an appointment to see Mr Bolt and discuss some investments. Would that be possible?'

'Certainly, yes. This is Mr Bolt's secretary speaking. Could I have your name?'

'Halley. John Halley.'

'You would be a new client, Mr Halley?'

'That's right.'

'I see. Well, now, Mr Bolt will be in the office tomorrow afternoon, and I could fit you in at three thirty. Would that suit you?'

'Thank you. That's fine. I'll be there.'

I put down the receiver and looked tentatively at Dolly.

'Would it be all right with you if I go out for the rest of the day?'

She smiled. 'Sid, dear, you're very sweet, but you don't have to ask my permission. The old man made it very clear that you're on your own now. You're not accountable to me or anyone else in the agency, except the old man himself. I'll grant you I've never known him give anyone quite such a free hand before, but there you are, my love, you can do what you like. I'm your boss no longer.'

'You don't mind?' I asked.

'No,' she said thoughtfully. 'Come to think of it, I

116

don't. I've a notion that what the old man has always wanted of you in this agency is a partner.'

'Dolly!' I was astonished. 'Don't be ridiculous.'

'He's not getting any younger,' she pointed out.

I laughed. 'So he picked on a broken-down jockey to help him out.'

'He picks on someone with enough capital to buy a partnership, someone who's been to the top of one profession and has the time in years to get to the top of another.'

'You're raving, Dolly dear. He nearly chucked me out yesterday morning.'

'But you're still here, aren't you? More here than ever before. And Joanie said he was in a fantastically good mood all day yesterday, after you'd been in to see him.'

I shook my head, laughing. 'You're too romantic. Jockeys don't turn into investigators any more than they turn into . . .'

'Well, what?' she prompted.

'Into auctioneers, then . . . or accountants.'

She shook her head. 'You've already turned into an investigator, whether you know it or not. I've been watching you these two years, remember? You look as if you're doing nothing, but you've soaked up everything the bloodhounds have taught you like a hungry sponge. I'd say, Sid love, if you don't watch out, you'll be part of the fixtures and fittings for the rest of your life.'

But I didn't believe her, and I paid no attention to what she had said.

I grinned. 'I'm going down to take a look at Seabury Racecourse this afternoon. Like to come?'

'Are you kidding?' she sighed. Her in-tray was six inches deep. 'I could have just done with a ride in that rocket car of yours, and a breath of sea air.'

I stacked the photographs together and returned them to the box, along with the negatives. There was a drawer in the table, and I pulled it open to put the photographs away. It wasn't empty. Inside lay a packet of sandwiches, some cigarettes, and a flat half bottle of whisky.

I began to laugh. 'Someone,' I said, 'will shortly come rampaging down from Missing Persons looking for his Missing Lunch.'

Seabury Racecourse lay about half a mile inland, just off a trunk road to the sea. Looking backwards from the top of the stands one could see the wide silver sweep of the English Channel. Between and on both sides the crowded rows of little houses seemed to be rushing towards the coast like Gadarene swine. In each little unit a retired schoolmaster or civil servant or clergyman – or their widows – thought about the roots they had pulled up from wherever it had been too cold or too dingy for their old age, and sniffed the warm south salt-laden air.

They had made it. Done what they'd always wanted. Retired to a bungalow by the sea.

I drove straight in through the open racecourse gates and stopped outside the weighing room. Climbing out, I stretched and walked over to knock on the door of the racecourse manager's office.

There was no reply. I tried the handle. It was locked. So was the weighing room, and everything else.

Hands in pockets, I strolled round the end of the stands to look at the course. Seabury was officially classified in Group Three: that is to say, lower than Doncaster and higher than Windsor when it came to receiving aid from the Betting Levy Board.

It had less than Grade Three stands: wooden steps with corrugated tin roofs for the most part, and draughts from all parts of the compass. But the track itself was a joy to ride on, and it had always seemed a pity to me that the rest of the amenities didn't match it.

There was no one about near the stands. Down at one end of the course, however, I could see some men and a tractor, and I set off towards them, walking down inside the rails, on the grass. The going was just about perfect for November racing, soft but springy underfoot, exactly right for tempting trainers to send their horses to the course in droves. In ordinary circumstances, that was. But as things stood at present, more trainers than Mark Witney were sending their horses elsewhere. A course which didn't attract runners didn't attract crowds to watch them. Seabury's gate receipts had been falling off for some time, but its expenses had risen; and therein lay its loss.

Thinking about the sad tale I had read in the balance sheets, I reached the men working on the course. They were digging up a great section of it and loading it on to a trailer behind the tractor. There was a pervasive unpleasant smell in the air.

An irregular patch about thirty yards deep, stretching nearly the whole width of the course, had been burned brown and killed. Less than half of the affected turf had already been removed, showing the greyish chalky mud underneath, and there was still an enormous amount to be shifted. I didn't think there were enough men working on it for there to be a hope of its being returfed and ready to race on in only eight days' time.

'Good afternoon,' I said to the men in general. 'What a horrible mess.'

One of them thrust his spade into the earth and came over, rubbing his hands on the sides of his trousers.

'Anything you want?' he said, with fair politeness.

'The racecourse manager. Captain Oxon.'

His manner shifted perceptibly towards the civil. 'He's not here today, sir. Hey! . . . aren't you Sid Halley?'

'That's right.'

He grinned, doing another quick change, this time towards brotherhood. 'I'm the foreman. Ted Wilkins.' I shook his outstretched hand. 'Captain Oxon's gone up to London. He said he wouldn't be back until tomorrow.'

'Never mind,' I said. 'I was just down in this part of the world and I thought I'd drop in and have a look at the poor old course.'

He turned with me to look at the devastation. 'Shame, isn't it?'

'What happened, exactly?'

'The tanker overturned on the road over there.' He pointed, and we began to walk towards the spot, edging round the dug up area. The road, a narrow secondary one, ran across near the end of the racecourse, with a wide semi-circle of track on the far side of it. During the races the hard road surface was covered thickly with tan or peat, or with thick green matting, which the horses galloped over without any trouble. Although not ideal, it was an arrangement to be found on many courses throughout the country, most famously with the Melling Road at Aintree, and reaching a maximum with five road crossings at Ludlow.

'Just here,' said Ted Wilkins, pointing. 'Worst place it could possibly have happened, right in the middle of the track. The stuff just poured out of the tanker. It turned right over, see, and the hatch thing was torn open in the crash.'

'How did it happen?' I asked. 'The crash, I mean?'

'No one knows, really.'

'But the driver? He wasn't killed, was he?'

'No, he wasn't even hurt much. Just shook up a

bit. But he couldn't remember what happened. Some people in a car came driving along after dark and nearly ran into the tanker. They found the driver sitting at the side of the road, holding his head and moaning. Concussion, it was, they say. They reckon he hit his head somehow when his lorry went over. Staggers me how he got out of it so lightly, the cab was fair crushed, and there was glass everywhere.'

'Do tankers often drive across here? Lucky it's never happened before, if they do.'

'They used not to,' he said, scratching his head. 'But they've been over here quite regularly now for a year or two. The traffic on the London road's getting chronic, see?'

'Oh ... did it come from a local firm, then?'

'Down the coast a bit. Intersouth Chemicals, that's the firm it belonged to.'

'How soon do you think we'll be racing here again?' I asked, turning back to look at the track. 'Will you make it by next week?'

He frowned. 'Strictly between you and me, I don't think there's a bleeding hope. What we needed, as I said to the Captain, was a couple of bulldozers, not six men with spades.'

'I would have thought so too.'

He sighed. 'He just told me we couldn't afford them and to shut up and get on with it. And that's what we've done. We'll just about have cut out all the dead turf by next Wednesday, at this rate of going on.'

'That doesn't leave any time for new turf to settle,'
I remarked.

'It'll be a miracle if it's laid, let alone settled,' he
agreed gloomily.

I bent down and ran my hand over a patch of brown
grass. It was decomposing and felt slimy. I made a face,
and the foreman laughed.

'Horrible, isn't it? It stinks too.'

I put my fingers to my nose and wished I hadn't.
'Was it slippery like this right from the beginning?'

'Yes, that's right. Hopeless.'

'Well, I won't take up any more of your time,' I said,
smiling.

'I'll tell Captain Oxon you came. Pity you missed
him.'

'Don't bother him. He must have a lot to worry
about just now.'

'One bloody crisis after another,' he nodded. 'So
long, then.' He went back to his spade and his heart-
breaking task, and I retraced the quarter mile up the
straight to the deserted stands.

I hesitated for a while outside the weighing room,
wondering whether to pick the lock and go in, and
knowing it was mainly nostalgia that urged me to do
it, not any conviction that it would be a useful piece of
investigation. There would always be the temptation, I
supposed, to use dubious professional skills for one's
own pleasure. Like doctors sniffing ether. I contented
myself with looking through the windows.

The deserted weighing room looked the same as ever: a large bare expanse of wooden board floor, with a table and some upright chairs in one corner, and the weighing machine itself on the left. Racecourse weighing machines were not all of one universal design. There weren't any left of the old type where the jockeys stood on a platform while weights were added to the balancing arm. That whole process was much too slow. Now there were either seats slung from above, in which one felt much like a bag of sugar, or chairs bolted to a base plate on springs: in both these cases the weight was quickly indicated by a pointer which swung round a gigantic clock face. In essence, modern kitchen scales vastly magnified.

The scales at Seabury were the chair-on-base-plate type, which I'd always found simplest to use. I recalled a few of the before-and-after occasions when I had sat on that particular spot. Some good, some bad, as always with racing.

Shrugging, I turned away. I wouldn't, I thought, ever be sitting there again. And no one walked over my grave.

Climbing into the car, I drove to the nearest town, looked up the whereabouts of Intersouth Chemicals, and an hour later was speaking to the personnel manager. I explained that on behalf of the National Hunt Committee I had just called in passing to find out if the driver of the tanker had fully recovered, or had remembered anything else about the accident.

The manager, fat and fiftyish, was affable but unhelpful. 'Smith's left,' he said briefly. 'We gave him a few days off to get over the accident, and then he came back yesterday and said his wife didn't fancy him driving chemicals any more, and he was packing it in.' His voice held a grievance.

'Had he been with you long?' I asked sympathetically.

'About a year.'

'A good driver, I suppose?'

'Yes, about average for the job. They have to be good drivers, or we don't use them, you see. Smith was all right, but nothing special.'

'And you still don't really know what happened?'

'No,' he sighed. 'It takes a lot to tip one of our tankers over. There was nothing to learn from the road. It was covered with oil and petrol and chemicals. If there had ever been any marks, skid marks I mean, they weren't there after the breakdown cranes had lifted the tanker up again, and the road was cleared.'

'Do your tankers use that road often?'

'They have done recently, but not any more after this. As a matter of fact, I seem to remember it was Smith himself who found that way round. Going over the racecourse missed out some bottle-neck at a junction, I believe. I know some of the drivers thought it a good idea.'

'They go through Seabury regularly then?'

'Sure, often. Straight line to Southampton and round to the oil refinery at Fawley.'

'Oh? What exactly was Smith's tanker carrying?'

'Sulphuric acid. It's used in refining petrol, among other things.'

Sulphuric acid. Dense; oily; corrosive to the point of charring. Nothing more instantly lethal could have poured out over Seabury's turf. They could have raced had it been a milder chemical, put sand or tan on the dying grass and raced over the top. But no one would risk a horse on ground soaked with vitriol.

I said, 'Could you give me Smith's address? I'll call round and see if his memory has come back.'

'Sure.' He searched in a file and found it for me. 'Tell him he can have his job back if he's interested. Another of the men gave notice this morning.'

I said I would, thanked him, and went to Smith's address, which proved to be two rooms upstairs in a suburban house. But Smith and his wife no longer lived in them. Packed up and gone yesterday, I was told by a young woman in curlers. No, she didn't know where they went. No, they didn't leave a forwarding address, and if I was her I wouldn't worry about his health as he'd been laughing and drinking and playing records to all hours the day after the crash, his concussion having cured itself pretty quick. Reaction, he'd said when she complained of the noise, against not being killed.

It was dark by then, and I drove slowly back into

London against the stream of headlights pouring out. Back to my flat in a modern block, a short walk from the office, down the ramp into the basement garage, and up in the lift to the fifth floor, home.

There were two rooms facing south, bedroom and sitting-room, and two behind them, bathroom and kitchen, with windows into an inner well. A pleasant sunny place, furnished in blond wood and cool colours, centrally heated, cleaning included in the rent. A regular order of groceries arrived week by week directly into the kitchen through a hatch, and rubbish disappeared down a chute. Instant living. No fuss, no mess, no strings. And damnably lonely, after Jenny.

Not that she had ever been in the place, she hadn't. The house in the Berkshire village where we had mostly lived had been too much of a battleground, and when she walked out I sold it, with relief. I'd moved into the new flat shortly after going to the agency, because it was close. It was also expensive: but I had no fares to pay.

I mixed myself a brandy with ice and water, sat down in an armchair, put my feet up, and thought about Seabury. Seabury, Captain Oxon, Ted Wilkins, Intersouth Chemicals, and a driver called Smith.

After that I thought about Kraye. Nothing pleasant about him, nothing at all. A smooth, phony crust of sophistication hiding ruthless greed; a seething passion for crystals, ditto for land; an obsession with the cleanliness of his body to compensate for the murk in his

127

mind; unconventional sexual pleasures; and the abnormal quality of being able to look carefully at a crippled hand and *then hit it*.

No. I didn't care for Howard Kraye one little bit.

CHAPTER SEVEN

'Chico,' I said. 'How would you overturn a lorry on a pre-determined spot?'

'Huh? That's easy. All you'd need would be some heavy lifting gear. A big hydraulic jack. A crane. Anything like that.'

'How long would it take?'

'You mean, supposing the lorry and the crane were both in position?'

'Yes.'

'Only a minute or two. What sort of lorry?'

'A tanker.'

'A petrol job?'

'A bit smaller than the petrol tankers. More the size of milk ones.'

'Easy as kiss your hand. They've got a low centre of gravity, mind. It'd need a good strong lift. But dead easy, all the same.'

I turned to Dolly. 'Is Chico busy today, or could you spare him?'

Dolly leaned forward, chewing the end of a pencil

and looking at her day's chart. The cross-over blouse did its stuff.

'I could send someone else to Kempton...' She caught the direction of my eyes and laughed, and retreated a whole half inch. 'Yes, you can have him.' She gave him a fond glance.

'Chico,' I said. 'Go down to Seabury and see if you can find any trace of heavy lifting gear having been seen near the racecourse last Friday... those little bungalows are full of people with nothing to do but watch the world go by... you might check whether anything was hired locally, but I suppose that's a bit much to hope for. The road would have to have been closed for a few minutes before the tanker went over, I should think. See if you can find anyone who noticed anything like that... detour signs, for instance. And after that, go to the council offices and see what you can dig up among their old maps on the matter of drains.' I told him the rough position of the subsiding trench which had made a slaughterhouse of the hurdle race, so that he should know what to look for on the maps. 'And be discreet.'

'Teach your grandmother to suck eggs,' he grinned.

'Our quarry is rough.'

'And you don't want him to hear us creep up behind him?'

'Quite right.'

'Little Chico,' he said truthfully, 'can take care of himself.'

After he had gone I telephoned Lord Hagbourne and described to him in no uncertain terms the state of Seabury's turf.

'What they need is some proper earth moving equipment, fast, and apparently there's nothing in the kitty to pay for it. Couldn't the Levy Board . . .?'

'The Levy Board is no fairy godmother,' he interrupted. 'But I'll see what can be done. Less than half cleared, you say? Hmm. However, I understand that Captain Oxon assured Weatherbys that the course would be ready for the next meeting. Has he changed his mind?'

'I didn't see him, sir. He was away for the day.'

'Oh.' Lord Hagbourne's voice grew a shade cooler. 'Then he didn't ask you to enlist my help?'

'No.'

'I don't see that I can interfere then. As racecourse manager it is his responsibility to decide what can be done and what can't, and I think it must be left like that. Mm, yes. And of course he will consult the Clerk of the Course if he needs advice.'

'The Clerk of the Course is Mr Fotherton, who lives in Bristol. He is Clerk of the Course there, too, and he's busy with the meetings there tomorrow and Monday.'

'Er, yes, so he is.'

'You could ring Captain Oxon up in an informal way and just ask how the work is getting on,' I suggested.

'I don't know . . .'

'Well, sir, you can take my word for it that if things

131

dawdle on at the same rate down there, there won't be any racing at Seabury next weekend. I don't think Captain Oxon can realize just how slowly those men are digging.'

'He must do,' he protested. 'He assured Weatherbys . . .'

'Another last minute cancellation will kill Seabury off,' I said with some force.

There was a moment's pause. Then he said reluctantly, 'Yes, I suppose it might. All right then. I'll ask Captain Oxon and Mr Fotherton if they are both satisfied with the way things are going.'

And I couldn't pin him down to any more direct action than that, which was certainly not going to be enough. Protocol would be the death of Seabury, I thought.

Monopolizing Dolly's telephone, I next rang up the Epping police and spoke to Chief-Inspector Cornish.

'Any more news about Andrews?' I asked.

'I suppose you have a reasonable personal interest.' His chuckle came down the wire. 'We found he did have a sister after all. We called her at the inquest yesterday for identification purposes as she is a relative, but if you ask me she didn't really know. She took one look at the bits in the mortuary and was sick on the floor.'

'Poor girl, you couldn't blame her.'

'No. She didn't look long enough though to identify

anyone. But we had your identification for sure, so we hadn't the heart to make her go in again.'

'How did he die? Did you find out?'

'Indeed we did. He was shot in the back. The bullet ricocheted off a rib and lodged in the sternum. We got the experts to compare it with the one they dug out of the wall of your office. Your bullet was a bit squashed by the hard plaster, but there's no doubt that they are the same. He was killed with the gun he used on you.'

'And was it there, underneath him?'

'Not a sign of it. They brought in "murder by persons unknown". And between you and me, that's how it's likely to stay. We haven't a lead to speak of.'

'What lead do you have?' I asked.

His voice had a smile in it. 'Only something his sister told us. She has a bedsitter in Islington, and he spent the evening there before breaking into your place. He showed her the gun. She says he was proud of having it; apparently he was a bit simple. All he told her was that a big chap had lent it to him to go out and fetch something, and he was to shoot anyone who got in his way. She didn't believe him. She said he was always making things up, always had, all his life. So she didn't ask him anything about the big chap, or about where he was going, or anything at all.'

'A bit casual,' I said. 'With a loaded gun under her nose.'

'According to the neighbours she was more

interested in a stream of men friends than in anything her brother did.'

'Sweet people, neighbours.'

'You bet. Anyway we checked with anyone we could find who had seen Andrews the week he shot you, and he hadn't said a word to any of them about a gun or a "big chap", or an errand in Cromwell Road.'

'He didn't go back to his sister afterwards?'

'No, she'd told him she had a guest coming.'

'At one in the morning? The neighbours must be right. You tried the racecourses, of course? Andrews is quite well known there, as a sort of spivvy odd-job messenger boy.'

'Yes, we mainly tried the racecourses. No results. Everyone seemed surprised that such a harmless person should have been murdered.'

'Harmless!'

He laughed. 'If you hadn't thought him harmless, you'd have kept out of his way.'

'You're so right,' I said with feeling. 'But now I see a villain in every respectable citizen. It's very disturbing.'

'Most of them are villains, in one way or another,' he said cheerfully. 'Keeps us busy. By the way, what do you think of Sparkle's chances – this year in the Hennessy . . .?'

When eventually I put the telephone down Dolly grabbed it with a sarcastic 'Do you mind?' and asked the switchboard girl to get her three numbers in a row, 'without interruptions from Halley'. I grinned, got the packet of photographs out of the plywood table drawer, and looked through them again. They didn't tell me any more than before. Ellis Bolt's letters to Kraye. Now you see it, now you don't. A villain in every respectable citizen. Play it secretly, I thought, close to the chest, in case the eyes looking over your shoulder give you away. I wondered why I was so oppressed by a vague feeling of apprehension, and decided in irritation that a bullet in the stomach had made me nervous.

When Dolly finished her calls I took the receiver out of her hand and got through to my bank manager.

'Mr Hopper? This is Sid Halley ... yes, fine thanks, and you? Good. Now, would you tell me just how much I have in both my accounts, deposit and current?'

'They're quite healthy, actually,' he said in his gravelly bass voice. 'You've had several dividends in lately. Hang on a minute, and I'll send for the exact figures.' He spoke to someone in the background and then came back. 'It's time you re-invested some of it.'

'I do have some investments in mind,' I agreed. 'That's what I want to discuss with you. I'm planning to buy some shares this time from another stockbroker, not through the bank. Er ... please don't think that I'm dissatisfied; how could I be, when you've done so well for me. It's something to do with my work at the agency.'

'Say no more. What exactly do you want?'

'Well, to give you as a reference,' I said. 'He's sure to want one, but I would be very grateful if you would

135

make it as impersonal and as strictly financial as possible. Don't mention either my past occupation or my present one. That's very important.'

'I won't, then. Anything else?'

'Nothing . . . oh, yes. I've introduced myself to him as John Halley. Would you refer to me like that if he gets in touch with you?'

'Right. I'll look forward to hearing from you one day what it's all about. Why don't you come in and see me? I've some very good cigars.' The deep voice was amused. 'Ah, here are the figures . . .' He told me the total, which for once was bigger than I expected. That happy state of affairs wouldn't last very long, I reflected, if I had to live for two years without any salary from Radnor. And no one's fault but my own.

Giving Dolly back her telephone with an ironic bow, I went upstairs to Bona Fides. Jack Copeland's mud coloured jersey had a dark blue darn on the chest and a fraying stretch of ribbing on the hip. He was picking at a loose thread and making it worse.

'Anything on Kraye yet?' I asked. 'Or is it too early?'

'George has got something on the prelim, I think,' he answered. 'Anybody got any scissors?' A large area of jersey disintegrated into ladders. 'Blast.'

Laughing, I went over to George's desk. The prelim was a sheet of handwritten notes in George's concertinaed style. 'Leg mat, 2 yrs. 2 prev, 1 div, 1 sui dec,' it began, followed by a list of names and dates.

'Oh, yeah?' I said.

'Yeah.' He grinned. 'Kraye was legally married to Doria Dawn, née Easterman, two years ago. Before that he had two other wives. One killed herself; the other divorced him for cruelty.' He pointed to the names and dates.

'So clear,' I agreed. 'When you know how.'

'If you weren't so impatient you'd have a legible typed report. But as you're here . . .' He went on down the page, pointing. 'Geologists think him a bit eccentric . . . quartz has no intrinsic value, most of it's much too common, except for the gem stones, but Kraye goes round trying to buy chunks of it if they take his fancy. They know him quite well along the road at the Geology Museum. But not a breath of any dirty work. Clubs . . . he belongs to these three, not over-liked, but most members think he's a brilliant fellow, talks very well. He gambles at Crockfords, ends up about all square over the months. He travels, always first-class, usually by boat, not air. No job or profession, can't trace him on any professional or university lists. Thought to live on investments, playing the stock market, etc. Not much liked, but considered by most a clever, cultured man, by one or two a hypocritical gasbag.'

'No talk of him being crooked in any way?'

'Not a word. If you want him dug deeper?'

'If you can do it without him finding out.'

George nodded. 'Do you want him tailed?'

'No, I don't think so. Not at present.' A twenty-four-hour tail was heavy on man-power and expensive to the client, quite apart from the risk of the quarry noticing and being warned of the hunt. 'Anything on his early life?' I asked.

George shook his head. 'Nothing. Nobody who knows him now has known him longer than about ten years. He either wasn't born in Britain, or his name at birth wasn't Kraye. No known relatives.'

'You've done marvels, George. All this in one day.'

'Contacts, chum, contacts. A lot of phoning, a bit of pubbing, a touch of gossip with the local tradesmen ... nothing to it.'

Jack, moodily poking his fingers through the cobweb remains of his jersey, looked at me over the half-moon specs and said that there wasn't a prelim on Bolt yet because ex-sergeant Carter, who was working on it, hadn't phoned in.

'If he does,' I said, 'let me know? I've an appointment with Bolt at three thirty. It would be handy to know the set-up before I go.'

'OK.'

After that I went down and looked out of the windows of the Racing Section for half an hour, idly watching life go by in the Cromwell Road and wondering just what sort of mess I was making of the Kraye investigation. A novice chaser in the Grand National, I thought wryly; that was me. Though, come to think of it, I had once ridden a novice in the National, and got round, too. Slightly cheered, I took Dolly out to a

drink and a sandwich in the snack bar at the Air Ter-
minal, where we sat and envied the people starting off
on their travels. So much expectation in the faces as if
they could fly away and leave their troubles on the
ground. An illusion, I thought sourly. Your troubles
flew with you; a drag in the mind . . . a deformity in the
pocket.

I laughed and joked with Dolly, as usual. What else
can you do?

The firm of Charing, Street, and King occupied two
rooms in a large block of offices belonging to a bigger
firm, and consisted entirely of Bolt, his clerk, and a
secretary.

I was shown the door of the secretary's office, and
went into a dull, tidy, fog-coloured box of a room with
cold fluorescent lighting and a close-up view of the fire-
escape through the grimy window. A woman sat at a
desk by the right-hand wall, facing the window, with
her back towards me. A yard behind her chair was a
door with ELLIS BOLT painted on a frosted glass panel.
It occurred to me that she was most awkwardly placed
in the room, but that perhaps she liked sitting in a
potential draught and having to turn round every time
someone came in.

She didn't turn round, however. She merely moved
her head round a fraction towards me and said, 'Yes?'

'I have an appointment with Mr Bolt,' I said. 'At three thirty.'

'Oh, yes, you must be Mr Halley. Do sit down. I'll see if Mr Bolt is free now.'

She pointed to an easy chair a step ahead of me, and flipped a switch on her desk. While I listened to her telling Mr Bolt I was there, in the quiet voice I had heard on the telephone, I had time to see she was in her late thirties, slender, upright in her chair, with a smooth wing of straight, dark hair falling down beside her cheek. If anything, it was too young a hair style for her. There were no rings on her fingers, and no nail varnish either. Her clothes were dark and uninteresting. It seemed as though she were making a deliberate attempt to be unattractive, yet her profile, when she half turned and told me Mr Bolt would see me, was pleasant enough. I had a glimpse of one brown eye quickly cast down, the beginning of a smile on pale lips, and she presented me again squarely with the back of her head.

Puzzled, I opened Ellis Bolt's door and walked in. The inner office wasn't much more inspiring than the outer; it was larger and there was a new green square of carpet on the linoleum, but the greyish walls pervaded, along with the tidy dullness. Through the two windows was a more distant view of the fire-escape of the building across the alley. If a drab conventional setting equalled respectability, Bolt was an honest stockbroker;

and Carter, who had phoned in just before I left, had found nothing to suggest otherwise.

Bolt was on his feet behind his desk, hand out-stretched. I shook it, he gestured me to a chair with arms, and offered me a cigarette.

'No, thank you, I don't smoke.'

'Lucky man,' he said benignly, tapping ash off one he was half through, and settling his pin-striped bulk back into his chair.

His face was rounded at every point, large round nose, round cheeks, round heavy chin: no planes, no impression of bone structure underneath. He had exceptionally heavy eyebrows, a full mobile mouth, and a smug self-satisfied expression.

'Now, Mr Halley, I believe in coming straight to the point. What can I do for you?'

He had a mellifluous voice, and he spoke as if he enjoyed the sound of it.

I said, 'An aunt has given me some money now rather than leave it to me in her will, and I want to invest it.'

'I see. And ...at made you come to me? Did some-one recommend . . .?' He tailed off, watching me with eyes that told me he was no fool.

'I'm afraid . . .' I hestitated, smiling apologetically to take the offence out of the words, 'that I literally picked you with a pin. I don't know any stockbrokers. I didn't know how to get to know one, so I picked up a classified directory and stuck a pin into the list of names, and it was yours.'

'Ah,' he said paternally, observing the bad fit of Chico's second best suit, which I had borrowed for the occasion, and listening to me reverting to the accent of my childhood.

'Can you help me?' I asked.

'I expect so, I expect so. How much is this er, gift?' His voice was minutely patronizing, his manner infinitesimally bored. His time, he suspected, was being wasted.

'Fifteen hundred pounds.'

He brightened a very little. 'Oh, yes, definitely, we can do something with that. Now, do you want growth mainly or a high rate of yield?'

I looked vague. He told me quite fairly the difference between the two, and offered no advice.

'Growth, then,' I said tentatively. 'Turn it into a fortune in time for my old age.'

He smiled without much mirth, and drew a sheet of paper towards him.

'Could I have your full name?'

'John Halley ... John Sidney Halley,' I said truthfully. He wrote it down.

'Address?' I gave it.

'And your bank?' I told him that too.

'And I'll need a reference, I'm afraid.'

'Would the bank manager do?' I asked. 'I've had an

account there for two years ... he knows me quite well.'

'Excellent.' He screwed up his pen. 'Now, do you have any idea what companies you'd like shares in, or will you leave it to me?'

'Oh, I'll leave it to you. If you don't mind, that is. I don't know anything about it, you see, not really. Only it seems silly to leave all that money around doing nothing.'

'Quite, quite.' He was bored with me. I thought with amusement that Charles would appreciate my continuing his strategy of the weak front. 'Tell me, Mr Halley, what do you do for a living?'

'Oh ... um ... I work in a shop,' I said. 'In the men's wear. Very interesting, it is.'

'I'm sure it is.' There was a yawn stuck in his throat.

'I'm hoping to be made an assistant buyer next year,' I said eagerly.

'Splendid. Well done.' He'd had enough. He got cumbrously to his feet and ushered me to the door. 'All right, Mr Halley, I'll invest your money safely for you in good long term growth stock, and send you the papers to sign in due course. You'll hear from me in a week or ten days. All right?'

'Yes, Mr Bolt, thank you very much indeed,' I said respectfully. He shut the door gently behind me.

There were now two people in the outer office. The woman with her back still turned, and a spare middle-aged man with a primly folded mouth, and tough stringy tendons pushing his collar away from his neck. He was quite at home, and with an incurious, unhurried glance at me he went past into Bolt's office. The clerk, I presumed.

The woman was typing addresses on envelopes. The twenty or so that she had done lay in a slithery stack on her left: on her right an open file provided a list of names. I looked over her shoulder casually, and then with quickened interest. She was working down the first page of a list of Seabury shareholders.

'Do you want something, Mr Halley?' she asked politely, pulling one envelope from the typewriter and inserting another with a minimum of flourish.

'Well, er, yes,' I said diffidently. I walked round to the side of her desk and found that one couldn't go on round to the front of it: a large old fashioned table with bulbous legs filled all the space between the desk and the end of the room. I looked at this arrangement with some sort of understanding and with compassion.

'I wondered,' I said, 'if you could be very kind and tell me something about investing money, and so on. I didn't like to ask Mr Bolt too much, he's a busy man. And I'd like to know a bit about it.'

'I'm sorry, Mr Halley.' Her head was turned away from me, bent over the Seabury investors. 'I've a job to do, as you see. Why don't you read the financial columns in the papers, or get a book on the subject?'

I had a book all right. *Outline of Company Law.* One thing I had learned from it was that only stockbrokers –

apart from the company involved – could send circulars to shareholders. It was illegal if private citizens did it. Illegal for Kraye to send letters to Seabury shareholders offering to buy them out: legal for Bolt.

'Books aren't as good as people at explaining things,' I said. 'If you are busy now, could I come back when you've finished work and take you out for a meal? I'd be so grateful if you would, if you possibly could.'

A sort of shudder shook her. 'I'm sorry, Mr Halley, but I'm afraid I can't.'

'If you will look at me, so that I can see all of your face,' I said, 'I will ask you again.'

Her head went up with a jerk at that, but finally she turned round and looked at me.

I smiled. 'That's better. Now, how about coming out with me this evening?'

'You guessed?'

I nodded. 'The way you've got your furniture organized . . . Will you come?'

'You still want to?'

'Well, of course. What time do you finish?'

'About six, tonight.'

'I'll come back. I'll meet you at the door, down in the street.'

'All right,' she said. 'If you really mean it, thank you. I'm not doing anything else tonight . . .'

Years of hopeless loneliness showed raw in the simple words. Not doing anything else tonight or most nights. Yet her face wasn't horrific; not anything as bad as I had been prepared for. She had lost an eye, and wore a false one. There had been some extensive burns and undoubtedly some severe fracture of the facial bones, but plastic surgery had repaired the damage to a great extent, and it had all been a long time ago. The scars were old. It was the inner wound which hadn't healed.

Well . . . I knew a bit about that myself, on a smaller scale.

CHAPTER EIGHT

She came out of the door at ten past six wearing a
neat, well cut dark overcoat and with a plain silk scarf
covering her hair, tied under her chin. It hid only a
small part of the disaster to her face, and seeing her
like that, defenceless away from the shelter she had
made in her office, I had an uncomfortably vivid vision
of the purgatory she suffered day in and day out on
the journeys to work.

She hadn't expected me to be there. She didn't look
round for me when she came out, but turned directly
up the road towards the tube station. I walked after
her and touched her arm. Even in low heels she was
taller than I.

'Mr Halley!' she said. 'I didn't think . . .'

'How about a drink first?' I said. 'The pubs are
open.'

'Oh no . . .'

'Oh yes. Why not?' I took her arm and steered her
firmly across the road into the nearest bar. Dark oak,
gentle lighting, brass pump handles, and the lingering

smell of lunchtime cigars: a warm beckoning stop for
city gents on their way home. There were already half
a dozen of them, prosperous and dark-suited, adding
fizz to their spirits.

'Not here,' she protested.

'Here.' I held a chair for her to sit on at a small
table in a corner, and asked her what she would like
to drink.

'Sherry, then . . . dry . . .'

I took the two glasses over one at a time, sherry for
her, brandy for me. She was sitting on the edge of the
chair, uncomfortably, and it was not the one I had put
her in. She had moved round so that she had her back
to everyone except me.

'Good luck, Miss . . .?' I said, lifting my glass.

'Martin. Zanna Martin.'

'Good luck, Miss Martin.' I smiled.

Tentatively she smiled back. It made her face much
worse: half the muscles on the disfigured right side
didn't work and could do nothing about lifting the
corner of her mouth or crinkling the skin round the
socket of her eye. Had life been even ordinarily kind
she would have been a pleasant looking, assured
woman in her late thirties with a loving husband and a
growing family: years of heartbreak had left her a shy,
lonely spinster who dressed and moved as though she
would like to be invisible. Yet, looking at the sad trav-
esty of her face, one could neither blame the young

men who hadn't married her nor condemn her own efforts at effacement.

'Have you worked for Mr Bolt long?' I asked peaceably, settling back lazily into my chair and watching her gradually relax into her own.

'Only a few months . . .' She talked for some time about her job in answer to my interested questions, but unless she was supremely artful, she was not aware of anything shady going on in Charing, Street, and King. I mentioned the envelopes she had been addressing, and asked what was going into them.

'I don't know yet,' she said. 'The leaflets haven't come from the printers.'

'But I expect you typed the leaflet anyway,' I said idly.

'No, actually I think Mr Bolt did that one himself. He's quite helpful in that way, you know. If I'm busy he'll often do letters himself.'

Will he, I thought. Will he, indeed. Miss Martin, as far as I was concerned, was in the clear. I bought her another drink and extracted her opinion about Bolt as a stockbroker. Sound, she said, but not busy. She had worked for other stockbrokers, it appeared, and knew enough to judge.

'There aren't many stockbrokers working on their own any more,' she explained, 'and . . . well . . . I don't like working in a big office, you see . . . and it's getting more difficult to find a job which suits me. So many stockbrokers have joined up into partnerships of three or more; it reduces overheads terrifically, of course, and it means that they can spend more time in the House . . .'

'Where are Mr Charing, Mr Street, and Mr King?' I asked.

Charing and Street were dead, she understood, and King had retired some years ago. The firm now consisted simply and solely of Ellis Bolt. She didn't really like Mr Bolt's offices being contained inside those of another firm. It wasn't private enough, but it was the usual arrangement nowadays. It reduced overheads so much . . .

When the city gents had mostly departed to the bosoms of their families, Zanna Martin and I left the pub and walked through the empty city streets towards the Tower. We found a quiet little restaurant where she agreed to have dinner. As before, she made a straight line for a corner table and sat with her back to the room.

'I'm paying my share,' she announced firmly when she had seen the prices on the menu. 'I had no idea this place was so expensive, or I wouldn't have let you choose it . . . Mr Bolt mentioned that you worked in a shop.'

'There's Aunty's legacy,' I pointed out. 'The dinner's on Aunty.'

She laughed. It was a happy sound if you didn't look at her, but I found I was already able to talk to her without continually, consciously thinking about her face. One got used to it after a very short while. Some time, I thought, I would tell her so.

I was still on a restricted diet, which made social eating difficult enough without one-handedness thrown in, but did very well on the clear soup and Dover sole, expertly removed from the bone by a waiter. Miss Martin, shedding inhibitions visibly, ordered lobster cocktail, fillet steak, and peaches in kirsch. We drank wine, coffee, and brandy, and took our time.

'Oh!' she said ecstatically at one point. 'It is so long since I had anything like this. My father used to take me out now and then, but since he died . . . well, I can't go to places like this myself . . . I sometimes eat in a café round the corner from my rooms, they know me there . . . it's very good food really, chops, eggs and chips . . . you know . . . things like that.' I could picture her there, sitting alone, with her ravaged head turned to the wall. Lonely unhappy Zanna Martin. I wished I could do something – anything – to help her.

Eventually, when she was stirring her coffee, she said simply. 'It was a rocket, this.' She touched her face. 'A firework. The bottle it was standing in tipped over just as it went off, and it came straight at me. It hit me on the cheek bone and exploded . . . It wasn't anybody's fault . . . I was sixteen.'

'They made a good job of it,' I said.

She shook her head, smiling the crooked tragic smile. 'A good job from what it was, I suppose, but . . . they said if the rocket had struck an inch higher it would have gone through my eye into my brain and killed me. I often wish it had.'

She meant it. Her voice was calm. She was stating a fact.

'Yes,' I said.

'It's strange, but I've almost forgotten about it this evening, and that doesn't often happen when I'm with anyone.'

'I'm honoured.'

She drank her coffee, put down her cup, and looked at me thoughtfully.

She said, 'Why do you keep your hand in your pocket all the time?'

I owed it to her, after all. I put my hand palm upward on the table, wishing I didn't have to.

She said 'Oh!' in surprise, and then, looking back at my face, 'So you do know. That's why I feel so . . . so easy with you. You do understand.'

I shook my head. 'Only a little. I have a pocket; you haven't. I can hide.' I rolled my hand over (the back of it was less off-putting), and finally retreated it on to my lap.

'But you can't do the simplest things,' she exclaimed. Her voice was full of pity. 'You can't tie your shoe-laces, for instance. You can't even eat steak in a restaurant without asking someone else to cut it up for you . . .'

'Shut up,' I said abruptly. 'Shut up, Miss Martin.

Don't you dare to do to me what you can't bear yourself.'

'Pity . . .' she said, biting her lip and staring at me unhappily. 'Yes, it's so easy to give . . .'

'And embarrassing to receive.' I grinned at her. 'And my shoes don't have shoe-laces. They're out of date, for a start.'

'You can know as well as I do what it feels like, and yet do it to someone else . . .' She was very upset.

'Stop being miserable. It was kindness. Sympathy.'

'Do you think,' she said hesitantly, 'that pity and sympathy are the same thing?'

'Very often, yes. But sympathy is discreet and pity is tactless. Oh . . . I'm so sorry.' I laughed. 'Well . . . it was sympathetic of you to feel sorry I can't cut up my own food, and tactless to say so. The perfect example.'

'It wouldn't be so hard to forgive people for just being tactless,' she said thoughtfully.

'No,' I agreed, surprised. 'I suppose it wouldn't.'

'It might not hurt so much . . . just tactlessness?'

'It mightn't . . .'

'And curiosity . . . that might be easier, too, if I just thought of it as bad manners, don't you think? I mean tactlessness and bad manners wouldn't be so hard to stand. In fact *I* could be sorry for *them*, for not knowing better how to behave. Oh why, why didn't I think of that years ago, when it seems so simple now. So sensible.'

'Miss Martin,' I said with gratitude. 'Have some more brandy ... you're a liberator.'

'How do you mean?'

'Pity is bad manners and can be taken in one's stride, as you said.'

'You said it,' she protested.

'Indeed I didn't, not like that.'

'All right,' she said with gaiety. 'We'll drink to a new era. A bold front to the world. I will put my desk back to where it was before I joined the office, facing the door. I'll let every caller see me. I'll...' Her brave voice nearly cracked. 'I'll just think poorly of their manners if they pity me too openly. That's settled.'

We had some more brandy. I wondered inwardly whether she would have the same resolve in the morning, and doubted it. There had been so many years of hiding. She too, it seemed, was thinking along the same lines.

'I don't know that I can do it alone. But if you will promise me something, then I can.'

'Very well,' I said incautiously. 'What?'

'Don't put your hand in your pocket tomorrow. Let everyone see it.'

I couldn't. Tomorrow I would be going to the races. I looked at her, appalled, and really understood only then what she had to bear, and what it would cost her to move her desk. She saw the refusal in my face, and some sort of light died in her room. The gaiety collapsed, the defeated, defenceless look came back, the liberation was over.

'Miss Martin . . .' I swallowed.

'It doesn't matter,' she said tiredly. 'It doesn't matter. And anyway, it's Saturday tomorrow. I only go in for a short while to see to the mail and anything urgent from today's transactions. There wouldn't be any point in changing the desk.'

'And on Monday?'

'Perhaps.' It meant no.

'If you'll change it tomorrow and do it all next week, I'll do what you ask,' I said, quaking at the thought of it.

'You can't,' she said sadly. 'I can see that you can't.'

'If you can, I must.'

'But I shouldn't have asked you . . . you work in a shop.'

'Oh.' That I had forgotten. 'It won't matter.'

An echo of her former excitement crept back.

'Do you really mean it?'

I nodded. I had wanted to do something – anything – to help her. Anything. My God.

'Promise?' she said doubtfully.

'Yes. And you?'

'All right,' she said, with returning resolution. 'But I can only do it if I know you are in the same boat . . . I couldn't let you down then, you see.'

I paid the bill, and although she said there was no need, I took her home. We went on the underground to Finchley. She made straight for the least conspicuous seat and sat presenting the good side of her face to the carriage. Then, laughing at herself, she apologized for doing it.

'Never mind,' I said, 'the new era doesn't start until tomorrow,' and hid my hand like a proper coward.

Her room was close to the station (a deliberately short walk, I guessed) in a large prosperous looking suburban house. At the gate she stopped.

'Will . . . er . . . I mean, would you like to come in? It's not very late . . . but perhaps you are tired.'

She wasn't eager, but when I accepted she seemed pleased.

'This way, then.'

We went through a bare tidy garden to a black painted front door adorned with horrible stained glass panels. Miss Martin fumbled endlessly in her bag for her key and I reflected idly that I could have picked that particular lock as quickly as she opened it legally. Inside there was a warm hall smelling healthily of air freshener, and at the end of a passage off it, a door with a card saying 'Martin'.

Zanna Martin's room was a surprise. Comfortable, large, close carpeted, newly decorated, and alive with colour. She switched on a standard lamp and a rosy table lamp, and drew burnt orange curtains over the black expanse of french windows. With satisfaction she showed me the recently built tiny bathroom leading out of her room, and the suitcase sized kitchen beside it, both of which additions she had paid for herself. The people who owned the house were very understanding, she said. Very kind. She had lived there for eleven years. It was home.

Zanna Martin had no mirrors in her home. Not one.

She bustled in her little kitchen, making more coffee: for something to do, I thought. I sat relaxed on her long comfortable modern sofa and watched how, from long habit, she leant forward most of the time so that the heavy shoulder length hair swung down to hide her face. She brought the tray and set it down, and sat on the sofa carefully on my right. One couldn't blame her.

'Do you ever cry?' she said suddenly.

'No.'

'Not ... from frustration?'

'No.' I smiled. 'Swear.'

She sighed. 'I used to cry often. I don't any more, though. Getting older, of course. I'm nearly forty. I've got resigned now to not getting married ... I knew I was resigned to it when I had the bathroom and kitchen built. Up to then, you see, I'd always pretended to myself that one day ... one day, perhaps ... but I don't expect it any more, not any more.'

'Men are fools,' I said inadequately.

'I hope you don't mind me talking like this? It's so seldom that I have anyone in here, and practically never anyone I can really talk to ...'

I stayed for an hour, listening to her memories, her experiences, her whole shadowed life. What, I chided

157

myself, had ever happened to me that was one tenth as bad? I had had far more ups than downs.

At length she said, 'How did it happen with you? Your hand . . .'

'Oh, an accident. A sharp bit of metal.' A razor sharp racing horse-shoe attached to the foot of a horse galloping at thirty miles an hour, to be exact. A hard kicking slash as I rolled on the ground from an easy fall. One of those things.

Horses race in thin light shoes called plates, not the heavy ones they normally wear: blacksmiths change them before and after, every time a horse runs. Some trainers save a few shillings by using the same racing plates over and over again, so that the leading edge gradually wears down to the thickness of a knife. But jagged knives, not smooth. They can cut you open like a hatchet.

I'd really known at once when I saw my stripped wrist with the blood spurting out in a jet and the broken bones showing white, that I was finished as a jockey. But I wouldn't give up hope, and insisted on the surgeons sewing it all up, even though they wanted to take my hand off there and then. It would never be any good, they said; and they were right. Too many of the tendons and nerves were severed. I persuaded them to try twice later on to rejoin and graft some of them and both times it had been a useless agony. They had refused to consider it again.

Zanna Martin hesitated on the brink of asking for

details, and fortunately didn't. Instead she said, 'Are you married? Do you know, I've talked so much about myself, that I don't know a thing about you.'

'My wife's in Athens, visiting her sister.'

'How lovely,' she sighed. 'I wish . . .'

'You'll go one day,' I said firmly. 'Save up, and go in a year or two. On a bus tour or something. With people anyway. Not alone.'

I looked at my watch, and stood up. 'I've enjoyed this evening a great deal. Thank you so much for coming out with me.'

She stood and formally shook hands, not suggesting another meeting. So much humility, I thought: so little expectation. Poor, poor Miss Martin.

'Tomorrow morning . . .' she said tentatively, at the door.

'Tomorrow,' I nodded. 'Move that desk. And I . . . I promise I won't forget.'

I went home cursing that fate had sent me someone like Zanna Martin. I had expected Charing, Street, and King's secretary to be young, perhaps pretty, a girl I could take to a café and the pictures and flirt with, with no great involvement on either side. Instead it looked as if I should have to pay more than I'd meant to for my inside information on Ellis Bolt.

CHAPTER NINE

'Now look,' said Lord Hagbourne, amidst the bustle of
Kempton races, 'I've had a word with Captain Oxon
and he's satisfied with the way things are going. I really
can't interfere any more. Surely you understand that?'

'No, sir, I don't. I don't think Captain Oxon's feelings
are more important than Seabury Racecourse. The
course should be put right quickly, even if it means
overruling him.'

'Captain Oxon,' he said with a touch of sarcasm,
'knows more about his job than you do. I give more
weight to his assurance than to your quick look at the
track.'

'Then couldn't you go and see for yourself? While
there is still time.'

He didn't like being pushed. His expression said so,
plainly. There was no more I could say, either, without
risking him ringing up Radnor to cancel the whole
investigation.

'I may . . . er . . . I may find time on Monday,' he said
at last, grudgingly. 'I'll see. Have you found anything

concrete to support your idea that Seabury's troubles were caused maliciously?'

'Not yet, sir.'

'A bit far-fetched, if you ask me,' he said crossly. 'I said so to begin with, if you remember. If you don't turn something up pretty soon . . . it's all expense, you know.'

He was intercepted by a passing Steward who took him off to another problem, leaving me grimly to reflect that so far there was a horrid lack of evidence of any sort. What there was, was negative.

George had still found no chink in Kraye's respectability, ex-sergeant Carter had given Bolt clearance, and Chico had come back from Seabury with no results all along the line.

We'd met in the office that morning, before I went to Kempton.

'Nothing,' said Chico. 'I wagged me tongue off, knocking at every front door along that road. Not a soggy flicker. The bit which crosses the racecourse wasn't closed by diversion notices, that's for sure. There isn't much traffic along there, of course. I counted it. Only forty to the hour, average. Still, that's too much for at least some of the neighbours not to notice if there'd been anything out of the ordinary.'

'Did anyone see the tanker, before it overturned?'

'They're always seeing tankers, nowadays. Several complaints about it, I got. No one noticed that one, especially.'

'It can't be coincidence . . . just at that spot at that time, where it would do most harm. And the driver packing up and moving a day or two afterwards, with no forwarding address.'

'Well . . .' Chico scratched his ear reflectively. 'I got no dice with the hiring of lifting gear either. There isn't much to be had, and what there was was accounted for. None of the little bungalows saw anything in that line, except the breakdown cranes coming to lift the tanker up again.'

'How about the drains?'

'No drains,' he said. 'A blank back to Doomsday.'

'Good.'

'Come again.'

'If you'd found them on a map, the hurdle race accident would have been a genuine accident. This way, they reek of tiger traps.'

'A spot of spade work after dark? Dodgy stuff.'

I frowned. 'Yes. And it had to be done long enough before the race meeting for the ground to settle, so that the line of the trench didn't show . . .'

'And strong enough for a tractor to roll over it.'

'Tractor?'

'There was one on the course yesterday, pulling a trailer of dug up turf.'

'Oh yes, of course. Yes, strong enough to hold a tractor . . . but wheels wouldn't pierce the ground like a horse's legs. The weight is more spread.'

'True enough.'

'How fast was the turf-digging going?' I asked.

'Fast? You're joking.'

It was depressing. So was Lord Hagbourne's shilly-shallying. So, acutely, was the whole day, because I kept my promise to Zanna Martin. Pity, curiosity, surprise, embarrassment, and revulsion, I encountered the lot. I tried hard to look on some of the things that were said as tactlessness or bad manners, but it didn't really work. Telling myself it was idiotic to be so sensitive didn't help either. If Miss Martin hadn't kept her side of the bargain, I thought miserably, I would throttle her.

Halfway through the afternoon I had a drink in the big upstairs bar with Mark Witney.

'So that's what you've been hiding all this time in pockets and gloves,' he said.

'Yes.'

'Bit of a mess,' he commented.

'I'm afraid so.'

'Does it hurt still?'

'No, only if I knock it. And it aches sometimes.'

'Mm,' he said sympathetically. 'My ankle still aches too. Joints are always like that; they mend, but they never forgive you.' He grinned. 'The other half? There's time; I haven't a runner until the fifth.'

We had another drink, talking about horses, and I reflected that it would be easy if they were all like him.

'Mark,' I said as we walked back to the weighing room, 'do you remember whether Dunstable ran into any sort of trouble before it packed up?'

'That's going back a bit.' He pondered. 'Well, it certainly wasn't doing so well during the last year or two, was it? The attendances had fallen off, and they weren't spending any money on paint.'

'But no specific disasters?'

'The Clerk of the Course took an overdose, if you call that a disaster. Yes, I remember now, the collapse of the place's prosperity was put down to the Clerk's mental illness. Brinton, I think his name was. He'd been quietly going loco and making hopeless decisions all over the place.'

'I'd forgotten,' I said glumly. Mark went into the weighing room and I leant against the rails outside. A suicidal Clerk of the Course could hardly have been the work of Kraye, I thought. It might have given him the idea of accelerating the demise of Seabury, though. He'd had plenty of time over Dunstable, but owing to a recent political threat of nationalization of building land, he might well be in a hurry to clinch Seabury. I sighed, disregarded as best I could a stare of fascinated horror from the teenage daughter of a man I used to ride for, and drifted over to look at the horses in the parade ring.

At the end of the too long afternoon I drove back to my flat, mixed a bigger drink than usual, and spent the evening thinking, without any world-shattering results. Late the next morning, when I was similarly engaged, the door bell rang, and I found Charles outside.

'Come in,' I said with surprise: he rarely visited the flat, and was seldom in London at weekends. 'Like some lunch? The restaurant downstairs is quite good.'

'Perhaps. In a minute.' He took off his overcoat and gloves and accepted some whisky. There was something unsettled in his manner, a ruffling of the smooth urbane exterior, a suggestion of a troubled frown in the high domed forehead.

'OK,' I said. 'What's the matter?'

'Er . . . I've just driven up from Aynsford. No traffic at all, for once. Such a lovely morning, I thought the drive would be . . . oh damn it,' he finished explosively, putting down his glass with a bang. 'To get it over quickly . . . Jenny telephoned from Athens last night. She's met some man there. She asked me to tell you she wants a divorce.'

'Oh,' I said. How like her, I thought, to get Charles to wield the axe. Practical Jenny, eager for a new fire, hacking away the dead wood. And if some of the wood was still alive, too bad.

'I must say,' said Charles, relaxing, 'you make a thorough job of it.'

'Of what?'

'Of not caring what happens to you.'

'I do care.'

'No one would suspect it,' he sighed. 'When I tell you your wife wants to divorce you, you just say, "Oh." When that happened,' he nodded to my arm, 'the first thing you said to me afterwards when I arrived full of sorrow and sympathy was, if I remember correctly, and I do, "Cheer up, Charles. I had a good run for my money." '

'Well, so I did.' Always, from my earliest childhood, I had instinctively shied away from too much sympathy. I didn't want it. I distrusted it. It made you soft inside, and an illegitimate child couldn't afford to be soft. One might weep at school, and one's spirit would never recover from so dire a disgrace. So the poverty and the sniggers, and later the lost wife and the smashed career had to be passed off with a shrug, and what one really felt about it had to be locked up tightly inside, out of view. Silly, really, but there it was.

We lunched companionably together downstairs, discussing in civilized tones the mechanics of divorce. Jenny, it appeared, did not want me to use the justified grounds of desertion: I, she said, should 'arrange things' instead. I must know how to do it, working for the agency. Charles was apologetic: Jenny's prospective husband was in the Diplomatic Service like Tony, and would prefer her not to be the guilty party.

Had I, Charles inquired delicately, already been . . . er . . . unfaithful to Jenny? No, I replied, watching him light his cigar, I was afraid I hadn't. For much of the time, owing to one thing and another, I hadn't felt well enough. That, he agreed with amusement, was a reasonable excuse.

I indicated that I would fix things as Jenny wanted, because it didn't affect my future like it did hers. She would be grateful, Charles said. I thought she would very likely take it for granted, knowing her.

When there was little else to say on the subject, we switched to Kraye. I asked Charles if he had seen him again during the week.

'Yes, I was going to tell you. I had lunch with him in the Club on Thursday. Quite accidentally. We both just happened to be there alone.'

'That's where you met him first, in your club?'

'That's right. Of course he thanked me for the weekend, and so on. Talked about the quartz. Very interesting collection, he said. But not a murmur about the St Luke's Stone. I would have liked to have asked him straight out, just to see his reaction.' He tapped off the ash, smiling. 'I did mention you, though, in passing, and he switched on all the charm and said you had been extremely insulting to him and his wife, but that of course you hadn't spoiled his enjoyment. Very nasty, I thought it. He was causing bad trouble for you. Or at least, he intended to.'

'Yes,' I said cheerfully. 'But I did insult him, and I also spied on him. Anything he says of me is fully merited.' I told Charles how I had taken the photographs, and all that I had discovered or guessed during the past week. His cigar went out. He looked stunned.

'Well, you wanted me to, didn't you?' I said. 'You started it. What did you expect?'

'It's only that I had almost forgotten . . . this is what you used to be like, always. Determined. Ruthless,

167

even.' He smiled. 'My game for convalescence has turned out better than I expected.'

'God help your other patients,' I said, 'if Kraye is standard medicine.'

We walked along the road towards where Charles had left his car. He was going straight home again.

I said, 'I hope that in spite of the divorce I shall see something of you? I should be sorry not to. As your ex-son-in-law, I can hardly come to Aynsford any more.'

He looked startled. 'I'll be annoyed if you don't, Sid. Jenny will be living all round the world, like Jill. Come to Aynsford whenever you want.'

'Thank you,' I said. I meant it, and it sounded like it.

He stood against his car, looking down at me from his straight six feet.

'Jenny,' he said casually, 'is a fool.'

I shook my head. Jenny was no fool. Jenny knew what she needed, and it wasn't me.

When I went into the office (on time) the following morning, the girl on the switchboard caught me and said Radnor wanted me straight away.

'Good morning,' he said. 'I've just had Lord Hagbourne on the telephone telling me it's time we got results and that he can't go to Seabury today because his car is being serviced. Before you explode, Sid . . . I told him that you would take him down there now, at once, in your own car. So get a move on.'

168

I grinned. 'I bet he didn't like that.'

'He couldn't think of an excuse fast enough. Get round and collect him before he comes up with one.'

'Right.'

I made a quick detour up to the Racing Section where Dolly was adjusting her lipstick. No cross-over blouse today. A disappointment.

I told her where I was going, and asked if I could use Chico.

'Help yourself,' she said resignedly. 'If you can get a word in edgeways. He's along in Accounts arguing with Jones-boy.'

Chico, however, listened attentively and repeated what I had asked him. 'I'm to find out exactly what mistakes the Clerk of the Course at Dunstable made, and make sure that they and nothing else were the cause of the course losing money.'

'That's right. And dig out the file on Andrews and the case you were working on when I got shot.'

'But that's all dead,' he protested, 'the file's down in records in the basement.'

'Send Jones-boy down for it,' I suggested, grinning. 'It's probably only a coincidence, but there is something I want to check. I'll do it tomorrow morning. OK?'

'If you say so, chum.'

Back at my flat, I filled up with Extra and made all speed round to Beauchamp Place. Lord Hagbourne, with a civil but cool good morning, lowered himself into the passenger seat, and we set off for Seabury. It took him about a quarter of an hour to get over having been manoeuvred into something he didn't want to do, but at the end of that time he sighed and moved in his seat, and offered me a cigarette.

'No, thank you, sir. I don't smoke.'

'You don't mind if I do?' He took one out.

'Of course not.'

'This is a nice car,' he remarked, looking round.

'It's nearly three years old now. I bought it the last season I was riding. It's the best I've ever had, I think.'

'I must say,' he said inoffensively, 'that you manage extremely well. I wouldn't have thought that you could drive a car like this with only one effective hand.'

'Its power makes it easier, actually. I took it across Europe last spring . . . good roads, there.'

We talked on about cars and holidays, then about theatres and books, and he seemed for once quite human. The subject of Seabury we carefully by-passed. I wanted to get him down there in a good mood; the arguments, if any, could take place on the way back; and it seemed as if he was of the same mind.

The state of Seabury's track reduced him to silent gloom. We walked down to the burnt piece with Captain Oxon, who was bearing himself stiffly and being pointedly polite. I thought he was a fool: he should have fallen on the Senior Steward and begged for instant help.

Captain Oxon, whom I had not met before, though he said he knew me by sight, was a slender pleasant looking man of about fifty, with a long pointed chin and a slight tendency to watery eyes. The present offended obstinacy of his expression looked more like childishness than real strength. A colonel manqué, I thought uncharitably, and no wonder.

'I know it's not really my business,' I said, 'but surely a bulldozer would shift what's left of the burnt bit in a couple of hours? There isn't time to settle new turf, but you could cover the whole area with some tons of tan and race over it quite easily, like that. You must be getting tan anyway, to cover the road surface. Surely you could just increase the order?'

Oxon looked at me with irritation. 'We can't afford it.'

'You can't afford another cancellation at the last minute,' I corrected.

'We are insured against cancellations.'

'I doubt whether an insurance company would stand this one,' I said. 'They'd say you could have raced if you'd tried hard enough.'

'It's Monday now,' remarked Lord Hagbourne thoughtfully. 'Racing's due on Friday. Suppose we call in a bulldozer tomorrow; the tan can be unloaded and spread on Wednesday and Thursday. Yes, that seems sound enough.'

'But the cost . . .' began Oxon.

'I think the money must be found,' said Lord Hagbourne. 'Tell Mr Fotherton when he comes over that I have authorized the expenditure. The bills will be met, in one way or another. But I do think there is no case for not making an effort.'

It was on the tip of my tongue to point out that if Oxon had arranged for the bulldozer on the first day he could have saved the price of casual labour for six hand-diggers for a week, but as the battle was already won, I nobly refrained. I continued to think, however, that Oxon was a fool. Usually the odd custom of giving the managerships of racecourses to ex-army and navy officers worked out well, but conspicuously not in this case.

The three of us walked back up to the stands, Lord Hagbourne pausing and pursing his lips at their dingy appearance. I reflected that it was a pity that Seabury had a Clerk of the Course whose heart and home were far away on the thriving course at Bristol. If I'd been arranging things, I'd have seen to it a year ago, when the profits turned to loss, that Seabury had a new Clerk entirely devoted to its own interests, someone moreover whose livelihood depended on it staying open. The bungle, delay, muddle, too much politeness and failure to take action shown by the Seabury executive had been of inestimable value to the quietly burrowing Kraye.

Mr Fotherton might have been worried, as he said, but he had done little except mention it in passing to Charles in his capacity as Steward at some other meeting. Charles, looking for something to divert my mind from my stomach, and perhaps genuinely anxious about

Seabury, had tossed the facts to me. In his own particular way, naturally.

The casualness of the whole situation was horrifying. I basely wondered whether Fotherton himself had a large holding in Seabury shares and therefore a vested interest in its demise. Planning a much closer scrutiny of the list of shareholders, I followed Lord Hagbourne and Captain Oxon round the end of the stands, and we walked the three hundred yards or so through the racecourse gates and down the road to where Captain Oxon's flat was situated above the canteen in the stable block.

On Lord Hagbourne's suggestion he rang up a firm of local contractors while we were still there, and arranged for the urgent earth-moving to be done the following morning. His manner was still ruffled, and it didn't improve things when I declined the well-filled ham and chutney sandwiches he offered, though I would have adored to have eaten them, had he but known. I had been out of hospital for a fortnight, but I had another fortnight to go before things like new bread, ham, mustard, and chutney were due back on the agenda. Very boring.

After the sandwiches Lord Hagbourne decided on a tour of inspection, so we all three went first round the stable block, into the lads' hostel, through the canteen to the kitchen, and into all the stable administrative offices. Everywhere the story was the same. Except for the rows of wooden boxes which had been thrown

173

up cheaply after the old ones burned down, there was no recent maintenance and no new paint.

Then we retraced our steps up the road, through the main gate, and across to the long line of stands with the weighing room, dining-rooms, bars, and cloakrooms built into the back. At one end were the secretary's office, the press room and the Stewards' room: at the other, the first-aid room and a store. A wide tunnel like a passage ran centrally through the whole length of the building, giving secondary access on one side to many of the rooms, and on the other to the steps of the stands themselves. We painstakingly covered the lot, even down to the boiler room and the oil bunkers, so I had my nostalgic look inside the weighing room and changing room after all.

The whole huge block was dankly cold, very draughty, and smelt of dust. Nothing looked new, not even the dirt. For inducing depression it was hard to beat, but the dreary buildings along in the cheaper rings did a good job of trying.

Captain Oxon said the general dilapidation was mostly due to the sea air, the racecourse being barely half a mile from the shore, and no doubt in essence he was right. The sea air had had a free hand for far too long.

Eventually we returned to where my car was parked inside the gate, and looked back to the row of stands: forlorn, deserted, decaying on a chilly early November

afternoon, with a salt-laden drizzle just beginning to
blur the outlines.

'What's to be done?' said Lord Hagbourne glumly,
as we drove through the rows of bungalows on our way
home.

'I don't know.' I shook my head.

'The place is dead.'

I couldn't argue. Seabury had suddenly seemed to
me to be past saving. The Friday and Saturday fixtures
could be held now, but as things stood the gate money
would hardly cover expenses. No company could go on
making a loss indefinitely. Seabury could plug the gap
at present by drawing on their reserve funds, but as I'd
seen from their balance sheets at Company House, the
reserves only amounted to a few thousands. Matters
were bound to get worse. Insolvency waited round a
close corner. It might be more realistic to admit that
Seabury had no future and to sell the land at the highest
price offered as soon as possible. People were, after all,
crying out for flat land at the seaside. And there was
no real reason why the shareholders shouldn't be
rewarded for their long loyalty and recent poor dividends and receive eight pounds for each one they had
invested. Many would gain if Seabury came under the
hammer, and no one would lose. Seabury was past
saving: best to think only of the people who would
benefit.

My thoughts stopped with a jerk. This, I realized,
must be the attitude of the Clerk, Mr Fotherton, and

of the Manager, Oxon, and of all the executive. This explained why they had made surprisingly little attempt to save the place. They had accepted defeat easily and seen it not only to be harmless, but to many, usefully profitable. As it had been with other courses, big courses like Hurst Park and Birmingham, so it should be with Seabury.

What did it matter that yet another joined the century's ghost ranks of Cardiff, Derby, Bournemouth, Newport? What did it matter if busy people like Inspector Cornish of Dunstable couldn't go racing much because their local course had vanished? What did it matter if Seabury's holiday makers went to the bingo halls instead?

Chasing owners, I thought, should rise up in a body and demand that Seabury should be preserved, because no racecourse was better for their horses. But of course they wouldn't. You could tell owners how good it was, but unless they were horsemen themselves, it didn't register. They only saw the rotten amenities of the stands, not the splendidly sited well-built fences that positively invited their horses to jump. They didn't know how their horses relished the short springy turf underfoot, or found the arc and cambers of the bends perfect for maintaining an even speed. Corners at many other racecourses threw horses wide and broke up their stride, but not those at Seabury. The original course builder had been brilliant, and regular visits from the Inspector of Courses had kept his work fairly intact.

Fast, true run, unhazardous racing, that's what Seabury gave.

Or had done, before Kraye.

Kraye and the executive's inertia between them . . . I stamped on the accelerator in a surge of anger and the car swooped up the side of the South Downs like a bird. I didn't often drive fast any more: I did still miss having two hands on the wheel. At the top, out of consideration for my passenger's nerves, I let the speedometer ribbon slide back to fifty.

He said, 'I feel like that about it too.'

I glanced at him in surprise.

'The whole situation is infuriating,' he nodded. 'Such a good course basically, and nothing to be done.'

'It could be saved,' I said.

'How?'

'A new attitude of mind . . .' I tailed off.

'Go on,' he said. But I couldn't find the words to tell him politely that he ought to chuck out all the people in power at Seabury; too many of them were probably his ex-school chums or personal friends.

'Suppose,' he said after a few minutes, 'that you had a free hand, what would you do?'

'One would never get a free hand. That's half the trouble. Someone makes a good suggestion, and someone else squashes it. They end up, often as not, by doing nothing.'

'No, Sid, I mean you personally. What would you do?'

'I?' I grinned. 'What I'd do would have the National Hunt Committee swooning like Victorian maidens.'

'I'd like to know.'

'Seriously?'

He nodded. As if he could ever be anything else but serious.

I sighed. 'Very well then. I'd pinch every good crowd-pulling idea that any other course has thought of, and put them all into operation on the same day.'

'What, for instance?'

'I'd take the whole of the reserve fund and offer it as a prize for a big race. I'd make sure the race was framed to attract the really top chasers. Then I'd go round to their trainers personally and explain the situation, and beg for their support. I'd go to some of the people who sponsor Gold Cup races and cajole them into giving five hundred pound prizes for all the other races on that day. I'd make the whole thing into a campaign. I'd get Save Seabury discussed on television, and in the sports columns of newspapers. I'd get people interested and involved. I'd make helping Seabury the smart thing to do. I'd get someone like the Beatles to come and present the trophies. I'd advertise free car-parking and free race cards, and on the day I'd have the whole place bright with flags and bunting and tubs of flowers to hide the lack of paint. I'd make sure everyone on the staff understood that a friendly welcome must be given to the customers. And I'd insist that the catering firm used its imagination. I'd fix the meeting for the beginning of April, and pray for a sunny spring day. That,' I said, running down, 'would do for a start.'

'And afterwards?' He was non-committal.

'A loan, I suppose. Either from a bank or from private individuals. But the executive would have to show first that Seabury could be a success again, like it used to be. No one falls over himself to lend to a dying business. The revival has to come before the money, if you see what I mean.'

'I do see,' he agreed slowly, 'but . . .'

'Yes. But. It always comes to But. But no one at Seabury is going to bother.'

We were silent for a long way.

Finally I said, 'This meeting on Friday and Saturday . . . it would be a pity to risk another last-minute disaster. Hunt Radnor Associates could arrange for some sort of guard on the course. Security patrols, that kind of thing.'

'Too expensive,' he said promptly. 'And you've not yet proved that it is really needed. Seabury's troubles still look like plain bad luck to me.'

'Well . . . a security patrol might prevent any more of it.'

'I don't know. I'll have to see.' He changed the subject then, and talked firmly about other races on other courses all the way back to London.

CHAPTER TEN

Dolly lent me her telephone with resignation on Tuesday morning, and I buzzed the switchboard for an internal call to Missing Persons.

'Sammy?' I said. 'Sid Halley, down in Racing. Are you busy?'

'The last teenager has just been retrieved from Gretna. Fire away. Who's lost?'

'A man called Smith.'

Some mild blasphemy sped three storeys down the wire.

I laughed. 'I think his name really is Smith. He's a driver by trade. He's been driving a tanker for Inter-south Chemicals for the last year. He left his job and his digs last Wednesday; no forwarding address.' I told him about the crash, the suspect concussion, and the revelry by night.

'You don't think he was planted on purpose on the job a year ago? His name likely wouldn't be Smith in that case . . . make it harder.'

'I don't know. But I think it's more likely he was a

bona fide Intersouth driver who was offered a cash payment for exceptional services rendered.'

'OK, I'll try that first. He might give Intersouth as a reference, in which case they'll know if he applies for another job somewhere, or I might trace him through his union. The wife might have worked, too. I'll let you know.'

'Thanks.'

'Don't forget, when the old man buys you a gold-plated executive desk I want my table back.'

'You'll want for ever,' I said, smiling. It had been Sammy's lunch.

On the table in question lay the slim file on the Andrews case that Jones-boy had unearthed from the basement. I looked round the room.

'Where's Chico?' I asked.

Dolly answered. 'Helping a bookmaker to move house.'

'He's doing *what*?' I goggled.

'That's right. Long-standing date. The bookmaker is taking his safe with him and wants Chico to sit on it in the furniture van. It had to be Chico, he said. No one else would do. The paying customer is always right, so Chico's gone.'

'Damn.'

She reached into a drawer. 'He left you a tape,' she said.

'Undamn, then.'

She grinned and handed it to me, and I took it over

to the recorder, fed it through on to the spare reel, and listened to it in the routine office way, through the earphones.

'After wearing my plates down to the ankles,' said Chico's cheerful voice, 'I found out that the worst things your Clerk of the Course did at Dunstable were to frame a lot of races that did the opposite of attract any decent runners, and be stinking rude to all and sundry. He was quite well liked up to the year before he killed himself. Then everyone says he gradually got more and more crazy. He was so rude to people who worked at the course that half of them wouldn't put up with it and left. And the local tradesmen practically spat when I mentioned his name. I'll fill you in when I see you, but there wasn't anything like Seabury – no accidents or damage or anything like that.'

Sighing, I wiped the tape clean and gave it back to Dolly. Then I opened the file on my table and studied its contents.

A Mr Mervyn Brinton of Reading, Berks, had applied to the agency for personal protection, having had reason to believe that he was in danger of being attacked. He had been unwilling to say why he might be attacked, and refused to have the agency make inquiries. All he wanted was a bodyguard. There was a strong possibility, said the report, that Brinton had tried a little amateurish blackmail, which had backfired. He had at length revealed that he possessed a certain letter, and was afraid of being attacked and having it stolen. After much persuasion by Chico Barnes, who pointed out that Brinton could hardly be guarded for the rest of his life, Brinton had agreed to inform a certain party that the letter in question was lodged in a particular desk drawer in the Racing Section of Hunt Radnor Associates. In fact it was not; and had not at any time been seen by anyone working for the agency. However, Thomas Andrews came, or was sent, to remove the letter, was interrupted by J. S. Halley (whom he wounded by shooting), and subsequently made his escape. Two days later Brinton telephoned to say he no longer required a bodyguard, and as far as the agency was concerned the case was then closed.

The foregoing information had been made available to the police in their investigation into the shooting of Halley.

I shut the file. A drab little story, I thought, of a pathetic little man playing out of his league.

Brinton.

The Clerk of the Course at Dunstable had also been called Brinton.

I sat gazing at the short file. Brinton wasn't an uncommon name. There was probably no connection at all. Brinton of Dunstable had died a good two years before Brinton of Reading had asked for protection. The only visible connection was that at different ends of the scale both the Dunstable Brinton and Thomas Andrews had earned their living on the racecourse. It wasn't much. Probably nothing. But it niggled.

I went home, collected the car, and drove to Reading.

A nervous grey haired elderly man opened the front door on a safety chain, and peered through the gap.

'Yes?'

'Mr Brinton?'

'What is it?'

'I'm from Hunt Radnor Associates. I'd be most grateful for a word with you.'

He hesitated, chewing an upper lip adorned with an untidy pepper and salt moustache. Anxious brown eyes looked me up and down and went past me to the white car parked by the kerb.

'I sent a cheque,' he said finally.

'It was quite in order,' I assured him.

'I don't want any trouble ... it wasn't my fault that that man was shot.' He didn't sound convinced.

'Oh, no one blames you for that,' I said. 'He's perfectly all right now. Back at work, in fact.'

His relief showed, even through the crack. 'Very well,' he said, and pushed the door shut to take off the chain.

I followed him into the front room of his tall terrace house. The air smelt stale and felt still, as if it had been hanging in the same spot for days. The furniture was of the hard-stuffed and brown shellacked substantial type that in my plywood childhood I had thought the peak of living, unobtainable; and there were cases of tropical butterflies on the walls, and carved ornaments from somewhere like Java or Borneo on several small tables. A life abroad, retirement at home, I thought. From colour and heat to suburban respectability in Reading.

'My wife has gone out shopping,' he said, still nervously. 'She'll be back soon.' He looked hopefully out of the lace curtained window, but Mrs Brinton didn't oblige him by coming to his support.

I said, 'I just wanted to ask you, Mr Brinton, if you were by any chance related to a Mr William Brinton, one time Clerk of Dunstable racecourse.'

He gave me a long agonized stare, and to my consternation sat down on his sofa and began to cry, his shaking hands covering his eyes and the tears splashing down on to his tweed-clad knees.

'Please . . . Mr Brinton . . . I'm so sorry,' I said awkwardly.

He snuffled and coughed, and dragged a handkerchief out to wipe his eyes. Gradually the paroxysm passed, and he said indistinctly, 'How did you find out? I told you I didn't want anyone asking questions . . .'

'It was quite accidental. Nobody asked any questions, I promise you. Would you like to tell me about it? Then I don't think any questions will need to be asked at all, from anyone else.'

'The police . . .' he said doubtfully, on a sob. 'They came before. I refused to say anything, and they went away.'

'Whatever you tell me will be in confidence.'

'I've been such a fool . . . I'd like to tell someone, really.'

I pictured the strung up, guilt-ridden weeks he'd endured, and the crying fit became not only understandable but inevitable.

'It was the letter, you see,' he said sniffing softly. 'The letter William began to write to me, though he never sent it . . . I found it in a whole trunk of stuff that was left when he . . . killed himself. I was in Sarawak then, you know, and they sent me a cable. It was a shock . . . one's only brother doing such a . . . a terrible thing. He was younger than me. Seven years. We weren't very close, except when we were children. I wish . . . but it's too late now. Anyway, when I came home I fetched all his stuff round from where it had been stored and put it up in the attic here, all his racing books and things. I didn't know what to do with them, you see. I wasn't interested in them, but it seemed . . . I don't know . . . I couldn't just burn them. It was months before I bothered to sort them out, and then I found the letter . . .' His voice faltered and he looked at me appealingly, wanting to be forgiven.

'Kitty and I had found my pension didn't go anywhere near as far as we'd expected. Everything is so terribly expensive. The rates . . . we decided we'd have to sell the house again though we'd only just bought it, and Kitty's family are all close. And then . . . I thought . . . perhaps I could sell the letter instead.'

'And you got threats instead of money,' I said.

'Yes. It was the letter itself which gave me the idea . . .' He chewed his moustache.

'And now you no longer have it,' I said matter of factly, as if I knew for certain and wasn't guessing. 'When you were first threatened you thought you could still sell the letter if Hunt Radnor kept you safe, and then you got more frightened and gave up the letter, and then cancelled the protection because the threats had stopped.'

He nodded unhappily. 'I gave them the letter because that man was shot . . . I didn't realize anything like that would happen. I was horrified. It was terrible. I hadn't thought it could be so dangerous, just selling a letter . . . I wish I'd never found it. I wish William had never written it.'

So did I, as it happened.

'What did the letter say?' I asked.

He hesitated, his fear showing. 'I might cause more trouble. They might come back.'

'They won't know you've told me,' I pointed out. 'How could they?'

'I suppose not.' He looked at me, making up his mind. There's one thing about being small: no one is ever afraid of you. If I'd been big and commanding I don't think he'd have risked it. As it was, his face softened and relaxed and he threw off the last threads of reticence.

'I know it by heart,' he said. 'I'll write it down for you, if you like. It's easier than saying it.'

I sat and waited while he fetched a ball point pen and a pad of large writing paper and got on with his task. The sight of the letter materializing again in front of his eyes affected him visibly, but whether to fear or remorse or sorrow, I couldn't tell. He covered one side of the page, then tore it off the pad and shakily handed it over.

I read what he had written. I read it twice. Because of these short desperate sentences, I reflected unemotionally, I had come within spitting distance of St Peter.

'That's fine,' I said. 'Thank you very much.'

'I wish I'd never found it,' he said again. 'Poor William.'

'Did you go to see this man?' I asked, indicating the letter as I put it away in my wallet.

'No, I wrote to him . . . he wasn't hard to find.'

'And how much did you ask for?'

Shame-faced, he muttered, 'Five thousand pounds.'

Five thousand pounds had been wrong, I thought. If he'd asked fifty thousand, he might have had a chance. But five thousand didn't put him among the big-power boys, it just revealed his mediocrity. No wonder he had been stamped on, fast.

'What happened next?' I asked.

'A big man came for the letter, about four o'clock one afternoon. It was awful. I asked him for the money and he just laughed in my face and pushed me into a chair. No money, he said, but if I didn't hand over the letter at once he'd . . . he'd teach me a thing or two.

That's what he said, teach me a thing or two. I explained that I had put the letter in my box at the bank and that the bank was closed and that I couldn't get it until the next morning. He said that he would come to the bank with me the next day, and then he went away . . .'

'And you rang up the agency almost at once? Yes. What made you choose Hunt Radnor?'

He looked surprised. 'It was the only one I knew about. Are there any others? I mean, most people have heard of Hunt Radnor, I should think.'

'I see. So Hunt Radnor sent you a bodyguard, but the big man wouldn't give up.'

'He kept telephoning . . . then your men suggested setting a trap in his office, and in the end I agreed. Oh, I shouldn't have let him, I was such a fool. I knew all the time, you see, who was threatening me, but I couldn't tell your agency because I would have had to admit I'd tried to get money . . . illegally.'

'Yes. Well, there's only one more thing. What was he like, the man who came and threatened you?'

Brinton didn't like even the memory of him. 'He was very strong. Hard. When he pushed me it was like a wall. I'm not . . . I mean, I've never been good with my fists, or anything like that. If he'd started hitting me I couldn't have stopped him . . .'

'I'm not blaming you for not standing up to him,' I pointed out. 'I just want to know what he looked like.'

'Very big,' he said vaguely. 'Huge.'

'I know it's several weeks ago, but can't you possibly

remember more than that? How about his hair? Anything odd about his face? How old? What class?'

He smiled for the first time, the sad wrinkles folding for a moment into some semblance of faded charm. If he'd never taken his first useless step into crime, I thought, he might still have been a nice gentle innocuous man, fading without rancour towards old age, troubled only by how to make a little pension go a long way. No tearing, destructive guilt.

'It's certainly easier when you ask questions like that. He was beginning to go bald, I remember now. And he had big blotchy freckles on the backs of his hands. It's difficult to know about his age. Not a youth, though; more than thirty. I think. What else did you ask? Oh yes, class. Working class, then.'

'English?'

'Oh yes, not foreign. Sort of cockney, I suppose.'

I stood up, thanked him, and began to take my leave. He said, begging me still for reassurance, 'There won't be any more trouble?'

'Not from me or the agency.'

'And the man who was shot?'

'Not from him either.'

'I tried to tell myself it wasn't my fault . . . but I haven't been able to sleep. How could I have been such a fool? I shouldn't have let that young man set any trap . . . I shouldn't have called in your agency . . . and it cost another chunk of our savings . . . I ought never to have tried to get money for that letter . . .'

'That's true, Mr Brinton, you shouldn't. But what's done is done, and I don't suppose you'll start anything like that again.'

'No, no,' he said with pain. 'I wouldn't. Ever. These last few weeks have been . . .' His voice died. Then he said more strongly, 'We'll have to sell the house now. Kitty likes it here, of course. But what I've always wanted myself is a little bungalow by the sea.'

When I reached the office I took out the disastrous letter and read it again, before adding it to the file. Being neither the original nor a photocopy, but only a reproduction from memory, it wasn't of the slightest use as evidence. In the older Brinton's small tidy script, a weird contrast to the heart-broken contents, it ran:

Dear Mervy, dear big brother,

I wish you could help me, as you did when I was little. I have spent fifteen years building up Dunstable racecourse, and a man called Howard Kraye is making me destroy it. I have to frame races which nobody likes. Very few horses come now, and the gate receipts are falling fast. This week I must see that the race card goes to the printers too late, and the Press room telephones will all be out of order. There will be a terrible muddle. People must think I am mad. I can't

escape him. He is paying me as well, but I
must do as he says. I can't help my nature,
you know that. He has found out about a boy
I was living with, and I could be prosecuted.
He wants the racecourse to sell for housing.
Nothing can stop him getting it. My
racecourse, I love it.

I know I shan't send this letter. Mervy, I
wish you were here. I haven't anyone else.
Oh dear God, I can't go on much longer, I
really can't.

At five to six that afternoon I opened the door of
Zanna Martin's office. Her desk was facing me and so
was she. She raised her head, recognized me, and
looked back at me in a mixture of pride and
embarrassment.

'I did it,' she said. 'If you didn't, I'll kill you.'

She had combed her hair even further forward, so
that it hung close round her face, but all the same
one could see the disfigurement at first glance. I had
forgotten, in the days since Friday, just how bad it was.

'I felt the same about you,' I said grinning.

'You really did keep your promise?'

'Yes, I did. All day Saturday and Sunday, most of
yesterday and most of today, and very nasty it is, too.'

She sighed with relief. 'I'm glad you've come. I
nearly gave it up this morning. I thought you wouldn't

do it, and you'd never come back to see if I had, and that I was being a proper idiot.'

'Well, I'm here,' I said. 'Is Mr Bolt in?'

She shook her head. 'He's gone home. I'm just packing up.'

'Finished the envelopes?' I said.

'Envelopes? Oh, those I was doing when you were here before? Yes, they're all done.'

'And filled and sent?'

'No, the leaflets haven't come back from the printers yet, much to Mr Bolt's disgust. I expect I'll be doing them tomorrow.'

She stood up, tall and thin, put on her coat and tied the scarf over her hair.

'Are you going anywhere this evening?' I asked.

'Home,' she said decisively.

'Come out to dinner,' I suggested.

'Aunty's legacy won't last long, the way you spend. I think Mr Bolt has already invested your money. You'd better save every penny until after settlement day.'

'Coffee, then, and the flicks?'

'Look,' she said hesitantly, 'I sometimes buy a hot chicken on my way home. There's a fish and chip shop next to the station that sells them. Would you . . . would you like to come and help me eat it? In return, I mean, for Friday night.'

'I'd enjoy that,' I said, and was rewarded by a pleased half-incredulous laugh.

'Really?'

'Really.'

As before, we went to Finchley by underground, but this time she sat boldly where her whole face showed. To try to match her fortitude, I rested my elbow on the seat arm between us. She looked at my hand and then at my face, gratefully, almost as if we were sharing an adventure.

As we emerged from the tube station she said, 'You know, it makes a great deal of difference if one is accompanied by a man, even ...' she stopped abruptly.

'Even,' I finished, smiling, 'if he is smaller than you and also damaged.'

'Oh dear ... and much younger, as well.' Her real eye looked at me with rueful amusement. The glass one stared stonily ahead. I was getting used to it again.

'Let me buy the chicken,' I said, as we stopped outside the shop. The smell of hot chips mingled with diesel fumes from a passing lorry. Civilization, I thought. Delightful.

'Certainly not.' Miss Martin was firm and bought the chicken herself. She came out with it wrapped in newspaper. 'I got a few chips and a packet of peas,' she said.

'And I,' I said firmly, as we came to an off-licence, 'am getting some brandy.' What chips and peas would do to my digestion I dared not think.

We walked round to the house with the parcels and went through into her room. She moved with a light step.

'In that cupboard over there,' she said, pointing, as she peeled off her coat and scarf, 'there are some glasses and a bottle of sherry. Will you pour me some? I expect you prefer brandy, but have some sherry if you'd like. I'll just take these things into the kitchen and put them in the oven to keep hot.'

While I unscrewed the bottles and poured the drinks I heard her lighting her gas stove and unwrapping the parcels. There was dead quiet as I walked across the room with her sherry, and when I reached the door I saw why. She held the chicken in its piece of greaseproof paper absently in one hand: the bag of chips lay open on the table with the box of peas beside it: and she was reading the newspaper they had all been wrapped in.

She looked up at me in bewilderment.

'You,' she said. 'It's you. This is you.'

I looked down where her finger pointed. The fish and chip shop had wrapped up her chicken in the *Sunday Hemisphere*.

'Here's your sherry,' I said, holding it out to her.

She put down the chicken and took the glass without appearing to notice it.

'Another Halley,' she said. 'It caught my eye. Of course I read it. And it's your picture, and it even refers to your hand. You are Sid Halley.'

'That's right.' There was no chance of denying it.

'Good heavens. I've known about you for years. Read about you. I saw you on television, often. My

195

father loved watching the racing, we always had it on when he was alive . . .' She broke off and then said with increased puzzlement, 'Why on earth did you say your name was John and that you worked in a shop? Why did you come to see Mr Bolt? I don't understand.'

'Drink your sherry, put the chicken in the oven before it freezes and I'll tell you.' There was nothing else to do: I didn't want to risk her brightly passing on the interesting titbit of news to her employer.

Without demur she put the dinner to heat, came to sit on the sofa, opposite to where I apprehensively waited in an armchair, and raised her eyebrows in expectation.

'I don't work in a shop,' I admitted. 'I am employed by a firm called Hunt Radnor Associates.'

Like Brinton, she had heard of the agency. She stiffened her whole body and began to frown. As casually as I could, I told her about Kraye and the Seabury shares; but she was no fool and she went straight to the heart of things.

'You suspect Mr Bolt too. That's why you went to see him.'

'Yes, I'm afraid so.'

'And me? You took me out simply and solely to find out about him?' Her voice was bitter.

I didn't answer at once. She waited, and somehow her calmness was more piercing than tears or temper could have been. She asked so little of life.

At last I said, 'I went to Bolt's office as much to take out his secretary as to see Bolt himself, yes.'

The peas boiled over, hissing loudly. She stood up slowly. 'At least that's honest.'

She went into the tiny kitchen and turned out the gas under the saucepan.

I said, 'I came to your office this afternoon because I wanted to look at those leaflets Bolt is sending to Seabury shareholders. You told me at once that they hadn't come from the printers. I didn't need to accept your invitation to supper after that. But I'm here.'

She stood in the kitchen doorway, holding herself straight with an all too apparent effort.

'I suppose you lied about that too,' she said in a quiet rigidly controlled voice, pointing to my arm. 'Why? Why did you play such a cruel game with me? Surely you could have got your information without that. Why did you make me change my desk round? I suppose you were laughing yourself sick all day Saturday thinking about it.'

I stood up. Her hurt was dreadful.

I said, 'I went to Kempton races on Saturday.'

She didn't move.

'I kept my promise.'

She made a slight gesture of disbelief.

'I'm sorry,' I said helplessly.

'Yes. Goodnight Mr Halley. Goodnight.'

I went.

CHAPTER ELEVEN

Radnor held a Seabury conference the next morning, Wednesday, consisting of himself, Dolly, Chico, and me: the result, chiefly, of my having the previous afternoon finally wrung grudging permission from Lord Hagbourne to arrange a twenty-four hour guard at Seabury for the coming Thursday, Friday, and Saturday.

The bulldozing had been accomplished without trouble, and a call to the course that morning had established that the tan was arriving in regular lorry loads and was being spread. Racing, bar any last minute accidents, was now certain. Even the weather was co-operating. The glass was rising; the forecast was dry, cold, and sunny.

Dolly proposed a straight patrol system, and Radnor was inclined to agree. Chico and I had other ideas.

'If anyone intended to sabotage the track,' Dolly pointed out, 'they would be frightened off by a patrol. Same thing if they were planning something in the stands themselves.'

Radnor nodded. 'Safest way of making sure racing

takes place. I suppose we'll need at least four men to do it properly.'

I said, 'I agree that we need a patrol tonight, tomorrow night, and Friday night, just to play safe. But tomorrow, when the course will be more or less deserted ... what we need is to pinch them at it, not to frighten them off. There's no evidence yet that could be used in a court of law. If we could catch them in mid-sabotage, so to speak, we'd be much better off.'

'That's right,' said Chico. 'Hide and pounce. Much better than scaring them away.'

'I seem to remember,' said Dolly with a grin, 'that the last time you two set a trap the mouse shot the cheese.'

'Oh God, Dolly, you slay me,' said Chico, laughing warmly and for once accepting her affection.

Even Radnor laughed. 'Seriously, though,' he said. 'I don't see how you can. A racecourse is too big. If you are hiding you can only see a small part of it. And surely if you show yourself your presence would act like any other patrol to stop anything plainly suspicious being done? I don't think it's possible.'

'Um,' I said. 'But there's one thing I can still do better than anyone else in this agency.'

'And what's that?' said Chico, ready to argue.

'Ride a horse.'

'Oh,' said Chico. 'I'll give you that, chum.'

'A horse,' said Radnor thoughtfully. 'Well, that's certainly an idea. Nobody's going to look suspiciously at a horse on a racecourse, I suppose. Mobile, too. Where would you get one?'

'From Mark Witney. I could borrow his hack. Seabury's his local course. His stables aren't many miles away.'

'But can you still...?' began Dolly, and broke off. 'Well, don't glare at me like that, all of you. I can't ride with two hands, let alone one.'

'A man called Gregory Philips had his arm amputated very high up,' I said, 'and went on racing in point-to-points for years.'

'Enough said,' said Dolly. 'How about Chico?'

'He can wear a pair of my jodhpurs. Protective colouring. And lean nonchalantly on the rails.'

'Stick insects,' said Chico cheerfully.

'That's what you want, Sid?' said Radnor.

I nodded. 'Look at it from the worst angle; we haven't anything on Kraye that will stand up. We might not find Smith, the tanker driver, and even if we do, he has everything to lose by talking, and nothing to gain. When the racecourse stables burned down a year ago, we couldn't prove it wasn't an accident; an illicit cigarette end. Stable lads do smoke, regardless of bans.

'The so-called drain which collapsed – we don't know if it was dug a day, a week, or six weeks before it did its work. That letter William Brinton of Dunstable wrote to his brother, it's only a copy from memory that we've got, no good at all for evidence. All it proves, to our own satisfaction, is that Kraye is capable of anything. We can't show it to Lord Hagbourne, because I obtained it in confidence, and he still isn't a hundred per cent convinced that Kraye has done more than buy shares. As I see it, we've just got to give the enemy a chance to get on with their campaign.'

'You think they will, then?'

'It's awfully likely, isn't it? This year there isn't another Seabury meeting until February. A three months' gap. And if I read it right, Kraye is in a hurry now because of the political situation. He won't want to spend fifty thousand buying Seabury and then find building land has been nationalized overnight. If I were him, I'd want to clinch the deal and sell to a developer as quickly as possible. According to the photographs of the share transfers, he already holds twenty-three per cent of the shares. This is almost certainly enough to swing the sale of the company if it comes to a vote. But he's greedy. He'll want more. But he'll only want more if he can get it soon. Waiting for February is too risky. So yes, I do think if we give him a chance that he will organize some more damage this week.'

'It's a risk,' said Dolly. 'Suppose something dreadful happens and we neither prevent it nor catch anyone doing it?'

They kicked it round among the three of them for several minutes, the pros and cons of the straight

patrols versus cat and mouse. Finally Radnor turned
back to me and said 'Sid?'

'It's your agency,' I said seriously. 'It's your risk.'

'But it's your case. It's still your case. You must
decide.'

I couldn't understand him. It was all very well for him
to have given me a free hand so far, but this wasn't the
sort of decision I would have ever expected him to pass
on.

Still ... 'Chico and I, then,' I said. 'We'll go along
tonight and stay all day tomorrow. I don't think we'll
let even Captain Oxon know we're there. Certainly not
the foreman, Ted Wilkins, or any of the other men.
We'll come in from the other side from the stands, and
I'll borrow the horse for mobility. Dolly can arrange
official patrol guards with Oxon for tomorrow night ...
suggest he gives them a warm room, Dolly. He ought
to have the central heating on by then.'

'Friday and Saturday?' asked Radnor, non-
committally.

'Full guards, I guess. As many as Lord Hagbourne
will sub for. The racecourse crowds make cat and
mouse impossible.'

'Right,' said Radnor, decisively. 'That's it, then.'

When Dolly, Chico, and I had got as far as the door
he said, 'Sid, you wouldn't mind if I had another look
at those photographs? Send Jones-boy down with them
if you're not needing them.'

'Sure,' I agreed. 'I've pored over them till I know

them by heart. I bet you'll spot something at once that I've missed.'

'It often works that way,' he said, nodding.

The three of us went back to the Racing Section, and via the switchboard I traced Jones-boy, who happened to be in Missing Persons. While he was on his way down I flipped through the packet of photographs yet again. The share transfers, the summary with the list of bank accounts, the letters from Bolt, the ten pound notes, and the two sheets of dates, initials, and figures from the very bottom of the attaché case. It had been clear all along that these last were lists either of receipts or expenditure: but by now I was certain they were the latter. A certain W.L.B. had received regular sums of fifty pounds a month for twelve months, and the last date for W.L.B. was four days before William Leslie Brinton, Clerk of Dunstable Racecourse, had taken the quickest way out. Six hundred pounds and a threat; the price of a man's soul.

Most of the other initials meant nothing to me, except the last one, J.R.S., which looked as if they could be the tanker driver's. The first entry for J.R.S., for one hundred pounds, was dated the day before the tanker overturned at Seabury, the day before Kraye went to Aynsford for the weekend.

In the next line, the last of the whole list, a further sum of one hundred and fifty pounds was entered against J.R.S. The date of this was that of the following Tuesday, three days ahead when I took the photographs. Smith had packed up and vanished from his job and digs on that Tuesday.

Constantly recurring among the other varying initials were two Christian names, Leo and Fred. Each of these was on the regular payroll, it seemed. Either Leo or Fred, I guessed, had been the big man who had visited and frightened Mervyn Brinton. Either Leo or Fred was the 'Big Chap' who had sent Andrews with a gun to the Cromwell Road.

I had a score to settle with either Leo or Fred.

Jones-boy came in for the photographs. I tapped them together back into their box and gave them to him.

'Where, you snotty nosed little coot, is our coffee?' said Chico rudely. We had been downstairs when Jones-boy did his rounds.

'Coots are bald,' observed Dolly dryly, eyeing Jones-boy's luxuriant locks.

Jones-boy unprintably told Chico where he could find his coffee.

Chico advanced a step, saying, 'You remind me of the people sitting on the walls of Jerusalem.' He had been raised in a church orphanage, after all.

Jones-boy also knew the more basic bits of Isaiah. He said callously, 'You did it on the doorstep of the Barnes cop shop, I believe.'

Chico furiously lashed out a fist to Jones-boy's head.

Jones-boy jumped back, laughed insultingly, and the
box he was holding flew high out of his hand, opening
as it went.

'Stop it you two, damn you,' shouted Dolly, as the
big photographs floated down on to her desk and on
to the floor.

'Babes in the Wood,' remarked Jones-boy, in great
good humour from having got the best of the slanging
match. He helped Dolly and me pick up the photographs, shuffled them back into the box in no sort of
order, and departed grinning.

'Chico,' said Dolly severely, 'you ought to know
better.'

'The bossy-mother routine bores me sick,' said Chico
violently.

Dolly bit her lip and looked away. Chico stared at
me defiantly, knowing very well he had started the row
and was in the wrong.

'As one bastard to another,' I said mildly, 'pipe
down.'

Not being able to think of a sufficiently withering
reply fast enough Chico merely scowled and walked out
of the room. The show was over. The office returned to
normal. Typewriters clattered, someone used the tape
recorder, someone else the telephone. Dolly sighed and
began to draw up her list for Seabury. I sat and thought
about Leo. Or Fred. Unproductively.

After a while I ambled upstairs to Bona Fides, where
the usual amount of telephone shouting filled the air.

George, deep in a mysterious conversation about mothballs, saw me and shook his head. Jack Copeland, freshly attired in a patchily faded green sleeveless pullover, took time out between calls to say they were sorry, but they'd made no progress with Kraye. He had, Jack said, very craftily covered his tracks about ten years back. They would keep digging, if I liked. I liked.

Up in Missing Persons Sammy said it was too soon for results on Smith.

When I judged that Mark Witney would be back in his house after exercising his second lot of horses, I rang him up and asked him to lend me his hack, a pensioned-off old steeplechaser of the first water.

'Sure,' he said. 'What for?'

I explained what for.

'You'd better have my horse box as well,' he commented. 'Suppose it pours with rain all night? Give you somewhere to keep dry, if you have the box.'

'But won't you be needing it? The forecast says clear and dry anyway.'

'I won't need it until Friday morning. I haven't any runners until Seabury. And only one there, I may say, in spite of it being so close. The owners just won't have it. I have to go all the way to Banbury on Saturday. Damn silly with another much better course on my door-step.'

'What are you running at Seabury?'

He told me, at great and uncomplimentary length, about a half blind, utterly stupid, one paced habitual non-jumper with which he proposed to win the novice chase. Knowing him, he probably would. We agreed that Chico and I should arrive at his place at about eight that evening, and I rang off.

After that I left the office, went across London by underground to Company House in the City, and asked for the files of Seabury Racecourse. In a numbered chair at a long table, surrounded by earnest men and women clerks poring over similar files and making copious notes, I studied the latest list of investors. Apart from Kraye and his various aliases, which I now recognized on sight from long familiarity with the share transfer photographs, there were no large blocks in single ownership. No one else held more than three per cent of the total: and as three per cent meant that roughly two and a half thousand pounds was lying idle and not bringing in a penny in dividends, it was easy to see why no one wanted a larger holding.

Fotherton's name was not on the list. Although this was not conclusive, because a nominee name like 'Mayday Investments' could be anyone at all, I was more or less satisfied that Seabury's Clerk was not gambling on Seabury's death. All the big share movements during the past year had been to Kraye, and no one else.

A few of the small investors, holding two hundred or so shares each, were people I knew personally. I wrote down their names and addresses, intending to ask them to let me see Bolt's circular letter when it arrived. Slower than via Zanna Martin, but surer.

My mind shied away from Zanna Martin. I'd had a bad night thinking about her. Her and Jenny, both.

Back in the office I found it was the tail-end of the lunch hour, with nearly all the desks still empty. Chico alone was sitting behind his, biting his nails.

'If we're going to be up all night,' I suggested, 'we'd better take the afternoon off for sleep.'

'No need.'

'Every need. I'm not as young as you.'

'Poor old grandpa.' He grinned suddenly, apologizing for the morning. 'I can't help it. That Jones-boy gets on my wick.'

'Jones-boy can look after himself. It's Dolly . . .'

'It's not my bloody fault she can't have kids.'

'She wants kids like you want a mother.'

'But I don't . . .' he began indignantly.

'Your own,' I said flatly. 'Like you want your own mother to have kept you and loved you. Like mine did.'

'You had every advantage, of course.'

'That's right.'

He laughed. 'Funny thing is I like old Dolly, really. Except for the hen bit.'

'Who wouldn't?' I said amicably. 'You can sleep on my sofa.'

He sighed. 'You're going to be less easy than Dolly to work for, I can see that.'

'Eh?'

'Don't kid yourself, mate. Sir, I mean.' He was lightly ironic.

The other inmates of the office drifted back, including Dolly, with whom I fixed for Chico to have the afternoon free. She was cool to him and unforgiving, which I privately thought would do them both good.

She said, 'The first official patrol will start on the racecourse tomorrow at six p.m. Shall I tell them to find you and report?'

'No,' I said definitely. 'I don't know where I'll be.'

'It had better be the usual then,' she said. 'They can report to the old man at his home number when they are starting the job, and again at six a.m. when they go off and the next lot take over.'

'And they'll ring him in between if anything happens?' I said.

'Yes. As usual.'

'It's as bad as being a doctor,' I said smiling.

Dolly nodded, and half to herself she murmured, 'You'll find out.'

Chico and I walked round to my flat, pulled the curtains, and did our best to sleep. I didn't find it easy at two-thirty in the afternoon: it was the time for racing, not rest. It seemed to me that I had barely drifted off when the telephone rang: I looked at my watch on my way to answer it in the sitting-room and found it was only ten to five. I had asked for a call at six.

It was not the telephone exchange, however, but Dolly.

'A message has come for you by hand, marked very

urgent. I thought you might want it before you go to
Seabury.'

'Who brought it?'

'A taxi driver.'

'Shunt him round here, then.'

'He's gone, I'm afraid.'

'Who's the message from?'

'I've no idea. It's a plain brown envelope, the size
we use for interim reports.'

'Oh. All right, I'll come back.'

Chico had drowsily propped himself up on one
elbow on the sofa.

'Go to sleep again,' I said. 'I've got to go and see
something in the office. Won't be long.'

When I reached the Racing Section again I found that
whatever had come for me, something else had gone.
The shaky lemon coloured table. I was deskless again.

'Sammy said he was sorry,' explained Dolly, 'but he
has a new assistant and nowhere to park him.'

'I had things in the drawer,' I complained. Shades
of Sammy's lunch, I thought.

'They're here,' Dolly said, pointing to a corner of her
desk. 'There was only the Brinton file, a half bottle of
brandy, and some pills. Also I found this on the floor.'
She held out a flat crackly cellophane and paper packet.

'The negatives of those photographs are in here,' I
said, taking it from her. 'They were in the box, though.'

'Until Jones-boy dropped it.'

'Oh yes.' I put the packet of negatives inside the

Brinton file and pinched a large rubber band from Dolly to snap round the outside.

'How about that mysterious very urgent message?' I asked.

Dolly silently and considerately slit open the envelope in question, drew out the single sheet of paper it contained and handed it to me. I unfolded it and stared at it in disbelief.

It was a circular, headed Charing, Street, and King, Stockbrokers, dated with the following day's date, and it ran:

> Dear Sir or Madam,
> We have various clients wishing to purchase
> small parcels of shares in the following lists
> of minor companies. If you are considering
> selling your interests in any of these, we
> would be grateful if you would get in touch
> with us. We would assure you of a good fair
> price, based on today's quotation.

There followed a list of about thirty companies, of which I had heard of only one. Tucked in about three-quarters of the way down was Seabury Racecourse.

I turned the page over. Zanna Martin had written on the back in a hurried hand.

> This is only going to Seabury shareholders.
> Not to anyone owning shares in the other

companies. The leaflets came from the
printers this morning, and are to be posted
tomorrow. I hope it is what you want. I'm
sorry about last night.

Z.M.

'What is it?' asked Dolly.

'A free pardon,' I said light-heartedly, slipping the
circular inside the Brinton file along with the negatives.
'Also confirmation that Ellis Bolt is not on the side of
the angels.'

'You're a nut,' she said. 'And take these things off
my desk. I haven't room for them.'

I put the pills and brandy in my pocket and picked
up the Brinton file.

'Is that better?'

'Thank you, yes.'

'So long, then, my love. See you Friday.'

On the walk back to the flat I decided suddenly to
go and see Zanna Martin. I went straight down to the
garage for my car without going up and waking Chico
again, and made my way eastwards to the City for the
second time that day. The rush hour traffic was so bad
that I was afraid I would miss her, but in fact she was
ten minutes late leaving the office and I caught her up
just before she reached the underground station.

'Miss Martin,' I called. 'Would you like a lift home?'

She turned round in surprise.

'Mr Halley!'

'Hop in.'

She hopped. That is to say, she opened the door, picked up the Brinton file which was lying on the passenger seat, sat down, tidily folded her coat over her knees, and pulled the door shut again. The bad side of her face was towards me, and she was very conscious of it. The scarf and the hair were gently pulled forward.

I took a pound and a ten shilling note out of my pocket and gave them to her. She took them, smiling.

'The taxi-man told our switchboard girl you gave him that for bringing the leaflet. Thank you very much.'

I swung out through the traffic and headed for Finchley.

She answered obliquely. 'That wretched chicken is still in the oven, stone cold. I just turned the gas out yesterday, after you'd gone.'

'I wish I could stay this evening instead,' I said, 'but I've got a job on for the agency.'

'Another time,' she said tranquilly. 'Another time, perhaps. I understand that you couldn't tell me at first who you worked for, because you didn't know whether I was an ... er, an accomplice of Mr Bolt's, and afterwards you didn't tell me for fear of what actually happened, that I would be upset. So that's that.'

'You are generous.'

'Realistic, even if a bit late.'

We went a little way in silence. Then I asked, 'What would happen to the shares Kraye owns if it were proved he was sabotaging the company? If he were convicted, I mean. Would his shares be confiscated, or would he still own them when he came out of jail?'

'I've never heard of anyone's shares being confiscated,' she said, sounding interested. 'But surely that's a long way in the future?'

'I wish I knew. It makes a good deal of difference to what I should do now.'

'How do you mean?'

'Well . . . an easy way to stop Kraye buying too many more shares would be to tell the racing press and the financial press that a take-over is being attempted. The price would rocket. But Kraye already holds twenty-three per cent, and if the law couldn't take it away from him, he would either stick to that and vote for a sell out, or if he got cold feet he could unload his shares at the higher price and still make a fat profit. Either way, he'd be sitting pretty financially, in jail or out. And either way Seabury would be built on.'

'I suppose this sort of thing's happened before?'

'Take-overs, yes, several. But only one other case of sabotage. At Dunstable. Kraye again.'

'Haven't any courses survived a take-over bid?'

'Only Sandown, publicly. I don't know of any others, but they may have managed it in secrecy.'

'How did Sandown do it?'

'The local council did it for them. Stated loudly that planning permission would not be given for building. Of course the bid collapsed then.'

'It looks as though the only hope for Seabury, in that case, is that the council there will act in the same way. I'd try a strong lobby, if I were you.'

'You're quite a girl, Miss Martin,' I said smiling. 'That's a very good idea. I'll go and dip a toe into the climate of opinion at the Town Hall.'

She nodded approvingly. 'No good lobbying against the grain. Much better to find out which way people are likely to move before you start pushing!'

Finchley came into sight. I said, 'You do realize, Miss Martin, that if I am successful at my job, you will lose yours?'

She laughed. 'Poor Mr Bolt. He's not at all bad to work for. But don't worry about my job. It's easy for an experienced stockbroker's secretary to get a good one, I assure you.'

I stopped at her gate, looking at my watch. 'I'm afraid I can't come in. I'm already going to be a bit late.'

She opened the door without ado and climbed out. 'Thank you for coming at all.' She smiled, shut the door crisply, and waved me away.

I drove back to my flat as fast as I could, fuming slightly at the traffic. It wasn't until I switched off the engine down in the garage and leaned over to pick it up that I discovered the Brinton file wasn't there. And then remembered Miss Martin holding it on her lap during the journey, and me hustling her out of the car. Zanna Martin still had Brinton's file. I hadn't time to go back for it, and I couldn't ring her up because I didn't know the name of the owner of the house she lived in. But surely, I reassured myself, surely the file would be safe enough where it was until Friday.

CHAPTER TWELVE

Chico and I sat huddled together for warmth in some gorse bushes and watched the sun rise over Seabury Racecourse. It had been a cold clear night with a tingle of nought degrees centigrade about it, and we were both shivering.

Behind us, among the bushes and out of sight, Revelation, one-time winner of the Cheltenham Gold Cup, was breakfasting on meagre patches of grass. We could hear the scrunch when he bit down close to the roots, and the faint chink of the bridle as he ate. For some time Chico and I had been resisting the temptation to relieve him of his nice warm rug.

'They might try something now,' said Chico hopefully. 'First light, before anyone's up.'

Nothing had moved in the night, we were certain of that. Every hour I had ridden Revelation at a careful walk round the whole of the track itself, and Chico had made a plimsoll-shod inspection of the stands, at one with the shadows. There had been no one about. Not a sound but the stirring breeze, not a glimmer of light but from the stars and a waning moon.

Our present spot, chosen as the sky lightened and some concealment became necessary, lay at the farthest spot from the stands, at the bottom of the semi-circle of track cut off by the road which ran across the course. Scattered bushes and scrub filled the space between the track and boundary fence, enough to shield us from all but closely prying eyes. Behind the boundary fence were the little back gardens of the first row of bungalows. The sun rose bright and yellow away to our left and the birds sang around us. It was half-past seven.

'It's going to be a lovely day,' said Chico.

At ten past nine there was some activity up by the stands and the tractor rolled on to the course pulling a trailer. I unshipped my race glasses, balanced them on my bent up knees, and took a look. The trailer was loaded with what I guessed were hurdles, and was accompanied by three men on foot.

I handed the glasses to Chico without comment, and yawned.

'Lawful occasions,' he remarked, bored.

We watched the tractor and trailer lumber slowly round the far end of the course, pause to unload, and return for a refill. On its second trip it came close enough for us to confirm that it was in fact the spare hurdles that were being dumped into position, four or five at each flight, ready to be used if any were splintered in the races. We watched for a while in silence. Then I said slowly, 'Chico, I've been blind.'

'Huh?'

'The tractor,' I said. 'The tractor. Under our noses all the time.'

'So?'

'So the sulphuric acid tanker was pulled over by a tractor. No complicated lifting gear necessary. Just a couple of ropes or chains slung over the top of the tanker and fastened round the axles. Then you unscrew the hatches and stand well clear. Someone drives the tractor at full power up the course, over goes the tanker and out pours the juice. And Bob's your uncle!'

'Every racecourse has a tractor,' said Chico thoughtfully.

'That's right.'

'So no one would look twice at a tractor on a racecourse. Quite. No one would remark on any tracks it left. No one would mention seeing one on the road. So if you're right, and I'd say you certainly are, it wouldn't necessarily have been that tractor, the racecourse tractor, which was used.'

'I'll bet it was, though.' I told Chico about the photographed initials and payments. 'Tomorrow I'll check the initials of all the workmen here from Ted Wilkins downwards against that list. Any one of them might have been paid just to leave the tractor on the course, lying handy. The tanker went over on the evening before the meeting, like today. The tractor would have been in use then too. Warm and full of fuel. Nothing easier. And afterwards, straight on up the racecourse, and out of sight.'

'It was dusk,' agreed Chico. 'As long as no one came along the road in the minutes it took to unhitch the ropes or chains afterwards, they were clear. No traffic diversions, no detours, nothing.'

We sat watching the tractor lumbering about, gloomily realizing we couldn't prove a word of it.

'We'll have to move,' I said presently. 'There's a hurdle just along there, about fifty yards away, where those wings are. They'll be down here over the road soon.'

We adjourned with Revelation back to the horse box half a mile away down the road to the west and took the opportunity to eat our own breakfast. When we had finished Chico went back first, strolling along confidently in my jodhpurs, boots, and polo-necked jersey, the complete horseman from head to foot. He had never actually sat on a horse in his life.

After a while I followed on Revelation. The men had brought the hurdles down into the semicircular piece of track and had laid them in place. They were now moving farther away up the course, unloading the next lot. Unremarked, I rode back to the bushes and dismounted. Of Chico there was no sign for another half hour, and then he came whistling across from the road with his hands in his pockets.

When he reached me he said, 'I had another look round the stands. Rotten security, here. No one asked me what I was doing. There are some women cleaning here and there, and some are working in the stable block, getting the lads' hostel ready, things like that. I said good morning to them, and they said good morning back.' He was disgusted.

'Not much scope for saboteurs,' I said morosely. 'Cleaners in the stands and workmen on the course.'

'Dusk tonight,' nodded Chico. 'That's the most likely time now.'

The morning ticked slowly away. The sun rose to its low November zenith and shone straight into our eyes. I passed the time by taking a photograph of Revelation and another of Chico. He was fascinated by the tiny camera and said he couldn't wait to get one like it. Eventually I put it back into my breeches pocket, and shading my eyes against the sun took my hundredth look up the course.

Nothing. No men, no tractor. I looked at my watch. One o'clock. Lunch hour. More time passed.

Chico picked up the race glasses and swept the course.

'Be careful,' I said idly. 'Don't look at the sun with those. You'll hurt your eyes.'

'Do me a favour.'

I yawned, feeling the sleepless night catch up.

'There's a man on the course,' he said. 'One. Just walking.'

He handed me the glasses and I took a look. He was right. One man was walking alone across the racecourse; not round the track but straight across the rough grass in the middle. He was too far away for his features to be distinguishable and in any case he was wearing a fawn duffle coat with the hood up. I shrugged and lowered the glasses. He looked harmless enough.

With nothing better to do we watched him reach the far side, duck under the rails, and move along until he was standing behind one of the fences with only his head and shoulders in our sight.

Chico remarked that he should have attended to nature in the gents before he left the stands. I yawned again, smiling at the same time. The man went on standing behind the fence.

'What on earth is he doing?' said Chico, after about five minutes.

'He isn't doing anything,' I said, watching through the glasses. 'He's just standing there looking this way.'

'Do you think he's spotted us?'

'No, he couldn't. He hasn't any binocs, and we are in the bushes.'

Another five minutes passed in inactivity.

'He must be doing *something*,' said Chico, exasperated.

'Well, he isn't,' I said.

Chico took a turn with the glasses. 'You can't see a damn thing against the sun,' he complained. 'We should have camped up the other end.'

'In the car park?' I suggested mildly. 'The road to

the stables and the main gates runs along the other end. There isn't a scrap of cover.'

'He's got a flag,' said Chico suddenly. 'Two flags. One in each hand. White on the left, orange on the right. He seems to be waving them alternately. He's just some silly nit of a racecourse attendant practising calling up the ambulance and the vet.' He was disappointed.

I watched the flags moving, first white, then orange, then white, then orange, with a gap of a second or two between each wave. It certainly wasn't any form of recognizable signalling: nothing like semaphore. They were, as Chico had said, quite simply the flags used after a fall in a race: white to summon the ambulance for the jockey, orange to get attention for a horse. He didn't keep it up very long. After about eight waves altogether he stopped, and in a moment or two began to walk back across the course to the stands.

'Now what,' said Chico, 'do you think all that was in aid of?'

He swept the glasses all round the whole racecourse yet again. 'There isn't a soul about except him and us.'

'He's probably been standing by a fence for months waiting for a chance to wave his flags, and no one has been injured anywhere near him. In the end, the temptation proved too much.'

I stood up and stretched, went through the bushes to Revelation, undid the head collar with which he was tethered to the bushes, unbuckled the surcingle and pulled off his rug.

'What are you doing?' said Chico.

'The same as the man with the flags. Succumbing to an intolerable temptation. Give me a leg up.' He did what I asked, but hung on to the reins.

'You're mad. You said in the night that they might let you do it after this meeting, but they'd never agree to it before. Suppose you smash the fences?'

'Then I'll be in almighty trouble,' I agreed. 'But here I am on a super jumper looking at a heavenly course on a perfect day, with everyone away at lunch.' I grinned. 'Leave go.'

Chico took his hand away. 'It's not like you,' he said doubtfully.

'Don't take it to heart,' I said flippantly, and touched Revelation into a walk.

At this innocuous pace the horse and I went out on to the track and proceeded in the direction of the stands. Anti-clockwise, the way the races were run. Still at a walk we reached the road and went across its uncovered tarmac surface. On the far side of the road lay the enormous dark brown patch of tan, spread thick and firm where the burnt turf had been bulldozed away. Horses would have no difficulty in racing over it.

Once on the other side, on the turf again, Revelation broke into a trot. He knew where he was. Even with no crowds and no noise the fact of being on a familiar racecourse was exciting him. His ears were pricked, his step springy. At fourteen he had been already a year in retirement, but he moved beneath me like a four-year-old. He too, I guessed fancifully, was feeling the satanic tug of pleasure about to be illicitly snatched.

Chico was right, of course. I had no business at all to be riding on the course so soon before a meeting. It was indefensible. I ought to know better. I did know better. I eased Revelation gently into a canter.

There were three flights of hurdles and three fences more or less side by side up the straight, and the water jump beyond that. As I wasn't sure that Revelation would jump the fences in cold blood on his own (many horses won't), I set him at the hurdles.

Once he had seen these and guessed my intention I doubt if I could have stopped him, even if I'd wanted to. He fairly ate up the first flight and stretched out eagerly for the second. After that I gave him a choice, and of the two obstacles lying ahead, he opted for the fence. It didn't seem to bother him that he was on his own. They were excellent fences and he was a Gold Cup winner, born and bred for the job and being given an unexpected, much missed treat. He flew the fence with all his former dash and skill.

As for me, my feelings were indescribable. I'd sat on a horse a few times since I'd given up racing, but never found an opportunity of doing more than riding out quietly at morning exercise with Mark's string. And here I was, back in my old place, doing again what I'd ached for in two and a half years. I grinned with irrepressible joy and got Revelation to lengthen his stride for the water jump.

He took it with feet to spare. Perfect. There were no irate shouts from the stands on my right, and we swept away on round the top bend of the course, fast and free. Another fence at the end of the bend – Revelation floated it – and five more stretching away down the far side. It was at the third of these, the open ditch, that the man had been standing and waving the flags.

It's an undoubted fact that emotions pass from rider to horse, and Revelation was behaving with the same reckless exhilaration which gripped me: so after two spectacular leaps over the next two fences we both sped onwards with arms open to fate. There ahead was the guard rail, the four foot wide open ditch and the four foot six fence rising on the far side of it. Revelation, knowing all about it, automatically put himself right to jump.

It came, the blinding flash in the eyes, as we soared into the air. White, dazzling, brain shattering light, splintering the day into a million fragments and blotting out the world in a blaze as searing as the sun.

I felt Revelation falling beneath me and rolled instinctively, my eyes open and quite unable to see. Then there was the rough crash on the turf and the return of vision from light to blackness and up through grey to normal sight.

I was on my feet before Revelation, and I still had hold of the reins. He struggled up, bewildered and staggering, but apparently unhurt. I pulled him forward into an unwilling trot to make sure of his legs, and was relieved to find them whole and sound. It only remained to remount as quickly as possible, and this was infuriatingly difficult. With two hands I could have jumped up easily: as it was I scrambled untidily back into the saddle at the third attempt, having lost the reins altogether and bashed my stomach on the pommel of the saddle into the bargain. Revelation behaved very well, all things considered. He trotted only fifty yards or so in the wrong direction before I collected myself and the reins into a working position and turned him round. This time we by-passed the fence and all subsequent ones: I cantered him first down the side of the track, slowed to a trot to cross the road, and steered then not on round the bottom semi-circle but off to the right, heading for where the boundary fence met the main London road.

Out of the corner of my eye I saw Chico running in my direction across the rough grass. I waved him towards me with a sweep of the arm and reined in and waited for him where our paths converged.

'I thought you said you could bloody well ride,' he said, scarcely out of breath from the run.

'Yeah,' I said. 'I thought so once.'

He looked at me sharply. 'You fell off. I was watching. You fell off like a baby.'

'If you were watching . . . the horse fell, if you don't mind. There's a distinction. Very important to jockeys.'

'Nuts,' he said. 'You fell off.'

'Come on,' I said, walking Revelation towards the

boundary fence. 'There's something I have to find.' I told Chico what. 'In one of those bungalows, I should think. At a window or on the roof, or in a garden.'

'Sods,' said Chico forcefully. 'The dirty sods.'

I agreed with him.

It wasn't very difficult, because it had to be within a stretch of only a hundred yards or so. We went methodically along the boundary fence towards the London road, stopping to look carefully into every separate little garden, and at every separate little house. A fair number of inquisitive faces looked back.

Chico saw it first, propped into a high leafless branch of a tree growing well back in the second to last garden. Traffic whizzed along the London road only ten yards ahead, and Revelation showed signs of wanting to retreat.

'Look,' said Chico, pointing upwards.

I looked, fighting a mild battle against the horse. It was five feet high, three feet wide, and polished to a spotless brilliance. A mirror.

'Sods,' said Chico again.

I nodded, dismounted, led Revelation back to where the traffic no longer fretted him, and tied the reins to the fence. Then Chico and I walked along to the London road and round into the road of bungalows. Napoleon Close, it said. Napoleon wasn't *that* close, I reflected, amused.

We rang the door of the second bungalow. A man

and woman both came to the door to open it, elderly, gentle, inoffensive, and inquiring.

I came straight to the point, courteously. 'Do you know you have a mirror in your tree?'

'Don't be silly,' said the woman, smiling as at an idiot. She had fat wavy grey hair and was wearing a sloppy black cardigan over a brown wool dress. No colour sense, I thought.

'You'd better take a look,' I suggested.

'It's not a mirror, you know,' said the husband, puzzled. 'It's a placard. One of those advertisement things.'

'That's right,' said his wife contrapuntally. 'A placard.'

'We agreed to lend our tree . . .'

'For a small sum, really . . . only our pension . . .'

'A man put up the framework . . .'

'He said he would be back soon with the poster . . .'

'A religious one, I believe. A good cause . . .'

'We wouldn't have done it otherwise. . . .'

Chico interrupted. 'I wouldn't have thought it was a good place for a poster. Your tree stands farther back than the others. It isn't conspicuous.'

'I did think . . .' began the man doubtfully, shuffling in his checked woolly bedroom slippers.

'But if he was willing to pay rent for your particular tree, you didn't want to put him off,' I finished. 'An extra quid or two isn't something you want to pass on next door.'

They wouldn't have put it so bluntly, but they didn't demur.

'Come and look,' I said.

They followed me round along the narrow path beside their bungalow wall and into their own back garden. The tree stood halfway to the racecourse boundary fence, the sun slanting down through the leafless branches. We could see the wooden back of the mirror, and the ropes which fastened it to the tree trunk. The man and his wife walked round to the front, and their puzzlement increased.

'He said it was for a poster,' repeated the man.

'Well,' I said as matter of factly as I could, 'I expect it is for a poster, as he said. But at the moment, you see, it is a mirror. And it's pointing straight out over the racecourse; and you know how mirrors reflect the sunlight? We just thought it might not be too safe, you know, if anyone got dazzled, so we wondered if you would mind us moving it?'

'Why, goodness,' agreed the woman, looking with more awareness at our riding clothes, 'no one could see the racing with light shining in their eyes.'

'Quite. So would you mind if we turned the mirror round a bit?'

'I can't see that it would hurt, Dad,' she said doubtfully.

He made a nondescript assenting movement with his hand, and Chico asked how the mirror had been put up in the tree in the first place. The man had brought a ladder with him, they said, and no, they hadn't one themselves. Chico shrugged, placed me beside the tree, put one foot on my thigh, one on my shoulder, and was up in the bare branches like a squirrel. The elderly couple's mouths sagged open.

'How long ago?' I asked. 'When did the man put up the mirror?'

'This morning,' said the woman, getting over the shock. 'He came back just now, too, with another rope or something. That's when he said he'd be back with the poster.'

So the mirror had been hauled up into the tree while Chico and I had been obliviously sitting in the bushes, and adjusted later when the sun was at the right angle in the sky. At two o'clock. The time, the next day, of the third race, the handicap steeplechase. Some handicap, I thought, a smash of light in the eyes.

White flag: a little bit to the left. Orange flag: a little bit to the right. No flag: dead on target.

Come back tomorrow afternoon and clap a religious poster over the glass as soon as the damage was done, so that even the quickest search wouldn't reveal a mirror. Just another jinx on Seabury racecourse. Dead horses, crushed and trampled jockeys. A jinx. Send my horses somewhere else, Mr Witney, something always goes wrong at Seabury.

I was way out in one respect. The religious poster was not due to be put in place the following day.

CHAPTER THIRTEEN

'I think,' I said gently to the elderly couple, 'that it might be better if you went indoors. We will explain to the man who is coming what we are doing to his mirror.'

Dad glanced up the path towards the road, put his arm protectively round his wife's woolly shoulders, and said gratefully, 'Er . . . yes . . . yes.'

They shuffled rapidly through the back door into the bungalow just as a large man carrying an aluminium folding ladder and a large rolled up paper came barging through their front gate. There had been the squeak of his large plain dark blue van stopping, the hollow crunch of the handbrake being forcibly applied, the slam of the door and the scrape of the ladder being unloaded. Chico in the tree crouched quite still, watching.

I was standing with my back to the sun, but it fell full on the big man's face when he came into the garden. It wasn't the sort of face one would naturally associate with religious posters. He was a cross between a heavyweight wrestler and Mount Vesuvius. Craggy, brutally strong, and not far off erupting.

He came straight towards me across the grass, dropped the ladder beside him, and said inquiringly, 'What goes on?'

'The mirror,' I said, 'comes down.'

His eyes narrowed in sudden awareness and his body stiffened. 'There's a poster going over it,' he began quite reasonably, lifting the paper roll. Then with a rush the lava burst out, the paper flew wide, and the muscles bunched into action.

It wasn't much of a fight. He started out to hit my face, changed his mind, and ploughed both fists in below the belt. It was quite a long way down for him. Doubling over in pain on to the lawn, I picked up the ladder, and gave him a swinging swipe behind the knees.

The ground shook with the impact. He fell on his side, his coat swinging open. I lunged forward, snatching at the pistol showing in the holster beside his ribs. It came loose, but he brushed me aside with an arm like a telegraph pole. I fell, sprawling. He rolled over into a crouch, picked up the gun from the grass and sneered down into my face. Then he stood up like a released spring and on the way with force and deliberation booted his toe-cap into my navel. He also clicked back the catch on his gun.

Up in the tree Chico yelled. The big man turned and took three steps towards him, seeing him for the first time. With a choice of targets, he favoured the one still in a state to resist. The hand with the pistol pointed at Chico.

'Leo,' I shouted. Nothing happened. I tried again. 'Fred!'

The big man turned his head a fraction back to me and Chico jumped down on to him from ten feet up.

The gun went off with a double crash and again the day flew apart in shining splintering fragments. I sat on the ground with my knees bent up, groaning quietly, cursing fluently, and getting on with my business.

Drawn by the noise, the inhabitants of the bungalows down the line came out into the back gardens and looked in astonishment over the fences. The elderly couple stood palely at their window, their mouths again open. The big man had too big an audience now for murder.

Chico was overmatched for size and nearly equalled in skill. He and the big man threw each other round a bit while I crept doubled up along the path into the front garden as far as the gate, but the battle was a foregone conclusion, bar the retreat.

He came alone, crashing up the path, saw me hanging on to the gate and half raised the gun. But there were people in the road now, and more people peering out of opposite windows. In scorching fury he whipped at my head with the barrel, and I avoided it by leaving go of the gate and collapsing on the ground again.

Behind the gate, with the bars nice and comfortingly between me and his boot.

He crunched across the pavement, slammed into the van, cut his cogs to ribbons and disappeared out on to the London road in a cloud of dust.

Chico came down the garden path staggering, with blood sloshing out of a cut eyebrow. He looked anxious and shaken.

'I thought you said you could bloody well fight,' I mocked him.

He came to a halt beside me on his knees. 'Blast you.' He put his fingers to his forehead and winced at the result.

I grinned at him.

'You were running away,' he said.

'Naturally.'

'What have you got here?' He took the little camera out of my hand. 'Don't tell me,' he said, his face splitting into an unholy smile. 'Don't tell me.'

'It's what we came for, after all.'

'How many?'

'Four of him. Two of the van.'

'Sid, you slay me, you really do.'

'Well,' I said, 'I feel sick.' I rolled over and retched what was left of my breakfast on to the roots of the privet hedge. There wasn't any blood. I felt a lot better.

'I'll go and get the horse box,' said Chico, 'and pick you up.'

'You'll do nothing of the sort,' I said, wiping my

mouth on a handkerchief. 'We're going back into the garden. I want that bullet.'

'It's halfway to Seabury,' he protested, borrowing my handkerchief to mop the blood off his eyebrow.

'What will you bet?' I said. I used the gate again to get up, and after a moment or two was fairly straight. We presented a couple of reassuring grins to the audience, and retraced our way down the path into the back garden.

The mirror lay in sparkling pointed fragments all over the lawn.

'Pop up the tree and see if the bullet is there, in the wood. It smashed the mirror. It might be stuck up there. If not, we'll have to comb the grass.

Chico went up the aluminium ladder that time.

'Of all the luck,' he called. 'It's here.' I watched him take a penknife out of his pocket and carefully cut away at a section just off-centre of the back board of the ex-mirror. He came down and held the little misshapen lump out to me on the palm of his hand. I put it carefully away in the small waist pocket of my breeches.

The elderly couple had emerged like tortoises from their bungalow. They were scared and puzzled, understandably. Chico offered to cut down the remains of the mirror, and did, but we left them to clear up the resulting firewood.

As an afterthought, however, Chico went across the garden and retrieved the poster from a soggy winter rosebed. He unrolled it and showed it to us, laughing.

'Blessed are the meek: for they shall inherit the earth.'

'One of them,' said Chico, 'has a sense of humour.'

Much against his wishes, we returned to our observation post in the scrubby gorse.

'Haven't you had enough?' he said crossly.

'The patrols don't get here till six,' I reminded him. 'And you yourself said that dusk would be the likely time for them to try something.'

'But they've already done it.'

'There's nothing to stop them from rigging up more than one booby trap,' I pointed out. 'Especially as that mirror thing wouldn't have been one hundred per cent reliable, even if we hadn't spotted it. It depended on the sun. Good weather forecast, I know, but weather forecasts are as reliable as a perished hot-water bottle. A passing cloud would have wrecked it. I would think they have something else in mind.'

'Cheerful,' he said resignedly. He led Revelation away along the road to stow him in the horse box, and was gone a long time.

When he came back he sat down beside me and said, 'I went all round the stables. No one stopped me or asked what I was doing. Don't they have *any* security here? The cleaners have all gone home, but there's a woman cooking in the canteen. She said I was too early, to come back at half past six. There wasn't anyone about in the stands block except an old geyser with snuffles mucking about with the boiler.'

The sun was lower in the sky and the November afternoon grew colder. We shivered a little and huddled inside our jerseys.

Chico said, 'You guessed about the mirror before you set off round the course.'

'It was a possibility, that's all.'

'You could have ridden along the boundary fence, looking into the gardens like we did afterwards, instead of haring off over all those jumps.'

I grinned faintly. 'Yes. As I told you, I was giving in to temptation.'

'Screwy. You must have known you'd fall.'

'Of course I didn't. The mirror mightn't have worked very effectively. Anyway, it's better to test a theory in a practical way. And I just wanted to ride round there. I had a good excuse if I were hauled up for it. So I went. And it was grand. So shut up.'

He laughed. 'All right.' Restlessly he stood up again and said he would make another tour. While he was gone I watched the racecourse with and without the binoculars, but not a thing moved on it.

He came back quietly and dropped down beside me.

'As before,' he said.

'Nothing here, either.'

He looked at me sideways. 'Do you feel as bad as you look?'

'I shouldn't be surprised,' I said. 'Do you?'

He tenderly touched the area round his cut eyebrow. 'Worse. Much worse. Soggy bad luck, him slugging away at your belly like that.'

'He did it on purpose,' I said idly; 'and it was very informative.'

'Huh?'

'It showed he knew who I was. He wouldn't have needed to have attacked us like that if we'd just been people come over from the racecourse to see if we could shift the mirror. But when he spoke to me he recognized me, and he knew I wouldn't be put off by any poster eyewash. And his sort don't mildly back down and retreat without paying you off for getting in their way. He just hit where he knew it would have most effect. I actually saw him think it.'

'But how did he know?'

'It was he who sent Andrews to the office,' I said. 'He was the man Mervyn Brinton described; big, going a bit bald, freckles on the backs of his hands, cockney accent. He was strong-arming Brinton, and he sent Andrews to get the letter that was supposed to be in the office. Well . . . Andrews knew me, and I knew him. He must have gone back and told our big friend Fred that he had shot me in the stomach. My death wasn't reported in the papers, so Fred knew I was still alive and would put the finger on Andrews at once. Andrews wasn't exactly a good risk to Fred, just a silly spiv with no sense, so Fred, I guess, marched him straight off to

Epping Forest, and left him for the birds. Who did a fair job, I'll give them that.'

'Do you think,' said Chico slowly, 'that the gun Fred had today . . . is that why you wanted the bullet?'

I nodded. 'That's right. I tried for the gun too, but no dice. If I'm going on with this sort of work, pal, you'll have to teach me a spot of judo.'

He looked down doubtfully. 'With that hand?'

'Invent a new sport,' I said. 'One-armed combat.'

'I'll take you to the club,' he said smiling. 'There's an old Jap there who'll find a way if anyone can.'

'Good.'

Up at the far end of the racecourse a horse box turned in off the main road and trundled along towards the stables. The first of the next day's runners had apparently arrived.

Chico went to have a look.

I sat on in fading daylight, watching nothing happen, hugging myself against the cold and the re-awakened grinding ache in my gut, and thinking evil thoughts about Fred. Not Leo. Fred.

There were four of them, I thought. Kraye, Bolt, Fred, and Leo.

I had met Kraye: he knew me only as Sid, a despised hanger-on in the home of a retired admiral he had met at his club and had spent a weekend with.

I had met Bolt: he knew me as John Halley, a shop assistant wanting to invest a gift from an aunt.

I had met Fred: he knew my whole name, and that I

worked for the agency, and that I had turned up at Seabury.

I did not know if I had met Leo. But Leo might know *me*. If he had anything to do with racing, he definitely did.

It would be all right, I thought, as long as they did not connect all the Halleys and Sids too soon. But there was my wretched hand, which Kraye had pulled out of my pocket, which Fred could have seen in the garden, and which Leo, whoever he was, might have noticed almost anywhere in the last six days, thanks to my promise to Zanna Martin. Zanna Martin, who worked for Bolt. A proper merry-go-round, I thought wryly.

Chico materialized out of the dusk. 'It was Ping Pong, running in the first tomorrow. All above board,' he said. 'And nothing doing anywhere, stands or course. We might as well go.'

It was well after five. I agreed, and got up stiffly.

'That Fred,' said Chico, casually giving me a hand, 'I've been thinking. I've seen him before, I'm certain. At race meetings. He's not a regular. Doesn't work for a bookie, or anything like that. But he's about. Cheap rings, mostly.'

'Let's hope he doesn't burrow,' I said.

'I don't see why he should,' he said seriously. 'He can't possibly think you'd connect him with Andrews or with Kraye. All you caught him doing was fixing a poster in a tree. If I were him, I'd be sleeping easy.'

'I called him Fred,' I said.

'Oh,' said Chico glumly. 'So you did.'

We reached the road and started along it towards the horse box.

'Fred must be the one who does all the jobs,' said Chico. 'Digs the false drains, sets fire to stables, and drives tractors to pull over tankers. He's big enough for anything.'

'He didn't wave the flags. He was up the tree at the time.'

'Um. Yes. Who did?'

'Not Bolt,' I said. 'It wasn't fat enough for Bolt, even in a duffle coat. Possibly Kraye. More likely Leo, whoever he is.'

'One of the workmen, or the foreman. Yes. Well, that makes two of them for overturning tankers and so on.'

'It would be easier for two,' I agreed.

Chico drove the horse box back to Mark's, and then, to his obvious delight, my Merc back to London.

CHAPTER FOURTEEN

Chief-Inspector Cornish was pleased but trying to hide it.

'I suppose you can chalk it up to your agency,' he said, as if it were debatable.

'He walked slap into us, to be fair.'

'And slap out again,' he said dryly.

I grimaced. 'You haven't met him.'

'You want to leave that sort to us,' he said automatically.

'Where were you, then?'

'That's a point,' he admitted, smiling.

He picked up the matchbox again and looked at the bullet. 'Little beauty. Good clear markings. Pity he has a revolver, though, and not an automatic. It would have been nice to have had cartridge cases as well.'

'You're greedy,' I said.

He looked at the aluminium ladder standing against his wall, and at the poster on his desk, and at the rush-job photographs. Two clear prints of the van showing its number plates and four of Fred in action against

Chico. Not exactly posed portraits, those, but four different, characteristic, and recognizable angles taken in full sunlight.

'With all this lot to go on, we'll trace him before he draws breath.'

'Fine,' I said. And the sooner Fred was immobilized the better, I thought. Before he did any more damage to Seabury. 'You'll need a tiger net to catch him. He's a very tough baby, and he knows judo. And unless he has the sense to throw it away, he'll still have that gun.'

'I'll remember,' he said. 'And thanks.' We shook hands amicably as I left.

It was results day at Radnor's, too. As soon as I got back Dolly said Jack Copeland wanted me up in Bona Fides. I made the journey.

Jack gleamed at me over the half moons, pleased with his department. 'George's got him. Kraye. He'll tell you.'

I went over to George's desk. George was fairly smirking, but after he'd talked for two minutes, I allowed he'd earned it.

'On the off chance,' he said, 'I borrowed a bit of smooth quartz Kraye recently handled in the Geology Museum and got Sammy to do the prints on it. Two or three different sets of fingers came out, so we photographed the lot. None of them were on the British files, but I've given them the run around with the odd pal in Interpol and so on, just in case. And brother, have we hit pay dirt or have we.'

'We have?' I prompted, grinning.,

'And how. Your friend Kraye is in the ex-con library of the state of New York.'

'What for?'

'Assault.'

'Of a girl?' I asked.

George raised his eyebrows. 'A girl's father. Kraye had beaten the girl, apparently with her permission. She didn't complain. But her father saw the bruises and raised the roof. He said he'd get Kraye on a rape charge, though it seems the girl had been perfectly willing on that count too. But it looked bad for Kraye, so he picked up a chair and smashed it over the father's head and scarpered. They caught him boarding a plane for South America and hauled him back. The father's brain was damaged. There are long medical details, but what it all boils down to is that he couldn't co-ordinate properly afterwards. Kraye got off on the rape charge, but served four years for attacking the father.

'Three years after that he turned up in England with some money and a new name, and soon acquired a wife. The one who divorced him for cruelty. Nice chap.'

'Yes indeed,' I said. 'What was his real name?'

'Wilbur Potter,' said George sardonically. 'And you'll never guess. He was a geologist by profession. He worked for a construction firm, surveying. Always moving about. Character assessment: slick, a pusher, a good talker. Cut a few corners, always had more money than his salary, threw his weight about, but nothing indictable. The assault on the father was his first brush with the law. He was thirty-four at that time.'

'Messy,' I said. 'The whole thing.'

'Very,' George agreed.

'But sex violence and fraudulent take-overs aren't much related,' I complained.

'You might as well say it is impossible to have boils and cancer at the same time. Something drastically wrong with the constitution, and two separate symptoms.'

'I'll take your word for it,' I said.

Sammy up in Missing Persons had done more than photograph Kraye's fingerprints, he had almost found Smith.

'Intersouth rang us this morning,' he purred. 'Smith gave them as a reference. He's applied for a driving job in Birmingham.'

'Good,' I said.

'We should have his address by this afternoon.'

Downstairs in Racing I reached for Dolly's telephone and got through to Charing, Street, and King.

'Mr Bolt's secretary speaking,' said the quiet voice.

'Is Mr Bolt in?' I asked.

'I'm afraid not . . . er, who is that speaking, please?'

'Did you find you had a file of mine?'

'Oh . . .' she laughed. 'Yes, I picked it up in your car. I'm so sorry.'

'Do you have it with you?'

'No,' she said. 'I didn't bring it here. I thought it might be better not to risk Mr Bolt seeing it, as it's got Hunt Radnor Associates printed on the outside along with a red sticker saying "Ex Records, care of Sid Halley".'

'Yes, it would have been disaster,' I agreed with feeling.

'I left it at home. Do you want it in a hurry?'

'No, not really. As long as it's safe, that's the main thing. How would it be if I came over to fetch it the day after tomorrow – Sunday morning? We could go for a drive, perhaps, and have some lunch?'

There was a tiny pause. Then she said strongly, 'Yes, please. Yes.'

'Have the leaflets gone out?' I asked.

'They went yesterday.'

'See you on Sunday, Miss Martin.'

I put down Dolly's telephone to find her looking at me quizzically. I was again squatting on the corner of her desk, the girl from the typing pool having in my absence reclaimed her chair.

'The mouse got away again, I understand,' she said.

'Some mouse.'

Chico came into the office. The cut on his eyebrow

246

looked red and sore, and all the side of his face showed greyish bruising.

'Two of you,' said Dolly disgustedly, 'and he knocked you about like kids.'

Chico took this a lot better than if she had fussed maternally over his injury.

'It took more than two Lilliputians to peg down Gulliver,' he said with good humour. (They had a large library in the children's orphanage.)

'But only one David to slay Goliath.'

Chico made a face at her, and I laughed.

'And how are our collywobbles today?' he asked me ironically.

'Better than your looks.'

'You know why Sid's best friends don't know him?' said Chico.

'Why?' said Dolly, seriously.

'He suffers from Halley-tosis.'

'Oh God,' said Dolly. 'Take him away someone. Take him away. I can't stand it.'

On the ground floor I sat in a padded maroon armchair in Radnor's drawing-room office and listened to him saying there were no out-of-the-ordinary reports from the patrols at Seabury.

'Fison has just been on the telephone. Everything is normal for a race day, he says. The public will start arriving very shortly. He and Tom walked all round the course just now with Captain Oxon for a thorough check. There's nothing wrong with it, that they can see.'

There might be something wrong with it that they couldn't see. I was uneasy.

'I might stay down there tonight, if I can find a room,' I said.

'If you do, give me a ring at home, during the evening.'

'Sure.' I had disturbed his dinner, the day before, to tell him about Fred and the mirror.

'Could I have those photographs back, if you've finished with them?' I asked. 'I want to check that list of initials against the racecourse workmen at Seabury.'

'I'm sorry, Sid, I haven't got them.'

'Are they back upstairs . . .?'

'No, no, they aren't here at all. Lord Hagbourne has them.'

'But why?' I sat up straight, disturbed.

'He came here yesterday afternoon. I'd say on balance he is almost down on our side of the fence. I didn't get the usual caution about expenses, which is a good sign. Anyway, what he wanted was to see the proofs you told him we held which show it is Kraye who is buying the shares. Photographs of share transfer certificates. He knew about them. He said you'd told him.'

'Yes, I did.'

'He wanted to see them. That was reasonable, and I didn't want to risk tipping him back into indecision, so I showed them to him. He asked me very courteously if he could take them to show them to the Seabury executive. They held a meeting this morning, I believe. He thought they might be roused to some effective action if they could see for themselves how big Kraye's holding is.'

'What about the other photographs? The others that were in the box.'

'He took them all. They were all jumbled up, and he was in a hurry. He said he'd sort them out himself later.'

'He took them to Seabury?' I said uneasily.

'That's right. For the executive meeting this morning.' He looked at his watch. 'The meeting must be on at this moment, I should think. If you want them you can ask him for them as soon as you get there. He should have finished with them by then.'

'I wish you hadn't let him take them,' I said.

'It can't do any harm. Even if he lost them we'd still have the negatives. You could get another print done tomorrow, of your list.'

The negatives, did he but know it, were inaccessibly tucked into a mislaid file in Finchley. I didn't confess. Instead I said, unconvinced, 'All right. I suppose it won't matter. I'll get on down there, then.'

I packed an overnight bag in the flat. The sun was pouring in through the windows, making the blues and greens and blond wood furniture look warm and friendly. After two years the place was at last beginning to feel like home. A home without Jenny. Happiness without Jenny. Both were possible, it seemed. I certainly felt more myself than at any time since she left.

The sun was still shining, too, at Seabury. But not on a very large crowd. The poor quality of the racing was so obvious as to be pathetic: and it was in order that such a rotten gaggle of weedy quadrupeds could stumble and scratch their way round to the winning post, I reflected philosophically, that I had tried to pit my inadequate wits against Lord Hagbourne, Captain Oxon, the Seabury executive, Kraye, Bolt, Fred, Leo, old Uncle Tom Cobley and all.

There were no mishaps all day. The horses raced nonchalantly over the tan pitch at their speedy crawl, and no light flashed in their eyes as they knocked hell out of the fences on the far side. Round One to Chico and me.

As the fine weather put everyone in a good mood a shred of Seabury's former vitality temporarily returned to the place: enough, anyway, for people to notice the dinginess of the stands and remark that it was time something was done about it. If they felt like that, I thought, a revival shouldn't be impossible.

The Senior Steward listened attentively while I passed on Zanna Martin's suggestion that Seabury council should be canvassed, and surprisingly said that he would see it was promptly done.

In spite of these small headways, however, my spine

wouldn't stop tingling. Lord Hagbourne didn't have the photographs.

'They are only mislaid, Sid,' he said soothingly. 'Don't make such a fuss. They'll turn up.'

He had put them down on the table round which the meeting had been held, he said. After the official business was over, he had chatted, standing up. When he turned back to pick up the box, it was no longer there. The whole table had been cleared. The ashtrays were being emptied. The table was required for lunch. A white cloth was being spread over it.

What, I asked, had been the verdict of the meeting, anyway? Er, um, it appeared the whole subject had been shelved for a week or two: no urgency was felt. Shares changed hands slowly, very slowly. But they had agreed that Hunt Radnor could carry on for a bit.

I hesitated to go barging into the executive's private room just to look for a packet of photographs, so I asked the caterers instead. They hadn't seen it, they said, rushing round me. I tracked down the man and woman who had cleared the table after the meeting and laid it for lunch.

Any amount of doodling on bits of paper, said the waitress, but no box of photographs, and excuse me love, they're waiting for these sandwiches. She agreed to look for it, looked, and came back shaking her head. It wasn't there, as far as she could see. It was quite big, I said despairingly.

I asked Mr Fotherton, Clerk of the Course; I asked

Captain Oxon, I asked the secretary, and anyone else I could think of who had been at the meeting. None of them knew where the photographs were. All of them, busy with their racing jobs, said much the same as Lord Hagbourne.

'Don't worry, Sid, they're bound to turn up.'

But they didn't.

I stayed on the racecourse until after the security patrols changed over at six o'clock. The incomers were the same men who had been on watch the night before, four experienced and sensible ex-policemen, all middle-aged. They entrenched themselves comfortably in the Press room, which had windows facing back and front, effective central heating, and four telephones; better headquarters than usual on their night jobs, they said.

Between the last race (three-thirty) and six o'clock, apart from hunting without success for the photographs and driving Lord Hagbourne round to Napoleon Close for a horrified first-hand look at the smashed-up mirror, I persuaded Captain Oxon to accompany me on a thorough nook and cranny check-up of all the racecourse buildings.

He came willingly enough, his stiffness of earlier in the week having been thawed, I supposed, by the comparative success of the day; but we found nothing and no one that shouldn't have been there.

I drove into Seabury and booked into the Seafront Hotel, where I had often stayed in the past. It was only half full. Formerly, on racing nights, it had been crammed. Over a brandy in the bar the manager lamented with me the state of trade.

'Race meetings used to give us a boost every three weeks nearly all the winter. Now hardly anyone comes, and I hear they didn't even ask for the January fixture this year. I tell you, I'd like to see that place blooming again, we need it.'

'Ah,' I said. 'Then write to the Town Council and say so.'

'That wouldn't help,' he said gloomily.

'You never know. It might. Do write.'

'All right, Sid. Just to please you then. For old time's sake. Let's have another brandy on the house.'

I had an early dinner with him and his wife and afterwards went for a walk along the seashore. The night was dry and cold and the onshore breeze smelt of seaweed. The banked pebbles scrunched into trickling hollows under my shoes and the winter sand was as hard-packed as rock. Thinking about Kraye and his machinations, I had strolled quite a long way eastwards, away from the racecourse, before I remembered I had said I would ring Radnor at his home during the evening.

There was nothing much to tell him. I didn't hurry, and it was nearly ten o'clock when I got back to Seabury. The modernizations didn't yet run to telephones in all the bedrooms at the hotel, so I used the kiosk outside on the promenade, because I came to it first.

It wasn't Radnor who answered, but Chico, and I knew at once from his voice that things had gone terribly wrong.

'Sid . . .' he said. 'Sid . . . look, pal, I don't know how to tell you. You'll have to have it straight. We've been trying to reach you all the evening.'

'What . . .?' I swallowed.

'Someone bombed your flat.'

'*Bombed*,' I said stupidly.

'A plastic bomb. It blew the street wall right out. All the flats round yours were badly damaged, but yours . . . well, there's nothing there. Just a big hole with disgusting black sort of cobwebs. That's how they knew it was a plastic bomb. The sort the French terrorists used . . . Sid, are you there?'

'Yes.'

'I'm sorry, pal. I'm sorry. But that's not all. They've done it to the office, too.' His voice was anguished. 'It went off in the Racing Section. But the whole place is cracked open. It's . . . it's bloody ghastly.'

'Chico.'

'I know. I know. The old man's round there now, just staring at it. He made me stay here because you said you'd ring, and in case the racecourse patrols want anything. No one was badly hurt, that's the only good thing. Half a dozen people were bruised and cut, at your flats. And the office was empty, of course.'

254

'What time . . .?'

'The bomb in the office went off about an hour and a half ago, and the one in your flat was just after seven. The old man and I were round there with the police when they got the radio message about the office. The police seem to think that whoever did it was looking for something. The people who live underneath you heard someone moving about upstairs for about two hours shortly before the bomb went off, but they just thought it was you making more noise than usual. And it seems everything in your flat was moved into one pile in the sitting-room and the bomb put in the middle. The police said it meant that they hadn't found what they were looking for and were destroying everything in case they had missed it.'

'Everything . . .' I said.

'Not a thing was left. God, Sid, I wish I didn't have to . . . but there it is. Nothing that was there exists any more.'

The letters from Jenny when she loved me. The only photograph of my mother and father. The trophies I won racing. The lot. I leant numbly against the wall.

'Sid, are you still there?'

'Yes.'

'It was the same thing at the office. People across the road saw lights on and someone moving about inside, and just thought we were working late. The old man said we must assume they still haven't found what they were looking for. He wants to know what it is.'

'I don't know,' I said.

'You must.'

'No. I don't.'

'You can think on the way back.'

'I'm not coming back. Not tonight. It can't do any good. I think I'll go out to the racecourse again, just to make sure nothing happens there too.'

'All right. I'll tell him when he calls. He said he'd be over in Cromwell Road all night, very likely.'

We rang off and I went out of the kiosk into the cold night air. I thought that Radnor was right. It was important to know what it was that the bomb merchants had been looking for. I leaned against the outside of the box, thinking about it. Deliberately not thinking about the flat, the place that had begun to be home, and all that was lost. That had happened before, in one way or another. The night my mother died, for instance. And I'd ridden my first winner the next day.

To look for something, you had to know it existed. If you used bombs, destroying it was more important than finding it. What did I have, which I hadn't had long (or they would have searched before) which Kraye wanted obliterated?

There was the bullet which Fred had accidentally fired into the mirror. They wouldn't find that, because it was somewhere in a police ballistics laboratory. And if they had thought I had it, they would have looked for it the night before.

There was the leaflet Bolt had sent out, but there

were hundreds of those, and he wouldn't want the one I had, even if he knew I had it.

There was the letter Mervyn Brinton had re-written for me, but if it were that it meant . . .

I went back into the telephone box, obtained Mervyn Brinton's number from directory inquiries, and rang him up.

To my relief, he answered.

'You are all right, Mr Brinton?'

'Yes, yes. What's the matter?'

'You haven't had a call from the big man? You haven't told anyone about my visit to you, or that you know your brother's letter by heart?'

He sounded scared. 'No. Nothing's happened. I wouldn't tell anyone. I never would.'

'Fine,' I reassured him. 'That's just fine. I was only checking.'

So it was not Brinton's letter.

The photographs, I thought. They had been in the office all the time until Radnor gave them to Lord Hagbourne yesterday afternoon. No one outside the agency, except Lord Hagbourne and Charles, had known they existed. Not until this morning, when Lord Hagbourne took them to Seabury executive meeting, and lost them.

Suppose they weren't lost, but stolen. By someone who knew Kraye, and thought he ought to have them. From the dates on all those documents Kraye would know exactly when the photographs had been taken. And where.

My scalp contracted. I must assume, I thought, that they had now connected all the Halleys and Sids.

Suddenly fearful, I rang up Aynsford. Charles himself answered, calm and sensible.

'Charles, please will you do as I ask, at once, and no questions? Grab Mrs Cross, go out and get in the car and drive well away from the house and ring me back at Seabury 79411. Got that? Seabury 79411.'

'Yes,' he said, and put down the telephone. Thank God, I thought, for a naval training. There might not be much time. The office bomb had exploded an hour and a half ago; London to Aynsford took the same.

Ten minutes later the bell began to ring. I picked up the receiver.

'They say you're in a call box,' Charles said.

'That's right. Are you?'

'No, the pub down in the village. Now, what's it all about?'

I told him about the bombs, which horrified him, and about the missing photographs.

'I can't think what else it can be that they are looking for.'

'But you said that they've got them.'

'The negatives,' I said.

'Oh. Yes. And they weren't in your flat or the office?'

'No. Quite by chance, they weren't.'

'And you think if they're still looking, that they'll come to Aynsford?'

'If they are desperate enough, they might. They might think you would know where I keep things ... And even have a go at making you tell them. I asked you to come out quick because I didn't want to risk it. If they are going to Aynsford, they could be there at any minute now. It's horribly likely they'll think of you. They'll know I took the photos in your house.'

'From the dates. Yes. Right. I'll get on to the local police and ask for a guard on the house at once.'

'Charles, one of them ... well, if he's the one with the bombs, you'll need a squad.' I described Fred and his van, together with its number.

'Right.' He was still calm. 'Why would the photographs be so important to them? Enough to use bombs, I mean?'

'I wish I knew.'

'Take care.'

'Yes,' I said.

I did take care. Instead of going back into the hotel, I rang up.

The manager said, 'Sid, where on earth are you, people have been trying to reach you all the evening ... the police too.'

'Yes, Joe, I know. It's all right. I've talked to the people in London. Now, has anyone actually called at the hotel, wanting me?'

'There's someone up in your room, yes. Your father-in-law, Admiral Roland.'

'Oh really? Does he look like an Admiral?'

'I suppose so,' he sounded puzzled.

'A gentleman?'

'Yes, of course.' Not Fred, then.

'Well, he isn't my father-in-law. I've just been talking to him in his house in Oxfordshire. You collect a couple of helpers and chuck my visitor out.'

I put down the receiver sighing. A man up in my room meant everything I'd brought to Seabury would very likely be ripped to bits. That left me with just the clothes I stood in, and the car . . .

I fairly sprinted round to where I'd left the car. It was locked, silent and safe. No damage. I patted it thankfully, climbed in, and drove out to the racecourse.

CHAPTER FIFTEEN

All was quiet as I drove through the gates and switched off the engine. There were lights on – one shining through the windows of the Press room, one outside the weighing room door, one high up somewhere on the stands. The shadows in between were densely black. It was a clear night with no moon.

I walked across to the Press room, to see if the security patrols had anything to report.

They hadn't.

All four of them were fast asleep.

Furious, I shook the nearest. His head lolled like a pendulum, but he didn't wake up. He was sitting slumped in his chair. One of them had his arms on the table and his head on his arms. One of them sat on the floor, his head on the seat of the chair and his arms hanging down. The fourth lay flat, face downwards, near the opposite wall.

The stupid fools, I thought violently. Ex-policemen letting themselves be put to sleep like infants. It shouldn't have been possible. One of their first rules in

261

guard work was to take their own food and drink with them and not accept sweets from strangers.

I stepped round their heavily breathing bulks and picked up one of the Press telephones to ring Chico for reinforcements. The line was dead. I tried the three other instruments. No contact with the exchange on any of them.

I would have to go back and ring up from Seabury, I thought. I went out of the Press room but in the light pouring out before I shut the door I saw a dim figure walking towards me from the direction of the gate.

'Who's that?' he called imperiously, and I recognized his voice. Captain Oxon.

'It's only me, Sid Halley,' I shouted back. 'Come and look at this.'

He came on into the light, and I stood aside for him to go into the Press room.

'Good heavens. What on earth's the matter with them?'

'Sleeping pills. And the telephones don't work. You haven't seen anyone about who ought not to be?'

'No. I haven't heard anything except your car. I came down to see who had come.'

'How many lads are there staying overnight in the hostel? Could we use some of those to patrol the place while I ring the agency to get some more men?'

'I should think they'd love it,' he said, consideringly. 'There are about five of them. They shouldn't be in bed yet. We'll go over and ask them, and you can use the telephone from my flat to ring your agency.'

'Thanks,' I said. 'That's fine.'

I looked round the room at the sleeping men. 'I think perhaps I ought to see if any of them tried to write a message. I won't be a minute.'

He waited patiently while I looked under the head and folded arms of the man at the table and under the man on the floor, and all round the one with his head on the chair seat, but none of them had even reached for a pencil. Shrugging, I looked at the remains of their supper, lying on the table. Half eaten sandwiches on grease-proof paper, dregs of coffee in cups and thermos flasks, a couple of apple cores, some cheese sections and empty wrappings, and an unpeeled banana.

'Found anything?' asked Oxon.

I shook my head in disgust. 'Not a thing. They'll have terrible headaches when they wake up, and serve them right.'

'I can understand you being annoyed . . .' he began. But I was no longer really listening. Over the back of the chair occupied by the first man I had shaken was hanging a brown leather binoculars case: and on its lid were stamped three black initials: L.E.O. Leo. *Leo.*

'Something the matter?' asked Oxon.

'No.' I smiled at him and touched the strap of the binoculars. 'Are these yours?'

'Yes. The men asked if I could lend them some. For the dawn, they said.'

'It was very kind of you.'

'Oh. Nothing.' He shrugged, moving out into the night. 'You'd better make the phone call first. We'll tackle the boys afterwards.'

I had absolutely no intention of walking into his flat.

'Right,' I said.

We went out of the door, and I closed it behind us.

A familiar voice, loaded with satisfaction, spoke from barely a yard away. 'So you've got him, Oxon. Good.'

'He was coming . . .' began Oxon in anxious anger, knowing that 'got him' was an exaggeration.

'No,' I said, and turned and ran for the car.

When I was barely ten yards from it someone turned the lights on. The headlights of my own car. I stopped dead.

Behind me one of the men shouted and I heard their feet running. I wasn't directly in the beam, but silhouetted against it. I swerved off to the right, towards the gate. Three steps in that direction, and the headlights of a car turning in through it caught me straight in the eyes.

There were more shouts, much closer, from Oxon and Kraye. I turned, half dazzled, and saw them closing in. Behind me now the incoming car rolled forward. And the engine of my Mercedes purred separately into life.

I ran for the dark. The two cars, moving, caught me again in their beams. Kraye and Oxon ran where they pointed.

I was driven across and back towards the stands like a coursed hare, the two cars behind inexorably finding me with their lights and the two men running with reaching, clutching hands. Like a nightmare game of 'He', I thought wildly, with more than a child's forfeit if I were caught.

Across the parade ring, across the flat tarmac stretch beyond it, under the rails of the unsaddling enclosure and along the weighing room wall. Sometimes only a foot from hooking fingers. Once barely a yard from a speeding bumper.

But I made it. Safe, panting, in the precious dark, on the inside of the door into the trainers' luncheon room and through there without stopping into the kitchen. And weaving on from there out into the members' lunch room, round acres of tables with upturned chairs, through the far door into the wide passage which cut like a tunnel along the length of the huge building, across it, and up a steep stone staircase emerging half way up the open steps of the stands, and sideways along them as far as I could go. The pursuit was left behind.

I sank down, sitting with one leg bent to run, in the black shadow where the low wooden wall dividing the Members from Tattersalls cut straight down the steps separating the stands into two halves. On top of the wall wire netting stretched up too high to climb: high enough to keep out the poorer customers from gate-crashing the expensive ring.

At the bottom of the steps lay a large expanse of

Members' lawn stretching to another metal mesh fence, chest high, and beyond that lay the whole open expanse of racecourse. Half a mile across it to the London road to Seabury, with yet another barrier, the boundary fence, to negotiate.

It was too far. I knew I couldn't do it. Perhaps once, with two hands for vaulting, with a stomach which didn't already feel as if it were tearing into more holes inside. But not now. Although I always mended fast, it was only two weeks since I had found the short walk to Andrews' body very nearly too much; and Fred's well-aimed attentions on the previous day had not been therapeutic.

Looking at it straight: if I ran, it had to be successful. My kingdom for a horse, I thought. Any reasonable cowboy would have had Revelation hitched to the rails, ready for a flying leap into the saddle and a thundering exit. I had a hundred and fifty mile an hour little white Mercedes: and someone else was sitting in it.

To run and be caught running would achieve nothing and be utterly pointless.

Which left just one alternative.

The security patrol hadn't been drugged for nothing. Kraye wasn't at Seabury for his health. Some more damage had been planned for this night. Might already have been done. There was just a chance, if I stayed to look, that I could find out what it was. Before they found *me*. Naturally.

If I ever have any children, they won't get me playing hide and seek.

Half an hour later the grim game was still in progress. My own car was now parked on the racecourse side of the stands, on the tarmac in Tattersalls where the bookies had called the odds that afternoon. It was facing the stands with the headlights full on. Every inch of the steps was lit by them, and since the car had arrived there I had not been able to use that side of the building at all.

The other car was similarly parked inside the racecourse gates, its headlights shining on the fronts of the weighing room, bars, dining-rooms, cloakrooms, and offices.

Presuming that each car still had a watching occupant, that left only Kraye and Oxon, as far as I could guess, to run me to ground: but I became gradually sure that there were three, not two, after me in the stands. Perhaps one of the cars was empty. But which? And it would be unlikely to have its ignition key in place.

Bit by bit I covered the whole enormous block. I didn't know what I was looking for, that was the trouble. It could have been anything from a plastic bomb downwards, but if past form was anything to go by, it was something which could appear accidental.

Bad luck. A jinx. Open, recognizable sabotage would be ruinous to the scheme.

Without a surveyor I couldn't be certain that part of the steps would not collapse the following day under the weight of the crowd, but I could find no trace of any structural damage at all, and there hadn't been much time: only five or six hours since the day's meeting ended.

There were no large quantities of food in the kitchen: the caterers appeared to have removed what had been left over ready to bring fresh the next day. A large double-doored refrigerator was securely locked. I discounted the possibility that Kraye could have thought of large scale food poisoning.

All the fire extinguishers seemed to be in their places, and there were no smouldering cigarette ends near tins of paraffin. Nothing capable of spontaneous combustion. I supposed another fire, so soon after the stables, might have been too suspicious.

I went cautiously, carefully, every nerve-racking step of the way, peering round corners, easing through doors, fearing that any moment one of them would pounce on me from behind.

They knew I was still there, because everywhere they went they turned on lights, and everywhere I went I turned them off. Opening a door from a lighted room on to a dark passage made one far too easy to spot; I turned off the lights before I opened any door. There had been three lights in the passage itself, but I had broken them early on with a broom from the kitchen.

Once when I was in the passage, creeping from the men's lavatories to the Tattersalls bar, Kraye himself appeared at the far end, the Members' end, and began walking my way. He came in through the faint glow from the car's headlights, and he hadn't seen me. One stride took me across the passage, one jump and a wriggle into the only cover available, the heap of equipment the bookmakers had left there out of the weather, overnight.

These were only their metal stands, their folded umbrellas, the boxes and stools they stood on: a thin, spiky, precarious heap. I crouched down beside them, praying I wouldn't dislodge anything.

Kraye's footsteps scraped hollowly as he trod towards my ineffective hiding place. He stopped twice, opening doors and looking into the storerooms which were in places built back under the steps of the stands. They were mostly empty or nearly so, and offered nothing to me. They were too small, and all dead ends: if I were found in one of them, I couldn't get out.

The door of the bar I had been making for suddenly opened, spilling bright light into the passage between me and Kraye.

Oxon's voice said anxiously, 'He can't have got away.'

'Of course not, you fool,' said Kraye furiously. 'But if you'd had the sense to bring your keys over with you

269

we'd have had him long ago.' Their voices echoed up and down the passage.

'It was your idea to leave so much unlocked. I could go back and fetch them.'

'He'd have too much chance of giving us the slip. But we're not getting anywhere with all this dodging about. We'll start methodically from this end and move down.'

'We did that to start with,' complained Oxon. 'And we missed him. Let me go back for the keys. Then as you said before we can lock all the doors behind us and stop him doubling back.'

'No,' said Kraye decisively. 'There aren't enough of us. You stay here. We'll go back to the weighing room and start all together.'

They began to walk away. The bar door was still open, lighting up the passage, which I didn't like. If anyone came in from the other end, he would see me for sure.

I shifted my position to crawl away along the wall for better concealment, and one of the bookmakers' metal tripods slid down and clattered off the side of the pile with an echoing noise like a dozen demented machine guns.

There were shouts from the two men down the passage.

'There he is.'

'Get him.'

I stood up and ran.

The nearest opening in the wall was a staircase up to a suite of rooms above the changing room and Members' dining-room. I hesitated a fraction of a second and then passed it. Up those steps were the executive's rooms and offices. I didn't know my way round up there, but Oxon did. He had a big enough advantage already in his knowledge of the building without my giving him a bonus.

I ran on, past the gents' cloaks, and finally in through the last possible door, that of a long bare dirty room smelling of beer. It was a sort of extra, subsidiary bar, and all it now contained was a bare counter backed by empty shelves. I nearly fell over a bucket full of crinkled metal bottle tops which someone had carelessly left in my way, and then wasted precious seconds to dart back to put the bucket just inside the door I'd come in by.

Kraye and Oxon were running. I snapped off the lights, and with no time to get clear through the far door out into the paddock, where anyway I would be lit by car headlights, I scrambled down behind the bar counter.

The door jerked open. There was a clatter of the bucket and a yell, and the sound of someone falling. Then the lights snapped on again, showing me just how tiny my hiding place really was, and two bottle tops rolled across the floor into my sight.

'For God's sake,' yelled Kraye in anger. 'You clumsy, stupid fool. Get up. Get up.' He charged down the room into the far door, the board floor bouncing slightly under his weight. From the clanking, cursing, and clattering of bottle tops I imagined that Oxon was extricating himself from the bucket and following. If it hadn't been so dangerous it would have been funny.

Kraye yanked the outside door open, stepped outside and yelled across to the stationary car to ask where I had gone. I felt rather than saw Oxon run down the room to join him. I crawled round the end of the counter, sprinted for the door I had come in by, flipped off the light again, slammed the door, and ran back up the passage. There was a roar from Kraye as he fumbled back into the darkened room, and long before they had emerged into the passage again, kicking bottle tops in all directions, I was safe in the opening of a little offshoot lobby to the kitchen.

The kitchens were safest to me because there were so many good hiding places and so many exits, but it wasn't much good staying there as I had searched them already.

I was fast running out of places to look. The boiler room had given me an anxious two minutes as its only secondary exit was into a dead end storeroom containing, as far as I could see, nothing but vast oil tanks with pipes and gauges. They were hard against the walls: nowhere to hide. The boiler itself roared, keeping the central heating going all through the night.

The weighing room was even worse, because it was big and entirely without cover. It contained nothing it shouldn't have: tables, chairs, notices pinned on the walls, and the weighing machine itself. Beyond, in the changing room, there were rows of pegs with saddles on, the warm, banked-up coke stove in the corner, and a big wicker basket full of helmets, boots, weight cloths, and other equipment left by the valets overnight. A dirty cup and saucer. A copy of *Playboy*. Several raincoats. Racing colours on pegs. A row of washed breeches hanging up to dry. It was the most occupied looking part of the stands, the place I felt most at home in and where I wanted to go to ground, like an ostrich in familiar sand. But on the far side of the changing room lay only the washroom, another dead end.

Opening out of the weighing room on the opposite side to the changing room was the Stewards' room, where in the past like all jockeys I'd been involved in cases of objections-to-the-winner. It was a bare room: a large table, chairs round it, sporting pictures, small threadbare carpet. A few of the Stewards' personal possessions lay scattered about, but there was no concealment.

A few doors here and there were locked, in spite of Oxon having left the keys in his flat. As usual I had the bunch of lock-pickers in my pocket and with shortened breath I spent several sticky minutes letting myself into one well secured room off the Members' bar. It proved to be the liquor store: crates of spirits, champagne, wine, and beer. Beer from floor to ceiling, and a porter's

273

trolley to transport it. It was a temptation to lock myself in there, and wait for the caterers to rescue me in the morning. This was one door that Oxon would not expect to find me on the far side of.

In the liquor store I might be safe. On the other hand, if I were safe the racecourse might not be. Reluctantly I left again; but I didn't waste time locking up. With the pursuit out of sight, I risked a look upstairs. It was warm and quiet, and all the lights were on. I left them on, figuring that if the watchers in the cars saw them go out they would know too accurately where I was.

Nothing seemed to be wrong. On one side of a central lobby there was the big room where the executive held their meetings and ate their lunch. On the other side there was a sort of drawing-room furnished with light armchairs, with two cloakrooms leading off it at the back. At the front, through double glass doors, it led out into a box high up on the stands. The private box for directors and distinguished guests, with a superb view over the whole course.

I didn't go out there. Sabotaging the Royal Box wouldn't stop a race meeting to which royalty weren't going anyway. And besides, whoever was in my car would see me opening the door.

Retreating, I went back, right through the dining-board room and out into the servery on the far side. There I found a storeroom with plates, glass, and cutlery, and in the storeroom also a second exit. A small service lift down to the kitchens. It worked with ropes, like the one in the office in the Cromwell Road . . . like the office lift *had* worked, before the bomb.

Kraye and Oxon were down in the kitchen. Their angry voices floated up the shaft, mingled with a softer murmuring voice which seemed to be arguing with them. Since for once I knew where they all were, I returned with some boldness to the ground again. But I was worried. There seemed to be nothing at all going wrong in the main building. If they were organizing yet more damage somewhere out on the course itself, I didn't see how I could stop it.

While I was still dithering rather aimlessly along the passage the kitchen door opened, the light flooded out, and I could hear Kraye still talking. I dived yet again for the nearest door and put it between myself and them.

I was, I discovered, in the ladies' room, where I hadn't been before: and there was no second way out. Only a double row of cubicles, all with the doors open, a range of washbasins, mirrors on the walls with a wide shelf beneath them, a few chairs, and a counter like that in the bar. Behind the counter there was a rail with coat hangers.

There were heavy steps in the passage outside. I slid instantly behind the counter and pressed myself into a corner. The door opened.

'He won't be in here,' said Kraye. 'The light's still on.'

'I looked in here not five minutes ago, anyway,' agreed Oxon.

The door closed behind them and their footsteps went away. I began to breathe again and my thudding heart slowed down. But for a couple of seconds only. Across the room someone coughed.

I froze. I couldn't believe it. The room had been empty when I came in, I was certain. And neither Kraye nor Oxon had stayed . . . I stretched my ears, tense, horrified.

Another cough. A soft, single cough.

Try as I could, I could hear nothing else. No breathing. No rustle of clothing, no movement. It didn't make sense. If someone in the room knew I was behind the counter, why didn't they do something about it? If they didn't know, why were they so unnaturally quiet?

In the end, taking a conscious grip on my nerves, I slowly stood up.

The room was empty.

Almost immediately there was another cough. Now that my ears were no longer obstructed by the counter, I got a clearer idea of its direction. I swung towards it. There was no one there.

I walked across the room and stared down at the washbasin. Water was trickling from one of the taps. Even while I looked at it the tap coughed. Almost laughing with relief I stretched out my hand and turned it off.

The metal was very hot. Surprised, I turned the

water on again. It came spluttering out of the tap, full of air bubbles and very hot indeed. Steaming. How stupid, I thought, turning it off again, to have the water so hot at this time of night . . .

Christ, I thought. The boiler.

CHAPTER SIXTEEN

Kraye and Oxon's so-called methodical end to end search, which had just failed to find me in the ladies', was proceeding from the Members' end of the stands towards Tattersalls. The boiler, like myself, was in the part they had already put behind them. I switched out the ladies' room lights, carefully eased into the passage, and via the kitchen, the Members' dining-room, the gentlemen's cloaks, and another short strip of passage returned to the boiler room.

Although there was no door through, I knew that on the far side of the inside wall lay to the left the weighing room and to the right the changing room, with the dividing wall between. From both those rooms, when it was quiet, as it was that night, one could quite clearly hear the boiler's muffled roar.

The light that I had switched off was on again in the boiler room. I looked round. It all looked as normal as it had before, except ... except that away to the right there was a very small pool of water on the floor.

Boilers. We had had a lesson on them at school.

Sixteen or seventeen years ago, I thought hopelessly. But I remembered very well the way the master had begun the lesson.

'The first thing to learn about boilers,' he said, 'is that they explode.'

He was an excellent teacher: the whole class of forty boys listened from then on with avid interest. But since then the only acquaintance I'd had with boilers was down in the basement of the flats, where I sometimes drank a cup of orange tea with the caretaker. A tough ex-naval stoker, he was, and a confirmed student of racing form. Mostly we'd talked about horses, but sometimes about his job. There were strict regulations for boilers, he'd said, and regular official inspections every three months, and he was glad of it, working alongside them every day.

The first thing to learn about boilers is that they explode.

It's no good saying I wasn't frightened, because I was. If the boiler burst it wasn't simply going to make large new entrances into the weighing room and changing room, it was going to fill every cranny near it with scalding tornadoes of steam. Not a death I looked on with much favour.

I stood with my back against the door and tried desperately to remember that long ago lesson, and to work out what was going wrong.

It was a big steam boiler. An enormous cylinder nine feet high and five feet in diameter. Thick steel, with dark red anti-rust paint peeling off. Fired at the bottom not by coke, which it had been built for, but by the more modern roaring jet of burning oil. If I opened the fire door I would feel the blast of its tremendous heat.

The body of the cylinder would be filled almost to the top with water. The flame boiled the water. The resulting steam went out of the top under its own fierce pressure in a pipe which – I followed it with my eye – led into a large yellow-painted round-ended cylinder slung horizontally near the ceiling. This tank looked rather like a zeppelin. It was, if I remembered right, a calorifier. Inside it, the steam pipe ran in a spiral, like an immobile spring. The tank itself was supplied direct from the mains with the water which was to be heated, the water going to the central heating radiators, and to the hot taps in the kitchen, the cloakrooms and the jockeys' washrooms. The scorching heat from the spiral steam pipe instantly passed into the mains water flowing over it, so that the cold water entering the calorifier was made very hot in the short time before it left at the other end.

The steam, however, losing its head in the process, gradually condensed back into water. A pipe led down the wall from the calorifier into a much smaller tank, an ordinary square one, standing on the floor. From the bottom of this yet another pipe tracked right back across the room and up near the boiler itself to a bulbous metal contraption just higher than my head.

An electric pump. It finished the circuit by pumping the condensed water up from the tank on the floor and returning it to the boiler, to be boiled, steamed, and condensed all over again. Round and round, continuously.

So far, so good. But if you interfered with the circuit so that the water didn't get back into the boiler, and at the same time kept the heat full on at the bottom, all the water inside the cylinder gradually turned to steam. Steam, which was strong enough to drive a liner, or pull a twelve coach train, but could in this case only get out at all through a narrow, closely spiralled pipe.

This type of boiler, built not for driving an engine but only for heating water, wasn't constructed to withstand enormous pressures. It was a toss-up, I thought, whether when all the water had gone the fast expanding air and steam found a weak spot to break out of before the flames burnt through the bottom. In either case, the boiler would blow up.

On the outside of the boiler there was a water gauge, a foot-long vertical glass tube held in brackets. The level of water in the tube indicated the level of water in the boiler. Near the top of the gauge a black line showed what the water level ought to be. Two thirds of the way down a broad red line obviously acted as a warning. The water in the gauge was higher than the red line by half an inch.

To put it mildly, I was relieved. The boiler wasn't bulging. The explosion lay in the future: which gave me more time to work out how to prevent it. As long as it would take Oxon and Kraye to decide on a repeat search, perhaps.

I could simply have turned out the flame, but Kraye and Oxon would notice that the noise had stopped, and merely light it again. Nothing would have been gained. On the other hand, I was sure that the flame was higher than it should have been at night, because the water in the ladies' tap was nearly boiling.

Gingerly I turned the adjusting wheel on the oil line. Half a turn. A full turn. The roaring seemed just as loud. Another turn: and that time there was a definite change. Half a turn more. It was perceptibly quieter. Slowly I inched the wheel around more, until quite suddenly the roar turned to a murmur. Too far. Hastily I reversed. At the point where the murmur was again a roar, I left it.

I looked consideringly at the square tank of condensed water on the floor. It was this, overflowing, which was making the pool of water; and it was overflowing because the contents were not being pumped back into the boiler. If they've broken the pump, I thought despairingly, I'm done. I didn't know the first thing about electric pumps.

Another sentence from that faraway school lesson floated usefully through my mind. *For safety's sake, every boiler must have two sources of water.*

I chewed my lower lip, watching the water trickle down the side of the tank on to the floor. Even in the few minutes I had been there the pool had spread. One source of water was obviously knocked out. Where and what was the other?

There were dozens of pipes in the boiler room; not only oil pipes and water pipes, but all the electric cables were installed inside tubes as well. There were about six separate pipes with stopcocks on them. It seemed to me that all the water for the entire building came in through the boiler room.

Two pipes, apparently rising mains, led from the floor up the wall and into the calorifier. Both had stopcocks, which I tested. Both were safely open. There was no rising main leading direct into the boiler.

By sheer luck I was half way round the huge cylinder looking for an inlet pipe when I saw the lever type door handle move down. I leapt for the only vestige of cover, the space between the boiler and the wall. It was scorching hot there: pretty well unbearable.

Kraye had to raise his voice to make himself heard over the roaring flame.

'You're sure it's still safe?'

'Yes, I told you, it won't blow up for three hours yet. At least three hours.'

'The water's running out already,' Kraye objected.

'There's a lot in there.' Oxon's voice came nearer. I could feel my heart thumping and hear the pulse in my ears. 'The level's not down to the caution mark on the gauge yet,' he said. 'It won't blow for a long time after it goes below that.'

'We've got to find Halley,' Kraye said. 'Got to.' If Oxon moved another step he would see me. 'I'll work from this end; you start again from the other. Look in every cupboard. The little rat has gone to ground somewhere.'

Oxon didn't answer audibly. I had a sudden glimpse of his sleeve as he turned, and I shrank into my hiding place.

Because of the noise of the boiler I couldn't hear them go away through the door, but eventually I had to risk that they had. The heat where I stood was too appalling. Moving out into the ordinarily hot air in the middle of the room was like diving into a cold bath. And Oxon and Kraye had gone.

I slipped off my jacket and wiped the sweat off my face with my shirt sleeve. Back to the problem: water supply.

The pump *looked* all right. There were no loose wires, and it had an undisturbed, slightly greasy, slightly dirty appearance. With luck, I thought, they hadn't damaged the pump, they'd blocked the pipe where it left the tank. I took off my tie and shirt as well, and put them with my jacket on the grimy floor.

The lid of the tank came off easily enough, and the water, when I tested it, proved to be no more than uncomfortably hot. I drank some in my cupped palm. The running and the heat had made me very thirsty, and although I would have preferred it iced, no water could have been purer; or more tasteless, though I was not inclined to be fussy on that point.

I stretched my arm down into the water, kneeling beside the tank. As it was only about two feet deep I could touch the bottom quite easily, and almost at once my searching fingers found and gripped a loose object. I pulled it out.

It was a fine mesh filter, which should no doubt have been in place over the opening of the outlet pipe.

Convinced now that the pipe was blocked from this end, I reached down again into the water. I found the edge of the outlet, and felt carefully into it. I could reach no obstruction. Bending over further, so that my shoulder was half in the water, I put two fingers as far as they would go into the outlet. I could feel nothing solid, but there did seem to be a piece of string. It was difficult to get it between two fingers firmly enough to pull as hard as was necessary, but gradually with a series of little jerks I managed to move the plug backwards into the tank.

It came away finally so suddenly that I nearly overbalanced. There was a burp from the outlet pipe of the tank and on the other side of the room a sharp click from the pump.

I lifted my hand out of the water to see what had blocked the pipe, and stared in amazement. It was a large mouse. I had been pulling its tail.

Accidental sabotage, I thought. The same old pattern. However unlikely it was that a mouse should dive into a tank, find the filter conveniently out of place, and get stuck just inside the outlet pipe, one would have a hard job proving that it was impossible.

I carefully put the sodden little body out of sight in the small gap between the tank and wall. With relief I noticed that the water level was already going down slightly, which meant that the pump was working properly and the boiler would soon be more or less back to normal.

I splashed some more water out of the tank to make a larger pool should Kraye or Oxon glance in again, and replaced the lid. Putting on my shirt and jacket I followed with my eyes the various pipes in and out of the boiler. The lagged steam exit pipe to the calorifier. The vast chimney flue for the hot gases from the burning oil. The inlet pipe from the pump. The water gauge. The oil pipe. There had to be another water inlet somewhere, partly for safety, partly to keep the steam circuit topped up.

I found it in the end running alongside and behind the inlet pipe from the pump. It was a gravity feed from a stepped series of three small unobtrusive tanks fixed high on the wall. Filters, I reckoned, so that the mains water didn't carry its mineral salts into the boiler and fur it up. The filter tanks were fed by a pipe which branched off one of the rising mains and had its own stopcock.

Reaching up, I tried to turn it clockwise. It didn't

move. The mains water was cut off. With satisfaction, I turned it on again.

Finally, with the boiler once more working exactly as it should, I took a look at the water gauge. The level had already risen to nearly halfway between the red and black marks. Hoping fervently Oxon wouldn't come back for another check on it, I went over to the door and switched off the light.

There was no one in the passage. I slipped through the door, and in the last three inches before shutting it behind me stretched my hand back and put the light on again. I didn't want Kraye knowing I'd been in there.

Keeping close to the wall, I walked softly down the passage towards the Tattersalls end. If I could get clear of the stands there were other buildings out that way to give cover. The barns, cloakrooms and tote buildings in the silver ring. Beyond these lay the finishing straight, the way down to the tan patch and the bisecting road. Along that, bungalows, people, and telephones.

That was when my luck ran out.

CHAPTER SEVENTEEN

I was barely two steps past the door of the Tattersalls bar when it opened and the lights blazed out on to my tiptoeing figure. In the two seconds it took Oxon to realize what he was seeing I was six running paces down towards the way out. His shouts echoed in the passage mingled with others farther back, and I still thought that if Kraye too were behind me I might have a chance. But when I was within ten steps of the end another figure appeared there, hurrying, called by the noise.

I skidded nearly to a stop, sliding on one of the scattered bottle tops, and crashed through the only possible door, into the same empty bar as before. I raced across the board floor, kicking bottle tops in all directions, but I never got to the far door. It opened before I reached it: and that was the end.

Doria Kraye stood there, maliciously triumphant. She was dressed theatrically in white slender trousers and a shiny short white jacket. Her dark hair fell smoothly, her face was as flawlessly beautiful as ever:

and she held rock steady in one elegant long-fingered hand the little .22 automatic I had last seen in a chocolate box at the bottom of her dressing-case.

'The end of the line, buddy boy,' she said. 'You stay just where you are.'

I hesitated on the brink of trying to rush her.

'Don't risk it,' she said. 'I'm a splendid shot. I wouldn't miss. Do you want a knee-cap smashed?'

There was little I wanted less. I turned round slowly. There were three men coming forward into the long room. Kraye, Oxon, and Ellis Bolt. All three of them looked as if they had long got tired of the chase and were going to take it out on the quarry.

'Will you walk,' said Doria behind me, 'or be dragged?'

I shrugged. 'Walk.'

All the same, Kraye couldn't keep his hands off me. When, following Doria's instructions, I walked past him to go back out through the passage he caught hold of my jacket at the back of my neck and kicked my legs. I kicked back, which wasn't too sensible, as I presently ended up on the floor. There was nothing like little metal bottle tops for giving you a feeling of falling on little metal bottle tops, I thought, with apologies to Michael Flanders and Donald Swann.

'Get up,' said Kraye. Doria stood beside him, pointing at me with a gun.

I did as he said.

'Right,' said Doria. 'Now, walk down the passage

and go into the weighing room. And Howard, for God's sake wait till we get there, or we'll lose him again. Walk, buddy boy. Walk straight down the middle of the passage. If you try anything, I'll shoot you in the leg.'

I saw no reason not to believe her. I walked down the centre of the passage with her too close behind for escape, and with the two men bringing up the rear.

'Stop a minute,' said Kraye, outside the boiler room.

I stopped. I didn't look round.

Kraye opened the door and looked inside. The light spilled out, adding to that already coming from the other open doors along the way.

'Well?' said Oxon.

'There's more water on the floor.' He sounded pleased, and shut the door without going in for a further look. Not all of my luck had departed, it seemed.

'Move,' he said. I obeyed.

The weighing room was as big and bare as ever. I stopped in the middle of it and turned round. The four of them stood in a row, looking at me, and I didn't at all like what I read in their faces.

'Go and sit there,' said Doria, pointing.

I went on across the floor and sat where she said, on the chair of the weighing machine. The pointer immediately swung round the clock face to show my weight. Nine stone seven. It was, I was remotely interested to see, exactly ten pounds less than when I had last raced. Bullets would solve any jockey's weight problem, I thought.

The four of them came closer. It was some relief to find that Fred wasn't among them, but only some. Kraye was emitting the same livid fury as he had twelve days ago at Aynsford. And then, I had merely insulted his wife.

'Hold his arms,' he said to Oxon. Oxon was one of those thin wiry men of seemingly limitless strength. He came round behind me, clamped his fingers round my elbows and pulled them back. With concentration Kraye hit me several times in the face.

'Now,' he said, 'where are they?'

'What?' I said indistinctly.

'The negatives.'

'What negatives?'

He hit me again and hurt his own hand. Shaking it out and rubbing his knuckles, he said, 'You know what negatives. The films you took of my papers.'

'Oh, those.'

'Those.' He hit me again, but less hard.

'In the office,' I mumbled.

He tried a slap to save his knuckles. 'Office,' I said.

He tried with his left hand, but it was clumsy. After that he sucked his knuckles and kept his hands to himself.

Bolt spoke for the first time, in his consciously beautiful voice. 'Fred wouldn't have missed them, especially as there was no reason for them to be concealed. He's too thorough.'

If Fred wouldn't have missed them, the bombs had been pure spite. I licked the inside of a split lip and thought about what I would like to do to Fred.

'Where in the office?' said Kraye.

'Desk.'

'Hit him,' said Kraye. 'My hand hurts.'

Bolt had a go, but it wasn't his sort of thing.

'Try with this,' said Doria, offering Bolt the gun, but it was luckily so small he couldn't hold it effectively.

Oxon let go of my elbows, came round to the front, and looked at my face.

'If he's decided not to tell you, you won't get it out of him like that,' he said.

'I told you,' I said.

'Why not?' said Bolt.

'You're hurting yourselves more than him. And if you want my opinion, you won't get anything out of him at all.'

'Don't be silly,' said Doria scornfully. 'He's so small.'

Oxon laughed without mirth.

'If Fred said so, the negatives weren't at his office,' asserted Bolt again. 'Nor in his flat. And he didn't bring them with him. Or at least, they weren't in his luggage at the hotel.'

I looked at him sideways, out of an eye which was beginning to swell. And if I hadn't been so quick to have him flung out of my hotel room, I thought sourly, he wouldn't have driven through the racecourse gate at exactly the wrong moment. But I couldn't have foreseen it, and it was too late to help.

'They weren't in his car either,' said Doria. 'But this was.' She put her hand into her shining white pocket and brought out my baby camera. Kraye took it from her, opened the case, and saw what was inside. The veins in his neck and temples became congested with blood. In a paroxysm of fury he threw the little black toy across the room so that it hit the wall with a disintegrating crash.

'Sixteen millimetre,' he said savagely. 'Fred must have missed them.'

Bolt said obstinately, 'Fred would find a needle in a haystack. And those films wouldn't have been hidden.'

'He might have them in his pocket,' suggested Doria.

'Take your coat off,' Kraye said. 'Stand up.'

I stood up, and the base-plate of the weighing machine wobbled under my feet. Oxon pulled my coat down over the back of my shoulders, gave a tug to get the sleeves off, and passed the jacket to Kraye. His own hand he thrust into my trouser pockets. In the right one, under my tie, he found the bunch of lock pickers.

'Sit down,' he said. I did so, exploring with the back of my hand some of the damage to my face. It could have been worse, I thought resignedly, much worse. I would be lucky if that were all.

'What are those?' said Doria curiously, taking the jingling collection from Oxon.

Kraye snatched them from her and slung them after the camera. 'Skeleton keys,' he said furiously. 'What he used to unlock my cases.'

'I don't see how he could,' said Doria, 'with that . . . that . . . *claw*.' She looked down where it lay on my lap.

A nice line in taunts, I thought, but a week too late. Thanks to Zanna Martin, I was at least learning to live with the claw. I left it where it was.

'Doria,' said Bolt calmly, 'would you be kind enough to go over to the flat and wait for Fred to ring? He may already have found what we want at Aynsford.'

I turned my head and found him looking straight at me, assessingly. There was a detachment in the eyes, an unmoved quality in the rounded features; and I began to wonder whether his stolid coolness might not in the end prove even more difficult to deal with than Kraye's rage.

'Aynsford,' I repeated thickly. I looked at my watch. If Fred had really taken his bombs to Aynsford, he should by now be safely in the bag. One down, four to go. Five of them altogether, not four. I hadn't thought of Doria being an active equal colleague of the others. My mistake.

'I don't want to,' said Doria, staying put.

Bolt shrugged. 'It doesn't matter. I see that the nega-tives aren't at Aynsford, because the thought of Fred looking for them there doesn't worry Halley one little bit.'

The thought of what Fred might be doing at Aynsford or to Charles himself didn't worry any of them either. But more than that I didn't like the way Bolt was reasoning. In the circumstances, a clear-thinking opponent was something I could well have done without.

'We must have them,' said Kraye intensely. 'We must. Or be certain beyond doubt that they were destroyed.' To Oxon he said, 'Hold his arms again.'

'No,' I said, shrinking back.

'Ah, that's better. Well?'

'They were in the office.' My mouth felt stiff.

'Where?'

'In Mr Radnor's desk, I think.'

He stared at me, eyes narrowed, anger half under control, weighing up whether I were telling the truth or not. He certainly couldn't go to the office and make sure.

'Were,' said Bolt suddenly.

'What?' asked Kraye, impatiently.

'Were,' said Bolt. 'Halley said were. The negatives *were* in the office. Now that's very interesting indeed, don't you think?'

Oxon said, 'I don't see why.'

Bolt came close to me and peered into my face. I didn't meet his eyes, and anything he could read from my bruised features he was welcome to.

'I think he knows about the bombs,' he said finally.

'How?' said Doria.

'I should think he was told at the hotel. People in London must have been trying to contact him. Yes, I think we can take it for granted he knows about the bombs.'

'What difference does that make?' said Oxon.

Kraye knew. 'It means he thinks he is safe saying the negatives were in the office, because we can't prove they weren't.'

'They were,' I insisted, showing anxiety.

Bolt pursed his full moist lips. 'Just how clever is Halley?' he said.

'He was a jockey,' said Oxon flatly, as if that automatically meant an IQ of 70.

Bolt said, 'But they took him on at Hunt Radnor's.'

'I told you before,' said Oxon patiently, 'I asked various people about that. Radnor took him on as an adviser, but never gave him anything special to do, and if that doesn't show that he wasn't capable of much, I don't know what does. Everyone knows that his job is only a face saver. It sounds all right, but it means nothing really. Jobs are quite often given in that way to top jockeys when they retire. No one expects them to *do* much, it's just their name that's useful for a while. When their news value has gone, they get the sack.'

This all too true summing up of affairs depressed me almost as deeply as my immediate prospects.

'Howard?' said Bolt.

'I don't know,' said Kraye slowly. 'He doesn't strike me as being in the least clever. Very much the opposite. I agree he did take those photographs, but I think you are quite right in believing he doesn't know why we want them destroyed.'

That, too, was shatteringly correct. As far as I had been able to see, the photographs proved nothing conclusively except that Kraye had been buying Seabury shares under various names with Bolt's help. Kraye and Bolt could not be prosecuted for that. Moreover the whole of Seabury executive had seen the photographs at the meeting that morning, so their contents were no secret.

'Doria?' Bolt said.

'He's a slimy spying little creep, but if he was clever he wouldn't be sitting where he is.'

You couldn't argue with that, either. It had been fairly certain all along that Kraye was getting help from somebody working at Seabury, but even after knowing about Clerk of the Course Brinton's unwilling collaboration at Dunstable, I had gone on assuming that the helper at Seabury was one of the labourers. I hadn't given more than a second's flicker of thought to Oxon, because it didn't seem reasonable that it should be him. In destroying the racecourse he was working himself out of a job, and good jobs for forty-year-old ex-army captains weren't plentiful enough to be lost lightly. As he certainly wasn't mentally affected like Brinton, he wasn't being blackmailed into doing it against his will.

I had thought him silly and self important, but not a rogue. As Doria said, had I been clever enough to suspect him, I wouldn't be sitting where I was.

Bolt went on discussing me as if I weren't there, and as if the decision they would come to would have ordinary everyday consequences.

He said, 'You may all be right, but I don't think so, because since Halley has been on the scene everything's gone wrong. It was he who persuaded Hagbourne to get the course put right, and he who found the mirror as soon as it was up. I took him without question for what he said he was when he came to see me – a shop assistant. You two took him for a wretched little hanger-on of no account. All that, together with the fact that he opened your locked cases and took good clear photographs on a miniature camera, adds up to just one thing to me. Professionalism. Even the way he sits there saying nothing is professional. Amateurs call you names and try to impress you with how much they know. All he has said is that the negatives were in the office. I consider we ought to forget every previous impression we have of him and think of him only as coming from Hunt Radnor.'

They thought about this for five seconds. Then Kraye said, 'We'll have to make sure about the negatives.'

Bolt nodded. If reason hadn't told me what Kraye meant, his wife's smile would have done. My skin crawled.

'How?' she said interestedly.

Kraye inspected his grazed knuckles. 'You won't beat it out of him,' said Oxon. 'Not like that. You haven't a hope.'

'Why not?' said Bolt.

Instead of replying, Oxon turned to me. 'How many races did you ride with broken bones?'

I didn't answer. I couldn't remember anyway.

'That's ridiculous,' said Doria scornfully. 'How could he?'

'A lot of them do,' said Oxon. 'And I'm sure he was no exception.'

'Nonsense,' said Kraye.

Oxon shook his head. 'Collar bones, ribs, forearms, they'll ride with cracks in any of those if they can keep the owners and trainers from finding out.'

Why couldn't he shut up, I thought savagely. He was making things much much worse; as if they weren't appalling enough already.

'You mean,' said Doria with sickening pleasure, 'that he can stand a great deal?'

'No,' I said. 'No.' It sounded like the plea it was. 'You can only ride with cracked bones if they don't hurt.'

'They must hurt,' said Bolt reasonably.

'No,' I said. 'Not always.' It was true, but they didn't believe it.

'The negatives were in the office,' I said despairingly. 'In the office.'

'He's scared,' said Doria delightedly. And that too was true.

It struck a chord with Kraye. He remembered Aynsford. 'We know where he's most easily hurt,' he said. 'That hand.'

'No,' I said in real horror.

They all smiled.

My whole body flushed with uncontrollable fear. Racing injuries were one thing: they were quick, one didn't expect them, and they were part of the job.

To sit and wait and know that a part of one's self which had already proved a burden was about to be hurt as much as ever was quite something else. Instinctively I put my arm up across my face to hide from them that I was afraid, but it must have been obvious.

Kraye laughed insultingly. 'So there's your brave clever Mr Halley for you. It won't take much to get the truth.'

'What a pity,' said Doria.

They left her standing in front of me holding the little pistol in an unswerving pink nailed hand while they went out and rummaged for what they needed. I judged the distance to the door, which was all of thirty feet, and wondered whether the chance of a bullet on the way wasn't preferable to what was going to happen if I stayed where I was.

Doria watched my indecision with amusement.

'Just try it, buddy boy. Just try it.'

I had read that to shoot accurately with an automatic pistol took a great deal of skill and practice. It was possible that all Doria had wanted was the power feeling of owning a gun and she couldn't aim it. On the other hand she was holding it high and with a nearly straight arm, close to where she could see along the sights. On balance, I thought her claim to be a splendid shot had too much probability to be risked.

It was a pity Doria had such a vicious soul inside her beautiful body. She looked gay and dashing in her white Courrèges clothes, smiling a smile which seemed warm and friendly and was as safe as the yawn of a python. She was the perfect mate for Kraye, I thought. Fourth, fifth, sixth time lucky, he'd found a complete complement to himself. If Kraye could do it, perhaps one day I would too . . . but I didn't know if I would even see tomorrow.

I put the back of my hand up over my eyes. My whole face hurt, swollen and stiff, and I was developing a headache. I decided that if I ever got out of this I wouldn't try any more detecting. I had made a proper mess of it.

The men came back, Oxon from the Stewards' room lugging a wooden spoke-backed chair with arms, Kraye and Bolt from the changing rooms with the yard-long poker from the stove and the rope the wet breeches had been hung on to dry. There were still a couple of pegs clinging to it.

Oxon put the chair down a yard or two away and Doria waved the gun a fraction to indicate I should sit in it. I didn't move.

'God,' she said disappointedly, 'you really are a little worm, just like at Aynsford. Scared to a standstill.'

'He isn't a shop assistant,' said Bolt sharply. 'And don't forget it.'

I didn't look at him. But for him and his rejection of Charles' usefully feeble Halley image, I might not have been faced with quite the present situation.

Oxon punched me on the shoulder. 'Move,' he said.

I stood up wearily and stepped off the weighing machine. They stood close round me. Kraye thrust out a hand, twisted it into my shirt, and pushed me into the chair. He, Bolt, and Oxon had a fine old time tying my arms and legs to the equivalent wooden ones with the washing line. Doria watched, fascinated.

I remembered her rather unusual pleasures.

'Like to change places?' I said tiredly.

It didn't make her angry. She smiled slowly, put her gun in a pocket, and leaned down and kissed me long and hard on the mouth. I loathed it. When at length she straightened up she had a smear of my blood on her lip. She wiped it off on her hand, and thoughtfully licked it. She looked misty-eyed and languorous, as if she had had a profound sexual experience. It made me want to vomit.

'Now,' said Kraye. 'Where are they?' He didn't seem

302

to mind his wife kissing me. He understood her, of course.

I looked at the way they had tied the rope tightly round and round my left forearm, leaving the wrist bare, palm downwards. A hand, I thought. What good, anyway, was a hand that didn't work.

I looked at their faces, one by one. Doria, rapt. Oxon, faintly surprised. Kraye, confident, flexing his muscles. And Bolt, calculating and suspicious. None of them within a mile of relenting.

'Where are they?' Kraye repeated, lifting his arm.

'In the office,' I said helplessly.

He hit my wrist with the poker. I'd hoped he might at least try to be subtle, but instead he used all his strength and with that one first blow smashed the whole shooting match to smithereens. The poker broke through the skin. The bones cracked audibly like sticks.

I didn't scream only because I couldn't get enough breath to do it. Before that moment I would have said I knew everything there was to know about pain, but it seems one can always learn. Behind my shut eyes the world turned yellow and grey, like sun shining through mist, and every inch of my skin began to sweat. There had never been anything like it. It was too much, too much. And I couldn't manage any more.

'Where are they?' said Kraye again.

'Don't,' I said. 'Don't do it.' I could hardly speak.

Doria sighed deeply.

I opened my eyes a slit, my head lolling weakly back,

303

too heavy to hold up. Kraye was smiling, pleased with his efforts. Oxon looked sick.

'Well?' said Kraye.

I swallowed, hesitating still.

He put the tip of the poker on my shattered bleeding wrist and gave a violent jerk. Among other things it felt like a fizzing electric shock, up my arms into my head and down to my toes. Sweat started sticking my shirt to my chest and my trousers to my legs.

'Don't,' I said. 'Don't.' It was a croak; a capitulation; a prayer.

'Come on, then,' said Kraye, and jolted the poker again.

I told them. I told them where to go.

CHAPTER EIGHTEEN

They decided it should be Bolt who went to fetch the negatives.

'What is this place?' he said. He hadn't recognized the address.

'The home of . . . a . . . girl friend.'

He dispassionately watched the sweat run in trickles down my face. My mouth was dry. I was very thirsty.

'Say . . . I sent you,' I said, between jagged breaths. 'I . . . asked her . . . to keep them safe . . . They . . . are with . . . several other things . . . The package . . . you want . . . has a name on it . . . a make of film . . . Jigoro . . . Kano.'

'Jigoro Kano. Right,' Bolt said briskly.

'Give me . . .' I said, 'some morphine.'

Bolt laughed. 'After all the trouble you've caused us? Even if I had any, I wouldn't. You can sit there and sweat it out.'

I moaned. Bolt smiled in satisfaction and turned away.

'I'll ring you as soon as I have the negatives,' he said

to Kraye. 'Then we can decide what to do with Halley.
I'll give it some thought on the way up.' From his tone
he might have been discussing the disposal of a block
of worthless stocks.

'Good,' said Kraye. 'We'll wait for your call over in
the flat.'

They began to walk towards the door. Oxon and
Doria hung back, Doria because she couldn't tear her
fascinated, dilated eyes away from watching me, and
Oxon for more practical reasons.

'Are you just going to leave him here?' he asked in
surprise.

'Yes. Why not?' said Kraye. 'Come on, Doria darling.
The best is over.'

Unwillingly she followed him, and Oxon also.

'Some water,' I said. 'Please.'

'No,' said Kraye.

They filed past him out of the door. Just before he
shut it he gave me a last look compounded of triumph,
contempt, and satisfied cruelty. Then he switched off
all the lights and went away.

I heard the sound of a car starting up and driving
off. Bolt was on his way. Outside the windows the night
was black. Darkness folded round me like a fourth
dimension. As the silence deepened I listened to the
low hum of the boiler roaring safely on the far side of
the wall. At least, I thought, I don't have to worry
about that as well. Small, small consolation.

The back of the chair came only as high as my

shoulders and gave no support to my head. I felt deathly tired. I couldn't bear to move: every muscle in my body seemed to have a private line direct to my left wrist, and merely flexing my right foot had me panting. I wanted to lie down flat. I wanted a long cold drink. I wanted to faint. I went on sitting in the chair, wide awake, with a head that ached and weighed a ton, and an arm which wasn't worth the trouble.

I thought about Bolt going to Zanna Martin's front door, and finding that his own secretary had been helping me. I wondered for the hundredth time what he would do about that: whether he would harm her. Poor Miss Martin, whom life had already hurt too much.

Not only her, I thought. In the same file was the letter Mervyn Brinton had written out for me. If Bolt should see that, Mervyn Brinton would be needing a bodyguard for life.

I thought about the people who had borne the beatings and brutalities of the Nazis and of the Japanese and had often died without betraying their secrets. I thought about the atrocities still going on throughout the world, and the ease with which man could break man. In Algeria, they said, unbelievable things had been done. Behind the Iron Curtain, brainwashing wasn't all. In African jails who knew?

Too young for World War Two, safe in a tolerant society, I had had no thought that I should ever come to such a test. To suffer or to talk. The dilemma which stretched back to antiquity. Thanks to Kraye, I now knew what it was like at first hand. Thanks to Kraye, I didn't understand how anyone could keep silent unto death.

I thought: I wanted to ride round Seabury racecourse again, and to go back into the weighing room, and to sit on the scales; and I've done all those things.

I thought: a fortnight ago I couldn't let go of the past. I was clinging to too many ruins, the ruins of my marriage and my racing career and my useless hand. They were gone for good now, all of them. There was nothing left to cling to. And every tangible memory of my life had blown away with a plastic bomb. I was rootless and homeless: and liberated.

What I refused to think about was what Kraye might still do during the next few hours.

Bolt had been gone for a long time when at last Kraye came back. It had seemed half eternity to me, but even so I was in no hurry for it to end.

Kraye put the lights on. He and Doria stood just inside the doorway, staring across at me.

'You're sure there's time?' said Doria.

Kraye nodded, looking at his watch. 'If we're quick.'

'Don't you think we ought to wait until Ellis rings?' she said. 'He might have thought of something better.'

'He's late already,' said Kraye impatiently. They had clearly been arguing for some time. 'He should have rung by now. If we're going to do this, we can't wait any longer.'

'All right,' she shrugged. 'I'll go and take a look.'

'Be careful. Don't go in.'

'No,' she said. 'Don't fuss.'

They both came over to where I sat. Doria looked at me with interest, and liked what she saw.

'He looks ghastly, doesn't he? Serves him right.'

'Are you human?' I said.

A flicker of awareness crossed her lovely face, as if deep down she did indeed know that everything she had enjoyed that night was sinful and obscene, but she was too thoroughly addicted to turn back. 'Shall I help you?' she said to Kraye, not answering me.

'No. I can manage. He's not very heavy.'

She watched with a smile while her husband gripped the back of the chair I was sitting in and began to tug it across the floor towards the wall. The jerks were almost past bearing. I grew dizzy with the effort of not yelling my head off. There was no one close enough to hear me if I did. Not the few overnight stable lads fast asleep three hundred yards away. Only the Krayes, who would find it sweet.

Doria licked her lips, as if at a feast.

'Go on,' said Kraye. 'Hurry.'

'Oh, all right,' she agreed crossly, and went out through the door into the passage.

Kraye finished pulling me across the room, turned the chair round so that I was facing the wall with my knees nearly touching it and stood back, breathing deeply from the exertion.

On the other side of the wall the boiler gently roared. One could hear it more clearly at such close quarters. I knew I had no crashing explosion, no flying bricks, no killing steam to worry about. But the sands were running out fast, all the same.

Doria came back and said in a puzzled voice, 'I thought you said there would be water all down the passage.'

'That's right.'

'Well, there isn't. Not a drop. I looked into the boiler room and it's as dry as a bone.'

'It can't be. It's nearly three hours since it started overflowing. Oxon warned us it must be nearly ready to blow. You must be wrong.'

'I'm not,' she insisted. 'The whole thing looks perfectly normal to me.'

'It can't be.' Kraye's voice was sharp. He went off in a hurry to see for himself, and came back even faster.

'You're right. I'll go and get Oxon. I don't know how the confounded thing works.' He went straight on out of the main door, and I heard his footsteps running. There was no urgency except his own anger. I shivered.

Doria wasn't certain enough of the boiler's safety to spend any time near me, which was about the first really good thing which had happened the whole night. Nor did she find the back of my head worth speaking to: she liked to see her worms squirm. Perhaps she had even lost her appetite, now things had gone wrong. She waited uneasily near the door for Kraye to come back, fiddling with the catch.

Oxon came with him, and they were both running. They charged across the weighing room and out into the passage.

I hadn't much left anyway, I thought. A few tatters of pride, perhaps. Time to nail them to the mast.

The two men walked softly into the room and down to where I sat. Kraye grasped the chair and swung it violently round. The weighing room was quiet, undisturbed. There was only blackness through the window. So that was that.

I looked at Kraye's face, and wished on the whole that I hadn't. It was white and rigid with fury. His eyes were two black pits.

Oxon held the mouse in his hand. 'It must have been Halley,' he said, as if he'd said it before. 'There's no one else.'

Kraye put his right hand down on my left, and systematically began to take his revenge. After three long minutes I passed out.

*

I clung to the dark, trying to hug it round me like a blanket, and it obstinately got thinner and thinner, lighter and lighter, noisier and noisier, more and more painful, until I could no longer deny that I was back in the world.

My eyes unstuck themselves against my will.

The weighing room was full of people. People in dark uniforms. Policemen. Policemen coming through every door. Bright yellow lights at long last shining outside the window. Policemen carefully cutting the rope away from my leaden limbs.

Kraye and Doria and Oxon looked smaller, surrounded by the dark blue men. Doria in her brave white suit instinctively and unsuccessfully tried to flirt with her captors. Oxon, disconcerted to his roots, faced the facts of life for the first time.

Kraye's fury wasn't spent. His eyes stared in hatred across the room.

He shouted, struggling in strong restraining arms, 'Where did you send him? Where did you send Ellis Bolt?'

'Ah, Mr Potter,' I said into a sudden oasis of silence. 'Mr Wilbur Potter. Find out. But not from me.'

CHAPTER NINETEEN

Of course I ended up where I had begun, flat on my back in a hospital. But not for so long, that time. I had a pleasant sunny room with a distant view of the sea, some exceedingly pretty nurses, and a whole stream of visitors. Chico came first, as soon as they would let him, on the Sunday afternoon.

He grinned down at me.

'You look bloody awful.'

'Thanks very much.'

'Two black eyes, a scabby lip, a purple and yellow complexion, and a three day beard. Glamorous.'

'It sounds it.'

'Do you want to look?' he asked, picking up a hand mirror from a chest of drawers.

I took the mirror and looked. He hadn't exaggerated. I would have faded into the background in a horror movie.

Sighing, I said, 'X certificate, definitely.'

He laughed, and put the mirror back. His own face still bore the marks of battle. The eyebrow was healing, but the bruise showed dark right down his cheek.

'This is a better room than you had in London,' he remarked, strolling over to the window. 'And it smells OK. For a hospital, that is.'

'Pack in the small talk and tell me what happened,' I said.

'They told me not to tire you.'

'Don't be an ass.'

'Well, all right. You're a bloody rollicking nit in many ways, aren't you?'

'It depends how you look at it,' I agreed peaceably.

'Oh sure, sure.'

'Chico, give,' I pleaded. 'Come on.'

'Well, there I was harmlessly snoozing away in Radnor's armchair with the telephone on one side and some rather good chicken sandwiches on the other, dreaming about a willing blonde and having a ball, when the front door bell rang.' He grinned. 'I got up, stretched, and went to answer it. I thought it might be you, come back after all and with nowhere to sleep. I knew it wouldn't be Radnor, unless he'd forgotten his key. And who else would be knocking on his door at two o'clock in the morning? But there was this fat geezer standing on the doorstep in his city pinstripes, saying you'd sent him. "Come in, then," I said, yawning my head off. He came in, and I showed him into Radnor's sort of study place, where I'd been sitting.

' "Sid sent you?" I asked him. "What for?"

'He said he understood your girlfriend lived here.

314

God, mate, don't ever try snapping your mouth shut at the top of a yawn. I nearly dislocated my jaw. Could he see her, he said. Sorry it was so late, but it was extremely important.

' "She isn't here," I said. "She's gone away for a few days. Can I help you?"

' "Who are you?" he said, looking me up and down. 'I said I was her brother. He took a sharpish look at the sandwiches and the book I'd been reading, which had fallen on the floor, and he could see I'd been asleep, so he seemed to think everything was OK, and he said, "Sid asked me to fetch something she is keeping for him. Do you think you could help me find it?"

' "Sure," I said. "What is it?"

'He hesitated a bit but he could see that it would look too weird if he refused to tell me, so he said, "It's a packet of negatives. Sid said your sister had several things of his, but the packet I want has a name on it, a make of films. Jigoro Kano."

' "Oh?" I said innocently. "Sid sent you for a packet marked Jigoro Kano?"

' "That's right," he said, looking round the room. "Would it be in here?"

' "It certainly would," I said.'

Chico stopped, came over beside the bed, and sat on the edge of it, by my right toe.

'How come you know about Jigoro Kano?' he said seriously.

'He invented judo,' I said. 'I read it somewhere.'

Chico shook his head. 'He didn't really invent it. In 1882 he took all the best bits of hundreds of versions of ju-jitsu and put them into a formal sort of order, and called it judo.'

'I was sure you would know,' I said, grinning at him.

'You took a very sticky risk.'

'You had to know. After all, you're an expert. And there were all those years at your club. No risk. I knew you'd know. As long as I'd got the name right, that is. Anyway, what happened next?'

Chico smiled faintly.

'I tied him into a couple of knots. Arm locks and so on. He was absolutely flabbergasted. It was really rather funny. Then I put a bit of pressure on. You know. The odd thumb screwing down to a nerve. God, you should have heard him yell. I suppose he thought he'd wake the neighbours, but you know what London is. No one took a blind bit of notice. So then I asked him where you were, when you sent him. He didn't show very willing, I must say, so I gave him a bit more. Poetic justice, wasn't it, considering what they'd just been doing to you? I told him I could keep it up all night, I'd hardly begun. There was a whole bookful I hadn't touched on. It shook him, it shook him bad.'

Chico stood up restlessly and walked about the room.

'You know?' he said wryly. 'He must have had a lot to lose. He was a pretty tough cookie, I'll give him that. If I hadn't been sure that you'd sent him to me as a sort of SOS, I don't think I'd have had the nerve to hurt him enough to bust him.'

'I'm sorry,' I said.

He looked at me thoughtfully. 'We both learnt about it, didn't we? You on the receiving end, and me ... I didn't like it. Doing it, I mean. I mean, the odd swipe or two and a few threats, that's usually enough, and it doesn't worry you a bit, you don't give it a second thought. But I've never hurt anyone like that before. Not seriously, on purpose, beyond bearing. He was crying, you see ...'

Chico turned his back to me, looking out of the window.

There was a long pause. The moral problems of being on the receiving end were not so great, I thought. It was easier on the conscience altogether.

At last Chico said, 'He told me, of course. In the end.'

'Yes.'

'I didn't leave a mark on him, you know. Not a scratch ... He said you were at Seabury racecourse. Well, I knew that was probably right, and that he wasn't trying the same sort of misdirection you had, because you'd told me yourself that you were going there. He said that you were in the weighing room and that the boiler would soon blow up. He said that he hoped it would kill you. He seemed half out of his mind with rage about you. How he should have known better than to believe you, he should have realized that you

317

were as slippery as a snake; he'd been fooled once
before . . . He said he'd taken it for granted you were
telling the truth when you broke down and changed
your story about the negatives being in the office,
because you . . . because you were begging for mercy
and morphine and God knows what.'

'Yes,' I said. 'I know all about that.'

Chico turned away from the window, his face light-
ening into a near grin. 'You don't say,' he said.

'He wouldn't have believed it if I'd given in sooner,
or less thoroughly. Kraye would have done, but not
him. It was very annoying.'

'Annoying,' said Chico. 'I like that word.' He paused,
considering. 'At what moment exactly did you think of
sending Bolt to me?'

'About half an hour before they caught me,' I admitted. 'Go on. What happened next?'

'There was a ball of string on Radnor's writing desk,
so I tied old Fatso up with that in an uncomfortable
position. Then there was the dicey problem of who to
ring up to get the rescue squads on the way. I mean,
the Seabury police might think I was some sort of a
nut, ringing up at that hour and telling such an odd
sort of story. At the best, they might send a bobby or
two out to have a look, and the Krayes would easily
get away. And I reckoned you'd want them rounded
up red-handed, so to speak. I couldn't get hold of
Radnor on account of the office phones being plastic-
ated. So, well I rang Lord Hagbourne.'

'You didn't!'

'Well, yes. He was OK, he really was. He listened to what I told him about you and the boiler and the Krayes and so on, and then he said, "Right", he'd see that half the Sussex police force turned up at Seabury racecourse as soon as possible.'

'Which they did.'

'Which they did,' agreed Chico. 'To find that my old pal Sid had dealt with the boiler himself, but was otherwise in a fairly ropy state.'

'Thanks,' I said. 'For everything.'

'Be my guest.'

'Will you do me another favour?'

'Yes, what?'

'I was supposed to take someone out to lunch today. She'll be wondering why I didn't turn up. I'd have got one of the nurses to ring her, but I still don't know her telephone number.'

'Are you talking about Miss Zanna Martin? The poor duck with the disaster area of a face?'

'Yes,' I said, surprised.

'Then don't worry. She wasn't expecting you. She knows you're here.'

'How?'

'She turned up at Bolt's office yesterday morning, to deal with the mail apparently, and found a policeman waiting on the doorstep with a search warrant. When he had gone she put two and two together smartly and trailed over to the Cromwell Road to find out what

319

was going on. Radnor had gone down to Seabury with Lord Hagbourne, but I was there poking about in the ruins, and we sort of swapped info. She was a bit upset about you, mate, in a quiet sort of way. Anyhow, she won't be expecting you to take her out to lunch.'

'Did she say anything about having one of our files?'

'Yes. I told her to hang on to it for a day or two. There frankly isn't anywhere in the office to put it.'

'All the same, you go over to where she lives as soon as you get back, and collect it. It's the Brinton file. And take great care of it. The negatives Kraye wanted are inside it.'

Chico stared. 'You're not serious.'

'Why not?'

'But everyone ... Radnor, Lord Hagbourne, even Kraye and Bolt, and the police ... everyone has taken it for granted that what you said first was right, that they were in the office and were blown up.'

'It's lucky they weren't,' I said. 'Get some more prints made. We've still got to find out why they were so hellishly important. And don't tell Miss Martin they were what Kraye wanted.'

The door opened and one of the pretty nurses came in.

'I'm afraid you'll have to go now,' she said to Chico. She came close beside the bed and took my pulse. 'Haven't you any sense?' she exclaimed, looking at him angrily. 'A few quiet minutes was what we said. Don't talk too much, and don't let Mr Halley talk at all.'

'You try giving *him* orders,' said Chico cheerfully, 'and see where it gets you.'

'Zanna Martin's address,' I began.

'No,' said the nurse severely. 'No more talking.'

I told Chico the address.

'See what I mean?' he said to the nurse. She looked down at me and laughed. A nice girl behind the starch.

Chico went across the room and opened the door.

'So long, then, Sid. Oh, by the way, I brought this for you to read. I thought you might be interested.'

He pulled a glossy booklet folded lengthwise out of an inner pocket and threw it over on to the bed. It fell just out of my reach, and the nurse picked it up to give it me. Then suddenly she held on to it tight.

'Oh no,' she said. 'You can't give him that!'

'Why not?' said Chico. 'What do you think he is, a baby?'

He went out and shut the door. The nurse clung to the booklet, looking very troubled. I held out my hand for it.

'Come on.'

'I think I ought to ask the doctors . . .'

'In that case,' I said, 'I can guess what it is. Knowing Chico. So be a dear and hand it over. It's quite all right.'

She gave it to me hesitantly, waiting to see my

321

reaction when I caught sight of the bold words on the cover.

'Artificial Limbs. The Modern Development.'

I laughed. 'He's a realist,' I said. 'You wouldn't expect him to bring fairy stories.'

CHAPTER TWENTY

When Radnor came the next day he looked tired, dispirited, and ten years older. The military jauntiness had gone from his bearing, there were deep lines around his eyes and mouth, and his voice was lifeless.

For some moments he stared in obvious distress at the white-wrapped arm which stopped abruptly four inches below the elbow.

'I'm sorry about the office,' I said.

'For God's sake . . .'

'Can it be rebuilt? How bad is it?'

'Sid . . .'

'Are the outside walls still solid, or is the whole place a write-off?'

'I'm too old,' he said, giving in, 'to start again.'

'It's only bricks and mortar that are damaged. You haven't got to start again. The agency is you, not the building. Everyone can work for you just as easily somewhere else.'

He sat down in an armchair, rested his head back, and closed his eyes.

'I'm tired,' he said.

'I don't suppose you've had much sleep since it happened.'

'I am seventy-one,' he said flatly.

I was utterly astounded. Until that day I would have put him in the late fifties.

'You can't be.'

'Time passes,' he said. 'Seventy-one.'

'If I hadn't suggested going after Kraye it wouldn't have happened,' I said with remorse. 'I'm so sorry . . . so sorry . . .'

He opened his eyes. 'It wasn't your fault. If it was anyone's it was my own. You wouldn't have let Hagbourne take those photographs to Seabury, if it had been left to you. I know you didn't like it, that I'd given them to him. Letting the photographs go to Seabury was the direct cause of the bombs, and it was my mistake, not yours.'

'You couldn't possibly tell,' I protested.

'I should have known better, after all these years. I think . . . perhaps I may not see so clearly . . . consequences, things like that.' His voice died to a low, miserable murmur. 'Because I gave the photographs to Hagbourne . . . you lost your hand.'

'No,' I said decisively. 'It's ridiculous to start blaming yourself for that. For heaven's sake snap out of it. No one in the agency can afford to have you in this frame of mind. What are Dolly and Jack Copeland and

324

Sammy and Chico and all the others to do if you don't
pick up the pieces?'

He didn't answer.

'My hand was useless, anyway,' I said. 'And if I'd
been willing to give in to Kraye I needn't have lost it.
It had nothing whatever to do with you.'

He stood up.

'You told Kraye a lot of lies,' he said.

'That's right.'

'But you wouldn't lie to me.'

'Naturally not.'

'I don't believe you.'

'Concentrate on it. It'll come in time.'

'You don't show much respect for your elders.'

'Not when they behave like bloody fools,' I agreed.

He blew down his nostrils, smouldering inwardly. But
all he said was, 'And you? Will you still work for me?'

'It depends on you. I might kill us all next time.'

'I'll take the risk.'

'All right then. Yes. But we haven't finished this
time, yet. Did Chico get the negatives?'

'Yes. He had two sets of prints done this morning.
One for him, and he gave me one to bring to you. He
said you'd want them, but I didn't think . . .'

'But you did bring them?' I urged.

'Yes, they're outside in my car. Are you sure . . .?'

'For heaven's sake,' I said in exasperation. 'I can
hardly wait.'

*

By the following day I had acquired several more pillows, a bedside telephone, and a reputation for being a difficult patient.

The agency restarted work that morning, squeezing into Radnor's own small house. Dolly rang to say it was absolute hell, there was only one telephone instead of thirty, the blitz spirit was fortunately in operation, not to worry about a thing, there was a new word going round the office, it was Halleylujah, and goodbye, someone else's turn now.

Chico rang a little later from a call box.

'Sammy found that driver, Smith,' he said. 'He went to see him in Birmingham yesterday. Now that Kraye's in jug Smith is willing to turn queen's evidence. He agreed that he did take two hundred and fifty quid, just for getting out of his cab, unclipping the chains when the tanker had gone over, and sitting on the side of the road moaning and putting on an act. Nice easy money.'

'Good,' I said.

'But that's not all. The peach of it is he still has the money, most of it, in a tin box, saving it for a deposit on a house. That's what tempted him, apparently, needing money for a house. Anyway, Kraye paid him the second instalment in tenners, from one of the blocks you photographed in his case. Smith still has one of the actual tenners in the pictures. He agreed to part with that for evidence, but I can't see anyone making him give the rest back, can you?'

'Not exactly!'

'So we've got Kraye nicely tied up on malicious damage.'

'That's terrific,' I said. 'What are they holding him on now?'

'GBH. And the others for aiding and abetting.'

'Consecutive sentences, I trust.'

'You'll be lucky.'

I sighed. 'All the same, he still owns twenty-three per cent of Seabury's shares.'

'So he does,' agreed Chico gloomily.

'How bad exactly is the office?' I asked.

'They're surveying it still. The outside walls look all right, it's just a case of making sure. The inside was pretty well gutted.'

'We could have a better lay-out,' I said. 'And a lift.'

'So we could,' he said happily. 'And I'll tell you something else which might interest you.'

'What?'

'The house next door is up for sale.'

I was asleep when Charles came in the afternoon, and he watched me wake up, which was a pity. The first few seconds of consciousness were always the worst: I had the usual hellish time, and when I opened my eyes, there he was.

'Good God, Sid,' he said in alarm. 'Don't they give you anything?'

I nodded, getting a firmer grip on things.

'But with modern drugs, surely . . . I'm going to complain.'

'No.'

'But Sid.'

'They do what they can, I promise you. Don't look so upset. It'll get better in a few days. Just now it's a bore, that's all . . . Tell me about Fred.'

Fred had already been at the house when the police guard arrived at Aynsford. Four policemen had gone there, and it took all four to hold him, with Charles going back and helping as well.

'Did he do much damage?' I asked. 'Before the police got there?'

'He was very methodical, and very quick. He had been right through my desk and all the wardroom. Every envelope, folder, and notebook had been ripped apart, and the debris was all in a heap, ready to be destroyed. He'd started on the dining-room when the police arrived. He was very violent. And they found a box of plastic explosive lying on the hall table, and some more out in the van.' He paused. 'What made you think he would come?'

'They knew I took the photographs at Aynsford, but how would they know I got them developed in London? I was afraid they might think I'd had them done locally, and that they'd think you'd know where the negatives were, as it was you who inveigled Kraye down there in the first place.'

328

He smiled mischievously. 'Will you come to Aynsford for a few days when you get out of here?'

'I've heard that somewhere before,' I said. 'No thanks.'

'No more Krayes,' he promised. 'Just a rest.'

'I'd like to, but there won't be time. The agency is in a dicky state. And I've just been doing to my boss what you did to me at Aynsford.'

'What's that?'

'Kicking him out of depression into action.'

His smile twisted in amusement.

'Do you know how old he is?' I said.

'About seventy, why?'

I was surprised. 'I'd no idea he was that age, until he told me yesterday.'

Charles squinted at the tip of his cigar. He said, 'You always thought I asked him to give you a job, didn't you? And guaranteed your wages.'

I made a face at him, embarrassed.

'You may care to know it wasn't like that at all. I didn't know him personally, only by name. He sought me out one day in the club and asked me if I thought you'd be any good at working with him. I said yes, I thought you would. Given time.'

'I don't believe it.'

He smiled. 'I told him you played a fair game of chess. Also that you had become a jockey simply through circumstances, because you were small and your mother died, and that you could probably succeed at something else just as easily. He said that from what he'd seen of your racing you were the sort of chap he needed. He told me then how old he was. That's all. Nothing else. Just how old he was. But we both understood what he was saying.'

'I nearly threw it away,' I said. 'If it hadn't been for you . . .'

'Oh yes,' he said wryly. 'You have a lot to thank me for. A lot.'

Before he went I asked him to look at the photographs, but he studied them one by one and handed them back shaking his head.

Chief-Inspector Cornish rang up to tell me Fred was not only in the bag but sewn up.

'The bullets match all right. He drew the same gun on the men who arrested him, but one of them fortunately threw a vase at him and knocked it out of his hand before he could shoot.'

'He was a fool to keep that gun after he had shot Andrews.'

'Stupid. Crooks often are, or we'd never catch them. And he didn't mention his little murder to Kraye and the others, so they can't be pinched as accessories to that. Pity. But it's quite clear he kept it quiet. The Sussex force said that Kraye went berserk when he found out. Apparently he mostly regretted not having known about your stomach while he had you in his clutches.'

'Thank God he didn't!' I exclaimed with feeling.

Cornish's chuckle came down the wire. 'Fred was supposed to look for Brinton's letter at your agency himself, but he wanted to go to a football match up North or something, and sent Andrews instead. He said he didn't think there'd be a trap, or anything subtle like that. Just an errand, about on Andrews' level. He said he only lent him the gun for a lark, he didn't mean Andrews to use it, didn't think he'd be so silly. But then Andrews went back to him scared stiff and said he'd shot you, so Fred says he suggested a country ramble in Epping Forest and the gun went off by accident! I ask you, try that on a jury! Fred says he didn't tell Kraye because he was afraid of him.'

'What! Fred afraid?'

'Kraye seems to have made an adverse impression on him.'

'Yes, he's apt to do that,' I said.

I read Chico's booklet from cover to cover. One had to thank the thalidomide children, it appeared, for the speed-up of modern techniques. As soon as my arm had properly healed I could have a versatile gas-powered tool-hand with a swivelling wrist, activated by small pistons and controlled by valves, and operated by my shoulder muscles. The main snag to that, as far as I could gather, was that one always had to carry the small gas cylinders about, strapped on, like a permanent skin diver.

Much more promising, almost fantastic, was the latest invention of British and Russian scientists, the myo-electric arm. This worked entirely by harnessing the tiny electric currents generated in one's own remaining muscles, and the booklet cheerfully said it was easiest to fit on someone whose amputation was recent. The less one had lost of a limb, the better were one's chances of success. That put me straight in the guinea seats.

Finally, said the booklet with a justifiable flourish of trumpets, at St Thomas's Hospital they had invented a miraculous new myo-electric hand which could do practically everything a real one could except grow nails.

I missed my real hand, there was no denying it. Even in its deformed state it had had its uses, and I suppose that any loss of so integral a part of oneself must prove a radical disturbance. My unconscious mind did its best to reject the facts: I dreamed each night that I was whole, riding races, tying knots, clapping . . . anything which required two hands. I awoke to the frustrating stump.

The doctors agreed to inquire from St Thomas's how soon I could go there.

On Wednesday morning I rang up my accountant and asked when he had a free day. Owing to an unexpected cancellation of plans, he said, he would be free on

Friday. I explained where I was and roughly what had happened. He said that he would come to see me, he didn't mind the journey, a breath of sea air would do him good.

As I put the telephone down my door opened and Lord Hagbourne and Mr Fotherton came tentatively through it. I was sitting on the edge of the bed in a dark blue dressing-gown, my feet in slippers, my arm in a cradle inside a sling, chin freshly shaved, hair brushed, and the marks of Kraye's fists fading from my face. My visitors were clearly relieved at these encouraging signs of revival, and relaxed comfortably into the armchairs.

'You're getting on well, then, Sid?' said Lord Hagbourne.

'Yes, thank you.'

'Good, good.'

'How did the meeting go?' I asked. 'On Saturday?'

Both of them seemed faintly surprised at the question.

'Well, you did hold it, didn't you?' I said anxiously.

'Why yes,' said Fotherton. 'We did. There was a moderately good gate, thanks to the fine weather.' He was a thin, dry man with a long face moulded into drooping lines of melancholy, and on that morning he kept smoothing three fingers down his cheek as if he were nervous.

Lord Hagbourne said, 'It wasn't only your security men who were drugged. The stable lads all woke up

333

feeling muzzy, and the old man who was supposed to look after the boiler was asleep on the floor in the canteen. Oxon had given them all a glass of beer. Naturally, your men trusted him.'

I sighed. One couldn't blame them too much. I might have drunk with him myself.

'We had the inspector in yesterday to go over the boiler thoroughly,' said Lord Hagbourne. 'It was nearly due for its regular check anyway. They said it was too old to stand much interference with its normal working, and that it was just as well it hadn't been put to the test. Also that they thought that it wouldn't have taken as long as three hours to blow up. Oxon was only guessing.'

'Charming,' I said.

'I sounded out Seabury Council,' said Lord Hagbourne. 'They're putting the racecourse down on their agenda for next month. Apparently a friend of yours, the manager of the Seafront Hotel, has started a petition in the town urging the council to take an interest in the racecourse on the grounds that it gives a seaside town prestige and free advertising and is good for trade.'

'That's wonderful,' I said, very pleased.

Fotherton cleared his throat, looked hesitantly at Lord Hagbourne, and then at me.

'It has been discussed...' he began. 'It has been decided to ask you if you... er... would be interested in taking on . . . in becoming Clerk of the Course at Seabury.'

'Me?' I exclaimed, my mouth falling open in astonishment.

'It's getting too much for me, being Clerk of two courses,' he said, admitting it a year too late.

'You saved the place on the brink of the grave,' said Lord Hagbourne with rare decisiveness. 'We all know it's an unusual step to offer a Clerkship to a professional jockey so soon after he's retired, but Seabury executive are unanimous. They want you to finish the job.'

They were doing me an exceptional honour. I thanked them, and hesitated, and asked if I could think it over.

'Of course, think it over,' said Lord Hagbourne. 'But say yes.'

I asked them then to have a look at the box of photographs, which they did. They both scrutinized each print carefully, one by one, but they could suggest nothing at the end.

Zanna Martin came to see me the next afternoon, carrying some enormous, sweet-smelling bronze chrysanthemums. A transformed Zanna Martin, in a smart dark green tweed suit and shoes chosen for looks more than sturdy walking. Her hair had been re-styled so that it was shorter and curved in a bouncy curl on her

335

cheek. She had even tried a little lipstick and powder, and had tidied her eyebrows into a shapely line. The scars were just as visible, the facial muscles as wasted as ever, but Miss Martin had come to terms with them at last.

'How super you look,' I said truthfully.

She was embarrassed, but very pleased. 'I've got a new job. I had an interview yesterday, and they didn't even seem to notice my face. Or at least they didn't say anything. In a bigger office, this time. A good bit more than I've earned before, too.'

'How splendid,' I congratulated her sincerely.

'I feel new,' she said.

'I too.'

'I'm glad we met.' She smiled, saying it lightly. 'Did you get that file back all right? Your young Mr Barnes came to fetch it.'

'Yes, thank you.'

'Was it important?'

'Why?'

'He seemed very odd when I gave it to him. I thought he was going to tell me something about it. He kept starting to, and then he didn't.'

I would have words with Chico, I thought.

'It was only an ordinary file,' I said. 'Nothing to tell.'

On the off-chance, I got her to look at the photographs. Apart from commenting on the many examples of her own typing, and expressing surprise that anybody should have bothered to photograph such ordinary papers, she had nothing to say.

She rose to go, pulling on her gloves. She still automatically leaned forward slightly, so that the curl swung down over her cheek.

'Goodbye, Mr Halley. And thank you for changing everything for me. I'll never forget how much I owe you.'

'We didn't have that lunch,' I said.

'No.' She smiled, not needing me any more. 'Never mind. Some other time.' She shook hands. 'Goodbye.'

She went serenely out of the door.

'Goodbye, Miss Martin,' I said to the empty room. 'Goodbye, goodbye, goodbye.' I sighed sardonically at myself, and went to sleep.

Noel Wayne came loaded on Friday morning with a bulging briefcase of papers. He had been my accountant ever since I began earning big money at eighteen, and he probably knew more about me than anyone else on earth. Nearly sixty, bald except for a grey fringe over the ears, he was a small, round man with alert black eyes and a slow-moving mills-of-God mind. It was his advice more than my knowledge which had turned my earnings into a modest fortune via the stock markets, and I seldom did anything of any importance financially without consulting him first.

'What's up?' he said, coming straight to the point as soon as he had taken off his overcoat and scarf.

I walked over to the window and looked out. The weather had broken. It was drizzling, and a fine mist lay over the distant sea.

'I've been offered a job,' I said, 'Clerk of the Course at Seabury.'

'No!' he said, as astonished as I had been. 'Are you going to accept?'

'It's tempting,' I said. 'And safe.'

He chuckled behind me. 'Good. So you'll take it.'

'A week ago I definitely decided not to do any more detecting.'

'Ah.'

'So I want to know what you think about my buying a partnership in Radnor's agency.'

He choked.

'I didn't think you even liked the place.'

'That was a month ago. I've changed since then. And I won't be changing back. The agency is what I want.'

'But has Radnor *offered* a partnership?'

'No. I think he might have done eventually, but not since someone let a bomb off in the office. He's hardly likely to ask me to buy a half share of the ruins. And he blames himself for this.' I pointed to the sling.

'With reason?'

'No,' I said rather gloomily. 'I took a risk which didn't come off.'

'Which was?'

338

'Well, if you need it spelled out, that Kraye would only hit hard enough to hurt, not to damage beyond repair.'

'I see.' He said it calmly, but he looked horrified. 'And do you intend to take similar risks in future?'

'Only if necessary.'

'You always said the agency didn't do much crime work,' he protested.

'It will from now on, if I have anything to do with it. Crooks make too much misery in the world.' I thought of the poor Dunstable Brinton. 'And listen, the house next door is for sale. We could knock the two into one. Radnor's is bursting at the seams. The agency has expanded a lot even in the two years I've been there. There seems more and more demand for his sort of service. Then the head of Bona Fides, that's one of the departments, is a natural to expand as an employment consultant on the managerial level. He has a gift for it. And insurance – Radnor's always neglected that. We don't have an insurance investigation department. I'd like to start one. Suspect insurance claims; you know. There's a lot of work in that.'

'You're sure Radnor will agree, if you suggest a partnership?'

'He may kick me out. I'd risk it though. What do you think?'

'I think you've gone back to how you used to be,' he said thoughtfully. 'Which is good. Nothing but good. But . . . well, tell me what you really think about that.'

He nodded at my chopped off arm. 'None of your flippant lies, either. The truth.'

I looked at him and didn't answer.

'It's only a week since it happened,' he said, 'and as you still look the colour of a grubby sheet I suppose it's hardly fair to ask. But I want to know.'

I swallowed. There were some truths which really couldn't be told. I said instead, 'It's gone. Gone, like a lot of other things I used to have. I'll live without it.'

'Live, or exist?'

'Oh live, definitely. Live.' I reached for the booklet Chico had brought, and flicked it at him. 'Look.'

He glanced at the cover and I saw the faint shock in his face. He didn't have Chico's astringent brutality. He looked up and saw me smiling.

'All right,' he said soberly. 'Yes. Invest your money in yourself.'

'In the agency,' I said.

'That's what I mean,' he said. 'In the agency. In yourself.'

He said he'd need to see the agency's books before a definite figure could be reached, but we spent an hour discussing the maximum he thought I should prudently offer Radnor, what return I could hope for in salary and dividends, and what I should best sell to raise the sum since it was agreed.

When we had finished I trotted out once more the infuriating photographs.

'Look them over, will you?' I said. 'I've shown them

to everyone else without result. These photographs were the direct cause of the bombs in my flat and the office, and of me losing my hand, and I can't see why. It's driving me ruddy well mad.'

'The police . . .' he suggested.

'The police are only interested in the one photograph of a ten pound note. They looked at the others, said they could see nothing significant, and gave them back to Chico. But Kraye couldn't have been worried about that bank note, it was ten thousand to one we'd come across it again. No, it's something else. Something not obviously criminal, something Kraye was prepared to go to any lengths to obliterate immediately. Look at the time factor . . . Oxon only pinched the photographs just before lunch, down at Seabury. Kraye lived in London. Say Oxon rang him and told him to come and look: Oxon couldn't leave Seabury, it was a race day. Kraye had to go to Seabury himself. Well, he went down and looked at the photographs and saw . . . what? What? My flat was being searched by five o'clock.'

Noel nodded in agreement. 'Kraye was desperate. Therefore there was something to be desperate about.' He took the photographs and studied them one by one.

Half an hour later he looked up and stared blankly out of the window at the wet grey skies. For several minutes he stayed completely still, as if in a state of suspended animation: it was his way of concentrated thinking. Finally he stirred and sighed. He moved his short neck as if it were stiff, and lifted the top photograph off the pile.

'This must be the one,' he said.

I nearly snatched it out of his hand.

'But it's only the summary of the share transfers,' I said in disappointment. It was the sheet headed S.R., Seabury Racecourse, which listed in summary form all Kraye's purchases of Seabury shares. The only noticeable factor in what had seemed to me merely a useful at-a-glance view of his total holding, was that it had been typed on a different typewriter, and not by Zanna Martin. This hardly seemed enough reason for Kraye's hysteria.

'Look at it carefully,' said Noel. 'The three left hand columns you can disregard, because I agree they are simply a tabulation of the share transfers, and I can't see any discrepancies.'

'There aren't,' I said. 'I checked that.'

'How about the last column, the small one on the right?'

'The banks?'

'The banks.'

'What about them?' I said.

'How many different ones are there?'

I looked down the long list, counting. 'Five. Barclays, Piccadilly. Westminster, Birmingham. British Linen Bank, Glasgow. Lloyds, Doncaster. National Provincial, Liverpool.'

'Five bank accounts, in five different towns. Perfectly

respectable. A very sensible arrangement in many ways. He can move round the country and always have easy access to his money. I myself have accounts in three different banks: it avoids muddling my clients' affairs with my own.'

'I know all that. I didn't see any significance in his having several accounts. I still don't.'

'Hm,' said Noel. 'I think it's very likely that he has been evading income tax.'

'Is that all?' I said disgustedly.

Noel looked at me in amusement, pursing his lips. 'You don't understand in the least, I see.'

'Well, for heaven's sake, you wouldn't expect a man like Kraye to pay up every penny he was liable for like a good little citizen.'

'You wouldn't,' agreed Noel, grinning broadly.

'I'll agree he might be worried. After all, they sent Al Capone to jug in the end for tax evasion. But over here, what's the maximum sentence?'

'He'd only get a year, at the most,' he said, 'but . . .'

'And he would have been sure to get off with a fine. Which he won't do now, after attacking me. Even so, for that he'll only get three or four years, I should think, and less for the malicious damage. He'll be out and operating again far too soon. Bolt, I suppose, will be struck off, or whatever it is with stockbrokers.'

'Stop talking,' he said, 'and listen. While it's quite normal to have more than one bank account, an Inspector of Taxes, having agreed your tax liability, may ask you to sign a document stating that you have disclosed to him *all* your bank accounts. If you fail to mention one or two, it constitutes a fraud, and if you are discovered you can then be prosecuted. So, suppose Kraye has signed such a document, omitting one or two or even three of the five accounts? And then he finds a photograph in existence of his most private papers, listing all five accounts as undeniably his?'

'But no one would have noticed,' I protested.

'Quite. Probably not. But to him it must have seemed glaringly dangerous. Guilty people constantly fear their guilt will be visible to others. They're vibratingly sensitive to anything which can give them away. I see quite a lot of it in my job.'

'Even so . . . bombs are pretty drastic.'

'It would entirely depend on the sum involved,' he said primly.

'Huh?'

'The maximum fine for income tax evasion is twice the tax you didn't pay. If for example you amassed ten thousand pounds but declared only two, you could be fined a sum equal to twice the tax on eight thousand pounds. With surtax and so on, you might be left with almost nothing. A nasty set-back.'

'To put it mildly,' I said in awe.

'I wonder,' Noel said thoughtfully, putting the tips of his fingers together, 'just how much undeclared loot Kraye has got stacked away in his five bank accounts?'

'It must be a lot,' I said, 'for bombs.'

'Quite so.'

There was a long silence. Finally I said, 'One isn't required either legally or morally to report people to the Inland Revenue.'

He shook his head.

'But we could make a note of those five banks, just in case?'

'If you like,' he agreed.

'Then I think I might let Kraye have the negatives and the new set of prints,' I said. 'Without telling him I know why he wants them.'

Noel looked at me inquiringly, but didn't speak.

I grinned faintly. 'On condition that he makes a free, complete, and outright gift to Seabury Racecourse Company of his twenty-three per cent holding.'